WEIGHT *of* MEMORY

sands press
Brockville, Ontario

WEIGHT *of* MEMORY

BY KRISTINA BRUNE

sands press

sands press

A Division of 3244601 Canada Inc.
300 Central Avenue West
Brockville, Ontario
K6V 5V2

Toll Free 1-800-563-0911 or 613-345-2687
http://www.sandspress.com

ISBN 978-1-988281-96-4
Copyright © Kristina Brune 2021
All Rights Reserved

For information on bulk purchases of this book or any book published by Sands Press, please call 1-800-563-0911.

1ST Printing

To book an author for your live event, please call: 1-800-563-0911

Sands Press is a literary publisher interested in new and established authors wishing to develop and market their product. For more information please visit our website at www.sandspress.com.

To Chip. None of this would have happened without you.
You are my rock and my best friend and the love of my life.
To Nate. I miss you so much it hurts, but I'm good.

CHAPTER ONE

Lara

"Where's Mommy?"

Lara Kemp heard her husband Alex call out as he shut the door. She heard Tessa's little footsteps on the kitchen tile, Alex putting his lunchbox on the counter and kicking off his work boots. These were normally comforting sounds, ones she looked forward to every day. But that day she heard it from far away, the sounds registering like so much background noise. And she didn't care.

"Where's Mommy?" Alex asked Tessa. "Do you think she ran away?"

"No, Daddy! Mommy peekin' boo!" Tessa answered. Lara could hear the smile in her little girl's voice.

"You think Mommy's playing peek-a-boo? I think you're right. We're just gonna have to find her!"

She heard them opening doors, pulling back the shower curtain, Tessa giggling and yelling, "Not here!" each time a new hiding spot didn't reveal Mommy. Still Lara didn't move. She was lying on her side, on the floor of her closet, her body curled around an old, gray sweatshirt. She didn't know how long she'd been there.

"Lara?" Alex was really calling for her now, the playful tone gone, concern and fear creeping into his voice.

Alex and Tessa were in the master bedroom now. She heard the sound of Tessa's old lovey, a stuffed bear with a rattle inside and a blanket he wore like a cape attached to his neck. Light flooded the closet as Alex flipped on the switch and Tessa pushed the door open wide.

"Found Mommy!" Lara felt Tessa's little hands on her head. When Lara didn't move, Tessa said, "Mommy?"

"Lara? What's wrong?" Alex was kneeling next to her now, shaking her shoulder. "Lara, come on. What is it?"

"Mommy o-tay?" Tessa sounded like she was near tears. *I should comfort her,* Lara thought. *Pop up, grab her and kiss her chubby little cheeks and tell her Mommy is just fine.* But Mommy wasn't just fine. Not today.

Instead, she said, "I can't do it anymore, Alex. I can't. I can't. I can't breathe. I picked up the phone to call him and I dialed the number and it rang and rang and then someone answered and it wasn't him and ... I just can't. I can't. I can't. I can't." She was sobbing, unable to catch her breath.

She felt his hand rest on her shoulder for a brief second. He picked Tessa up, and said brightly, "Mommy is so tired she fell asleep in her closet. She needs to finish her nap, silly Mommy. How about a snack and some *Paw Patrol?*"

"O-tay." Tessa sounded resigned. Could a two-year-old sound resigned? If so, she did. *I did that,* thought Lara. *I can't get my shit together and I'm breaking my fucking kid.* Still she didn't get up.

Minutes later, Alex came back in. He sat on the floor with her. He put his hands on her shoulders and pulled her into a sitting position. *Always picking me up.*

"What happened, babe?" He tugged the sweatshirt out of her loose grasp and sighed when he saw what it was. Gray and faded, two sizes too big for her, it had holes on the cuffs and you could barely tell that it had once been a senior class sweatshirt. The faded letters on the back read: "Class of '98, kiss our class goodbye!"

"My dad's birthday is in a couple of weeks and I wanted to get him this whiskey. When we were kids he always used to tell my mom, 'Only the rich people drink'... whatever the name of this whiskey is. But I couldn't remember what it was. So I just called. I had to ask him, you know? A woman answered his phone. It's not his number anymore." The words tumbled out of her in a stream.

Alex sighed. "Well. I mean, that's normal, babe ..." he seemed unsure about what to say. "Did you try writing it down in the journal, like Dr. Martinez said? He said it might help to—"

"I don't want to fucking write it down in a journal! I want to know the name of the whiskey and if I can't remember, I want to ask Ben!" she yelled without meaning to—a little piece of the big ball of anger that lived in her chest chipping off and coming out before she could stop it. She saw Alex flinch. Fresh tears sprang to her eyes. Now she'd made her baby and her husband sad.

"I don't know what to say anymore," said Alex.

"There's nothing to say. I just have to get my shit together. That's it." Lara took the sweatshirt back from Alex and roughly wiped her eyes with it.

"It's not that simple and you know it."

"He's going to stay dead, Alex. I have to find a way to deal with that. I should have found a way to deal with it months ago. I'm pathetic." She let the anger fuel her and finally got to her feet. She shoved Ben's sweatshirt onto the top shelf and grabbed dirty clothes off the floor, forcing them into the already-full hamper.

People thought that sadness was the hard part of grief. They warned you about depression or suicide. What no one ever talked about was the anger. The overwhelming, red-hot, make-you-blind-with-rage anger. No one told you it would be a daily—sometimes hourly—struggle to keep it at bay and not unleash it on everyone around you. Or how it was always right there at the surface of every emotion. She could go from feeling happy, sad, desperate, whatever—to angry in an instant. Sometimes it scared her how quickly the anger overwhelmed her, driving out all logic and control.

Lara worked hard at keeping it tucked away. When it did threaten to overwhelm her, as it was doing now, she let it out into her muscles, driving her to move—to clean the house or go on a run or hammer out the work emails she'd been putting off. If she didn't let it do something, it would take over.

"Lara, come on. Stop." If Alex was surprised by her sudden change in emotions from sadness to anger, he shouldn't have been. That was just how she was now.

She pushed past Alex and walked into their room. "I'm going to use the bathroom and then I'll start dinner." She didn't wait for him to reply before she walked into their bathroom and closed the door.

The rest of the evening passed quietly but Lara occasionally felt Alex's eyes on her as she drained spaghetti noodles, as she changed Tessa's diaper, as they watched TV. She felt the weight of her sadness, her depression, and her grief settling over her, dragging her down. She moved slowly, barely responding to stimuli around her.

She knew she should say something to him, try to explain. Maybe apologize for letting herself turn into a crying mess on the floor of the closet. Again. But instead she said nothing. Really, there was nothing to say.

It had been a little over a year since her brother, Ben, had died suddenly, the victim of hypertrophic cardiomyopathy—a fancy way to say he had an undetected heart condition that sometimes caused young athletes to die suddenly of a heart attack. It caught up to Ben in the middle of his kitchen floor, about five minutes after he'd returned home after a run. His wife, Cate, found him only minutes later but it was already too late. He was thirty-four.

Lara had been beyond devastated. She and her brother were very close—she was the baby and her big brother was her rock. He was only a little more than a year older than her and they'd always been close. Together, they'd navigated their parents' messy marriage and messier divorce. They attended the same college, and though she and Alex had moved away briefly, when they had returned to St. Louis they'd moved to a house just a few miles from Ben and Cate.

Her brother was her best friend. With Ben gone, it felt like her life was cleaved in two: before—when everything wasn't perfect, but it was good enough and at least it made sense—and after—when everything sucked and nothing made sense.

Most days, she felt like everything had changed and her life was completely unrecognizable. Not only had she lost Ben, but her relationships with her parents, her friends, and Alex had changed. She felt alone. She had Tessa, which was the only thing that still made her honestly, simply, happy, but she was screwing that up, too.

Lara just didn't know how to deal with the pain of losing Ben. It was all-encompassing, both physical and mental. She was constantly distracted, unable to focus. She forgot to do simple tasks like pay the cable bill. She forgot to switch a load of laundry from the washer to the dryer for so long that the clothes began to smell like mildew and she had to wash them again. But the world expected her to move on.

The grief also made her heart race, her stomach churn, and her body feel exhausted and achy. Too many days her body and her mind just could not summon up the strength to do the things that needed to be done—to help Alex with the small day-to-day tasks that made up their life together.

But if she was honest, she didn't really care that much if none of those things got done. She knew she should, but she just couldn't see an end to any of it. What was the point? None of it mattered. Ben was going to stay dead. She'd never have her brother back. She'd never really feel happy again.

Her only choice was to find a way to deal with it. She had to find a way to still live some sort of a life. If she didn't, Alex would eventually take Tessa and leave. And rightfully so. She didn't want that to happen, but she also couldn't see how anything would ever change.

"Are we going to talk about this?" Alex was looking at her. He'd paused the television where the Cards were playing the Cubs. They were only a game and a half apart in the race for the pennant, and the Cards needed to win this game to keep their lead.

She didn't want to do this again, have the same conversation they'd had who knows how many times in the last year.

"What do you want me to say, Alex? It hurts. I can't cope. My brother is dead. I can't talk to my parents. I can't talk to anyone. No one understands. It builds up and builds up and some days I just end up on the floor of the closet."

"Then you need to get help. You stopped going to Dr. Martinez, even though I told you I thought you weren't ready. We can't function like this anymore."

Same old song. Alex didn't deserve any of her anger. He'd put up with so much, had been there for her and picked her up, literally and figuratively, countless times. But his words still pissed her off and before she could bite it back, she retorted, "*We* can't function or *you* can't function like this anymore?"

"I don't know. What I do know is you're not okay. And I'm trying to do what I can. I've been working a lot of overtime because I know work has been slow for you. But then I come home and there's laundry to do and no groceries and you're in the closet ..." his voice trailed off.

Lara's stomach tightened and she felt heat rise up in her cheeks. She knew she wasn't working enough. As a freelance graphic designer, she had the ability to make great money, if she took the time to market her services and seek out new clients. But since Ben had died, she'd only managed to hang onto her few retainered clients. That was okay, but it brought in far less than she usually made and they were feeling the pinch. She knew she could do better. She *should* do better. But like with everything else, she just couldn't summon up the will to care. Hearing Alex admit that it was causing him stress made her feel guilty—which supercharged her anger. It was a vicious cycle.

"Well I'm *so sorry* my grief is *such* an inconvenience for you. I'll make sure I get over it and get back to keeping the laundry caught up and having food on the table every night when you get home."

"You know it's not about any of that. You know it's not about the damn laundry or making dinner. It's about *you*. You're not okay! We're not okay!" he was yelling now and she could feel tears filling her eyes.

"You never talk to me. When was the last time we went out together? When was the last time you asked me how work was going or what I think about *anything*? I miss my wife!"

Alex's voice grew quiet. Quiet, but not soft. Angry quiet. "And I'm not going to put our daughter in a situation where she's not safe."

"What does that mean?" Lara stood, staring at him, challenging him.

"You know exactly what I mean, Lara. What the hell were you doing yesterday? Do you know how it felt when the daycare called me, asking why we were late to pick Tessa up? You said you were 'on your way,' but I could hear that you weren't even in the car yet. Then I get home and Tessa is sitting in the living room, crying, hungry, with a full diaper—"

"I told you I was working on that project and lost track of time."

"Bullshit. That's never once happened before." Alex was standing now, too, and Lara could feel the anger and the heat coming off of both of them. This was too much. She wanted to crawl out of her skin; she wanted to get away; she wanted to scream.

"Fuck. You. Don't imply that I can't take care of my own daughter!"

"Well apparently you can't!"

Lara felt like she'd been slapped and an overwhelming desire to hit him washed over her. She balled her fists and she almost hit him. For a second she thought about how good it would feel to finally give her anger a physical outlet.

And just as quickly as the desire to lash out and hit her husband flooded her, it receded, and she was horrified at herself. She ran down the hall and locked herself in the bathroom, Alex calling after her. She ignored him.

She sat on the floor, with her back against the door, and sobbed. *This isn't the way my life is supposed to go,* she thought. She was supposed to marry the love of her life, have kids, be happy. She'd had it all just a year ago. Then Ben died and now it was all slipping away. She couldn't see that there was a way out, that there was any way for her to get better. She was ruining her life, but more than that, she was ruining Alex and Tessa's lives. They'd be better off without her.

She had actually been okay the first couple of months after Ben died. First there was the shock, of course, and she had functioned on autopilot. Lara helped make decisions at the funeral home. She helped her mom, dad, and Cate decide other terrible things like what Ben should wear in his casket and whether or not they wanted the old ladies at the church to have lunch after the service or if they'd cater something. It had kept her busy.

Then there were those few days right before and after the funeral. Family and friends came in from out of town. People congregated around Lara's kitchen table. There had been so much laughter. Tears, of course, but also laughter as they talked about Ben and shared their favorite stories about him. The funeral was horrible, but Lara felt cocooned—wrapped up in the support of her family and friends, who were grieving, too. She thought it would always be like that, everyone working to keep his memory alive.

She couldn't have been more wrong. Over the next weeks and months, everyone went home and back to their lives. *Of course* they went back to their lives—they had to. They had jobs and kids and other obligations and couldn't drown in the grief of losing Ben. When she was thinking clearly, Lara didn't really expect them to do otherwise. But *she* couldn't go back to her life.

She'd tried, and for a couple of months it even looked like she was going to succeed. She rode the wave of shock and continued to function almost normally, making decisions, getting back to work, taking care of Tessa. Nothing was the same, but she thought she was doing okay.

Then one day, out of the blue, it had slammed into her like a speeding semi into an oblivious bug. It was the day before Thanksgiving. Her friends and even some family were avoiding her like her grief was something they could catch like a cold that would really dampen their holiday plans. She was staring down a long list of "firsts" without Ben—double Thanksgiving at Mom's and then at Dad's, where Mom would guilt them for leaving to visit their father, and Dad and his new wife would be drunk the whole evening. Then Christmas. Then New Year's, when their traditional double date at the Chase Park Plaza in downtown St. Louis obviously wouldn't be happening. Then it would be his birthday. All of these milestones were going to pass this year, and the next, and every year after for the rest of her life. A lifetime without her best friend seemed impossible. She simply didn't want to do it. And she was so angry that she didn't have a choice.

So she'd picked a fight with Alex about something stupid that day. She'd known she was doing it, tried to tell herself to stop, that he didn't deserve it and it certainly wasn't going to make her feel better. She didn't care. She picked the fight and instead of letting it go like he had been doing over the past months, Alex fought back. Told her she was being unreasonable and to stop taking everything out on him.

That was the first time she'd let the fury take the wheel. Lara felt it crawling along her skin, heating her limbs, making her heart race. It wanted out and she wanted to let it run. So she exploded.

All of the pain, anger, grief, and fear came out that day in one long, screaming rant at her husband. Later, she wouldn't even remember exactly what she'd said, but she knew she laid it all at his feet, accusing him of not being there for her, not supporting her, and not even trying to understand what she was going through. Tessa was crying and Alex just stood there and took it, the fight knocked out of him by the force of her words. He didn't try to stick up for himself or calm her down or even walk away. He just stood there.

When she was done, she packed a bag for herself and for Tessa. In a calm, steely voice, she told Alex she was leaving him, and drove away. Still he just stood there.

She made it about two miles before she realized that some automatic response seeded deep in her psyche was taking her to Ben's. She imagined Ben and Cate taking her and Tessa in, listening to her story and telling her everything was going to be okay. Then it hit her that she certainly couldn't go to Ben's house. Cate would take her in, of course, but it would be too hard to be in their apartment, with all of Ben's things. And she couldn't dump her problems on Cate, who was dealing with enough. Lara had nowhere to go. She began to cry so hard she had to pull over. When she was calm enough, she turned around and headed back home.

Lara walked back in the door, just minutes after she'd stormed out. Alex was sitting on the couch with his head in his hands. She was embarrassed. She didn't recognize the woman who had just screamed at her husband and told him she was leaving him. She looked at him, this man who had been trying so hard to be there for her, to provide her with whatever she needed, but who, just like her, didn't know how to fix this. *Who the hell am I and what have I done to my life?*

She had silently handed Tessa to him and went about unpacking the bag she'd packed not fifteen minutes before. When she was in slightly more control, she apologized. She couldn't look him in the face, but quietly said, "I'm sorry. I won't ever do that again. You didn't deserve to be yelled at like that and I don't want to leave."

Alex had just said, "Okay."

From that day on, she'd worked hard to keep her anger in check, but it felt impossible. Something had broken through the shock of Ben's death and there was no more pretending she was okay.

So she yelled at other drivers on the road or got overly impatient with a slow teller at the bank or picked just a *little* fight with Alex. Not one that would lead to a screaming match, but just enough so she could be a little bitchy. On the days she wasn't angry, she was sad and ended up on the closet floor, curled up around Ben's old sweatshirt. Some days, it was both. The only days she was okay were the rare days she was forced to go out into the world, to attend a meeting or go to a birthday party or take Tessa to the doctor. Then, she *had* to pretend, which was exhausting, so she usually ended those days by drinking too much wine and falling asleep.

She felt like a release valve that needed to be opened millimeter by millimeter, just to relieve the pressure. It was exhausting. And it obviously wasn't working. The worst part was that the anger didn't even touch the pain of the other things she'd lost since Ben died, things that she could have never even imagined could be lost.

Now, as she sat on the floor of her bathroom, taking stock of how she'd ended up there, she knew she'd become a drain on her family. There was no way she could deal with all of this without tearing her family apart. It would just be easier for Alex and Tessa if they didn't have to deal with her.

Lara opened the medicine cabinet and pulled out every prescription bottle they had. Antidepressants, muscle relaxers, the serious pain killers. Leftovers from a minor surgery, a battle with strep, a sore back. She counted how many were in each bottle. Surely it was enough. If she wanted to.

Lara contemplated what it would be like to swallow the pills and how it would feel. Would she just get tired and fall asleep? Would she get sick? What would Alex do when he found her? There was only one thing she was sure of: Alex didn't deserve everything she was putting him through. All he wanted was to help her and be there for her and she just crapped all over everything he said or did, never making an effort to meet him halfway.

She was so tired. So fucking tired. She didn't have the strength to keep going.

As she spread the pills along the counter, she thought about what her death would do to her family. Her parents were so far gone that she wouldn't be surprised if they weren't too far behind her. Ben's death had decimated them all.

Alex and Tessa were her main concern, of course. Alex would probably feel guilty and likely devastated, but eventually he'd find someone else, someone normal, someone not so broken. And Tessa was young. She might not even remember Lara. Lara couldn't decide whether that was better for her than growing up in the kind of home where Mommy couldn't get up off the floor and forgot to pick her up from daycare.

Because there was the truth of it. Lara could be as indignant as she wanted, tell Alex he was wrong, that of course she could take care of her own fucking kid. But she couldn't. Not well, at least. She'd never intentionally do anything to hurt Tessa, but she was in a fog of anger and grief and not even her baby's needs could break through it.

She didn't really want to commit suicide. She didn't really *want* to leave that legacy for her family. She'd spent hours begging God or whatever or whoever was out there to just make it easy on her and take her. It could be a car accident, or a brain aneurysm, or maybe she could just die in her sleep. But that hadn't happened no matter how hard she'd begged, and she just didn't want to do this anymore. She didn't want to face down a lifetime without Ben and this pain and weight in her chest that was never going to go away.

Lara was crying now, deep, racking sobs from the very bottom of her battered soul. She was so tired. Bone-tired down to her soul.

She filled a cup with water. Put six, seven, eight pills into her palm and just stood there. She closed her eyes.

As her tears slowed, Lara focused on breathing deeply. She

KRISTINA BRUNE

wanted to be calm as she made this decision. Taking deep breaths, she felt something right behind her right shoulder. Not movement. Not a touch. Something was just *there*.

"Ben?" Her eyes flew open, but she didn't move.

This happened to her every once in a while. It started two days after Ben's funeral. Lara had been in the car, on her way home from Target. They'd needed toilet paper and she had thought this one small task might help her feel a little bit normal. But every person she'd talked to or made eye contact with just seemed so damn *happy*. She didn't know how everyone could be so *happy* when she'd never be happy again. She'd left without buying anything and just wanted to make it home.

As she sat at a red light trying not to cry, she felt it. Just out of sight, behind her right shoulder. It was Ben. She didn't know how she knew. There was no sound, nothing there she could see. It was just him. She'd felt comforted for the first time since he died and she'd decided then and there that she wasn't going to overthink this or tell anyone about it. It was hers and she would enjoy it for as long as it lasted.

Feeling Ben—or whatever it was—here in her bathroom while she was honest-to-God thinking about killing herself made her start crying again. "Bubba," she breathed, tears choking her words. But he was gone.

She looked at the pills in her hand. The water glistening in the glass. *What the fuck am I doing?* she thought. *What in the fuck am I thinking?* She tossed the pills into the sink, knocking all the bottles over, and crumpled to the floor. Her legs bent underneath her, and her shoulder hit the bathroom cabinet as she fell against it.

"Lara?" she heard Alex jiggle the door handle. "Lara, what are you doing?" His voice rose. He sounded scared.

He must have heard the rattle of the bottles, the thud of her collapse. Jesus, what the *hell* was she thinking? She was crying so hard

23

she couldn't talk. She could hear Alex jiggling the door handle, calling for her to open the door, calling her name over and over. She heard the rattle of something in the doorknob and moments later Alex burst through the door.

He looked at the pills, the water, Lara sitting crumpled on the floor.

"Oh no baby, no baby, no, no, no," he repeated, his voice breaking. "What did you do? Lara, what did you do? What did you take? No baby, no, no, no."

She saw him reach for his phone and realized he was probably going to call 911. She managed to say, "I didn't take anything, I'm sorry, I'm sorry, I didn't take anything."

And then she was in his arms, clinging to his shirt. She could feel Alex's chest heave and he was crying, too. The hot, desperate tears just kept coming. "I'm sorry. I'm sorry," she whispered, over and over.

When Lara finally calmed down, her eyes swollen and burning, she asked Alex to leave her alone for a minute.

"I'm okay. I'm okay. I just need to splash some water on my face and I need to pick up this mess."

"I'm not leaving you—"

"Alex." She touched his arm. "I'm okay right now. It was so stupid. I wasn't thinking clearly, I wasn't actually going to … Just … just let me flush this—" she gestured to the pills scattered on the sink. "I want to do it."

He looked at her for a long moment and then said, "Nope. No way. I'll watch you do it. I'm not leaving you alone."

"Alex—"

"No."

She knew she was in no position to argue and his arms folded across his chest told her he wasn't going to budge. So she gathered the pills in her palm and dropped them into the toilet, flushing it quickly. She threw the empty bottles into the trash, dumped the water out of the glass, and placed it carefully on the sink.

She washed her face with cool water. Alex was still standing right there. She couldn't look at him.

He grabbed her shoulders, speaking softly but forcefully. "Don't you ever fucking do that to me. Ever. There is not a single thing that would fix. It would ruin my life and Tessa's life." He pushed her back gently and forced her chin up to look at him. "And it would piss Ben off, Lara. That's not the way out."

She looked away again.

"Look at me, Lara. You need help. I understand that you're depressed and I understand you feel hopeless and I should have gotten you, I don't know, more serious help, something, a long time ago, but that is *not the way*. Do you understand me?"

She nodded.

"Okay. Okay." Alex took a breath. "Do you need to go somewhere tonight?"

"What do you mean?"

"I don't know what I mean. I don't know if I need to take you to the hospital. I don't know if you can be left alone." This last he said almost in a whisper, to himself. Lara didn't know how to respond. She thought she would be okay, but if you'd asked her this morning if she'd end the evening in her bathroom, contemplating suicide and counting out pills, she would have said no.

"I'm okay. I don't need to go to the hospital. It was a really stupid thing to even think about. Really stupid. I don't want to die. I'm just so tired. I'm so tired." Her body felt a hundred pounds heavier, the crying and drama of the last hour draining her of any energy.

"Well I'm definitely not going to work tomorrow. I'll stay home and we'll make some calls, get you an appointment with Dr. Martinez and—"

"Can we just go to bed for now? I'm sorry, I just feel like I can't stand up anymore."

"Yeah. Okay."

Lara changed her clothes and climbed into bed. Alex changed, brushed his teeth, and sat down next to her.

"I'm sorry," she said, again.

"I'm sorry, too," he responded. "I'm here, babe. We're going to get through this." He ran his hand through her hair and she fell asleep almost immediately, exhaustion taking hold.

Some time later, she heard him turn the television on and felt the glow of the screen behind her eyelids. Clearly he wouldn't sleep tonight. She clutched the locket that hung around her neck in her hand. It was simple, a small, silver rectangle and contained some of Ben's ashes. She never took it off. As she held it, she wanted to apologize to Alex again, but before she could, she had fallen asleep.

The next morning, she woke up late, sun streaming in the windows. She glanced at the alarm clock. Nine-thirty. Alex wasn't in bed with her, but the bedroom door was wide open and she could hear the television on, Tessa babbling to herself.

Lara leaned back into the pillows and closed her eyes, fresh tears squeezing out as she thought about what she'd almost done last night. She didn't *want* to die. She was a mother and a wife and she loved Alex and Tessa and didn't want to leave them.

But even as she reassured herself, a small voice inside her head said, *But you're still here. And he's still dead. You still have to deal with it. You're still so tired. And it still hurts so fucking much.*

CHAPTER TWO

Lara

Lara was trying not to cry as she and Alex dropped Tessa off at daycare. She couldn't stop herself from imagining every terrible scenario that could possibly play out with a rambunctious two-year-old while they were gone. *What if something happens to her and Alex's parents can't get hold of us? Cell service kind of sucks in Grafton. What if something happens to* us, *and Tessa spends the rest of her life wondering why we left her to go drink wine?*

In the parking lot, when she turned around a second time to get one more glimpse of Tessa waving goodbye with her chubby little hand, Alex slung his arm around her. "She's gonna be fine."

"I know, I know. Trying to turn it off."

The day after she'd locked herself in the bathroom, she and Alex had called the Employee Assistance Program available through Alex's employer. They got the names of three counselors and after making a series of calls to talk with their receptionists, Lara made an appointment with Dr. Moore, who specialized in grief and had been counseling for more than thirty years. She begged for a time for the next day, explaining to him, as difficult as it was, that she needed help sooner rather than later.

That first appointment had gone well. Now, she was a month in, and while she wasn't exactly confident that she could get better, Lara thought if anyone could help her, Dr. Moore could.

She hadn't been super excited about this trip. Dr. Moore had recommended an intense therapy plan so she was going twice a week, but she still had days where it felt like too much. She'd skipped a couple of sessions, which she and Alex had fought about. He'd accused her of not taking it seriously. She'd accused him of not understanding that sometimes she was just too tired to deal with the emotional roller coaster that was a therapy session.

But she also had good days. Days where she got up in the morning and got dressed, took care of Tessa, had a productive day at work, and felt like there was light at the end of this long, dark tunnel. Like the day Alex had asked her about going on this trip.

"Hey babe," Alex had said, putting his lunchbox down on the counter and coming up

behind Lara, who was washing dishes in the sink. He turned her around and gave her a big, long hug. She smiled against his chest, enjoying the smell of him; a mixture of the outdoors, creosote, and just Alex.

"What's all this love for?" she asked, turning to give Alex a kiss on the cheek.

"Just because." Alex went to the pantry and picked out a bag of trail mix. "Okay. So I have an idea and you're not allowed to say no."

"Uh-oh," said Lara.

Alex popped a handful of trail mix in his mouth and chewed before saying, "I talked to my mom today. She and my dad miss Tessa and they wanted to know if we'd like them to take her next weekend, Friday and Saturday night. I made an executive decision and told them yes."

"Alex … I don't know. We've never left her for a whole weekend. I don't know if I feel up to it."

"I said you couldn't say no. I know we haven't left her for that long. But she was fine the night they watched her for Johnny's wedding and she's even older now so we don't have to worry so much about her schedule. She'll have a blast on the farm."

Lara didn't say anything.

"Come on. I made plans to go to Grafton for the weekend. We'll just relax, go shopping, visit Maisie. I need to just spend time with you."

Lara had wanted to say no. The thought of packing all of their stuff and driving all the way to Grafton felt exhausting. She felt comfortable at home, where she could control her surroundings and retreat to the closet.

"My mom and dad have already agreed to pick Tessa up from daycare early Friday afternoon. I got a room at the Ruebel. You've always wanted to stay there. We need this time away, babe."

Still Lara had hesitated. She worried it would be too hard being at Maisie's and would remind her of … well, of everything she was trying so hard *not* to be reminded of. She worried about being away from Tessa or that she would have a bad day while they were gone and not be able to get out of bed. She took a deep breath, opened her mouth to tell him no, but the look on his face stopped her. He already looked disappointed. He expected her to say no.

He deserves this, she told herself. He wasn't asking too much. She at least owed it to him to try.

"Okay!" She'd forced a smile. "Thank you for planning it. It'll be nice to get away."

Alex had let out a surprised laugh and said, "Really? It's gonna be great, babe. I promise." He kissed her on the forehead.

Lara nodded and began the hard work of talking herself into it. *It's going to be fine,* she told herself.

Alex put the trail mix away and began walking toward the living room.

"Now go ahead and start typing out the three-page list of instructions I know you're going to leave with my mom," he said.

"Hey!" Lara said, surprising herself by laughing as Alex ran out of the room before she could smack him with the dish towel. "Don't make fun of my instructions! Everyone loves them and they are *super* helpful!" she yelled after him.

It felt good to laugh.

Now, they were heading out of St. Louis, traveling west on

highway 270, then north again on 367, crossing the Lewis and Clark Bridge and entering Illinois. They didn't talk much. Alex held her hand, rubbing his thumb across hers. Lara looked out the window as they drove through Alton, taking in the familiar sights: the marina with everything from fishing boats to yachts parked in the slips, old-town Alton with its steep streets, bars and antique shops living side by side, and the eyesore that was the Alton Belle Casino, a riverboat-turned-casino, which someone had inexplicably decided to paint in various shades of pastel green, pink, blue, and purple.

They turned onto the Great River Road. The road stretched for 2,000 miles along the Mississippi, winding through ten states and hundreds of historic river towns, and was consistently named one of the best scenic routes in America.

Here between Alton and Grafton, the River Road cut right between the massive Mississippi River on one side and impossibly tall bluffs on the other. The bluffs, cut out of mostly limestone, rose like giants, towering over the road. Topped with trees, they seemed ready to crumble at any moment. If you craned your head way, way up, you could make out the large homes that sat on top of the bluffs, set back against trees and seeming to dangle right off the edge. There was a rumor that Tom Cruise and Nicole Kidman had once owned one of those bluff houses, but Lara never knew whether or not that was true.

As they wound along the road that followed the snaking path of the river, Lara took in the view. The leaves were changing, and reds, oranges, and yellows ran like fire along the cliffs, stark against the blue sky. Large barges moved grain, coal, gravel, and who knew what else slowly along the river. Bald eagles, seagulls, and ducks swooped in and out of the water. A large group of motorcycles passed them on one side and a family of bicyclists passed them on the other, where a bike path wound along the bluff side.

"I always forget how beautiful it is over here. The river makes me feel so small," she said. "When I was a kid, I wished I could travel down the river like Tom Sawyer."

Alex laughed. "When I was a kid all I ever saw was cornfields. All I could wish for was that my dad would let me drive the tractor."

They passed several small communities, the kind of "towns" that were made up of just a few houses and no real infrastructure or businesses to speak of. They were leftovers, forgotten, maintained only by those families that refused to leave because they'd been there forever.

The River Road turned into Grafton's main street that ran through town. The town sat right on the Mississippi River, just northeast of the northern St. Louis counties. Flooding was always a threat in Grafton, so the homes and businesses on the river side of the road were up on stilts, constructed on tall berms, or designed so the lower floors could be easily evacuated and material goods moved out.

Grafton itself had a population of just a little over 500, but it was a big tourist attraction. Small shops, mostly antique stores and kitschy boutiques, along with restaurants, wineries, and small bed and breakfasts, lined either side of the road. Some were right on the water and some were nestled up in the river bluffs, where you could watch the river wind for miles.

Most of the homes in Grafton were on the opposite side of the river, across the main road. The streets were steep, feeling nearly vertical as your car powered up them. Many of the older homes were painted in bright colors and newer condos had sprung up in recent years within walking distance of Main Street.

Lara and Alex parked on the street and headed into the Ruebel Hotel to check in. The Ruebel was a historic landmark in Grafton. The brick building looked like a page from a history book, a wild west hotel. It was also rumored to be haunted by a little girl named Abigail. In spite of having grown up nearby, Lara had never stayed overnight, visiting only to eat dinner in the restaurant.

They dropped off their bags in the room and Alex put his arms around Lara, nuzzling her neck. "So what should we do first? Want to take a nap?"

"Ha! I don't think you have sleeping in mind," she said, kissing him on the cheek. "I want to walk around. Let's go check out some of the shops. You know you can't resist a good antique store." Alex was a sucker for vintage stuff. Their home was dotted with antique fans, milk bottles, and old farming equipment Alex thought was interesting. Lara didn't like to admit it to Alex, but she thought it added a certain charm to their home and helped offset her more sparse, neutral decor preferences. At the very least they made great conversation starters.

"Okay, fine," he said, kissing her one more time on the spot right underneath her ear that always made her toes curl. "But are you *sure* you wouldn't rather stay here?"

Lara laughed and gently pushed him away. "You almost got me."

They walked down the main street in Grafton, stopping in the small shops and boutiques. When visiting Maisie as a child, Lara had spent hours walking through the musty, dusty antique shops. She'd been amazed at the breadth of items for sale—you could find everything from vintage clothing and custom-made art to ancient farming equipment and vintage toys. She'd been fascinated by the history contained in these pieces and wondered who had used them, who had made them? How had they landed here, in an antique shop in the middle of nowhere, on sale for a buck?

When Lara opened the door to Great Rivers Antiques, the musty smell unique to antique shops and flea markets—a little bit of dust, mold, and mothballs—hit her nose. It was packed full of items, floor-to-ceiling shelves lining the perimeter of the room. Tables and other furniture were set up in the middle of the space, piled high with items for sale. Old signs from gas stations, vintage advertisements, and unique artwork lined what little wall space was available.

Near the front of the store, a huge L-shaped desk sat in one corner, in front of the window overlooking the street. The desktop was covered with paperwork, a laptop, random items for sale, and a small television was playing *Wheel of Fortune* on mute. Behind the desk were boxes full of more stuff. Some of it appeared to be getting ready to ship, as bubble wrap and brown paper were overflowing from a few boxes.

An old man sat behind the desk, perched on a padded stool. His back was turned to the store, and he was engrossed in what looked like a large ledger, full of small, cramped writing. He didn't look up when Lara and Alex walked in.

"How's it going?" Alex, always polite, called out. The man looked up. He wore small wireframe glasses, a plain white button-down shirt with pens sticking out of the pocket, and suspenders clipped into blue jeans that looked like they'd seen better days. His gray hair was wispy—almost translucent—atop his head and the skin on his face, neck, and head had been reddened by years of exposure to the sun.

"Sorry, I didn't hear you folks come in. My bell fell off the door yesterday and without it, well ... let's just say the old ears aren't what they used to be."

"No problem, just looking around," Alex said.

"Alright. Let me know if I can help with anything."

Alex wandered away toward some old photographs of Grafton and the river. Lara found herself immediately drawn to the books. She let her fingers trail over the book spines, reading through the paperback bestsellers and the long-forgotten yellowed and musty titles. She spied a number of books she'd already read and remembered enjoying. She found herself thinking how odd it was that you could read a book once and forget so much of it. Lara thought she could read all of those books again and have a totally different experience. *I wish I could just read again,* she thought. She closed her eyes for a moment and pushed the thought away, before it got too big and ruined what good mood she'd managed to scrape together this weekend.

When she opened her eyes, Lara spotted the corner of a book on the floor, wedged between the wall and the shelf. It must have fallen and been pushed back there and no one had noticed. She knelt down and reached around to grab the book, gently prying it out.

She stood up, brushing dust off the cover. It was a leather-bound hardback, dark hunter green with gold gilt around the edges of the front, back, and spine. The gilt design included a border of leaves, with a large gold tree in the center. Under the tree were the title and author: *Memoriae* by Violet Marsh.

The book seemed to be in fairly good shape. The leather was worn on the corners and some of the gold gilt was rubbed away. She could see that the pages were yellowed, but they seemed to be tight with the binding. Lara opened the book to the title page, where it simply said *Memoriae,* and just a few lines underneath that, Violet Marsh, 1890. There was no table of contents. Lara turned to the first page.

The day my brother died was the day I felt like I lost my grip on the real world. When his heart stopped beating, I willed mine to do the same. But no matter how hard I tried, how hard I prayed for the sweet release that would allow me to join him, wherever he might be, here I remained. Trapped.

"Whoa," Lara whispered. Suddenly, she felt a hand on her shoulder. She jumped, her hand flying to her chest.

"Shit!" she said. She turned to see Alex's smiling face. He was clearly trying not to laugh.

"Sorry! I didn't mean to sneak up on you. I said your name, but you didn't hear me."

"I was looking at this book," she said, handing it to him. "Read those first couple of lines."

Alex read the words. "That's weird. Sounds a little like you, babe," he said kindly, brushing a dust bunny off her hand. He turned the book over. "I guess *Memoriae* means memory?"

"Probably. Sounds like Latin or something."

"Are you going to buy it?"

She almost said no. But there was something about it. Maybe she needed to hear Violet's story. "Yeah, I think I'm going to. Even if I don't read it, it's pretty. I'll put it on my desk or something." It was then that she noticed the pile of crap at Alex's feet. "What is all of that?"

He smiled sheepishly. "You know you can't take me into these places. I always find something I need! But look at all this stuff I found!"

Feigning annoyance, she said, "What are you going to bring home now?"

He showed her a vintage minnow trap for fishing that had a $20 sticker on it ("They're ten dollars at Wal-Mart!" she said); an admittedly gorgeous picture of the bend in the river just north of town, taken from the bluffs; and a beautiful old metal lantern that had just the right amount of rust peeking through the shiny black finish.

"But best of all is this!" he said, picking up a large, black case. He set it on a nearby table and carefully opened the clasps. Inside was a vintage typewriter.

"I've always wanted one of these," Lara said.

Alex smiled at her. "I know. It's in really great shape. Not that we're going to actually use it, but it works," he said, pushing a couple of keys.

"Alright, I'll admit those are some pretty good finds." She set her book inside the typewriter case and shut it. She picked up the picture and the lantern, leaving Alex to carry the rest. They walked to the cash register where the storeowner was still paging through the old ledger. He took his glasses off and stuck them in his shirt pocket.

"Find everything you need?"

"Probably more than we need," Lara said, laughing. He didn't respond and began ringing up their items. As he finished, Lara remembered the book. "Oh! We also have a book. I stuck it in the typewriter case and forgot. It's a hardback. I think the sign said they were all three dollars."

"Yep," he said.

Lara raised her eyebrows at Alex as if to say, *Not very talkative, this one.* Alex smiled and handed over some cash.

"Not from around here?" the storeowner asked as he made their change. It wasn't really a question, as most people who shopped in his store were probably tourists.

"Not really, no," said Lara. "My aunt lives here in Grafton and I spent a lot of time here as a kid. But I grew up in Jerseyville. We live in St. Louis now."

"Who's your aunt?"

"Maisie Beck."

His hands froze over the cash register drawer, for just a moment. "Maisie Beck, huh?" He seemed to recover and handed Alex his change.

"Yes. You know her?"

"Everyone knows Maisie. She's real involved in church." He took his glasses out of his pocket, put them back on, and pulled the old ledger toward him. "Thanks for coming."

"Um. Sure," Lara said.

"Was that weird or was it just me?" she asked Alex as they walked down the sidewalk.

"He's probably just a crabby old man. But he didn't seem to

36

want to talk about Maisie, huh?"

"I thought everyone here loves her. I *know* they do."

"Like I said, probably just a crabby old man."

"Yeah," Lara said, though she wasn't entirely convinced.

Lara and Alex walked around town some more, shopping, enjoying a bottle of wine and a cheese plate at Aeries Winery, which sat atop one of the bluffs. You could see for miles, across the river into Missouri, back toward Alton and farther north.

After they'd returned to the hotel to take a shower and get dressed before dinner, Lara could feel the strain of the day wearing on her. It was exhausting, constantly pushing down the pain and the grief so she could try to enjoy this time with Alex. But she ignored it, did her hair and makeup, and even held Alex's hand as they walked down the street toward the restaurant. Because it *did* feel nice to be out with just him. It had been a long time since they'd spent time alone without the pull of something else—Tessa or the laundry or work or her grief and depression.

As she finished her first glass of wine and ordered a decadent dinner, she felt herself slowly relax. They talked about Tessa and about the big project Alex and his crew were starting the next week. She told him about a new prospective client she'd had a meeting with. They watched a group of older people dancing to the music of a husband-wife duo and joked that they hoped their dance moves would be that good when they were in their seventies. Lara had forgotten how much this man could make her laugh and how handsome he looked in jeans and a button-down shirt.

As they opened their second bottle of wine, picking at what remained of their dinner, Alex swung his chair around to her side of their small, round table and put his hand on her shoulder. He absentmindedly ran his hand through the hair at the nape of her neck, making her shiver and lean into him. He kissed her on the top of her head and she rested her hand on his leg, drawing small circles with her thumb. She closed her eyes and, for the first time in a long time, felt content with where she was, in that moment.

It wasn't long before they'd finished the second bottle and Alex was whispering in her ear, making her giggle. When the waitress came back by, he asked for the check. They stumbled back down the street to the Ruebel, fell into bed, a little tipsy and a lot horny, just like it used to be.

John

When Maisie's niece and her husband left the store, John stood up, walked to the front door, and flipped the store sign to "Closed." He wasn't in the mood to talk to anyone else today, even though it was Friday and he might miss some sales from the weekend revelers.

He dimmed the store lights, then sat back down behind the counter and flipped on his lamp. He tried to get back into the ledger, but couldn't concentrate.

He sighed and turned the volume up on the small television he kept behind the counter. He usually enjoyed *Judge Judy*, but as the familiar strains of the introduction music came on, he found his mind drifting.

Lara looked a little bit like Maisie—dark, thick hair and big blue eyes. Well. Maisie sixty years ago. Now her dark hair was gray and while her eyes were still bright blue, they were framed in deep lines. He still occasionally found himself sneaking glances at her during church and around town. She was always smiling. Always had been the kind of person who could light up a room and grab the attention of men and women alike.

John, Maisie, and Cecille had grown up together in Grafton. They'd been born in the middle of the Great Depression and had lived close to each other on a steep residential street up in the bluffs. They'd weathered the war together, with the rest of the children in town, and when it was over they figured out how to navigate absent

38

(and, for some of them, dead) fathers and mothers, the ones left just doing their best to hold things down at home. When the war ended, the world had seemed wide open to them.

They spent all their free time together, at least what they had of it. Children back then were expected to help around the house and didn't have nearly so much time to play and get into trouble as kids these days, thank you very much. They had adventures along the river and explored the woods up on the bluffs. John had grown up with three sisters, so he was used to being around girls all the time. But Maisie and CiCi hadn't been like other girls. They hadn't been afraid to get dirty, didn't scream when a bug landed on their face, and didn't wear frilly dresses or put bows in their hair. He had male friends, of course, but was happy to spend most of his time with Maisie and CiCi.

But as so often happened when boys and girls grow up, when the trio turned thirteen, things between them began to change. He'd catch Maisie and CiCi laughing and talking together, but they'd stop as soon as he entered the room. They began to dress up a little more often, coming to school with big bows in their hair and ribboned socks to match their Mary Janes. And they began talking to other boys.

John vividly remembered their freshman year in high school when he'd come upon CiCi kissing William Dunson in a quiet hallway. They didn't notice him and he'd backed slowly away. That night, he and Maisie had plans to go to a Sadie Hawkins dance. She had asked him as a joke, telling him teasingly, "You're just the most logical choice." But when he accepted her invitation, he felt a little flutter of excitement he did his best to completely ignore. Then, when he picked her up, he noticed for the first time how her body had changed. She was somehow softer—her hair fuller, hips rounder. And she smelled good.

"What's wrong with you? Maisie said, when she caught him staring at her.

"N-nothing," he'd stammered. "You look nice."

To his great surprise, Maisie had blushed. Maisie never got embarrassed and her reaction to his compliment made him feel happy. That night, they danced together for the first time. As they walked home, John thought about holding her hand, but didn't. He didn't really understand what he was feeling and certainly wasn't sure what to do about it.

To his relief, the three of them met up the next day to go to their secret spot in the woods and everything seemed normal. Although he did catch Maisie looking at him as CiCi regaled them with a story about her date with William the night before. She'd rolled her eyes at him and smiled a smile that seemed kind of sad.

Over the next year, John and Maisie spent more time together and less time with CiCi. Something had changed between the girls, but Maisie never wanted to talk about it when he asked, so he eventually let it go. After a time—much longer than he wanted—they began dating and John couldn't have been happier.

He went through a lot of trouble to make sure he did nice things for Maisie, picking her flowers, buying her favorite candies, and leaving notes in her locker. Occasionally the thought would occur to him that Maisie never seemed quite as excited to spend time together or make out or do the things he thought about all the time. But he'd shake it off, reminding himself that she wasn't like other girls and didn't need a lot of attention and lovey-dovey stuff.

Then came the Korean War. It began their junior year and by the time they graduated, it was 1951, the war was in full swing, and John was eighteen. He decided to enlist in the Army, following in his father and grandfather's footsteps. He was sent to boot camp three short weeks after their graduation and had gone off to fight.

In the beginning, Maisie wrote to him frequently and he'd been glad when she'd told him she and CiCi had been spending more time together. CiCi had married William right after school, just before he'd also been sent to Korea.

But slowly, Maisie's letters became less frequent and more perfunctory in subject matter. She rarely talked about missing him like she had in the beginning and the letters read more like a recitation of the ins and outs of her days as a nursing student and less like a love letter. Eventually, about two weeks before the armistice would end the fighting, as it would turn out, he got his very own Dear John letter. Maisie told him how much she loved him and that he would always be one of her closest and dearest friends, but that she no longer wanted a romantic relationship.

John had been shocked and upset, but he was sure it was just because of the physical distance between them and that when he returned home, all would be well again. But he'd been wrong. William had died in the war and when John got home, he discovered that Maisie had moved into the small apartment CiCi and William had shared. And she wasn't planning on rekindling their relationship.

Maisie agreed to go to dinner with him just two days after his return, but made it clear it was just as friends. He asked her why she didn't love him anymore and what had happened. She'd been nice about it, but said that she felt like they'd been together for so long and it was time for her to go out into the world on her own.

He was ashamed to admit it, but he'd stormed out of the restaurant after throwing some bills down on the table. He didn't understand why she was doing this and felt helpless because clearly there was no way he could change her mind.

Eventually, he'd moved on, meeting Virginia and falling in love with her. She had been a wonderful wife and mother and he counted himself lucky. He'd gone to work for his father's manufacturing company and had been able to retire when he was fairly young. He and Virginia had opened Great Rivers Antiques and he'd enjoyed it much more than he'd thought he would. He'd had a good life. A great life.

Over the years, he, Maisie, and CiCi had remained cordial enough. They had to in a town this small. But they were never so close again and John did not seek out the women's company. When the rumors around town started about Maisie and CiCi, a lot of things clicked into place for John, but he didn't like to think about it. He didn't think he'd ever fully recovered from losing Maisie. He wished they could have stayed friends, and he was sure Maisie would have welcomed him back into her life, but it was too painful.

Now look at me, he thought. *I'm a silly old man, still pining away for his childhood sweetheart.*

But they'd always be tied together. Maybe that was why it was so hard for him to let it go. He and Maisie and CiCi had experienced something as kids that he hoped he'd never have to think of again.

John shook his head to chase out the thoughts and headed home for the evening.

Lara

The next morning Lara woke at six, looked at the clock and burrowed deeper into the fluffy white bedding, cuddling up to Alex and luxuriating at not waking up to an alarm. Eventually she fell back asleep.

Some time later she woke again when Alex stirred beside her, groaning.

"Why did I drink so much?" he mumbled into his pillow.

Lara laughed and turned over, rubbing his back. "Not feeling too good?"

"Like I got hit by a truck."

"We're too old to party, babe."

"Never drinking again."

Eventually, they rolled out of bed and got moving, grabbing coffee before they made the short drive to Aunt Maisie's small home. As they pulled into her driveway and parked, the front door opened and Maisie, apron tied around her waist, stepped onto the porch. Lara smiled and bounded up the stairs, wrapping Maisie in a huge hug. She breathed in the scent of Maisie's famous apple crumble pie and banana muffins, and the lavender she used for everything from freshening her laundry to sprinkling in her bath.

"My darling, it is so good to see you," Maisie whispered into her hair. "My sweet, sweet Lolly."

Tears pricked at Lara's eyes. She hadn't realized how badly she'd needed one of Maisie's hugs. She walked into Maisie's home and felt peace settle over her like a blanket. Maisie's house hadn't changed much in the many years she'd lived there. There were a few upgrades here and there—a new smart TV in the living room and stainless appliances in the kitchen—but for the most part it was like stepping back in time for Lara. The framed photographs of her family and of Grafton hung on the living room and hallway walls. The same yellow, red, and orange quilt was neatly folded along the back of the couch and the same lace curtains hung in the kitchen windows. It was like coming home.

Maisie pulled back, her hands grasping both of Lara's upper arms. "Let me look at you! You're as beautiful as ever!" Maisie looked past Lara and smiled broadly at Alex. "And who is this handsome drink of water? Couldn't possibly be Alex. Lara, you've gone and gotten yourself a sexy new boyfriend, haven't you?"

For all of Maisie's grandmotherly qualities, she also wasn't afraid to cuss like a sailor or make vaguely inappropriate comments about young men. It was one of the things Lara loved best about her.

Maisie had never married. A fiercely independent woman, she'd had one true love in her life and it was her best friend Cecille. They'd been inseparable for nearly seventy-five years, never living more than a few blocks from each other. They both became nurses, were active in their church, and were a strong force for feminism and civil rights in this fiercely Republican, Midwestern area.

They'd been in love, of course, hiding it in the shadows like "society" required. CiCi had gotten married when she was nineteen, at the pressure of her family, but her husband died in the Korean War and she'd never remarried. Instead she and Maisie chose to fill their days together.

When Lara asked Maisie once why they'd never moved out of Grafton, to a bigger city where they could live together and not have to pretend, Maisie had said, simply, that this was their home. It was where their roots were. "People around here know exactly who we are, even if they'd never say it," said Maisie. "You know I could never live with someone else in my house anyway, even CiCi! We tried that when we were young for a while and she's far too messy. And anyway, people aren't quite as willing to buy the roommate story when two women are in their seventies and not their twenties." She'd shrugged. "It's just what we've always known."

CiCi had died seven years before of breast cancer. Lara had worried about Maisie and tried to talk her into moving in with her and Alex, but Maisie had refused. She was the strongest person Lara knew.

"I'm so glad you all are here. Of course, I can't understand why you'd show up at my house without that baby, but I suppose I can spend some time with just you. But just this once," she admonished as she ushered them inside.

"Sorry, Maisie. My fault," Alex said. "We'll bring Tess next time for sure. We just needed to get away and I gave Lara no choice."

Alex's voice was perfectly normal, revealing none of the stress of the last year or so. But Maisie was perceptive.

"How are you, Lolly?" Maisie asked, as she set out muffins and coffee cups.

"I'm okay. I'm feeling better, I think."

Alex put his hand on her back and nodded.

"I'm getting the help I need. It's still really hard. But I'm figuring out how to deal with it. Anyway! Tell me what's happening here."

Maisie looked at her for a long moment, then gave in to Lara's change of subject, regaling them with tales from around town—who was marrying who, which businesses were in trouble, what stupid thing the town council had decided on.

Eventually Alex said, "Okay, Maisie. I know you have a list for me. Whatcha got? Need the gutters cleaned out? Leaves raked up? Lay it on me."

"No list today. You two need to get on with your day and go have some fun. You don't need to spend your time fixing shit for this old lady."

"Absolutely not," said Alex. "I'm not leaving here without getting something done. You better tell me or I'm going to go find something to do and you're finally going to end up with that old person handle in the shower you're always saying you don't need," he teased.

"You better not be thinking about me in the shower. Fine. Go clean out those gutters. It rained buckets the other day and I could hear all that water pouring out of the damn things. Oh!" Maisie stood up, clearly having just thought of something. "You know I was watching HGTV the other day and they were talking about gallery walls and I just loved that idea."

Maisie started leading Alex up the stairs, talking all the way. "So I got all these frames and old photos and started measuring the wall in my office and I saw this trick where you use pieces of paper to mark where you want each thing to go but I got so damn mad when ..."

Her voice trailed off as they went into her office. Lara took a deep breath and closed her eyes. She knew Maisie wasn't fooled by their bright smiles and assurances that everything was fine. She would want to know how Lara was really doing. Lara wouldn't lie to her.

She sighed as she thought back to that day just a month ago. She'd been so close to doing something she could never take back and now, sitting here in Maisie's kitchen, she still felt tired. The pain of losing Ben was still overwhelming. But there was a small glimmer of hope, somewhere deep inside her.

Lara heard Maisie's footsteps clunking down the stairs and she shoved aside her thoughts. Maisie sat down and put her hand on top of Lara's. "How are you really, love? I've been worried about you," she said.

Lara looked down at the table, tracing the ancient nicks and scratches in the wood with her fingertips. "Things have been pretty bad for a while. I spent so long pretending that everything was okay, that I could just deal with it. But I really wasn't okay. I—" She took a deep breath—"I'm really not okay."

"You know no one expects you to be okay."

Lara wiped a stray tear from her cheek. "I know that. Logically. But I just feel like … I don't know. It was just my brother, you know? Mom and Dad and Cate needed my help more than I needed them and—"

"No." Maisie interrupted her. "You know, I still pick up the phone to call my sister? She died twenty years ago, Lara." Maisie sighed. "I'm old. I've lost both of my parents. Countless friends. I lost CiCi. And Ben. I've lost cousins and grandparents and aunts and uncles. Of course, I can't speak to losing a child, but as much as I miss CiCi and Mama and Papa, losing my sister was the hardest loss of all."

Maisie took a sip of her now-cold coffee and wrapped her hands around the mug.

"Our relationships with our siblings are our longest and, I think, one of the most powerful relationships of our lives. They're not always easy but your siblings are the people in your life you can tell your secrets to but still stick with you. You can fight like cats and dogs and maybe not even speak for months or years but they will always be there. They know all of your history and all of your mistakes and are meant to be with you for the long haul. It's not fair that you lost Ben so soon. You don't have to rush your healing."

"I know that," Lara said. "But I can't be … catatonic, either. I have to find a way to live, right? It just feels really, really hard."

"You do have to live. I just don't want you to feel like there's some magical cure, or…I don't know, a timeline or something that you have to stick to. You just need to do what you need to do. And don't forget to talk about him. I know I sure miss him."

Lara smiled and held Maisie's hand, not trusting herself to speak. Her throat clenched and she swallowed the lump there. Lara worried that if she kept talking, she'd start crying for real and she didn't want to have a breakdown here in Maisie's kitchen. So she changed the subject, getting her phone out of her purse to show Maisie the latest pictures of Tessa.

When Alex came back in they talked for a while longer, but Maisie eventually shooed them out so they could enjoy their day.

Lara hugged her aunt good-bye and whispered, "Thank you so much, Maze. I love you."

"You're going to be okay, Lolly. You're going to be okay." Lara wanted to believe her.

Later that night, after they'd hiked through the woods at Pere Marquette State Park, taken a luxurious nap back at the Ruebel and had dinner and drinks, they went back to the hotel early, laughing because getting a good night's sleep sounded better than staying out late to party.

Alex fell asleep, snoring softly, but once she lay down, Lara didn't feel tired anymore. She turned on the television but there wasn't anything good, just a bunch of infomercials and a sitcom she didn't care for.

As she lay there, she stole a glance at Alex, sleeping so peacefully.

She still loved him so much, after all these years and everything they'd been through. She reached out and stroked back a stray lock of hair that had grown a little too long.

Things hadn't always been this way between them; difficult and fraught with grief and fear and misunderstanding. Once upon a time, they'd been easy together.

They'd met by chance, at a Halloween party at a school neither of them went to, in a town neither of them lived in. Lara had been visiting a friend at Tennessee State University. The party was at the off-campus sorority house where Lara's friend lived. Alex was attending a lineman training school in Georgia and was tagging along with a friend to his hometown of Nashville.

They started talking because Lara was dressed as a Barbie; short pink dress, platinum blonde wig, and stilettos. Alex was dressed as a chick magnet; he'd used a Sharpie to draw a plus sign on the front and minus sign on the back of an old white t-shirt, and Barbies were tied all over the shirt. They joked that Lara wouldn't be able to stay away from him all night.

Once they started talking they didn't stop. They discovered that they'd both grown up in Illinois, just a little more than an hour apart—Alex in the small town of Carlyle and Lara in Jerseyville. They both loved scary movies, had a passion for the *Harry Potter* books and Cardinals baseball, and had dreams of seeing the world. They were the same age, just turned twenty-one, and would both be graduating in the next couple of months. Alex had plans to move back home and get a job with a local utility or maybe travel around the country, chasing the aftermath of hurricanes and tornadoes. Lara, who was majoring in design at Southern Illinois University Edwardsville, didn't have any specific plans.

When Lara's friend gave her the puppy dog eyes because she wanted to leave the party with a guy she'd been crushing on for months, Lara didn't care. She said she'd find her way back to the sorority house. Alex's friend had fallen asleep on a couch and they left him there. Lara and Alex sat outside for the rest of the night, talking. She thought how odd—and sweet— it was that Alex hadn't tried to make a move on her, even though she probably would have been okay with it.

Finally, at 4:00 a.m., Alex reluctantly said he needed to get his friend home. Alex tried to wake him up first by shaking his arm, then by yelling at him. When that didn't work, he dumped water on his face, which resulted in him falling off the couch and yelling some not-so-polite words at Alex before he staggered out to Alex's truck. Laughing, Lara and Alex walked outside and leaned against the tailgate. They exchanged numbers, promising to keep in touch even though Alex had two months left in Georgia and Lara would be heading back to Edwardsville. Alex had kissed her, softly, almost chastely, and run his hand down her arm.

She'd been ecstatic when Alex called her the next day while she was driving home. They talked for two hours and it was just *easy*. They talked every day after that for the next two months, until they'd both graduated and Alex had moved back to Illinois. He got a job with an electrical contractor that served the metro east area and entered their apprenticeship. In two years, he'd be able to work anywhere. Lara got a job at an ad agency in St. Louis, where people brought their dogs into the office and funky, creative ideas were welcome.

After three years together, Alex booked a trip to Nashville, telling Lara they were going to the CMA Music Festival. But Alex also took her back to the sorority house where they'd met and proposed right there in the street where he first kissed her. They'd married in a small ceremony in Mexico and shortly after, Alex took a job in California and they moved into a small house two miles from the beach. They were happy. Lara worked for a small production company, dabbling in video animation. She loved living in California, where it was almost always sunny and she could go to the beach every day if she wanted. But they never intended to live there forever and after four years they moved back home, buying a house in a suburb of St. Louis. They took trips and had lazy Sundays in bed and built a small family of friends around them. They adopted a beagle named George, got pregnant with Tessa, and settled into life.

Then Ben died and here they were. She was a mess. Their marriage was a mess and she'd lost so much more than just her brother.

Lara sighed and rolled over again. She saw the black typewriter case sitting on the floor and got out of bed, opening it quietly. She pulled out *Memoriae* and brought it back to bed, switching on the lamp on the end table. She looked more closely at the cover, running her fingers over the gold gilt leaves and the full tree. She opened it, flipping through the pages. It wasn't very long and there were a ton of blank pages at the end of the book. It was a regular printed book, but as she flipped through the pages, skimming a passage here and there, she realized it was really more of a diary.

Lara began to read.

Amabel

Just after midnight, on the outskirts of town, Amabel's eyes flew open, her fingers tingling. She'd been asleep in her favorite chair, a late-night sitcom rerun playing quietly in the background.

Something had woken her up. She fumbled around for the remote, muting the sound on the television and listening intently. She heard nothing but the sound of her cat stretching from his perch on the back of her chair.

However, she knew well enough that she didn't wake up like this, fingers tingling, wide awake, for no reason. Something had woken her. *What was it?* She cast her mind out, trying to pick up on the energy that had found her. Eventually, she felt it. A low hum, nothing more than a vibration, really. Something powerful, but subdued.

She stilled her body and opened her mind. Yes, it was still there. And just the smallest bit louder.

"Oh my god," she whispered. Then she smiled. "I always knew it was here."

Her heart began to race and her stomach clenched, because in the deepest depths of her soul it felt real. True. And if it were true … well. She couldn't quite yet comprehend what that would mean.

She sat there for a long while, listening. It grew almost imperceptibly, yet steadily stronger, until around one thirty in the morning, when there was a sharp spike in energy that made her jump. After that, it fell silent.

CHAPTER THREE

Memoriae

The day my brother Henry died was the day I felt as though I lost my grip on the real world. When his heart stopped beating, I willed mine to do the same. But no matter how hard I tried, how hard I prayed for the sweet release that would allow me to join him, wherever he might be, here I remained. Trapped. My twin brother, the other half of me, my very best friend, was dead.

My father was lost to drink, only expending energy on the family business before he retreated to his study in the afternoons, rarely appearing again before breakfast. My mother was lost in a different way, to the demons that kept her in her room for days on end. She'd once had them under control but, after Henry's death, they had raged again. She rarely left her room, did not entertain visitors, and did not care whether or not our home fell to disrepair around her. They were empty husks. I was twenty-three and I was alone.

As I came out of the fog of losing Henry in the fall of 1889, I had to make a choice about my life and what lay ahead for me. Marriage was what was expected of me, of course, but it did not appeal to me. I wanted more. I wanted to travel, I wanted to write, I wanted to make decisions for myself. I wanted all of that. Or I had wanted it. Before.

Henry fueled the fire of my dreams, assuring me that he would help me escape the confines of society's expectations. I thought that with him—a powerful man—to help me, I might actually be able to do something different with my life. Because god forbid a woman achieve something on her own. Now, however, I did not know what would happen to me. I did not even know what I wanted any longer.

I was fortunate that my family had the means to allow me to do what I wanted thus far. We were not wealthy by traditional standards. They would have laughed us right out of society in New York or even Chicago, but oh, we were the talk of the town in Grafton. My father had built a successful ship building business that kept fishermen up and down the river in new boats. He mostly designed and sold fishing boats—the Marsh Skiff was in demand from St. Louis to New Orleans.

All of that was at risk now, however. Father spent more and more time in his office, drowning in his bottles of whiskey. I began to worry that he would allow the business to fall apart. And then what would we do? I began to ask him about the family's finances, waiting until he was just drunk enough to be willing to give me information he would have deemed "inappropriate for a lady" when sober. He told me that a large corporation from New Orleans had offered to buy the business, intending to expand along the Gulf of Mexico. It would provide enough money for he and mother to live comfortably for the rest of their days.

"And of course, Violet, you will be married soon."

"Of course, Father," I agreed quietly.

I encouraged him to see the deal through and waited for final word that it was done. Less than one year after my brother's death, the family business was sold. And good riddance as far as I was concerned. They had agreed to keep father on as a consultant of sorts, for which I was thankful. That would give him a reason to wait until at least noon to dip into the whiskey.

Mother was confined to her room most of the time, claiming pain from headaches. I thought it was simply a broken heart. The doctor came once a week to see her although there was little he could do. Hers was a sickness in her mind and in her heart and there was no medicine or procedure to fix it. Someone without mother's means would have been labeled crazy as a loon and sent to an asylum long ago. But she was alive and we could care for her and so our family continued to cling to life. Or a proximity of a life.

Despite my best efforts to keep track of what needed to be done and hire the appropriate help, the house began to fall into disrepair. The railing on the porch was broken, the sitting room needed fresh paint, there appeared to be water coming in through the roof in a small patch in the upstairs bath, and a shingle was hanging sideways on the north side of the house. These were small things that could be easily fixed by a handyman hired from town, but father had always handled that and now he didn't seem to care. When I asked him, he simply said, "What is the point, Violet?"

I knew that whether or not mother and father cared about the house or the Marsh family reputation, if we wanted to maintain our maid and our cook and our place in society, someone had to ensure the upkeep of our home continued. So although I grieved, I was left to manage the house. I did so, hiring and paying a man to make the occasional repairs. I also began to manage our staff, such as it was. To my surprise, I enjoyed managing the details. Or perhaps what I enjoyed was the distraction.

Even so, I had plenty of time to do nothing at all. I spent hours on our porch, looking at the river snake along the bluffs, knowing that at any moment it could carry me away and bring an end to my misery, should I so choose.

There was one letter from Henry that I read over and over, the ink faded, creases so fragile that they nearly tore each time I unfolded it.

July 18, 1888

My dearest sister,

I miss you! I hope all is well at home. Nothing of excitement to report here. We work, day in and day out. Father teaches me about the business and I occasionally feign interest. Of course I'm being difficult. I know I must learn how to manage operations if I expect to one day take his place. And of course I have no other option. Father found my journal and laughed at my writing. He'd never take me seriously if I told him that, more than anything, I would like to write books for the rest of my life. I suppose I must satisfy that need by filling journal after journal and writing to you, of course.

We witnessed a horrific death on the river today. A man fell overboard and we could not recover him. I will spare you the details, but suffice to say it's something I hope to never witness again. It made me think how little control we have of what happens to us. Here was this chap, his name was Albert, just doing his job, trying to provide for his family. Now what will happen to them?

We do not know what might occur in the next day or the next minute. If I should be taken from this earth, my dear sister, please know that you are my greatest friend. Should I die, my hope for you is that you find peace and love. Of course you will miss me! But you are stronger than any other woman and you have great things to do—things bigger than marriage or children or managing a house. Do not sacrifice your dreams.

I must go now, father has asked me to "Stop that confounded pencil scratching" and come inspect some machine or another.

All my love,

Henry

Henry was dead a month later. Had he had some feeling that he was going to die? I read the letter over and over trying to remind myself to heed his words and take his sound advice to keep moving forward. What he couldn't have known then was how desperately my soul would seek the comfort of his voice and his company.

When Henry and I were children, we had only each other for companionship. It hadn't started that way. My mother had once been engaged in raising us. She would tell us stories and we would take long walks along the river, spotting wildlife and crafting stories about the river monster of the deep. Our home was immaculate and often filled with visitors—my mother's friends and father's business companions.

However, when Henry and I were eight, my mother fell pregnant again. She'd had a difficult time falling pregnant and had suffered several miscarriages. Her spirit was dampened a little after each loss, but when this pregnancy seemed to progress normally, excitement befell the household. Mother began laboring late one winter's night. Father ordered us to the parlor, where we were to stay no matter what we heard. We endured the sounds of mother's pain, following father's orders to stay put.

At mother's final deep and powerful yell, the house fell silent. Only to be followed by another scream. Something different. Something ... primal. Mother was keening. The baby had been stillborn.

After that, everything changed. Mother was never able to recover. She stayed confined to her bed nearly every day. There were no more parties, no more walks along the river. Father paid just enough attention to us to ensure we were going to school and being fed by the housekeeper, Miss Ada, but beyond that, he was using his grief to fuel his business. Henry and I were left to occupy our own time. We only had each other.

We spent every moment we were not at school together. Henry passed up opportunities to play with his friends to stay with me, seeming to sense that the two of us needed each other more than we needed anyone else. We spent hours in the woods, taking our own nature walks, building elaborate fortresses, and exploring the banks of the river. Father would occasionally scold me for dirtying my dresses and "playing like a boy," but he didn't really care enough to follow through on any of his threats to teach me to "act like a proper girl."

We spent hours composing elaborate stories together, writing them down in our "Storybook," as we called it. We envisioned pirates sailing the seven seas, fanciful creatures who roamed the woods, and evil witches who lured children into their lairs. We were never happier than when we were in the middle of a story. We both had dreams of publishing our work one day.

And so the years passed. Father saw success and began to prime Henry to take over the business and me for marriage to a young bachelor with good breeding and good business sense. Mother began entertaining the occasional friend and even redecorated the sitting room. However, I would not be married off. I am a solitary person and had no desire to manage a home and be a man's vessel for children. I needed nothing in my life but my books and my garden. And I needed no person in my life but Henry. I knew that one day he would marry. I could only hope she wouldn't be someone flighty and frivolous, and instead would respect and nurture Henry's writing—and who would also accept his spinster sister.

Of course, I needn't have worried. Henry died. And I along with him, so it seemed.

CHAPTER FOUR

Lara

Lara startled awake, confused for a moment about where she was. She heard a door slam from somewhere in the hotel and then she remembered. Alex's arm was draped across her back. She glanced at the clock. It was only 4:00. She stumbled out of bed, feeling her way along the wall and into the bathroom.

As she got back into bed, her foot hit something on the floor. In the dim light of the bedside alarm clock, she saw the small green book sitting there on her side of the bed. She must have fallen asleep while reading it. Already sinking back into the pillows, she thought, *I'll pick it up when I wake up.*

When she woke again, sunlight was streaming through a small gap in the curtains. Alex was still asleep. She decided to take a shower and carefully swung her legs over the side of the bed, startled to see the little green book sitting on the nightstand, not lying flat, but standing up and propped open for balance. *I thought I left that sitting on the floor. I must have picked it up.* She felt unsettled, though. She thought for sure she'd left it where it had fallen. She shook her head and walked into the bathroom.

Lara and Alex ate brunch at a restaurant near the hotel, but didn't linger. They were ready to get back to Tessa. As their car wound down Great River Road, Lara felt okay. Not great. Nothing was fixed but she felt more relaxed than she had in a long time. The weekend had given her a glimpse of the way things could be—that she could be okay again. Someday.

"Thank you for planning this weekend, Alex. It's the first time in a long, long time that I felt like myself."

Alex put his hand on her leg and said, "I'm glad. I felt like we were us again, you know?"

"It was so much fun," she agreed. "And I didn't feel guilty about having fun. I think that's progress."

"Definitely. I'm proud of you. I think Ben would be proud of you, too."

Lara was surprised by the tears that sprang to her eyes at his words. She knew there was nothing wrong with having fun. And Alex was right. Ben would never want her to be miserable for the rest of her life. But it did make her wonder if it would ever be easy—if there would ever come a day where she moved through her life not thinking about Ben being dead. If she could ever just think of him and not be overwhelmingly sad. The thought scared her.

Alex looked at the expression on her face and said, "What's wrong?"

"Nothing. Not really."

Alex took her hand. "Having fun and not being sad for a while doesn't mean we're forgetting about him."

"I know that in my brain," she laughed. "It's just convincing the rest of me it's okay."

"You'll get there," Alex responded. And his voice was so sure, so confident in her, that she could almost believe it was true.

Amabel

Amabel had eventually made her way to bed, after being awoken in her chair. But the thought was beating in her head—*I always knew it was here. I always knew it was here.* She slept fitfully until she awoke at dawn.

She could barely feel it, no more powerful than the background hum of an air conditioner in summer. But she knew it was here and it was coming from the direction of Main Street.

She got dressed and ready for the day. She drove to town and sat at a table in front of the coffee shop's window. There she sat, for two hours. Listening. Waiting.

Until eventually the hum became a pinprick of concentrated energy, coming from across the street. From the front of the Ruebel, specifically from a young woman and a young man, maybe in their early thirties. He was handsome, in brown boots, dark jeans, and a flannel shirt. She wore an oversized sweater with jeans and her dark brown hair fell in soft waves around her shoulders. They held hands as they carried their bags to a car parked down the street. They looked happy enough, but Amabel could tell there was a deep sadness there, too. Something not masked very well by their smiles.

"She has it," she whispered to herself.

She wasn't quite sure what to do. She had so many questions. How did that woman get it? Where did it come from? *What is it?* She thought she knew the answer to that one. It was a window to the beyond, to wherever the soul goes when it dies. No. Not a window. That was too big. A keyhole? That was closer. She had trouble articulating it even to herself, based on what little she knew.

Whatever it was, all she knew in this moment was that she needed a plan. She couldn't very well go up to them on the street and ask them for it, tell them she knew they had it and she needed it. It was more likely they didn't even realize what it was.

She'd have to let them go for now. She'd find out who they were, however; she had to. Amabel pulled her cell phone out of her purse. Normally she hated the damn thing, but now she was glad to have a camera at the ready. She tried to use the fingerprint option to open the screen but the damn thing wouldn't work. She put in her passcode, navigating to the camera app, but by now the couple had moved down the street, their backs to Amabel's position at the table.

"Damn it!" she muttered. She snapped a picture of them walking away anyway.

She quickly gathered her things and left the shop. She realized the couple was probably parked not far away. She could try to catch up, snap a better picture, maybe check out the license plate. But by the time she was back on the sidewalk, she could no longer see them.

I'll figure out who she is, she reassured herself as she headed back home. It's finally happening.

Lara

When Lara and Alex returned home after their trip, Lara was a bit surprised when her improved mood seemed to carry into her daily life. Maybe the combination of therapy and the trip and feeling more connected to Alex was actually working. Whatever the reason, each day she found it just a bit easier to get out of bed. Her head felt a bit clearer. Sometimes, she even thought about Ben without choking up. And she was reading again.

When she lost Ben, she'd never expected to lose so much else in her life, but with his death she'd lost things she never even imagined could be lost.

First it was books. She *loved* to read. Some of her earliest memories were of "reading," looking at the pictures of *The Berenstain Bears* and *Ms. Frizzle and The Magic School Bus* and making up stories to go along with them. Eventually, when she learned to read, she read everything she could get her hands on, moving from children's books to the words of Judy Blume and Beverley Cleary, then on to *The Little House on the Prairie*, Nancy Drew, and *The Baby-Sitter's Club*.

As an adult, reading was the one hobby she consistently made time for. She'd read anywhere and everywhere, especially when the magic of technology meant she could have a book with her at any time on her phone. She usually read almost fifty books a year, everything from horror to historical fiction to trashy novels she would never admit she'd actually read twice. She'd never been picky. As long as it was entertaining and allowed her to escape from real life, she was in. Whatever problems or worries she had, Lara could put them all aside when she was lost in a book.

When Ben died, her love for reading simply disappeared. Anytime she tried to pick a book up, something about it would make her too angry or upset to continue. Literary books about death or grieving or family were out of the question, for obvious reasons. She tried romance, thinking that nothing was farther from the death of her brother than a novel with too much sex and not enough plot. But when the heroine inevitably got her heart broken, it made Lara cry. And crying about the book just led her to crying about Ben, so those were out. She tried murder mysteries—James Patterson and John Grisham and Sue Grafton—thinking that surely she could lose herself in a fun whodunit. But those made her angry that she couldn't somehow avenge Ben's death. She tried everything: young adult novels (emotions were much too raw), nonfiction (sometimes the real world was sadder than fiction), comedy (she just didn't feel like laughing), and everything in between.

Eventually she gave up and only read to Tessa. Without a book in her hand, she felt unmoored and wasn't sure what to do in her downtime. When she didn't have something to occupy her mind, her thoughts inevitably strayed to Ben and she wanted to avoid that at all costs. So she listened to podcasts. She watched a lot of television. She watched baseball and football with Alex. She didn't know why she could watch sappy dramas and edge-of-your-seat crime shows but couldn't read books. It was devastating, but she'd chalked it up to one more way her life was changed.

The next thing to disappear was her friends. Lara had always had a lot of friends, from college, from their time in California, even some childhood friends she'd remained close with. Alex's hours could sometimes be unpredictable, working nights and weekends, especially when the weather was bad. So she was always scheduling last minute girls' dinners or dates to the movies. She texted her closest friends constantly and they had group chats on Facebook where they'd share funny videos and memes. She loved her friends.

When Ben died, they really tried to help her. They showed up for her in those first few months in ways big and small, calling, texting, dropping off food, offering to watch Tessa. At first, Lara responded, did her best to ask after their lives, go to dinner, laugh over bottles of wine.

But eventually, she couldn't handle it. It was all fake. None of them knew how badly she was hurting and she thought if she told them—if she said, "Hey guys, most days I feel like I want to die and missing Ben hurts so badly that I don't shower or change my clothes for days"—that it would ruin everyone's good time. It's not like they could help, anyway. So she turned down more and more of their invitations and let texts go unanswered until eventually they stopped trying.

She'd come to accept this, too.

But there was something else, something she hadn't admitted to anyone. And it was the most painful thing of all, her real demon, the thing that kept her up at night, that beat over and over in her head on the days she was curled up on the closet floor.

She had lost her memories of Ben. She'd not only forgotten what his voice sounded like and couldn't conjure up his face without looking at a photo, but she couldn't remember anything. She had stories, sure—all of the classic Ben stories that everyone knew. These were the stories they'd shared in the days after he died and the ones she rehashed with Cate or Ben's friends when they got together for drinks. But they weren't her memories. When she tried to think of something new, some story from their childhood, it was blank. She'd stare at old pictures and remember nothing about that particular vacation or holiday or birthday party.

At first she thought it was a defense mechanism, her mind shutting down, just for a bit, to spare her the pain of dwelling on what she'd lost. But as time went on and her memories didn't come back she began to obsess about it. She'd lie in bed night after night, forcing herself to think back to their childhood, when they were teenagers, as recently as just a couple of years ago—and there was nothing. She'd force herself to try to remember, until she'd end up crying herself to sleep. She looked at pictures and watched videos and he'd be back with her for a few minutes, until she put them away. Then she was just left with the same vague, secondhand memories she'd gleaned from everyone else.

Now that Ben was dead, memories were all she had left of him and they were gone. She desperately wanted them back and felt indescribably guilty that she couldn't do such a simple thing as keep her brother's memory alive.

But reading *Memoriae* had caused a small shift in her. The book had captured her attention and she started to feel like maybe there was a chance she could eventually regain some of what she'd lost.

In the days after she and Alex returned home, she read every chance she got. It felt amazing to *want* to read again. She was captivated by Violet's story. Violet's struggle to cope with the loss of her brother made Lara feel not so alone, even if Violet was just a character in a book.

CHAPTER FIVE

Memoriae

As time wore on I spent day after day watching the river, biding my time—for what I was not entirely sure. I managed the house as best I could, attended church functions, and spent most of my time reading. Occasionally I visited with my friends, listening to their chatter, although I never again felt like I could truly engage with them. They were concerned with marriage and children and keeping a home. I was concerned with whether or not my parents would ever be well again or if I myself would finally meet the day that I simply couldn't get out of bed.

I found the walls of our home stifling and so I spent much of my time outdoors. I walked along the river, some days walking miles. Being outside and taking in the activity on the river allowed me to lose myself and finally quiet my mind.

I felt restless. I did not know what I should do. I did not know how I was ever going to build a life of meaning again. All of the things I wanted to tell Henry, all of the thoughts and feelings I wanted to share with just him, the questions I wanted to ask, had nowhere to go. It was all building up and I had no choice but to ignore it.

One day, as I walked along the river, I quite suddenly came upon what I believed to be a heap of old clothing or blankets. However, as I walked closer, I realized it was an old woman, sitting on a large rock, wrapped in a shawl. Her head was hanging low and the black shawl covered her face. I could only see her hands, gnarled and nearly skeletal. Wisps of white hair flowed out from the ends of the shawl, lifting in the light breeze.

I had never seen her before and in a town the size of Grafton, I would have recognized her had she lived there for any length of time. My instinct was to hurry toward her, to call out and see that she was well. However, as I got closer still, my steps slowed. Who was this woman? I did not know her, had never seen her. There was something unnatural about the way she sat so still. She was upright, so she was not unconscious—or worse—but so, so still.

I began to quietly turn around, with the intention of seeking out the town constable and asking him to check on her. But she called out to me.

"You are searching for that which you will not find in this place."

I stopped. "Excuse me?"

"You will not find what you so desperately seek here along the water. The water is a conduit for power, yes, but not the power of which you need."

What she was saying made no sense. Clearly she'd been in the bottle already this morning. "Good day, ma'am." I moved to walk away.

"You need the power of land. Not water. You need the power of those who can commune with the ones who have been interred into the earth before us."

I froze. "What did you say?"

She didn't look directly at me, but lifted her head and stared at the bluffs that rose along the river. Her skin was pale, innumerable wrinkles lining her face. Her eyes were glossy, white, and filmy.

"There are those among us who draw strength from the earth. The spirits of those gone before us are carried in the living, breathing soil from whence we all came and where we shall all return."

"And what makes you think I need to discuss any such thing?" My heart was pounding, even as I tried to convey disdain for what she was saying. She turned to look at me then and I could not tell whether her rheumy eyes saw me or not.

"I know."

"Well, you are mistaken," I said. But I did not walk away from her.

"I can help you find him again."

My breath caught in my chest. Could she possibly mean Henry? "H … h … how?" I stuttered.

"It is an ancient secret. One born of the people of this land and the people of the book."

"Can you do it?" The words left my lips before my mind could pull them back. My mind could make no sense of her words, other than the implication that she knew, somehow, how to communicate with the dead.

"No. That is not my role. I am to simply … connect those who have a need with the knowledge that will help them."

"Then how?"

"There is a text that provides the answers you seek. You see, the power is not in one person. The power is in the ancient readings, drawn from the soil of this land's ancestors and the magic of the book."

"Can you please speak plainly? None of this makes any sense at all."

"There is a sacred text that contains instructions for opening a path to speak with the one you seek most. I can access it."

"Where do I get it?" Again, the words tumbled out of me before I could consider them. Part of me could not believe I was engaging in a conversation with this woman. There was no reason for me to trust her and she was speaking of unbelievable things that couldn't possibly be true. But I had been waiting for so long for something— anything—to change in my life. To show me a path. If that path led to Henry, no matter how insane, how could I not try?

Oh, I had no hope of him coming back to life. I did not even entertain that thought. But the desperation I felt at missing him, the deep well of pain, propelled me forward. If I could just talk to him one more time. Just once more. Then maybe he could tell me what to do. About mother, about father, about the rest of my life that stretched out before me.

She had not yet answered my question. "Where is it?" I asked again.

She stood slowly, painfully, leaning on a long, smooth walking stick. I ignored my upbringing, which told me to help her. But I didn't want to touch her.

"Follow me," she said. She turned and began walking farther down the river's edge, toward a copse of trees. To my credit, I did not follow her immediately. I did stop and think, for more than a few moments, that perhaps this was not the safest course of action. But I could not ignore the voice that said, *Perhaps there is a way. Perhaps there is a way to connect with Henry again.* I knew it was wrong and most definitely not something I should pursue. But even stronger than my instinct to keep myself safe was the desperation of missing my brother.

So I followed her.

She led me farther down the river and into a patch of woods that lined the main road just outside of town. There was a small shack. Shack might be too kind a description. The woman's dwelling was not much more than four wooden walls leaning against each other, and looked as though if one wall crumbled the whole structure would collapse. Animal skins and woven nets with feathers tied to them were nailed to the walls around the front door. Pails of water and stacks of firewood lay around the building. Smoke drifted lazily from a hole in the roof. I did not want to go inside. However, she was standing in the doorway, gesturing for me to follow her.

I hesitated. I did not believe that this frail, old woman could harm me. But no one knew I was here. Not one single soul could attest to my whereabouts, and chances were that if I, who had lived here my whole life, had never known this woman's shack existed in this copse of woods, no one else did either and I would never be found.

But as I thought it through, I thought, why did I care? Who would miss me? Mother and Father would never notice if I were late coming home. It would take them days to wonder why I had not returned. I had no appointments with friends or otherwise in the coming days and church was still four days away. It would likely be our staff that would first suspect something was amiss. And I didn't even interact with them on a daily basis, so, really, there was no way of knowing how long it would take for anyone to miss me.

The thought both saddened and liberated me. How sad is a life where one believes one's absence could go days without being noticed? But also, how freeing it was to know that I could go anywhere—do anything—for days with no one questioning why or for how long. And if something terrible did happen to me in this shack, well. It was no real loss for the world. Mother and Father would just need to manage on their own.

Such were my jumbled thoughts as I took a deep breath and followed the woman into the building. In spite of its questionable exterior appearance, it was rather pleasant inside. Warm and dimly lit, I smelled the comforting aroma of the fire in the old stove, and the faint odor of herbs. It was, to no great surprise, sparsely furnished. A small straw mattress lay in the corner of the room, one lone blanket atop it. There were three shelves along the far wall that seemed to hold all of her possessions, and a small table and one chair near the fire.

I took all of this in quickly as the woman shut the door behind us and lit the candles that sat atop the table. I stood by the door, unwilling to move farther into the space. The woman sat down in the chair next to the fire.

"Please tell me what you meant," I said, trying not to sound too terribly demanding but also not wanting to stay here any longer than necessary.

"You are missing someone, yes? Someone who meant a great

deal to you?" She spoke quietly, her voice raspy and deep.

"Yes."

"And you would like to speak with this person."

"Yes."

"My family has lived here, near the power of the great river for one hundred years. We settled here after fleeing the persecution in the east. We lived alongside the ancestors of this land, who had learned to harness the power of the river for many things. Transportation, food, to quench thirst. But there are other secrets in the power of the river. Do you know how the great bluffs were formed?"

She was speaking, of course, of the great bluffs along the river, that rose out of the earth and towered above the water. "The river carved them over time." I tried to sound confident. And anyway, it was only slightly more than a guess. I seemed to remember some lesson in school about the land formations here, but couldn't be sure.

"Yes. Over time, slowly, drop by flowing drop, the river carved great gashes into the land itself. Its power was not forceful or loud. It was slow. Quiet. But as it stayed its course it began to change the fabric of the land." She paused, and began to twist a small ring around her middle finger. It was silver and thin, with carvings I could not make out etched along its smooth surface.

"Humans used to be much the same. From day to day, we did not make great changes to the land. The tribes here killed the buffalo, burned the wood, drank the water, but never caused major changes to the land. They respected it. They gave back. When we settled here, we were much the same. We built our homes and ate from the abundance of great Mother Earth, but we communed with Her. We thanked Her. We were quietly born and went quietly back to the dirt." She paused. "Until the settlers came, blasting rocks and building roads and polluting the air with machines. Now, each day, the land is changed. Each day, it is different."

She looked at me then, a piercing stare through those white

glossy eyes that made me want to turn away, but I did not.

"When man began to change the land, we began to lose our connection with the power of the earth. It was severed. Not completely, but it was worn away. Imagine the end of a fraying rope. It is still connected, but coming apart, piece by piece. Just a few of the strongest threads are holding both ends together. My people have managed to maintain a number of those frayed edges. It's difficult and they are becoming thinner every day. But that is not your concern. You'll want to know about the one piece that keeps the living tied to the dead."

I drew in a breath. "I am not sure what you mean exactly. Is this some kind of evil? I am sure it cannot be real."

"As I said, we lived alongside the ancestors of this land for a hundred years. It is not widely known, but we reached a sort of agreement with them."

I interrupted her then. "What do you mean? And who are your people?"

"The people who lived here since the beginning of time. The people whose land was ripped from them." As for my people. Well. Suffice it to say, girl, that we were driven out of the east. Out of Connecticut and out of Virginia and out of East Hampton. Out of Salem."

"Salem," I repeated quietly. So, she was a witch. Or thought she was one. It was then that I considered that I had aligned myself with an insane person on this day. Or that I was having some sort of hallucination.

"Of course you think I am insane. Witches do not belong in your world, do they, Violet?"

At the sound of my name on her tongue, I jumped as though I'd been slapped. I had not told her my name, of that I was certain.

"How do you know my name?"

"You may not believe, girl, but that doesn't mean it is not real."

She reached over and added a log to the fire. I could not think of a single thing to say.

"My people and the people of this land lived together peacefully," she continued. "We shared our histories. We shared our knowledge. Theirs, of the elements—the land, the water, the air. And ours, of our bodies and our minds. It was powerful, but it was simple. Remember, we were not trying to change the world. We were simply living in it.

"Until we found the one thing that could actually change the world. But perhaps not for the better. It could be harmful if not contained. On that, those of us who understood the power of the thing we had discovered, all agreed. So it was shared with only a chosen few. Now, the world is moving faster, moving on quickly. The natives have been forced to leave. My people have all but disappeared. It is only me. I am tasked with keeping it safe. Closed. Not allowing it to be opened. By anyone."

Her voice had moved from quiet and calm to melancholy. I had been enraptured with her tale and I paused to let it sink in. I had so many questions, I was not quite sure where to begin.

"What is it?" I eventually asked.

The old woman sighed. "It is a piece of canvas, woven with magic. But that is too simple an explanation for what it actually is. I could try to explain, but I do not know that it would even make sense to you."

"A piece of canvas holds all of this power? Destroy it! Burn it! How bad could it possibly be?" I couldn't believe all of this was over a simple piece of canvas. It was ridiculous.

"As I said, it is not that simple. It is what's inside of it, what is woven into its very fibers." She sighed. "I wish there was a way to explain it to you but I cannot, even after all this time. It is connected to the other side. Wherever our souls may go after we die, this can get you there."

"Pardon me?" I was sure I didn't understand and she could not possibly be implying what I thought she was.

"In the wrong hands, it would be dangerous. No one should have the power to speak with the dead. It is not natural and it is most assuredly not safe. So someone has to keep it closed. And you are the next in our line."

"Wonderful. What does this have to do with me? What do you mean, next in our line?"

She looked up at me then. "You are the next in our line to be tasked with keeping it. It has to stay closed."

"You are not making any sense at all."

The woman closed her eyes for a brief moment and took a deep breath, as though she were annoyed with me. But what could I do other than ask question after question? What she was saying was impossible and ridiculous.

"You are of our line of witches, Violet."

Before I could respond, she grabbed a handful of dried herbs sitting in a bowl on the table and threw it into the fire. It flamed in a burst of light and heat, emitting a pleasant, earthy smell.

She then indicated I should sit near the fire. Still stunned by her implication that she and I were somehow related, I did as she said. Reaching down, she took each of my hands in hers and closed her eyes, instructing me to do the same. I hesitated, but closed my eyes. I felt her place something in my hands. Before I could open my eyes, she said quietly, but in a tone that left no room for argument, "Do not open your eyes."

What happened next, I don't entirely remember. I know the woman began talking. I could not detail everything she said if I wanted to, but she began speaking in a low voice, so quiet I could barely hear though I sat right across from her. The object felt heavy, a coarse material that rubbed against my palms. It grew warm in my hand. At first, I tried to follow the thread of her words and remember as much as I could. I could only catch threads of words and phrases—it seemed to be a set of instructions.

I remember her saying, "Take hold of one thread of the fraying rope, imagine your brother holding the other end." But eventually the language began to change, evolving into something I could not understand. After that, I entered into some state that I can neither identify nor describe. I know not how much time passed.

Eventually, I became aware that she had stopped speaking and the gentle pressure of her hands and the object in mine had disappeared. I slowly opened my eyes, staring directly into her eyes. They were black as night. It seemed as though the pupil had completely overtaken the eye and I was looking into the depths of a starless sky. I nearly screamed, but in the next second I blinked, and when I looked again they were back to the same white, cloudy blankness.

I jerked my hands back to my middle, standing quickly and smoothing my skirts. "What was that? What have you done to me?"

She picked up an object from the table. I had not noticed it before. It was a small burlap sack, the top folded over the object inside. She held it out to me in one hand. I peeked inside and saw a book.

"Take this. Take it into the woods at dusk, along with three of Henry's things"—at this point I wasn't even surprised she knew Henry's name—"and as the sun sets, place them in a circle around you. Write down three of your favorite memories in the pages of this book." She placed her hand on its cover. "Sit in the circle of his things. Hold the book open to your memories, close your eyes, and let it come."

"Let what come?"

She didn't answer my question, instead saying, "Violet, you must be certain to only write down three memories in that book. Any more would be dangerous."

"I am so confused. Surely this cannot be real."

"You have all you need now." I wasn't sure what she meant, but I was sure I wanted to leave.

I took the book from her and placed it in my bag. As I prepared to leave, I stopped on the threshold of her door and turned to look at the woman. "Who are you?" I asked. "Are we related somehow? Why have I never seen you in town?"

"My name is Amelia."

Clearly she wasn't going to provide me any additional information. "What if this doesn't work? What if I have questions? What does it mean to be in possession of this book?"

"You are the one in need and you are the only one left to keep it. Use it wisely, Violet. Do not share it. There is strong magic there, but there is also dark magic. Only invoke its power in the name of finding the thread that leads to your brother. Nothing more," she said, moving to close the door.

I stepped back, out of her front door, clutching my handbag to my chest. "You will not hear from me again," she said, and closed the door.

I stood there for a moment, staring at her door. I did not even know if I believed her, and I had so many questions. I could not deny something had happened to me as I sat by her fire. But did I dare try what the witch suggested? It wasn't natural. It might even be evil. More likely, I had been taken for a fool.

But over the next couple of days, every time I had nearly talked myself out of it and considered chucking the book into the river, one thought repeated over and over in my head. *What if? What if? What if?*

CHAPTER SIX

Lara

Lara was keeping her appointments with Dr. Moore, even on the days she really didn't feel like going. Therapy was hard work, harder than she'd ever anticipated. She still found it almost impossible to be honest about how much she was hurting, but she was definitely making progress. She had bad days, days she had to force herself to get out of bed, but she did it.

On one particularly bad day, she'd finally broken down and decided to go to a grief support group.

She'd woken up sad, but had pushed through. But when Alex and Tessa came home, things had quickly fallen apart. Alex had had a bad day at work and had almost gotten hurt. Lara didn't want to hear about it, because the thought of something happening to Alex made her entire body run hot then cold in panic. She'd told him, not very kindly, that she didn't want to know. He'd rolled his eyes, muttered, "Thanks for letting me vent," and walked out.

Tessa had been crabby, too. She was fighting a cold and had a couple of molars coming in and nothing was making her happy. Finally, Lara gave Tessa some Tylenol, put her to bed early, and was in bed herself by eight.

When Alex came in, seeing her in bed already, he said, "You're going to bed?"

"Yeah. I'm tired."

"It's early."

"I know, Alex. I'm tired. I don't feel like being awake anymore."

"Okay …" He drew the word out, like he wanted to say more.

"What the hell, Alex? I'm tired. I want to go to bed. It's been a long day." She didn't understand why he was making such a big deal out of this.

"I just don't want—"

"What? You don't want what? You don't want me to turn back into a crying mess, spending all my time in bed? Give me a break. I'm going to bed early one night."

"Fine." He walked out of their room.

Lara blew out a frustrated breath. This back and forth, Alex always worried about her, looking for signs she was slipping, was exhausting. She understood and loved him for wanting to take care of her, but sometimes it felt stifling.

The next day wasn't any better. Lara's mother called her, crying. She'd found some of Ben's old school papers and projects and a poem he'd written for Mother's Day in 1989. As Lara listened to her sob, she'd only been able to offer an occasional, "Yeah, I know. Me too. I'm sorry, Mom." It was another conversation in which her mother had said, "Lara, you just can't understand how hard this is for me. No one understands."

Every time her mother said it, it made Lara feel angry and then guilty for feeling angry. She knew she was just the sister. She knew her grief didn't rate as high as her parents' or Cate's pain. She knew she should be finding a way to move on and the fact that it had been a year and she'd allowed her whole life to fall apart clearly meant that there was something wrong with her. That she was weak. Those thoughts made her more upset and it felt like a vicious, endless cycle.

It had not been a good day. So as she'd lain in bed that night, exhausted but still unable to sleep, she promised herself she'd go to a support group Dr. Moore recommended.

Now Lara was sitting on a hard plastic chair in the basement of St. Mary's church, waiting for the support group to start. There were ten other people and one facilitator, an older woman with short, grey hair cut into a sleek bob.

"Welcome to Hope and Healing, everyone. My name is June and

I'm the parish nurse. I'm so glad you're all here. We've all experienced loss and this group is meant to be a safe place to share your feelings. I have a short video for us to watch and then we'll move on to our discussion points and have time for sharing." June smiled warmly. "But before we start the video, I'd like everyone to introduce themselves and tell us a little bit about why you're here."

June turned to a young woman sitting to her right and said, "Sarah? Would you like to start?"

Sarah, whose ripped jeans, black boots, and dark makeup screamed "Angry Teenage Girl!" rolled her eyes and said, "I'm here because my mom signed me up?" She was doing that thing teenagers did, where everything out of their mouth sounds like a question.

"I guess she thinks I'm not dealing so well since my grandma died? I don't know. I mean, I'm fine. She was old, so what are you going to do?" It was clear she was trying to maintain a tough façade, but Lara could see she was barely holding back tears. Lara wanted to cross the circle and hug her.

After Sarah was Jim—wife, cancer, can't get rid of any of her stuff and it's been three years. Then Jack—husband, suicide, so angry at him that some days he's almost glad he's gone. Pam followed Jack—dad, brain aneurysm, trying to accept he won't be there to walk her down the aisle at her spring wedding. Ellen—daughter, cancer, no one needs to be told how fucked up that is.

See? Lara thought. *Could be worse.* Then she instantly felt terrible for thinking it.

Andrea—husband, car accident. Charles—wife, heart attack. On and on it went, a marching band of pain and grief that made Lara mad and sad and want to run out the door.

The woman sitting two chairs down from Lara started to speak. She was stunning. She was tall and wore no makeup but red lipstick, which made her deep brown skin and brown eyes stand out even more. Her natural, dark hair was cut short, soft black curls like a halo around her head.

"My name is Maryn. I'm here because my brother died two years ago and I still can't find a way to stop myself from picking up the phone to call him. He was my best friend. He was killed by a drunk driver and I'm so, so angry. My parents can't deal with any of it. I'm trying to help everyone but no one is helping me. I'm just so fucking pissed off!" Maryn shook her head back and forth quickly, once, twice, her fists clenched. She turned to June. "Sorry. I don't know what else to say."

June patted her hand and smiled. "It's okay. We've all been there. Anger is normal."

Lara quickly looked away when she realized she'd been staring at Maryn for what might have been an uncomfortably long time. But here was someone else who knew. She could have spoken those exact words. Maryn seemed to know exactly how she felt.

"I'm sorry. Can I say something?" Jim—wife, cancer—said.

"Sure," said June.

Jim looked at Maryn. "I'm sorry your brother died. But you're young. You have to find a way to move on. You can't let this ruin your life. You have the rest of your life ahead of you. It was just your brother."

Maryn looked at him blankly. Lara felt her heart pounding, anger bubbling up in her chest. She wanted to ask Jim if he seriously just said that out loud. Why did everyone act like losing a sibling wasn't that hard? Lara clenched her fists, telling herself that it was her first day in the group and that she shouldn't say anything yet, especially if she was going to speak in anger.

"Well, it's true we don't want our grief to take over our lives," said June. "But everyone's grief journey is different."

"I'm not going to minimize my grief because it's *just*"—Maryn rolled her eyes at the word just— "my brother. I'm so tired of people acting like I don't hurt as much as my parents hurt. Or that I'm not as affected as his wife and kids are. He was my best friend and he was more than that. He. Was. My. Brother."

Yes. Exactly, Lara thought.

Grieving a sibling had made Lara feel lost and alone in ways she could have never predicted. Of course, grief was lonely for everyone. No one processes pain the same way and all grievers come to a point where they just don't want to bother their family and friends with their pain, especially after what is considered an "appropriate" amount of grieving time. No one wants to be a buzzkill. So they keep silent and get on with their life, even though some days the pain feels just as fresh as day one, even if it's months or years later. Grievers just deal with it and pretend like everything is okay, even when things are most definitely not okay.

Jim had the grace to look slightly abashed. June was going on about not comparing your grief journey to anyone else's journey.

Lara had realized early on that there is an unspoken hierarchy of grief. Parents obviously get top spot in terms of what kind of grieving sucks the most. No one is supposed to bury a child. Running a close second comes spouses. Losing your life partner sucks for sure. After that, you have children of the deceased. Everyone expects that their parents will die at some point, but it's still not easy, especially if your parents die young. Then, maybe, comes the siblings.

Siblings get lost in some weird grief purgatory where people assume your pain isn't as intense as everyone else's. You're expected to be there for everyone else. Help your parents through their pain. Provide support for your sibling's spouse and children in their absence. Be the strong one who makes the decisions and makes the phone calls because no one else can handle it right now. Forget about the fact that you've lost someone who was your first friend, who had literally been there all of your life, and who was supposed to see this whole thing through until you were both too old to care.

"Do you want to share next?"

Lara startled, realizing June was speaking to her.

"Oh. Sorry. I ..." she trailed off. This was the part she hated the most. Saying the words out loud breathed life into her pain, making it something alive, something bigger than her that could take over if she let it. She closed her eyes and took a deep breath.

"My brother died, too. I ... I'm not doing well." She looked up, her eyes meeting Maryn's. And in that second, Lara understood what drew people to groups like this. There was a link between them. Everyone in this room knew loss—but here was someone who could understand how fucking awful it is to suddenly lose someone who was supposed to be your companion for life. Gone. In an instant.

Without saying a word Lara and Maryn were saying, *This hurts. I know. You don't have to explain why you haven't left your house in weeks or why you keep picking up the phone to call your dead brother.*

Holding Maryn's gaze she says, "It's been almost a year but I cannot function. My husband and I are fighting all the time and some days it feels like my whole life is falling apart. I'm pissed off, too." Lara couldn't say any more. She did not want to cry. She clenched her fists in her lap.

June, recognizing Lara needed a moment to regroup, said, "Thank you, Lara. We're glad you're here," and moved on.

After they watched the video—cheesy and sappy and entirely unhelpful—June asked questions of the group and encouraged everyone to share. Lara and Maryn didn't say any more. It was clear the vibe of this group was about finding peace and acceptance. No one talked about what it felt like to be really, really pissed off and what you were supposed to do if you felt like you just weren't going to be able to move on with your life.

After group was over, Lara and Maryn, by unspoken agreement, walked out of the room together and made their way down the dimly lit hallway.

"Well that fucking sucked." Lara surprised herself by laughing out loud at Maryn's statement.

"Yeah, it did. I guess it was your first time, too?"

"Yep. And last. I guess I can see how it might help some people who feel ready to move on. Whatever that means. I'm just not there yet. I don't want someone to tell me how to find peace. I want someone to tell me how I'm supposed to function. And how not to feel like ... like ..."

"Punching something? Or someone?" Lara replied.

"Exactly."

Lara surprised herself by laughing again. "Yeah. Everyone talks about anger as a stage of grief but I feel like anger is just who I am now. All anyone ever says about it is that you should let it go and try to move past it. If only it were that easy." Lara lapsed into silence, a little embarrassed she'd said so much to a complete stranger. They had walked out of the church's side door and were standing on the sidewalk.

"The anger sits in my chest, like something physical I can feel," Maryn said. "All the bullshit advice people give about trying to talk to him, or visiting his grave, or writing to him as a way to release some of those feelings ... it just makes me more angry that I can't actually talk to him."

"I tried to go to counseling a while ago and the counselor said we would work on 'building a new relationship' with my brother. I left and never went back to her. Build a new relationship with my dead brother? How do you build a relationship with someone who isn't there? Normally, that would earn you a mental health diagnosis."

Now Maryn laughed. "No kidding." The other support group members had streamed past them into the parking lot. June was the last one out the door, closing and locking it behind her.

"Thank you both so much for coming," she said as she smiled and walked past Lara and Maryn. "I hope to see both of you back again." Lara and Maryn just smiled and said thanks.

"It just fucking sucks," said Lara, not sure how to sum up the most honest conversation she'd had in almost a year.

"It just. Fucking. Sucks," Maryn responded, smiling sadly.

"Did we just become best friends?" The words were out of her mouth before Lara could stop herself and for a horrifying moment she thought for sure Maryn wouldn't understand the joke and run away from this clearly insane women.

"Yep!" Maryn said, laughing. "I love *Stepbrothers*."

"Oh thank god," Lara said with relief. "Otherwise I would have really sounded like I'd lost my mind."

"I'd love to get coffee sometime. It's been a really long time— well this is maybe the first time— I've been able to talk about my brother and laugh, too. It's nice to meet someone who gets it," Maryn said.

"I'd love that," said Lara. "Although I can't promise I'll be in anything more fancy than yoga pants. I'm not so good at getting out of the house these days."

"Let's make a rule that we can't wear anything other than yoga pants. Bras are optional, too," said Maryn.

"Count me in," Lara responded. The women exchanged numbers and began walking toward their cars.

As she opened her car door, Lara turned around and said, "Maryn?" When the other woman stopped and looked her way, Lara said, "What's your brother's name?"

Maryn smiled and said, "Will. And yours?"

"Ben. His name is Ben."

****

Lara and Maryn met for coffee two days later. They sat at a cafe for more than three hours, first ordering coffee, then lunch, and eventually another cup of coffee.

"What that guy said in group the other night pissed me off," Maryn said. "I've spent my life being marginalized and minimized as a black person and as a woman. I'm used to people treating me like I don't matter as much as everyone else. But I never would have imagined I'd experience the same thing when I lost Will. From day one, I've been the one who was supposed to be strong for everyone else. My parents need me, Will's kids need me, my grandparents need me." Maryn shook her head.

"You know, when I told an old family friend that my husband and I were thinking about still continuing to try for a baby, do you know what she said? She said, 'I really wish you would wait. I'm not sure your mom can handle it right now.'" Maryn laughed sadly and shook her head. "Sure. Stop doing the one thing that is keeping you clinging to life right now in order to make things easier for everyone else. It's how it's been since day one. No one gives a shit about me and my other siblings' grief."

"Yep. I feel totally forgotten. Every time someone asks after any of us, it's always, 'Oh, Lara, how are your mom and dad? How is Cate? How is your grandma? How's the freaking dog?'"

"Jesus, do we sound like whiny bitches or what?" Maryn laughed genuinely this time.

"Maybe," Lara said. "But I really don't care. It's not like we're wrong. A few weeks after Ben died, I went online to try to find some books about losing a sibling or even an online forum or something. There are a few websites, but not much. There's about a billion books about losing a child or a parent, but very little about losing a sibling. There are more books about losing a pet than losing a sibling."

"You're kidding."

"Nope. Look it up on Amazon. Meanwhile, I'm thinking, why isn't anyone talking about how hard it is to lose someone who's been your best friend for as long as you can remember?"

They talked a lot about Ben and Will but they eventually talked about their lives. Maryn told her about her husband Tim. They'd met while getting their undergraduate degrees in engineering at Illinois State University. "He was the only hot guy in my whole class who didn't also still have action figures in his room," she said with a laugh.

They'd moved to St. Louis from Chicago a couple years ago when Tim was offered a job at Boeing. Maryn told her what it had been like to grow up as a mixed-race woman in America who now worked in a male-dominated industry. She'd been working at a "small, boring ass manufacturing firm with a bunch of old white dudes," and had decided to get her Master's degree at St. Louis University. She eventually wanted to work on energy and nuclear engineering, finding cleaner sources of energy and improving nuclear power. She was close to her family and she and Tim visited them in Chicago often.

When they'd finally left that day, they'd hugged good-bye and Lara said, "Don't laugh at me, but I want to cry. I'm really glad we met."

"Me too," said Maryn. "Let's plan dinner. I think Alex and Tim will get along great. They can talk about football or some shit and we can continue to feel sorry for ourselves about our dead brothers."

Lara laughed. It was surprising and refreshing that Maryn wasn't afraid to make dead brother jokes. They had to laugh sometimes or they'd cry all the time.

As she drove home that afternoon, Lara found herself singing along to an old song on the radio. She was going to go home and get a couple hours of work in. She would take Tessa for a walk to the park tonight. She would cuddle up next to Alex in bed and read.

She felt hopeful.

****

Dr. Moore had been trying to convince Lara that one of the reasons she was having such a difficult time, other than the obvious fact that she missed her brother, was that she had a version of post-traumatic stress disorder. Lara had argued with Dr. Moore about that diagnosis for at least three sessions.

"I can't have PTSD," she insisted. "Soldiers and survivors of mass shootings have PTSD. They're the ones who've been through something truly traumatic. I mean, it's awful that my brother died. But it wasn't *traumatic*. I wasn't in danger. I wasn't even there. I just need to learn how to deal with it."

"It sounds like you don't think you deserve to have PTSD," Dr. Moore said.

"I don't! I just need to learn to deal with my grief."

It wasn't until Dr. Moore began asking some very pointed questions about the hours immediately following Ben's death, something she'd skillfully (or so she thought) been able to dodge thus far, that it clicked for her. She didn't like to think about that time. Even his funeral had seemed easier than those first few hours.

Cate had called Lara from the hospital and told her Ben was dead. She'd sounded robotic, had clearly been in shock. Lara called her parents. She had to be the one to tell them that their son was dead. She would never forget the anguished wail of her mother or the way her father had screamed at her. Then it had fallen to Lara to make phone calls notifying family and friends. The voices haunted her. Some screamed. Some were silent. Most cried. Many had just said, "No, no, no," over and over. Lara had called the funeral home and once she'd arrived at the hospital had talked to a nurse and a pastor about what was next, taking the pamphlet from the coroner's office and Ben's small bag of belongings.

It was in those hours that Lara's life—which had really been pretty rosy and safe, all things considered—had crashed down around her. It was the first time she'd really understood that *everything* could change in an instant. It was the most unsettling and anxiety-inducing feeling she'd ever experienced. Ever since, she'd felt completely out of control of her life, knowing that she was unable to stop something bad from happening again.

She didn't know how to go on as before, knowing that literally at any second, something awful could happen again. There was nothing to stop it. Nothing to stop Alex from getting electrocuted and dying at work. Nothing to stop Tessa from choking on a grape. Nothing to stop any of the billions of ways her life could be ruined again. She didn't know how to deal with that level of anxiety.

So she played out scenarios in her head. She considered the worst possible things that could happen to her and then spent long minutes letting her mind spiral, planning for what she would do if she got another phone call. If Alex died, she knew who'd she call first, the funeral home she would use, where she and Tessa would move. She knew what she'd do if one of her parents died. She knew what she would do if something happened to Tessa.

This spiraling, as she called it, helped her feel just a little more prepared. She knew, logically, that if she got a call that her daughter had died, no amount of planning would prepare her to deal with that. It was the only way she could contemplate that awful thing happening without completely falling apart.

When she wasn't morbidly planning for the deaths of everyone she loved, the voices of her loved ones played over and over and over again ... *Screaming. Silence. Crying. "No, no, no."* Ambulance lights nearly paralyzed her. The smell of a doctor's office reminded her of the hospital and made her start shaking. Every time her phone rang her stomach knotted until she answered and realized it was just a normal call. And forget it if there was a knock at the door or a phone call late at night—her body immediately reacted as though it was someone delivering more terrible news.

"You're having flashbacks, Lara," Dr. Moore said quietly. "And the spiraling? Your mind is trying to find a way to deal with the anxiety of the awful and unexpected happening again. It's PTSD. It might not be the same kind of PTSD a soldier returning from war might have, but it's the same type of illness."

Lara was silent for almost a full minute. She looked around the now-familiar office. The teal and black abstract painting that hung over Dr. Moore's chair. The scratchy grey fabric of the couch she was sitting on (because of course it was a couch, although she'd never actually laid down on it). The neat desk and tall bookshelf in the corner. Eventually, she looked back at Dr. Moore, his kind brown eyes, gray hair, and black-framed glasses looking back at her expectantly.

She thought about what he'd said and how she was coping (or not). She had to admit that it did *sound* like PTSD, but she hadn't been *traumatized*.

She let out a frustrated breath. "I just don't know. It doesn't seem right."

Dr. Moore put his iPad down on a side table, folded his hands in his lap, and leaned toward her.

"Lara, every type of grief is traumatic for those of us left behind, even if it's our hundred-year-old grandmother who lived a full life. But just like so many other things in life, there are degrees of trauma. Someone's sudden death is traumatic. Especially when it's someone who was young. Especially when it's someone who we couldn't help and who we didn't have the opportunity to say goodbye to. The sudden ripping of Ben from your life *is* a trauma. The hours after his death, when you had to be the bearer of bad news for so many people, *is* a trauma."

He fell silent and leaned back in his seat, watching her.

She closed her eyes and swallowed back tears. "Let's say that I do have PTSD. What do I do?"

"Well, you need to learn coping mechanisms to help you deal with the flashbacks and spiraling. And while you're not going to like this answer, you have to accept the fact that, yes, there are plenty of things in life we cannot change or stop from happening. No amount of planning or worrying about it can change that. It's just the way it is."

"That makes me feel like I can't breathe. Do you know that every night before I go to bed, I stare at Tessa and cry? And I beg God not to take her from me? Over and over, I say, 'Please don't take her from me. Please don't take her from me.' I wouldn't survive it." Lara began to cry.

Dr. Moore let her cry for a minute, kindly handing her a tissue. After she calmed down, he said, "Lara, before Ben died, what words would you have used to describe him?"

She smiled. "Funny. Sarcastic. Smart. Kind. My biggest supporter."

He smiled at her. "And when you describe him now?"

Lara looked down at her hands. "I tell people he died. That he was my best friend, but he died."

"Have you ever thought that his whole life doesn't have to be about his death?"

Lara's breath literally caught in her throat and for a moment she really couldn't breathe. "What did you say?"

"His whole life doesn't have to be about his death. He can be Ben, your best friend. Your brother who made you laugh. He doesn't always first have to be your brother who died."

Lara was looking at Dr. Moore blankly, but in her mind things were clicking into place so quickly she couldn't put it into words.

"Does that make sense?" Dr. Moore asked.

"Yes. It makes so much sense. I don't … you've just changed the way I'm seeing things for the first time since he died. He was—IS—so much more than his death."

"Exactly. I think by making his death the first thing you think or say about him, you're making that scary, awful thing—his death—the most *important* thing. Which is exacerbating your anxiety by focusing only on death—Ben's, Alex's, Tessa's."

Lara shook her head. "I really cannot explain to you how this is making me feel. I'll be honest, I thought 'breakthroughs' in therapy were bullshit."

Dr. Moore smiled.

"But I really think I'm having one. I honestly felt like Ben being dead *was* the most important thing about him now. But damn it, he deserves so much more than that."

They were silent for a long moment, as Lara looked out the window. She finally said, "Do you think if I can stop thinking only about his death, I can also stop obsessing so much about everyone else dying?"

"I think it will help."

Lara nodded. "I think so, too."

When Lara got home that evening, she couldn't wait to tell Alex about her talk with Dr. Moore.

"It makes so much sense. I mean, I know it's not a magical answer. Obviously I'm not going to be able to stop myself from having certain thoughts and just saying I have to change the way I feel and talk about Ben is much easier than actually doing it. But Dr. Moore is going to teach me breathing techniques and some other stuff I can do when my thoughts feel out of control. We're also going to work through the most difficult parts of those first days after Ben died. That makes me want to puke, but he thinks that laying it all out there will help."

"Good," Alex said. "I can't say I understand completely, only because I'm not going through it. But if you feel more in control and it's helping, I'm so glad."

Later that night, when Lara went into Tessa's room, she managed to ask God, *Please don't take her from me*, only once. And she didn't cry. It was a small victory, but it was hers all the same.

As she waited for sleep that night, she felt hopeful that if she could have this one small victory there might be others.

CHAPTER SEVEN

Memoriae

Eight days after my mysterious meeting with the witch, I could no longer deny the call of the book from my handbag.

I waited until Sunday afternoon, when Mother and Father were usually exhausted after church and sure to stay indoors resting. I walked into the woods and found a patch of sparse grass with plenty of dirt showing through the thin blades. I sat in the dirt, legs crossed, pressing into the earth, and placed three of Henry's things around me—his hat, his favorite book, and the pocket watch my grandfather had passed down to my father and my father to Henry. I had written down three of my favorite memories of Henry on one of the middle pages of the book.

I held the open book in my lap, my hands pressing into the pages, feeling the lines of my words in the paper, my memories made real. As I had written down my three favorite memories, other things had begun to come to me and I wrote them all down. The pain over losing him, the few details I knew about his death, the ways I had tried and failed to overcome my grief. It was cathartic. And now that I had finally worked up the courage to do what the witch had instructed me to, I was hopeful that I would somehow be able to move forward and figure out what I should do next in my life.

As dusk fell and as the last of the sun's bright rays touched the treetops, I closed my eyes and let it come as Amelia had said. Quietly, slowly, and without any conscious thought, I began to chant words that were not familiar to me, that I could not repeat here as I write this if I wanted to. But they overcame me and I repeated them over and over, the words seeming to gain momentum, streaming out of my mouth so quickly that I felt thoroughly out of control.

A strong, strange wind whipped up, blowing the branches and leaves that were scattered around me into an outward circle that cleared my little patch of earth of everything but the grass, the dirt, and Henry's possessions. I watched the leaves swirl around me, terrified but unable to move.

I feel like a mad person writing what happened next, but happen it did and I will not forget. Henry's hat flipped over on its end. The pages of his book began flipping open rapidly. The watch flew into a nearby tree, cracking the face. Then, as suddenly as it had started, the wind stopped abruptly, dropping debris in a perfect circle around me. Henry's items stilled.

I thought I should feel scared, but I did not. Instead, I felt a peace and calm settle around me that I had not known since Henry's death. The sun, making its final descent, shone brightly on my face for a moment and I smiled. I smiled! At that moment, I didn't know if this little ceremony had worked. All I knew was that I felt peace.

And then, he was there. Not physically. I could not have touched him and could not see him with my eyes. But Henry was there in the shape of every memory I ever had of him. A sharp and vivid memory of us as children, running along the river, flying a kite, came to me then, and I felt the wind in my hair. I felt his hand on my head, stroking lightly when the children at school had called me Violent Violet after I pushed a girl for pulling my braid. I smelled his cologne. I felt his arms embrace me in a hug. I felt the plush seat of the couch, the weight of Henry's feet in my lap, and the warmth of the fire as we read together in the sitting room. It was all there. I remembered it all.

Over and over since Henry's death I had lamented over the memories I would forget over the coming years—those pieces of Henry that would be lost forever to time. Yet here they all were. In my mind, as clear is if they had happened yesterday. I closed my eyes and sat until it was full dark, reveling in the memories washing over me.

Eventually, I opened my eyes and allowed them to adjust to the darkness. There was enough moonlight for me to locate my bag and the lantern I had brought. I stood shakily to my feet, lit the lantern, and gathered Henry's things, placing them in my bag. I made my way out of the woods.

I understood, now, what the witch had meant about threads and connection. I had, somehow, managed to take hold of the thread of my memories of my Henry and tug on it. In this way, I could keep him alive, through the things that connected us even in his death—the memories of the precious time we had together. I would not lose him and all we had experienced. The knowledge that I could conjure up his face, his laugh, the feel of him sitting next to me at the dinner table, brought me a sense of peace that I thought had been lost to me.

I did not understand what happened to me in those woods or how I did what I did. All I know is that it worked and I was forever grateful to the mysterious woman who had helped me.

CHAPTER EIGHT

Lara

When Lara finished *Memoriae,* she felt disappointed. Both that the story was over and that it hadn't given her more answers. As she'd read Violet's account of her run-in with the mysterious witch, Lara was frustrated. Without really admitting it to herself, she'd been hoping for a story that would uplift her and maybe even guide her to something that would help her overcome the pain of losing her brother. And even though it was ridiculous, in her heart of hearts, she'd wanted to know more about how Violet got her memories back. Lara was powerfully, painfully jealous of Violet's memories. It almost made her angry. She told herself that was silly. It was a book. A story. Violet was a character. But she'd somehow managed to regain *all* her memories of her brother and Lara wanted that so badly. If someone told her she could have even just one more minute with Ben or get just one more memory back in all its beautiful entirety, Lara wouldn't hesitate. She'd do it, no matter what it cost. But she also knew, logically, that it was wishful thinking.

Even so, Violet's story helped her see that there was still something left of Ben in her life.

After her experience in the woods, Violet went on to detail how it changed her outlook on her life and her future. With her memories of Henry intact, she was able to let go of some of the pain of her loss and move forward. She'd written her story down in the very notebook the witch had given her and started rebuilding her life.

Violet continued to help her mother and father manage the house, making the necessary improvements and repairs. She even got her mother treatment for, what was clear to Lara, a severe case of depression. Violet went on to get married and have children, sharing the memories of her brother with her family. She'd found peace. Lara had printed her favorite passage and taped it to her mirror.

The one thing we have after someone we love dies—the thing we have that is known and is true and that cannot be taken from us—is our memories of the ones we lost. It is a small comfort. It is not enough. Cruelly, memories fade over time. We forget the tenor of their laugh, the way their eyes crinkled at the corners when they smiled, how they tilted their head when you were in a deep discussion. We try to cling to them, but they slip away and it is yet another loss in a long string of things that have been ripped away from us.

It is cruel, but it is also simply the way things are. What I have come to realize is that my brother does not live in the specifics of my memories. When I laugh with my husband or hug my children, I am feeling the weight of them, smelling their skin, and taking in the lines and curves of their faces that I love so deeply. These are the kinds of things we think we need to cling to. But what I am really taking in is the power of our connection. The love that ties us together and our shared experiences form the weight of our memories that will carry us through the rest of our lives.

The passage gave Lara hope that maybe one day, she could get her memories back, too, and rebuild her own life.

****

The next couple of months passed uneventfully for Lara. She continued counseling, each week getting a little stronger and learning tools to help her cope on the bad days. She was able to focus on work and had even gotten two new clients. She and Alex carried some of the spark they'd re-ignited on their trip into their everyday life. They started scheduling once-monthly date nights and as he continued to be her rock, to lift her up over and over again, she felt closer to him than she had even since before Ben's death.

But possibly most important for her was her friendship with Maryn. The two had grown very close and joked that they'd replaced that awful first support group with a two-woman support group. It hadn't been easy for Lara to accept the PTSD diagnosis or to force herself to continue therapy on the days it was hard and made her sad. She talked to Alex about it, but she knew that if she burdened him with too much, it would strain their already-fragile marriage. She needed someone other than just him to vent to. And although she'd only known Maryn for a few months, it felt like they'd always been a part of each other's lives. Maryn helped her stay grounded and see that the therapy wasn't easy, but that it was working.

Lara marveled at how well Maryn seemed to be doing when it came to Will's death. Maryn always shrugged off her praise, saying, "I'm getting all of my therapy vicariously through you!" Lara suspected that it was just in Maryn's nature to put other people first.

As time went on, they talked less about the pain of losing Ben and Will and more about what they wanted for their lives. Alex and Tim also got along well and the two couples had spent a lot of time together, hosting dinners and barbecues at their houses, and going to Blues games. Maryn and Tim loved Tessa, even babysitting a few times when Lara and Alex needed a date night.

It also seemed as though *Memoriae* had broken her streak of not reading. She was reading again and it had made her so happy. She reread the entire *Harry Potter* series, caught up on a bunch of Stephen King and James Patterson novels, and read a couple of bestsellers she'd missed out on.

She made it through the holidays, even though it was hard. Tessa's excitement this year helped, as it was the first year she really understood Santa and she was obsessed. Every old man with gray hair was "Ho-ho;" she sang "Rudolph the deer," over and over again, and her excitement was contagious. Even Lara's parents weren't as dysfunctional and annoying as she thought they would be. They'd been drunk and medicated, sure, but they made it through.

Lara still had bad days, but for the most part she was able to deal with them, or, at the very least, just tell Alex she was having a bad day and he gave her the space she needed to decompress.

Things seemed to be looking up all around. Until one day a few weeks after the New Year, her mother called.

"Lara, you have to help me. I don't know what to do." Her mother sounded frantic. It took a lot of willpower for Lara to not roll her eyes. There was always some "emergency" her mother needed help with.

"What's wrong, Mom?"

"Well I called Cate because I would like some of Ben's things and she told me that it wasn't really a good time and she didn't know when it would be. Ben is my son! I don't see the harm in simply asking to have some of his things. I don't know why she has to be like this. Especially since she'll probably be moving that man in soon anyway."

Lara's mother had never had much love for Cate. Lara didn't understand why. Cate was sweet, and a very strong woman. She was an attorney and women attorneys didn't get out of law school and survive the first few years of work without growing a thick skin and learning to stand up for themselves. Cate and Lara had a lot in common and Lara loved her because she had been so good for Ben. Lara thought her mom had a problem with Cate because it was never Cate's plan to have a bunch of kids and stay home. She wanted bigger things for her career.

Lara missed her. Since Ben died, Lara and Cate had tried to spend time together, but both women found it hard. They were walking their own grief journeys and as the two people in the world who had loved Ben most, Lara felt like their grief was just too much for them to bear together. But they texted regularly and Lara had been excited for Cate when she'd told her she met a widower in an online support group who she'd been spending time with. She made it clear there wasn't romance there yet, but that she thought maybe there could be. Someday. Lara knew that Ben was just the kind of selfless and caring man who would want his wife to be happy in his absence, so she'd told Cate to go out and find happiness again.

As she listened to her mother complain about Cate, Lara felt the familiar anger she experienced every time her mother went on one of her rants trying to take over. Cate was a good woman who had made her brother happy and she deserved to have a life.

Lara took a deep breath and reminded herself of what Dr. Moore had told her about dealing with her mother. "You cannot change the way she deals with her grief, Lara," he'd said. "You can only change how you respond to her. It's not easy for you to deal with, but it's a temporary blip in your healing. You do not need to take on her pain and her anger in addition to your own."

"Mom. First of all, she's not going to be moving anyone in. And even if she did, she's an adult and she will have another relationship someday and it's really none of our business. Ben would have wanted her to be happy."

"But, Lara—"

"No, Mom," Lara was staying calm, but she also wasn't going to let her mother railroad her. "It's fine that you want some of Ben's things. Cate hasn't gotten rid of anything yet. I just don't think she's ready to move any of it. She's not trying to keep anything from you. It's just hard for her. I'm sure if there's something specific you'd like you could just tell her and she'd get it. Or tell me and I'll ask her about it."

Her mother didn't say anything for a long moment. "Mom?"

"Well, I guess no one cares about the pain I'm in and that having some of his things would really help me."

"Jesus, Mom! No one is saying that!" Lara felt her patience slipping away. She took another deep breath. "I'll talk to Cate and see what she's thinking. Okay?"

"I found his journal, you know."

"What?" Lara wanted to be sure she'd heard her mother correctly before she started yelling.

Ben had been organized almost to a fault. His drawers and cabinets were never overstuffed. His closet was organized by color. And he *never* missed a meeting or appointment, thanks to the calendar that he carried with him always, where he'd manage his schedule and to-do lists. He also used it to doodle, write down ideas, and make note of some of his favorite memories throughout the year. He insisted it was just a planner, but they liked to tease him about it being a journal.

When he died, no one could find his most recent calendar. He kept all of his old ones on a shelf in his office and a few months ago Lara and Cate had spent an hour going through all of them, laughing at his funny drawings and observations about his life and crying when they came across notes like, "Lara and Alex getting married today! So happy for my little sis."

"I found his journal," her mother said. "I guess he left it here when he'd been over to my house helping me clean up the basement. He must have set it down there and forgot about it. He died two days later."

"You have got to be kidding me, Mom! When did you find it?" Lara felt tense waiting for her mother's answer. She was barely holding back her anger now.

"Oh, a few months ago, I guess."

Lara didn't know why it had been so important to her, but she and Cate both had really wanted to find that journal. She supposed it was because his calendars were like a peek into Ben's mind. It would have been a way to sort of "hear" from him after his death.

"And you're just now telling me? You know how much I wanted to find that! You're so fucking selfish!"

"Well I'm *sorry*. You don't have to talk to me like that, though." It was an insincere apology and it pissed Lara off. This was so like her mother. She'd found something great and kept it to herself to use as ammunition later.

"I just wanted to hang onto it because I don't really have many of his things at all. Cate just—"

"No, Mom!" Lara cut her off for the second time in their short conversation. "You don't get to do that! You don't get to keep things like that from us. For the last time, Cate is not trying to keep things from you. She's just having a hard time getting rid of his stuff! If she'd found something as important as his journal she would have told you. It's not the same thing!"

Lara could hear her mother crying and now she did roll her eyes. Why did it always have to be this way? Why couldn't her mother ever think beyond her own grief? She needed to get off the phone.

Lara closed her eyes and tried to calm down.

"Can I come over and look at his journal? I'll even make us a digital copy so we can all have one."

"Fine," her mother said. "Can you come by today? I also need someone to figure out why my cable isn't working." Lara took a deep breath. Her "cable" was really her satellite dish and Lara had no idea how, but about every other month, her mother managed to disable or disconnect it from her televisions and wouldn't learn how to fix it herself.

"Sure, Mom. I have some time this afternoon if you'll be home."

Lara began to mentally brace herself for an afternoon with her mother. As much as she didn't feel like dealing with her, she really, really wanted to read Ben's journal.

When she got off the phone, she sent Cate a text. "The good news is that my mother found Ben's journal! The bad news is that she's been hanging onto it for months *eye roll* she can be so difficult. I'm sorry. I'm going over there this afternoon and I'm going to create a digital copy for all of us. I'm going to *try* to take it with me so you can have it. <3"

Cate responded just a few moments later. "Sigh. She's something else. But I am glad she found it. Thanks, Lara."

Lara could tell as soon as she walked into her mother's small apartment that it was not going to go well. The air was hazy with cigarette smoke and her mother hadn't greeted her at the door. "Mom?" she called as she let herself in.

"In here," her mother responded.

When Lara walked into the kitchen, she took in the scene in the combination kitchen/dining room. There were unwashed dishes in the sink, the trash can was full, and plates of uneaten food sat on the table. On the sideboard in the dining room, she saw her mother's shrine to Ben.

Lara had had one of her own in the months after Ben died. It sat atop her counter for nearly six months. A small vase held three roses from his casket bouquet, dead and crispy, blackened around the edges. Prayer cards from his funeral had sat in a dusty stack, the ugly angel picture on the front and sappy poem on the back, instructing her "not to cry anymore," letting her know that her loved one was "safely home." She remembered hating those poems almost as much as the stack of sympathy cards smeared with every trite and useless consolation people offer up when someone dies. Because people don't know what to say when someone dies, they say stupid things like: you'll see him again someday; he's in a better place; someday, it will hurt less; or everything happens for a reason. All bullshit, of course.

The shrine had sat there until one day Lara looked at it and, rather than finding comfort from all of the well-intended sentiments, it had made her want to punch something. On one particularly bad day, she'd knocked it to the ground with a scream and one strong sweep of her arm. Thinking back, Lara realized that she'd never picked it up and Alex must have taken care of it. She wondered if he'd kept it all.

Looking at her mother's framed photos of Ben, the stacks of cards, the dusty and crumbling roses, Lara felt immediately guilty. Maybe if she'd taken more time to come and check on her mother or offered to help more, maybe it wouldn't have gotten this bad. Maybe her mother needed more help than she realized. Then her mother opened her mouth.

"Well, here it is. Take it," she said, sliding the journal across the table. "I guess *I* don't need it anymore."

"Mom, please stop. We all want to have a piece of him. I'm going to make us all copies."

"Well who gets the original?" her mother challenged her.

Lara just shook her head. She had been so excited to see Ben's journal and now she didn't even want to open it. She decided she'd wait until she got home to read it. Without answering her mother's question, she just said, "Okay, what's going on with the satellite?"

Lara finished fixing it as quickly as she could. Mustering up every bit of willpower she had left, she asked her mom if she'd like to go to lunch. They'd spent a tense forty-five minutes at Panera, where Lara tried to make polite conversation while her mother complained about everything. It was exhausting.

When Lara was finally able to leave, she still had a couple of hours until Alex and Tessa got home, so she sat down on the couch with Ben's journal. Opening the first page was like a punch in the stomach. His sloppy handwriting, a little doodle of the Cardinals logo, and a picture of Cate paper clipped to the page were just so *Ben*. She surprised herself by laughing and smiling more than crying as she paged through the journal. It was mostly mundane business appointments, but occasionally she found a funny note about a night out he'd had with friends or a celebratory note about a Blues win against the Blackhawks.

When she reached the page dated just a couple of days after he died, she held the journal in her hands, rubbing her fingers over the last words he'd written there. "Dinner with Lara and Alex. Tell Lara about Mom's cat." They'd had plans to have dinner two days after Ben died. Ben clearly wanted to tell her some story about their mother, something that would have made all of them laugh and commiserate (because she didn't have a cat), then joking (kind of) about who would have to take care of her when she got old.

Having dealt with their mother just that day, Lara felt the stabbing pain of missing Ben and being able to talk to him (and complain) about their mother. As she closed the journal, she felt lonely and desperate and angry. Reading his journal was the closest she'd felt to Ben in a long time and she tried to focus on the comfort that brought her rather than the pain. But it was just so hard. It wasn't fair she had to deal with her parents alone. It wasn't fair Ben had never been able to tell her the funny story he'd wanted to share. She felt deep, painful sobs building from inside her chest.

All of the coping skills she'd worked on with Dr. Moore flew right out of her head and she cried for a long time, sitting on the couch, clutching his journal to her chest. She lay down, her sobs slowing into quiet tears. She let them fall down her face and collect on the pillow.

She was exhausted, but forced herself to sit up when she heard Alex's truck in the driveway. "Lara?" he called out when he came in through the garage. She sat up, hurriedly wiping tears from her face.

"I'm here, babe." She stood, reaching out to take Tessa from Alex. She hugged her daughter, breathing in the sweet scent of her head, a mixture of her baby shampoo and banana she must have smeared in her hair at breakfast. Lara smiled into Tessa's hair. Tessa began squirming, saying, "Down, Mama! Want *Paw Patrol!*"

"Okay, baby." At the sound of Lara's quiet voice, Tessa looked at her, placing one chubby little hand on her cheek. "Love Mama." Lara smiled even though this hurt her. Her two-year-old had spent too much time with a mother who wasn't whole, who cried too much. She could always read it. And while Lara loved that sometimes Tessa knew when she needed some extra love, she also hated that it was a lesson she'd learned so young.

"I love you too, baby." Lara kissed her cheek and set her down. Tessa toddled off, grabbed the remote and held it out to Lara. Lara turned on her favorite show and Tessa climbed onto the couch. Alex had been quietly watching them, not saying anything. When they walked into the kitchen, Alex said, "Are you okay?"

"Not really. It's been a really bad day. I went to my mother's."

"Oh, no. Why?"

Lara filled him in on the journal, the anger coming back as she realized it was another situation her mother had made about her own grief.

"Did she let you take it?" Alex asked.

"Yeah. It's here. I read it," she said, handing it to him. "I miss him so much." She began to cry and Alex set the book down on and wrapped his arms around her.

"Maybe you shouldn't torture yourself with his stuff."

"No. It was nice to read it. Just hard." She stepped out of Alex's hug and wiped her eyes again. "I'm not feeling so great. Are you okay with putting in a frozen pizza for dinner? I'm not that hungry and I think I'm going to lie down."

"Right now?"

"Yeah."

"Okay …" Alex sounded confused and worried. "You sure you don't want to stay up? Play with Tess?"

It had been at least two months since she'd had a really bad day and Lara could tell he was nervous this would be the start of a backslide for her, back to the days when she'd curl up on the closet floor. She wanted to reassure him she would be okay, but she didn't really feel okay right now.

"I'm sorry. I'm just going to lie down for a bit. Wake me up in like an hour, okay?"

"Okay."

Lara lay down on her bed, wrapping herself in her favorite blanket. She fell asleep immediately and woke to Alex gently pushing the hair back from her face.

"Hey babe. You alright?" he asked softly.

"Yeah. I'll be out in a minute." Lara went into the bathroom and splashed water on her face. She felt drained and was quiet for the rest of the evening. She told Alex that she was fine and that she just needed some time. It was obvious he wanted to ask her questions, but respected her request to just sit together and watch some mindless TV.

Lara forced herself to clean the kitchen and give Tessa a bath and read her a story even though she wanted to curl up on the couch and do nothing. As the night wore on, she found herself thinking up excuses about how she could justify taking the day off work tomorrow. She could feel the pull of the grief, calling her to let it all go again.

When they headed to bed, Lara lay there for a long time after Alex fell asleep. She felt tired, but couldn't sleep. For the first time in months, she found herself unable to stop thinking about Ben's death and his funeral. Then she started thinking about the cough Tessa had and wondered if that was a sign of something more serious and if she should call the doctor and, and, and ...

I have to stop this, she thought. She did not want to start obsessing again. Lara rolled over and looked at the clock on her nightstand and sighed. It was almost midnight. She was going to be tired tomorrow. She looked at the books on her nightstand. She was in the middle of a new thriller that had gotten rave reviews, but she wasn't crazy about it and it was a little sad. There were a couple of other books in the stack, but nothing sounded good.

She saw *Memoriae* sitting at the bottom of the pile and picked it up. It had been sitting on her nightstand since she'd finished it months before and the paper on which she'd written the quote was still taped to her mirror. She thought a lot about Violet Marsh and reminded herself over and over that she still held the weight of Ben's memory and that was something. Now, after this awful day, she thought maybe Violet might be able to help her feel a bit less alone. She opened the book's yellowed pages.

This time, as she read, she began making notes in the margin and in the blank pages. The bookworm in her rebelled, not wanting to mark up the book—she never even dog-eared pages to keep her place. But Lara had never been one for journaling, even though Dr. Moore and every expert out there recommended it and said it would help her. Following along with Violet's experience and writing down the parallels to her own life seemed to help her process some of her own feelings, without having to write long posts about the complicated emotions that came along with therapy.

That night, she read and wrote until her eyes grew heavy. She set the book down, switched off the lamp, and fell asleep immediately.

CHAPTER NINE

Lara

The next day she felt tired, but not as bad as she'd feared. Mostly she felt proud that she was actually using the tools she'd talked about so often with Dr. Moore. She'd had a bad day and listened to herself when she needed a rest. She talked to Alex. She stopped her spiraling thoughts. She could still feel the pull of the depression, always right there, and something, she realized, she might have to fight against for her whole life, but she had managed it.

She got up on time, made Alex's lunch, and kissed him goodbye. He seemed relieved to see her up and going. She dropped Tessa off at daycare and then texted Maryn. In the past she would have kept to herself all day, maybe crying some more and definitely paging through Ben's planner over and over again. But not today. She'd work and then get out of the house and talk to Maryn. She needed to talk to someone and process how she was feeling about the journal. She didn't have an appointment with Dr. Moore until next week, but Maryn was the next best thing.

They met for lunch at their favorite restaurant and settled in a back corner table. Maryn looked tired. She wasn't wearing her signature red lip and she had bags under her eyes.

"Are you okay?" Lara asked.

"Yeah, I'm fine. Why?"

"You just ... seem tired."

Maryn smiled, but it didn't quite reach her eyes. "Just a late night. A lot on my mind."

"What is it, Mar?"

"I just ..." Maryn shook her head a little. "I just have a big test coming up that I'm nervous about."

Lara didn't buy it. Maryn rarely lost her cool, especially when it came to classes.

Seeing that Lara didn't believe her, Maryn smiled again and said, "I'm serious, I'm fine. So what's up?"

Clearly Maryn wasn't going to tell her what was going on. Not yet. So Lara told her about the visit with her mother and reading Ben's journal. She told her how she'd felt the pull of the depression and how easy it had been to slide back into bed in the middle of the day.

When she was done, Maryn said, "Have I ever told you about the time I went crazy and tore Will's apartment apart?"

"No. What happened?"

Maryn sighed. She said that she'd been in shock in the days after his death and during his funeral. She had cried, but hadn't really felt the crushing pain that would come later.

"I felt cocooned, you know? Everyone, family, friends, and co-workers, were surrounding me and my family. We were telling stories about Will, sharing pictures, we actually laughed a lot. It felt like a celebration. I mean, it was fucking terrible. But there were moments when it was also … nice."

Lara nodded. She remembered the same feeling. Hearing stories from Ben's friends that she hadn't heard before, seeing pictures that she'd never seen, made it feel like Ben was still alive.

Maryn went on to describe what happened once all her family and friends went back to their lives. That was when she'd felt the grief crash upon her. She said she'd gone to his apartment to get an old sweatshirt of his that she wanted to keep. She walked in and saw all the same old photos in frames and that's when she realized that there wouldn't be any new stories or pictures of Will. And that thought literally brought her to her knees. There, in her brother's kitchen, she fell to the floor and began to cry.

"I think I kind of lost my mind for a bit. I became obsessed with the thought that I was going to find some secret note from Will, some message he'd left behind just for me."

Maryn shook her head and took a deep breath. "I tore everything apart. I looked in every drawer, every book, every closet. I took pictures off the walls, looked under mattresses and couch cushions. It looked like someone had tried to rob the place."

She laughed an unamused laugh. "I never found anything and his wife was so mad at me for the mess I made."

"Oh, Maryn."

"That wasn't the last time I temporarily lost my mind. There have been a lot of moments when I did things that were completely irrational or at the very least wouldn't have made sense to anyone else. But it was what I needed to do at the time. It was a release for me."

She reached for a napkin and smoothed it over her lap. "I guess the point of the story is that I think there are just moments when we have to give in to the grief. Even if just for a little bit. If we don't, it gets to be too much bottled inside and it's going to come out anyway. We have to just *feel* it sometimes, you know? The trick is pulling yourself out again. And you're here, Lara. You're not in bed and you're talking it through."

Lara nodded and thought about what Maryn had said. "Did I ever tell you about Ben's funeral and how I freaked out there?"

Maryn shook her head no.

"I had asked specifically that they not play that stupid arms of the angels song."

"Oh my god. It's the worst."

"*The worst*," Lara agreed. "But someone played it during the visitation. I think it was playing along with some slideshow or something."

Lara thought back to those first words and what had happened when they first played over the speakers in that small, stuffy room filled with people waiting to pay their respects to her and her family.

She'd been taking a break from the long line of visitors, sitting in one of the folding chairs. When she heard the song, she'd looked wildly around the room, looking for Alex or anyone who could make it stop. *Not this song. Not this song. Who is playing THIS SONG?*

"Lara? Are you okay?" Alex had appeared at her side, and placed his hand on her arm.

"N-no. Why—Who is playing this song? They weren't supposed to play this song!" her breath had caught in her chest and she realized she was shaking. As the song encouraged her to find some comfort in the arms of the angels, she felt her tenuous grasp on reality slipping away.

May you find some comfort here.

She must have looked wild because Alex looked scared and said, "I'll make sure the song gets turned off. Just stay here." He walked away, hurrying toward the table where someone's laptop was streaming a montage of video clips and photographs of Ben.

"I sat there, and folded over until my head was on my knees and I actually put my hands over my ears. I was just rocking back and forth and eventually Alex had to shake me—really shake me—to let me know it had been turned off. I felt ridiculous, but that song just … broke something open in me. It wasn't rational. It's just a song. I could have just walked out of the room. I guess that was the first time I really lost my mind, too."

Maryn smiled at her sadly. "But we're still here, huh?"

"Yeah. We are. For better or worse, I guess. It would have been really easy for me to let the journal become a reason to be sad all the time again. Not long ago it probably would have. It's really a choice, isn't it?"

"What do you mean?" Maryn asked.

"I think that in those first days and weeks the grief and pain was kind of out of my control. I was just reacting and trying to survive. Which is all anyone can do in that situation, I think. But I stayed in that mindset for a year—that grief was something happening to me and I couldn't do anything to change it. That's the wrong way to look at it. While I can't change the fact that Ben is gone, I *can* change the way I deal with it.

"It's like a light switch—it's really easy to flip on the anger or sadness. Easy because it hurts. It sucks. Those emotions are always right there at the surface, so it's easy to fall back to them. But I also have the option to turn that switch off after a while. I can move away from the bad feelings and focus on something better. I'm not saying we should never feel sad or angry because those things are healthy. But I can control how much I let those feelings control me." Lara looked down at her hands. It felt silly, to talk like this, like she was a therapist, but she supposed all those sessions with Dr. Moore were working.

"I never really thought about it like that. Like I have a choice."

"But you act like it, Mar. You've chosen joy a lot better than I've been able to."

Maryn laughed. "Sometimes. It's not always pretty."

"Maybe not. But you're more positive than I am."

"You're getting there."

"Yeah. And little things help. Like this book I'm reading. Well, rereading. I don't know if I ever told you about it. The one about the girl who loses her brother?"

"I'm not sure. What's it about?"

Lara gave her a brief rundown of *Memoriae*, but as she went on, she noticed that Maryn seemed distracted. She squirmed in her seat and didn't say much. Eventually, Lara just stopped talking about the book and said, "Maryn, what's going on?"

"Nothing. I'm sorry, I'm just tired. Look, I have a meeting with my advisor and need to prepare."

"Okay." Lara was confused. Maryn was never abrupt with her. "Hey."

Maryn looked up from where she was digging her keys out of her purse.

"Did I say something to upset you?" Lara couldn't figure out why Maryn was in such a rush to get out of there.

"No, of course not. I'm sorry. I just need to get going. I'll call you tomorrow, okay?"

"Sure."

What the hell is going on with her? Lara thought.

Over the next few days, Lara continued reading *Memoriae* and taking notes. She had even devoted two whole pages in the back of the book to her three favorite memories of Ben, just like Violet had.

She'd found it so comforting that she had kept going, writing down everything she could think of, good or bad. She wrote down every story she remembered friends and family telling about Ben in the days after his death. Getting detention at school because he brought a frog hidden in his lunchbox. The winning touchdown during his high school football team's trip to the state championship. College stories about running naked around his fraternity house. And the scary moments in their lives. When her mother had tried to force them to sleep in separate rooms after the divorce but they'd refused. The time Ben had broken his arm and she'd held his hand in the backseat on the way to the hospital.

I might not have any of my own memories to contribute, she thought bitterly, *but at least I can write down the memories everyone else shared with me.* It helped to write them down all the same. She was writing out her own feelings about grief and how she'd been trying so desperately to heal.

Lara was drawn again and again to a particular passage, right before Violet met the mysterious witch at the riverfront.

I felt restless. I did not know what I should do. I did not
know how I was ever going to build a life of meaning again.
All of the things I wanted to tell Henry, all of the thoughts

112

and feelings I wanted to share with just him, the questions I
wanted to ask, had nowhere to go. It was all building up and
I simply had to ignore it.

Lara had highlighted that and scribbled in the margin: "This. It's
like that quote, 'Grief is love with nowhere to go.' I want Ben. It feels
like no one else can help. I just want Ben and it feels unfair and cruel
that I can't even talk to him."

Lara put down the pen and rubbed her eyes. She turned back to
the spot where she'd left off reading.

CHAPTER TEN

Memoriae

I feel like a mad person writing what I think happened next, but happen it did and I will not forget. A strong, strange wind whipped up, blowing the branches and leaves that were scattered around me into an outward circle that cleared my little patch of earth of everything but the grass, the dirt, and Henry's possessions. Henry's hat flipped over on its end. The pages of his book began flipping open rapidly, some flying out, violently ripped from the binding. The watch flew into a nearby tree, cracking the face. Under the moaning of the wind I heard a low scream, one that seemed to be moving through the trees and getting closer to me.

Then, as suddenly as it had started, the wind stopped abruptly, dropping debris in a perfect circle around me. Henry's items stilled. I watched the leaves swirl settle around me, terrified but unable to move.

And then, something was there. Not physically. I could not have touched it and could not see anything with my eyes. But something was there. A sharp and vivid memory of us as children, running along the river, came to me then, and I felt the wind in my hair then felt the fear as I tripped, stumbling and bashing my head on a rock. I remembered holding Henry's hand as we listened to mother screaming from her room about the baby she had lost. I felt the cold terror spread from my stomach to my limbs as father told me the news of Henry's death.

I stood quickly, looking for my lantern, but it had blown over in the wind and rolled away from the circle. I didn't know what to do. I needed to get out of this place.

There was enough moonlight for me to locate my bag and the

lantern. It was only as I stood shakily to my feet, that I realized I was being guided by moonlight. Moonlight! It had been dusk when I started this ceremony. How had I lost so much time? My heart was pounding now. What had happened to me? I needed to get out of the woods. I lit the lantern, and gathered Henry's things, placing them in my bag. I made my way out of the woods, skirts gathered in my hands, walking as quickly as I could. I stopped frequently to listen, to ensure nothing was following me. I heard nothing but normal forest noises.

I did not feel like I was alone. The feeling dissipated a bit as I left the woods and made my way back to the house, but I just did not feel entirely at peace. I don't know what happened to me. But something did.

CHAPTER ELEVEN

Lara

Lara set the book down, her brows furrowed in confusion. She wasn't sure, but she thought this scene felt entirely different than the first time she had read it. Which, of course, didn't make any sense. But Lara thought for sure that when she'd read that passage the first time, it had felt peaceful and comforting. Violet had gotten all of her memories back—and they had been *good* memories. *This* wasn't the way she remembered it at all. Or was it? As she read the passage again, she became less sure. The first time she read it she'd been sad and depressed, so she thought it was possible that she didn't remember exactly.

"How is it?" Alex asked, looking up from the baseball game he was watching. It was Sunday and Tessa was napping.

"Oh, fine," she said. "You know, it's weird, I just got done reading this one part and I remember it being a little different the last time I read it. Which can't be true right?"

"Well you've been reading a lot lately, you're probably just getting it mixed up with other stories."

"Yeah, that's true. And I wasn't in such a great place the first time I read it, either." Lara laughed. "I was actually not doing well at all. I guess I just took away from the book what I needed to take away from it at the time."

It is odd, though, she thought, *that once you read a book you can't be sure it's exactly the same as the last time you read it.* Lara shook her head.

"Yep." Alex was looking back at the game. Lara wanted to keep reading, sure that the rest of the book would be just as she remembered it. But she heard Tessa talking to her baby doll and went in to pick her up.

The next day, Lara took Tessa to daycare and settled in to work. She had a new project, a book layout for a local author, and she was excited about it. It was a combination self-help book and workbook, so the design was interesting and fun. Lara was hoping to work with this client on future projects, so she wanted to knock this one out of the park.

After a while, Lara leaned back in her chair and stretched her arms over her head. Her back was aching and when she looked at the clock and realized she'd been working for almost three hours, she realized why. She needed a break.

Standing up, she decided to pick up the house and put a load of laundry in before she went back to the office. She started in the kitchen, putting some dirty dishes in the dishwasher and throwing away the junk mail that had accumulated on the counter. Lara took the trash bag out of the trashcan and headed toward the garage door to take it outside, almost tripping over one of Tessa's Crocs sitting on the small rug next to the door. She spotted the other one on the floor by the basement stairs. Rolling her eyes and smiling a little, she made a mental note to pick them up on her way back in.

Lara took the trash out and while she was outside watered some of the plants on the front porch and swept leaves and dirt off the steps. She went back into the house through the front door, cleaning up some of Tessa's toys in the living room and straightening the pillows on the couch before she headed back to the office. *I'll work for another hour then stop for lunch.*

Two hours later, the book layout was done and she was hungry and ready for a break. As Lara walked back into the kitchen, she remembered the shoes. Looking over at the door to the garage, she stopped in her tracks.

The shoes were in the middle of the rug, placed neatly side-by-side. "What the hell …" she said quietly. Those shoes had been thrown on the floor, at least three feet apart. Hadn't they? *You have to be misremembering,* she told herself. Shaking her head, she picked them up and placed them on the mat where they belonged. *Don't be stupid, Lara.*

She ate lunch and worked for a while longer before she went to pick Tessa up. She mostly forgot about the shoes.

That evening, they went for a walk after dinner, gave Tessa a bath, put her to bed, and settled in for the night. She and Alex wanted to catch up on the show they'd been binging on Netflix.

Suddenly, Alex paused the television. "Did you hear that?" Alex asked her.

"Hmm?" she said, looking at him. "I didn't hear anything."

"I thought I heard Tessa calling for you." They listened, not hearing anything. After a moment, Alex shrugged and turned the sound back on.

Less than a minute later Lara heard, "Mommy!"

"You were right," she said to Alex, getting up off the couch. As she walked out of the living room, heading down the hall, she heard, "Mom?"

"I'm coming, baby," she called.

Lara turned on the hallway light and walked into Tessa's room. "You okay, baby?" Lara knelt down next to the toddler bed, expecting Tessa to hold up her arms to be held. But she was fast asleep, arms thrown back over her head, mouth wide open. Lara stroked her cheek, but Tessa didn't move. Her breathing didn't change. She was dead asleep. Frowning, Lara stood up and looked at her daughter for a moment before she walked out of the room, turned off the hallway light, and made her way back to the living room.

"That was so weird," she said to Alex.

"What?"

"She was totally asleep."

"She was probably just dreaming and called out."

"No, I don't think so. She was *asleep*, asleep. Dead to the world."

"I know I heard her."

"Me, too." She shrugged and Alex resumed their show. It was only a moment before a disturbing thought occurred to her. Tessa was two. She always called Lara mommy or mama or occasionally Lara because they laughed when she did. She had never called her mom.

Lara tried to focus on the show they were watching, but she felt unsettled. Maybe Tessa had called out for her and she had said mom. She did occasionally spend time with older kids at daycare and she had older cousins who called their mother, mom. She could have picked it up from anywhere. But would she call out for Lara from a dead sleep and say mom and not mommy? Lara really didn't think so.

When the show was over, she was relieved. This had been a weird day and she just wanted to go to bed.

"I'm going to take a shower," Lara told Alex.

"Want some company?" he asked with a smile.

Lara wanted to say no, but she reminded herself that making her relationship with Alex a priority was part of her healing process. So she smiled and said, "Sure."

They showered together, going slow and taking their time. They made love and it was nice. Comfortable. It made her feel alive.

Alex rinsed off and stepped out of the shower. "I'm going to stay in for a while," Lara said. "Be out in a bit."

She heard Alex leave the bathroom, shutting the door behind him. Lara let the hot water run over her head, enjoying the softening of her muscles. Showers were sometimes the hardest part of her day. It was the only time she couldn't occupy her mind with a book, television, or work. And when her mind wasn't occupied it tended to go to places that she didn't want to go.

She forced her mind to clear while she shampooed and

conditioned her hair. She focused on the feeling of the soap in her hands, the loofah on her back, and the warm water pooling around her feet and running down her back.

She heard a noise outside of the shower. She froze. "Alex?" No answer. She heard a shuffling sound. "Alex, are you in here?" Still no answer. She didn't know why, but she didn't want to pull the curtain back. She stayed silent, listening hard, but didn't hear anything else.

Heart hammering, she tried to convince herself she must have imagined the sounds. She quickly finished rinsing and turned the water off. She listened for a moment and hearing nothing, she thought, *Just do it like a band aid. Quick. There's nothing there.* Taking a deep breath, she quickly pulled the curtain back.

There was nothing there. Steam fogged the mirror and her towel lay where she'd left it. Lara smiled and tried to laugh at herself. *You've got to calm down, Kemp.*

It wasn't until she went to take her robe off the back of the door that she realized the door was open.

She ran down the hallway, yelling for Alex. "Alex! Did you come back into the bathroom?"

"Huh?"

"Did you come back into the bathroom and open the door?" She could hear the panic in her voice and told herself to calm down.

"No. I've been out here the whole time. Why?"

"Fuck," she said. "Fuck. The door was open when I got out of the shower."

"Okayyyy ..."

"I heard you close the door. Didn't you?"

"I think so."

"You did. I know you did. I heard it." Lara looked down the hallway.

"Well maybe I didn't close it all the way. Not a big deal."

"But I heard something. Then I heard the door open."

"Babe, what are you getting at? You think someone opened the door?" Lara could tell Alex thought she was overreacting. She hadn't told him about the other weird things that had happened because she knew he would think she'd lost it and look at her exactly the way he was looking at her right now.

"I don't know. I don't know. You're probably right. Sorry. Just got a little spooked." Lara shook her head. "I'm going to get dressed and go to bed."

"I'll go with you," Alex said.

She got ready for bed, heart thudding the whole time. She climbed in next to Alex and pulled the covers up to her chin. *What a weird day,* she thought. *I must be super tired or getting sick or something.* There was a rational explanation for everything that had happened. Maybe she kicked the shoes as she walked out the door with the trash. It's entirely possible that Tessa had called out for mom. Or maybe she had said mommy and it just *sounded* like mom. And of course, Alex just didn't close the door to the bathroom all the way. All of that made perfect sense.

Lara read for a while, but *Memoriae* left her feeling unsettled and she really was tired. But she couldn't stop thinking about the sound she'd heard in her bathroom. It was a long time before she fell asleep.

CHAPTER TWELVE

Maryn

Maryn could feel it building, feel it start to spin out of her control.

"'Just keep an eye on it,' they said. 'It's not a big deal, nothing's going to happen. We just need to know what's going on. Just keep an eye on her,'" Maryn muttered to herself sarcastically as she sat at her kitchen table, drinking tea and trying to decide whether or not to call Clara. "My ass. There's some crazy shit going on right now. And now I'm talking to myself."

She wasn't happy she had been put in this position in the first place and on top of that, she'd been given almost no information. *This is exactly why it took me thirteen years to even get involved in this bullshit,* she thought. Now, here she was trying to manage a situation that she didn't understand with no help from anyone.

She decided she was too worked up to try to talk to Clara over the phone. She didn't want to say something she'd regret. So she typed out a quick text message instead. "We need to talk. Now."

As she waited for a response, Maryn thought about how she'd got here, caught up in this madness.

It had started in high school. Maryn's childhood had been good, all things considered. She lived in a diverse area of the city, which was important to her as a girl with a black dad and a white mom. She fit in and had plenty of friends. Her parents supported her dedication to swim team, shuttling her to and from practices and sitting at meets for hours. She and her friends were good kids for the most part, only getting into trouble with the occasional party or getting caught out past curfew.

During her junior year, she was experiencing more stress than she ever had before. She was taking AP classes and swimming six days a week. She was trying to decide where she wanted to go to college and figuring out how to apply and how she'd be able to afford it. As fall moved into winter, she felt herself withdrawing. She would sit down at her desk to do homework, her to-do list so long that she didn't even know where to start, and find herself staring into space instead.

She began to lose whole chunks of time, sitting there at her desk. At first it would be just a minute here or there. She'd find herself suddenly coming to, shaking her head and, thinking she'd just been daydreaming, she'd put her head down and get back to work. But slowly, she'd lose longer and longer periods of time, marked by the songs that passed on her CDs, with no memory of having listened to them.

She had no idea what happened during these blackouts. Nothing around her seemed to have changed. The only marked difference between before and after would be a slight tingling in her fingertips and a dull ache behind her eyes. Not a pain so much as a weight.

Her grades began to dip, ever so slightly, because she wasn't able to get all of her homework done on time and she spaced out when she tried to study. She tried to cram in as much work as she could during study hall, because she didn't seem to lose time while she was at school, but it wasn't enough to keep up.

By the time Christmas break came around, she was exhausted and instead of her regular list of As and maybe a couple of Bs, she had Bs and Cs on her second quarter report card. When her mother questioned her about it, Maryn almost told her what had been happening, but she knew her mom would freak out and want to take her to the doctor and get her checked for ADD or narcolepsy or something and Maryn didn't want the trouble. She just needed to focus.

Over winter break, she tried to relax, thinking it might help with the stress. She spent time with her friends, listening to them talk about boys, if there was a way to make their boobs bigger, what they thought college would be like. But Maryn never really joined in. It was like she was daydreaming, but couldn't remember the dream.

What she did notice when she forced herself to focus on what was going on around her was an intense reaction to whatever the people around her were experiencing. The first time she really noticed it, she was studying at the kitchen table and heard her mother and father in their room upstairs, arguing in low voices. She suddenly felt a searing anger toward her dad, then what felt like disgust toward her mother. She wanted to get up and join in the argument. She wanted to cry. She didn't understand why she was feeling this way. The argument had nothing to do with her and there was no reason for her to be so upset.

She gathered her books and took them into the basement living room where she could no longer hear them. She started experiencing similar emotions around her friends, the longing for a boy, the stress of filling out a college application, confusion about an upcoming exam. It got so difficult to separate her own emotions from others' that Maryn would have to grind her teeth, clench her fists, and rush away from whoever was emitting the most intense feelings.

She stopped spending time with people. Eventually her parents caught on and demanded she tell them what was wrong with her. She didn't know what to say.

"Well, Mom and Dad, it started with me blacking out. Now, I feel everyone else's emotions really intensely and I can't stand it." They'd think she'd lost her mind. So she told them it was the stress of junior year, and swim team, and planning for the future. They seemed to accept that and Maryn told herself she'd just have to ignore it. Double down on the work and try her best to ignore what was happening.

That worked for a while, until one night her parents had invited some neighbors over for dinner and she had a big history test the next day. There was nowhere for her to go in the house, but it was cold and raining, so she didn't feel like driving to the library. *I'll just study in my room and play my music really loud. It'll be okay.*

But it wasn't. As soon as she settled down to concentrate, she was gone. This time, when she came to, the study guide she'd been holding was burnt, crisp around the edge where she'd been holding it. Her skin wasn't burnt, but the paper had very clearly been burning slowly, the heat spreading up the paper, distorting and destroying the words.

With a gasp, Maryn dropped the paper on her desk, where it sat, no longer burning. "What the fuck?" she whispered. She looked around for a lighter, for matches, for anything that could explain the burnt paper, even though she knew there was no such thing in her room.

Her heart beating wildly, Maryn stood up, though she didn't know where to go or what to do. She gathered up her papers and books, stacking them neatly, knowing she was done studying for the night. She got ready for bed, but it was a long time before she fell asleep.

The next day, she'd woken late after a few restless hours of sleep. Bleary-eyed, she got ready for school. As she gathered her things to put in her backpack, she stole a glance at her study guide. Still burnt.

Fighting back tears, she said goodbye to her mom and headed to school. After getting stopped at every light, she pulled into the parking lot with only a couple of minutes to get to her first class on time. She ran through the parking lot, bursting through the side entrance closest to her locker.

She fumbled with her lock, needing to get just one book for her first class. As she slammed the door shut, she saw Mrs. White, the librarian, walking toward her as the hallway cleared of all the other students. Mrs. White was one of Maryn's favorite adults at the school. She was an old hippie (her words) and had long, light brown hair that was braided down her back. She favored leggings and flowing shirts that hid her slender frame. She was the teacher advisor for the yearbook, so Maryn had worked closely with her for the past two years as part of the yearbook club. She was the only teacher who seemed to understand that Maryn had a mind for both science and art and wanted to study engineering, but use her degree to make the world a more beautiful, better place. Mrs. White had encouraged her to explore unique summer internships at the local utility and city planning department.

Mrs. White was smiling and as she got closer, she said, "Running a little late, Maryn?"

"Yes. I didn't sleep very well and hit snooze one too many times," Maryn said apologetically, hoisting her backpack on her shoulder.

"What class do you have first period?"

"Spanish."

"Do you have a test or anything important?"

Maryn thought this was an odd question and her puzzlement must have shown on her face, because Mrs. White said, "I was just wondering if you had some time to talk. I can write you a note, tell Senora Rosa that we had some yearbook items to discuss."

"Um. Okay." Maryn was confused and couldn't think what Mrs. White could possibly want to talk to her about, but curiosity got the best of her and she followed Mrs. White down the hall toward the library.

That meeting would change her life.

Maryn shook her head clear of her memories as her phone pinged with a response from Clara. "Okay. Can you meet me for coffee Tuesday morning?"

Lara

It had been a few days since she and Maryn had met for lunch and Lara couldn't shake the feeling that something was wrong with her friend. She was worried about her. They'd texted a couple of times, and yesterday Maryn had cancelled plans they'd had together with Alex and Tim tonight, saying she had to study. It wasn't often she cancelled plans.

Maryn had been so supportive since they'd met and always seemed to have it together. Lara wondered if her strange behavior had something to do with Will or maybe she and Tim were fighting.

Lara had woken up determined to get hold of Maryn today and let her know she wasn't alone, whatever was going on. She'd texted her friend three times, but Maryn had only responded once, a short message saying everything was fine, she was just super busy and that she'd call her tomorrow.

Lara had been looking forward to getting dressed up and doing something fun, so she decided to plan a night at home after Tessa went to bed. She asked Alex to put Tessa to bed and ordered sushi from their favorite place and had it delivered. She set up the dining room table with candles and a bottle of wine. She even made a playlist on her phone of some of their favorite music. When Alex was done putting Tessa to bed, she ushered him into the dining room.

"Wow," he said. "This is nice. Thanks, babe." They ate, drank wine, and talked and laughed for two hours. When they had gone through two bottles of wine, they stumbled their way down the hallway.

"I am *not* sober," Lara said, laughing.

"Me either," Alex stage whispered. "If we wake the baby up, not it!"

Lara pushed him playfully into their room and closed the door behind her. He wrapped his arms around her and kissed her, running his hands through her hair, down her back, and grabbing her ass. She pushed him on the bed, landing on top of him.

Later, she lay next to him as he snored softly. *I should get up and check on Tessa and make sure the doors are locked*, she thought. She didn't want to get out of their comfortable bed, Alex's warm body pressed against her. But it would bother her all night if she didn't double check the locks and give Tessa one more kiss. She also wanted to get a glass of water. She'd need it in the morning.

She quietly got out of bed, wrapping her robe around her, and made her way down the dark hallway. The small night light they kept in the living room must have burned out because she couldn't see anything, so she spread out both of her arms, feeling her way down the hall. Just as she was getting ready to flip on the light in the kitchen, she heard a shuffling noise coming from the dining room. She froze as she heard it again. It sounded like fabric ruffling.

Her mind was screaming at her that she should yell for Alex, but she didn't want to wake Tessa up. And after all, it could be anything. It was probably the curtains moving as the heat kicked on and the air blew out of the floor vents. Reassured that she'd figured out what the noise was, she flipped on the kitchen light. Nothing looked out of place.

She checked that the door to the backyard was locked and walked through the dining room to the living room to check the front door. She looked at the dining room table where the remains of their dinner sat and her hands flew to her mouth.

"Oh my god," she moaned. The table runner, which she'd folded up and set on one of the chairs so they could eat, was now laid out along the length of the table. The tall glass vase filled with decorative rocks and candles that she used as a centerpiece was placed back neatly in the middle of the table. Their dirty dishes had been stacked nicely and their wine glasses sat side by side at the end of the table.

"What the fuck," she breathed. She knew they had not cleaned up before they made their way down to their bedroom. They must have, though. There was no other explanation for it.

Lara backed quickly out of the room, switching on the small light above the kitchen sink. She checked in on Tessa, kissing her softly on the cheek and checking that her video monitor was on. Lara got back into bed, took the video monitor from the nightstand, and turned it on. She pulled the covers up and around her shoulders and watched Tessa sleeping. She tried to convince herself it was nothing. Alex had just picked up the table while she went to the bathroom or something and she hadn't noticed. That had to be it.

Thirty minutes later she was still wide awake. She was sober now. She picked up *Memoriae*, hoping that reading would distract her.

CHAPTER THIRTEEN

Memoriae

In the days that followed my experience in the woods, I felt an unnatural heaviness around me. I did not want to get out of bed. I did not want to eat or manage the house or do anything, really. I forced myself to be presentable each day, in the event someone would visit in need of my attention, although I rarely commenced the day before noon.

I spent a lot of time thinking about Henry and I was plagued with thoughts of his death. I had surprisingly detailed visions about his death, even though I was not there. I could see the riverbank, see the sky growing dark and the wind picking up. I heard the screams of men as lightning hit the boat and saw Henry tumble off the side, violently hitting the side of the vessel, before his body was lost to the river. Saw a small trail of red blood in the churning white water. I heard my father screaming. My imagination seemed to have gone completely crazy. I had never asked father exactly what happened to Henry, because I didn't want to know. But now I couldn't stop thinking about what had happened to him.

To try to drive out these thoughts, I read his letters. I lay on his bed. I cried. I became consumed with trying to remember everything I could about him. I wrote down my favorite memories, the mundane memories, the memories I didn't want to remember. I felt sure that I was going to somehow forget every memory I had of him and then what would I be left with? Mostly, I visited his grave. Sometimes, I lay on the grass, letting my body feel heavy, wishing at times that I could sink right into the earth.

It was one such day that I found myself standing in the kitchen around noon, having just left my room for the first time, staring out into the back garden. I do not know how long I had been standing there. I had simply lost track of time and the tea that had been warm in my hand not long ago was now cold. I startled when I realized someone was knocking on the door.

I placed my cup on the counter, smoothed my skirts, and hurried to the door. When I opened it, I saw my friend Liza standing there. She was holding a small bouquet of flowers and a basket of sweet rolls.

"Hello, friend." Liza was smiling brightly

"Hello, Liza." I stood there, unable to think what I should say next.

"Violet?" Liza looked concerned now, a frown on her pretty face. "May I come in?"

"Oh! Of course. I'm sorry." I stepped aside, waving her into the foyer. Liza unwrapped the shawl from around her shoulders and draped it over her arm. She looked at me expectantly and I realized I had yet again missed a cue.

"Let's sit in the sitting room," I suggested, attempting to gain some semblance of my control back. I took the flowers from her as we walked down the hallway. "I'll just get a vase and some water for these, and be right in," I said as I stepped into the kitchen.

I walked into the room but stopped short when I saw my garden shoes placed neatly side-by-side, in front of the sink. They surely had not been there before. I looked around, making sure no one else was in the kitchen. Confused, I was unsure what to do. Was I in such a daze that I had moved the shoes myself and not remembered doing so? It was surely possible, but just minutes ago I had been standing right where the shoes were now placed.

Heart pounding, I felt frozen to the spot. Surely this was not an event of any importance. Surely it was as simple as me not noticing they had been sitting there the whole time. I looked around the kitchen one more time, not noticing anything out of place. I chose a vase, which I filled with water. I gathered a tray, setting down the things for tea and some cookies and pastries. Taking one last look at the shoes in the middle of the floor, I made my way back to the sitting room.

As I set the tray down, I could feel Liza's eyes on me.

"Violet, I do not want to speak out of turn, but are you quite alright? You look horribly pale."

"Oh, I'm just a little tired, I suppose. There's so much to do around here and it's just me, you know ..." My voice trailed off. I saw Liza take in the current state of the sitting room, which, upon my cursory inspection, revealed itself to be dusty and cluttered with days-old newspaper and even a number of used teacups. Instantly, I was embarrassed. When had things fallen into such disrepair? And what day was it? Wasn't the maid supposed to take care of exactly these types of tasks? I would need to have a talk with her.

Sensing my discomfort, Liza, ever the courteous friend, quickly began filling me in on the latest town gossip. She distracted me with her tales and I found myself laughing for the first time in what felt like a very long time. We drank tea and I ate three cookies, which was more than I had eaten in one sitting for days. When Liza finally stood to leave, she grasped both of my hands in her own.

"Violet. I know how difficult things have been for you. I want you to know that you do have friends."

"Thank you, Liza. It is much appreciated. I just need to pop out of it, as mother used to say. Catch up on some rest and all will be well." Liza smiled kindly at me and squeezed my hand.

Once I had seen Liza off, I went back to the kitchen to make yet another cup of tea. Her visit had cheered me. I resolved to do better, in all aspects of my life. I decided I would start with clearing the sitting room. When I finished my tea and had tidied the kitchen counters, I headed to the sitting room.

I stopped in the doorway. The table upon which our tea things had been set was clear of clutter. The vase that contained Liza's flowers was placed neatly in the center. Our cups and saucers were stacked neatly on the tray, along with the other teacups that had littered the room, and the tray had been placed on a sideboard.

I'm not ashamed to say that my legs turned watery and weak, and I slumped against the doorjamb, a low moan escaping my mouth. When I had recovered, I began calling for the maid. Perhaps she had come while I was in the kitchen and cleaned these things.

"Helen! Helen!" I called all throughout the house, to no avail. She was not in the house.

"Violet!" I heard my mother call from her room. "What is going on? Why are you screaming?"

"Sorry, mother!" I called from the hallway. "I'm looking for Helen."

"I've sent her to the pharmacy. Please be quiet, my head aches."

It was only my mother and me in the house. Helen wasn't here. None of us had cleared the sitting room.

After that day, I attempted to ignore it. I convinced myself—or I tried to convince myself—that it was impossible. I was a rational woman, not taken with dramatics. There were three adults and two employees living in this house and someone else could have simply stopped by the sitting room and straightened it up. Everything could be very easily explained.

Until it could not.

One day, I was heading upstairs to my room, hoping to rest before dinner. As I made my way up the stairs, I looked down the hall and saw a door opened just a crack. The door to Henry's room.

I knew it had not been open before. It was never open and had hardly been touched since his death. I did not want to see what awaited me there. I did not want to know if something—someone— had been inside my house and upset my dead brother's room. But I pressed on, simply because I felt I needed to know what I was dealing with.

With my light held before me, I made my way to Henry's room. I slowly pushed open the door and peered inside. At first, I noticed nothing out of place. His bed was made and his overcoat was hanging on a hook on the back of his door. His wardrobe was closed, his Sunday shoes placed neatly on the floor under the window. On his nightstand sat a pitcher for water, a book, and an open notebook. All was just as he'd left it all those months ago.

It wasn't until I looked more closely at the red notebook on the nightstand that I realized something wasn't quite right. It was open to the middle of the book and dark, black words were scrawled across both pages, reading: *"You can't. Don't. Don't."*

I stepped back quickly. It was Henry's handwriting, of that I was sure, but it was messy and I could tell it had been written in a hurry. What I couldn't accept was that it was there at all. I suppose it could have been there all along, but I had spent a lot of time simply sitting in this room, surrounded by his things, and I never touched anything. I hadn't been able to do so much as pick up the things on his nightstand and I was sure that this notebook had not been there before. Who had put it there? And why had Henry ever written those words?

I was fairly certain no one had touched the book or his room at all since he'd died. I could not think of an explanation.

Chapter Fourteen

Lara

Lara dropped the book and put her hands over her mouth. Her stomach felt cold and the hair was standing up on her arms.

"What the fuck," she whispered. Alex stirred next to her and she had a sudden desire to wake him up and tell him what was happening. What she thought was happening. What couldn't really be happening. Violet finding shoes in the middle of the kitchen floor, just as she had, would have been an odd coincidence. But the dishes …

Beyond just that, what was more concerning was the fact that she knew for certain she had not read any of this the first time she'd read the book. She knew now it was very, very different. She remembered the days after Violet's time in the woods as a time of healing for her. She and Liza had laughed during their visit and Liza had been one of the first people Violet had let back into her life as she tried to heal. Violet hadn't been depressed or sad and certainly hadn't found creepy shoes in the middle of the kitchen or suspected a ghost of picking up the sitting room. And what the hell did those words in Henry's book mean?

I have to be rational here, Lara thought. Did she really think that what was happening *in a book* was somehow also happening to her? Had she really just missed entire scenes the first time? It didn't make any sense. A book couldn't just *change.*

Ok, she thought. *I just forgot those parts or I was skimming over them. No big deal. No big deal.* She repeated this to herself over and over until she finally started to get drowsy.

Over the next week, Lara didn't pick the book up again. But the strange things she couldn't explain continued happening and she'd almost reached a breaking point. She was running out of explanations.

The morning after Lara and Alex's stay-at-home date, their dog George had sat in her room, staring at the nightstand where the book was in the drawer, growling and barking. Lara couldn't tear him away from it and only when she grabbed his collar and pulled him out of the room did he stop.

Two days later, she'd gotten out of the shower to find markings in the steam on the mirror. It was far from crystal-clear—it could have been made from droplets of water running through the steam. But it looked like the word *don't.*

The day after that, yesterday, something had happened that she could not explain away for the life of her. She was afraid she was losing her mind. She was beginning to think it was time to tell Alex what was going on even though she knew he still wouldn't believe her.

She'd had a lull in work—she was waiting to get some approvals back from a couple of clients—so she decided to get some deep cleaning done. Over the past year, she'd been lucky if she'd managed to help Alex with just the regular dusting, mopping, and wiping down counters. She knew that the big jobs she tried to do at least a few times a year—things like washing all the curtains, wiping down baseboards, dusting ceilings fans, and cleaning under the couch—had been neglected.

Lara turned on the latest episode of her favorite podcast and started by taking down the curtains in the living room and putting them in the washing machine. While that was running she filled the sink with warm water and a bit of soap and wiped down the baseboards. She refilled the sink with clean water and tackled the fans and light fixtures. Next, she reluctantly got out the vacuum and all of its attachments so she could clean under the couch. Using one of the long extension tubes, she swiped out all of the toys, pacifiers, socks, pens, and loose change that had accumulated, wondering how it was possible for so much crap to get under there. She scored when she found the missing half of her favorite pair of slippers and one of Alex's ball caps he thought he'd lost.

On her second swipe, the tube hit something hard and heavy. Lara braced the tube against the side of the object and carefully pulled it toward her. As the item emerged from under the couch, she realized what it was: a toy diary Tessa had gotten for Christmas. It was red and plastic, made to look like a real journal or diary, but inside it had dry erase pages so they could be used over and over. Lara smiled as she flipped through Tessa's childish scribbles and laughed at some of the animals Alex had drawn for Tessa; a puppy wearing a birthday hat and a pig in a bathtub. She was just about to close it when the diary flipped open to one of the last pages.

There, written in script that wasn't hers or Alex's, were three short sentences. *"You can't. Don't. Don't."*

"Oh, fuck! Fuck!" Lara screamed. Heart pounding, she slammed the book closed, tossing it on the couch. It fell at her feet and she was unable to move. She breathed deep and tried to slow her heart rate down. *You're okay. You're okay,* she repeated to herself. How did those same damn words get into that diary?

Gathering her courage, Lara quickly flipped through the rest of the pages looking for more of the strange writing but finding nothing. *What the hell,* she thought. She tried to think back to the last time she'd seen the diary. She couldn't remember, which was no surprise. But she knew it had been a long time. She suspected it had been under the couch for at least four months or so, because she didn't remember Tessa playing with it much beyond just a couple of days after Christmas.

What does that mean? And who the hell wrote it? Lara's thoughts were swirling. *This is too much.* She didn't want the diary anywhere near her. She picked it up and walked into the garage. Before she put it in a box, she flipped to the back pages, hoping the writing would be gone. Of course it wasn't. She rubbed at the words with her finger. They didn't rub off, so it wasn't dry erase marker. She scratched at the letters, but that didn't have any effect on them either. *There has to be some explanation for this.* She put it in a box and left it on a shelf.

Lara went back into the house and absentmindedly vacuumed under the couch, put the vacuum away, and switched the curtains from the washing machine to the dryer.

That night, she couldn't focus on anything. She was distracted, didn't hear Alex when he asked her questions, and when she'd been giving Tessa a bath, she didn't realize how long she'd been in there until Tessa said, "Mommy, I cold!"

She had to know what was happening in that book. She had to know if the things that had happened to her over the last week were happening to Violet, too. So after Tessa was asleep, she told Alex she was going to read in bed. She was relieved when he said he'd join her, as he wanted to finish the book he was reading, too. She thought that if she was going to do this, if she was going to read this book and see just how crazy it was going to get, she didn't want to be alone. Even if Alex had no clue what was going on.

CHAPTER FIFTEEN

Memoriae

That evening during dinner, Mother actually made her way downstairs to eat with Father and me. I was loath to bring up any subjects that might upset her, but I also wanted to ask both of them if they had been spending any time in Henry's room.

After making small talk about the weather and sharing some town gossip with Mother, I carefully asked, "So I was noticing that the house could use some small repairs, Father. Do you think we could speak about that tomorrow?"

"Well I suppose, if you think it is really necessary."

"Just some small things, like fixing the porch railing and perhaps freshening the paint in the sitting room." When Mother and Father had no comment, I pressed on. "Also, I was in Henry's room the other day and I think perhaps it time—"

"No." My mother's voice was quiet but brooked no argument.

"Mother, I don't want to dispose of anything, I think we can just tidy up, perhaps choose what we want to set aside for safekeeping." Mother had set down her silverware and was shaking her head back and forth.

"Leave it, Violet," said my father.

"Yes. Mother, can I just ask, have you been in his room lately? I wonder if it might provide you some comfort to be around his things."

"No, I have not," she said, placing her napkin on the table. "I have no desire to go in there. But I do not want a single thing removed." She stood up. "I have a headache. I'm going to retire to my room."

I sighed and stood, kissing her on the cheek. "Good night, Mama."

I sat back down, but was no longer hungry. I felt guilty for upsetting my mother.

"What possessed you to ask her about that tonight, the first time she's been down to dinner in weeks?" My father's tone was measured, careful. He was clearly trying to hold back his frustration.

"I am sorry, Father. I just … I just wish she could live some sort of life. I thought maybe having a task, helping me with things around the house, even Henry's room, might help her find a purpose. Clearly I was mistaken."

"Violet. Please know that I understand the burden that has been placed on you. When Henry died, your mother and I … well I don't have to tell you how difficult it's been. I—we—appreciate you taking on the responsibilities that you have." He patted my hand. "But I also know that we need to start thinking about your future and finding you a husband."

"It's okay, Daddy. I'm fine." I patted his hand and, not wanting to continue the discussion of my marrying, said, "Daddy, have you been in Henry's room lately?"

Eyes downcast, he said, "Not in many, many months, dear. It's too painful."

I nodded and squeezed his hand again. "I know, Daddy." Just then Helen came in to clear our dishes away and Father and I went our separate ways. He headed to his study, and I went into the kitchen to speak with Helen. She was the only other person who might have gone into Henry's room.

"Helen?" She turned from the sink, where she was rinsing off our plates. "May I ask you a question?"

"Of course, miss."

I picked up a cloth and stepped beside her to help dry the dishes. "Have you been in Henry's room lately?"

Helen's hands stilled for a moment, then resumed their work. "Not recently, miss, no. I will admit that in the weeks after he passed,

I did spend some small amount of time there, just dusting and, well, it was … nice."

I looked over at her, but she wouldn't meet my eyes. Helen had been with our family for almost twenty years. Of course she was missing Henry as much as the rest of us. I patted her shoulder and said, "I understand."

"But one day, oh, I suppose it was about six months ago, your mother happened to walk by while I was inside his room and gave me *very* clear instructions that I wasn't to enter the room for any purpose. I have honored her wishes."

"Thank you, Helen. For staying with us. I can't imagine it's been easy."

"Of course, miss." She squeezed my hand.

I was upset and confused and I didn't understand what was happening. Three days passed uneventfully and I started to hope that it had all been in my head. Then one night, a summer storm kicked up, plunging the world into darkness at five in the afternoon. The wind was blowing the trees, nearly doubling them over and the air had that strange charge of electricity it gets just before a storm hits full-force.

I went up to check on my mother, who was wide awake and staring at the storm outside. I sat with her quietly as rain began blowing sideways against the windows. We listened to thunder rumbling from not too far away. Wind whipped at the house, rattling the windows, and lightning lit up the sky. I've always loved a good summer storm and this one did not disappoint. It seemed to calm Mother, whose eyes grew heavy.

When I was sure she was asleep in her chair near the window, I walked downstairs and out onto the porch. I took the witch's book with me. I had begun writing again, detailing this story you're reading now, and had taken to carrying it with me almost all of the time, lest inspiration strike. I thought that maybe one day I would want to remember all that had happened to me.

The porch protected me from the wind and rain for the most part. I sat in a rocking chair and watched the storm, feeling the charge in my body as lightning struck close and thunder rumbled overhead. Eventually, the sky quieted and I made my way back inside.

As I walked through the front door, I heard a knocking coming from upstairs. It was quiet, just two light raps. I assumed it was Mother trying to get my attention. I sighed and quickly climbed the stairs, made my way to the end of the hall, and opened her door. But she was asleep. Confused, I spun around as I heard the knocking again, from right outside the room. Ice formed in the pit of my stomach.

I walked slowly down the hallway, feeling my way as I was afraid of lighting a lamp. As I passed each door, the knocking followed. I walked past my bedroom; *knock, knock.* Past Henry's closed room; *knock, knock.* The faster I walked, the faster the knocking followed me. Eventually I was running, gathering my skirts in my hand and tearing down the stairs.

As I reached the main foyer, I heard a loud, low scream coming from upstairs. It was getting closer to me and it was definitely following me. It was only then I realized that I had left Mother there, alone. Whatever was following me was up there with her and I hadn't given it a second thought. As the scream grew louder still, I paused with my hand on the doorknob. Could I really just leave Mother there, defenseless? I did not know if this thing was capable of hurting us, but dare I leave Mother to find out?

Abruptly, the screaming stopped. I stood stock-still for several moments, listening for any noise. I heard nothing. Carefully, I lit a lamp and made my way slowly up the stairs, pausing every few seconds to listen. I arrived at Mother's door and listened carefully. I could hear her deep, heavy breathing and let out a relieved breath. Surely the screaming would have woken her. Could she not hear it?

I slowly opened her door, needing to see that she was unharmed. I entered, the lamp held out in front of me, casting a small glow over her nightstand and then her bed. She sat peacefully, fast asleep and breathing evenly.

Not wanting to keep my back to the door, I turned slowly, arranging Mother's blanket carefully as I did so. I walked slowly out of the room, peering out into the hallway before I stepped out. There was nothing there.

I approached Henry's room cautiously. There was no sound. Nothing seemed disturbed at first glance. At least until I looked toward the notebook. It was open to another page and there was more black writing scrawled sloppily across the page. In Henry's familiar hand it read: "Love you, VV. Please stop. Not safe."

VV had been how I signed all of our stories. This was a message from Henry.

CHAPTER SIXTEEN

Lara

Lara woke with a start, sitting bolt-upright in bed. Something had woken her. Then she heard it again. A knock. Coming from somewhere above her head. She began crying quietly. This was too much. The words in the diary, what was happening to Violet. It was too much. She didn't even understand what she was reading anymore. Now she didn't even want to know what else happened to Violet. She was convinced the book was totally different from what she had read the first time and she didn't understand how it was possible.

The next morning, as soon as she got up, she put the book in a box and stuck it on the back of a shelf in the basement. She stood there for a moment, looking at the box. She was feeling conflicted and confused and couldn't make sense of why she both wanted to lock the book away but also keep it close.

It had once brought her so much comfort but now hinted at something so much darker, something not comforting at all. But. It also hinted at something else—something Lara couldn't really admit to herself, but niggled at the back of her mind anyway. She shook her head and headed back upstairs.

She and Alex ate breakfast and Lara played with Tessa, folded laundry, and tried to keep her mind off the book and what she'd read last night, but she couldn't calm down. She jumped at every sound, peered into every room before she walked in, and found herself straining to hear any odd noises.

Lara knew she had to tell Alex what was going on. After she put Tessa down for a nap, she couldn't wait any longer. She was too unsettled and nervous.

Lara walked slowly, reluctantly, toward the garage. Alex was trying to organize and get a handle on the toys, tools, and other items that had taken over the shelves.

"Alex?"

"Yeah?"

"We need to talk about something." The knots in Lara's stomach, already making her sick, tightened even more and she fought the urge to run away.

Alex looked at her, putting a jar of car wax he'd been holding back in the cabinet. "Okay ..."

Lara's hands closed into fists and she crossed her arms around her stomach. Taking a deep breath, she said, "I need to tell you about some things that have been happening to me. It's going to sound crazy and I've put off telling you for a while, but something happened yesterday and I can't ignore it anymore."

Tears welled up in her eyes and her throat felt constricted. She didn't want to go on.

Alex was frowning. "What's going on?"

"Okay. Um. It's just ..." she trailed off again.

Alex, getting nervous, said, "Lara, come on. You're freaking me out. What the hell is going on?"

"Do you remember when I told you about Tessa's shoes in the middle of the floor and the bathroom door being open last week?"

"Yeah."

"Those aren't the only weird things that have happened to me lately."

"Okay." Alex was looking at her expectantly, waiting for the rest. She hadn't lost him yet.

She took a deep breath. "There's more." She told him everything then. About the dishes, the words in the steam on the mirror, George barking at the drawer. And finally, the words in Tessa's diary. She hadn't looked at him throughout her telling, but lifted her eyes to meet his now.

He rubbed his hands over his face. "I don't know what to say, babe. What are you saying? I mean, do you think our house is haunted? I know we joked about it after we thought we heard that little kid's voice, but come on."

Lara knew this would be his first reaction, so she'd waited to tell him about the book.

"You know the book I bought in Grafton?"

"Yeah."

"Alex, trust me, I know how this is going to sound, okay, but you need to believe me. I liked the book so much that I started reading it again a few days ago. But it's different this time. The story has changed. In small ways at the beginning of the book, but as I got farther into it … it had changed a lot. It's scary. But the thing is …" Lara took deep breath, knowing that this would be the thing that might make him really concerned for her well-being.

"All of the weird things that have happened in the house? They're in the book now. The same things happened to the main character in the book."

There was a long moment of silence as Alex tried to take in what she was saying. "You're telling me that you read this book and the weird stuff that happened in the book started happening here?"

"Yeah. Well, kind of. I mean, I read it the first time and nothing happened. This time, the book was the same in the beginning, but shortly after I started reading it, weird shit started happening like with Tessa's shoes and us hearing that voice say, 'Mom.' Then I read those same things in the book. As I kept reading, more stuff started happening here. I was reading last night and the words in Tessa's diary … that same thing happened in the book—the main character found a book in her brother's room that she'd never seen before— it was red, just like Tessa's diary, and inside were those same words." She stopped short of telling him it had been a message from her

146

brother and that Lara had awoken to a knocking on their bedroom wall.

Alex was looking at her blankly. "I … Don't you think it's more likely that you just don't remember everything that happened the first time you read it?"

"Yeah of course I thought of that. But even if that were true, it doesn't explain why all of this is happening to me."

Alex took a rag in his hand and started twisting it around. She could tell he didn't believe her. He cleared his throat. "I don't know how to say this without sounding like an asshole. But I think I need to say it. Is it possible you read all this stuff, didn't remember it, and now you're somehow … I don't know, imagining that it's happening here?"

"You're not an asshole. I know how it sounds. It doesn't make sense to me, either. But look at this." Lara handed Alex Tessa's red diary and told him to flip to the last pages. There, just as black and bold as before were the same words. "You can't. Don't. Don't."

"That's not my handwriting or yours. Obviously Tessa didn't write it. And she got that thing for Christmas, played with it for just a couple of days and then it must have fallen behind the couch. I haven't seen it since and only found it because I finally vacuumed back there."

Alex was studying the writing. "Yeah, it's not your writing." He looked up from the notebook. "Lara, I really don't know what to say. I'm not even sure what you're trying to tell me."

"I don't know either, to be honest. I just don't feel … good about it. Whatever it is. I guess I just wanted you to know. So you could, you know, keep an eye out for anything out of the ordinary."

"Well, I will, but I think you're probably making something out of nothing."

Lara sighed. "I hope so. But I don't know." Lara didn't know what was going on, but she knew it was something. She was downplaying it to Alex because she knew it would take a lot of convincing for him to believe her.

The next evening, Lara was in the kitchen when she heard Maryn knock one quick rap on the front door before opening it, sticking her head in, and yelling, "Hello? I come bearing wine and cinnamon gummy bears!"

Lara called back, "In here! And move quick, I need some wine!"

Alex had to work overtime. Something about a bad transformer. He'd be home late, maybe not until the next morning. Lara had gone to pick up Tessa and, deciding she wasn't sure she wanted to be alone in the house all night, texted Maryn. "Want to come over and drink with me tonight? Alex is working late."

Always up to share a bottle of wine, Maryn had quickly responded, "Sure. I'll bring the wine and the gummies if you feed me popcorn." It wasn't until Lara read the text that she realized she'd been expecting Maryn to blow her off again.

As Lara opened a drawer to retrieve a corkscrew for the wine, Tessa came running down the hall, sweet and cuddly in her footie pajamas.

"Mary-nin!" Tessa loved Maryn. From the very first time they'd met, Tessa had formed a bond with her that no one could come between. Tessa wanted Maryn to read her books, color, play dolls, everything—because Maryn would do it, every single time.

Maryn and Tim didn't have kids. Maryn wanted them, but it just never seemed like the right time. She liked to joke that her time was running out (although she was only thirty) but Lara recognized her and Alex's own indecision in Maryn and Tim. She and Alex had waited for, what seemed to some people, a long time to have kids. They'd wanted to travel and Lara had wanted to focus on her career. There was just always a reason not to. But as she'd told Maryn before, if the decision hadn't been taken out of their hands by a surprise pregnancy, they might never have actually gotten around to it. But they had, and it was the best thing that had ever happened to them.

"Well hello, my little Tessa bug!" Maryn scooped her up onto her lap. "And how are you today? Wrestled any polar bears lately?"

Tessa giggled and said, "Yessss ..." This was their favorite game. Maryn would come up with some crazy adventure and ask Tessa about it. Tessa always said yes and then Maryn would tell her a whole story about Tessa the Brave and how she wrestled polar bears or swam with sharks or climbed to the tippy top of the tallest mountain. While Lara listened to Maryn's latest story and saw how she occasionally stopped to smell the top of Tessa's head or plant a kiss on her chubby cheek, she smiled. Maryn might be closer to a decision than she realized.

Lara watched them play, taking in Maryn's appearance. She looked even more ragged than she had the other day. She was wearing ratty old sweatpants and a stained T-shirt. She had no makeup on, not even her red lipstick. She didn't *always* wear makeup, but there was something about her face, the deep lines between her eyes and a sluggishness Lara had never seen before in her movements made it even more concerning.

"Okay, baby, it's time for bed." Tessa's smile faded quickly. Lara knew she was going to have to be the bad guy and was anticipating a meltdown from her daughter. She never wanted to let Maryn out of her sight.

"Hey Tessa bug, do you think Mommy would let *me* tuck you in tonight?" Maryn asked Tessa.

"Yes!" Tessa looked intently at Lara, the expression comically serious on her tiny features. "Right, Mommy? Mary-nin take me night-night?"

"Sure, baby," Lara smiled gratefully at Maryn. "But you have to give me some love first." Tessa gave her a quick kiss and a hug before she reached for Maryn again and they set off toward Tessa's room.

Maryn came back into the kitchen just a few minutes later. "You're like a baby whisperer," said Lara. "It takes me at least a half an hour to get her to sleep."

"Well it helps that I told her if she went to bed like a big girl, she could have donuts for breakfast."

"Thanks!" Lara said, laughing. "What if I don't have any donuts?"

"Eh, she'll forget about it by morning."

"Shows what you know about three-year-olds. They're like freaking elephants."

Lara wanted to ask Maryn if she was okay, but her strange behavior at lunch the other day made her hesitant. Lara didn't want to push but she wanted to be there for her friend. Noticing Maryn hadn't yet drunk her wine, Lara wondered if she was so tired because she was pregnant.

Just as Lara was getting ready to ask what was going on, Maryn smiled thinly and said, "So what's up? Usually when Alex works all night you can't wait to take a bath and put on your old lady pants."

Lara laughed. "Yeah, I know. I don't know …" She wanted to tell Maryn what was happening to her to see how her friend would react. Alex clearly didn't believe that there was anything out of the ordinary happening. But what if Maryn didn't believe her either? Some days she felt like the people in her life treated her with kid gloves because they were worried she wasn't going to be able to continue holding it together. She didn't want to give them a reason to worry. But this was not in her head.

"What is it, Lara?" Maryn's voice was gentle and concerned, but there was also something else there Lara couldn't quite put her finger on. It sounded almost like a challenge. Or an expectation.

"There's been some really weird stuff happening to me lately."

"What do you mean weird?"

Lara told her everything. The book, the shoes, the dishes, the diary. Maryn listened to every word, interrupting only to ask a question here or there. When Lara was done, she took a big drink of wine. *Not pregnant, then,* Lara thought as she waited to hear what Maryn would say.

There was an odd expression on Maryn's face. Lara couldn't tell if she was confused or scared or just didn't believe her. It somehow looked like a combination of all three. Maryn didn't say anything.

"You think I'm nuts, too," Lara said with a sigh.

"Um. No, sorry. Just trying to take it all in." Maryn looked away, staring into space.

"Here, look at the diary." She flipped Tessa's diary open to the page with the writing. Maryn looked closely at it, rubbing her fingers across it just as Lara had done.

"Who do you think is doing it? What do you think is going on?"

"You believe me?"

"Yeah. Yeah, I do. A lot of it could probably be explained away, like the shoes and the bathroom door. But there is no logical explanation I can think of for *that*—"She pointed at the diary. "Can I see the book?"

"I don't really want to get it out, to be honest," Lara said. "I was hoping if I stopped reading it and just put it away that everything would stop."

"Why don't you just get rid of it?" Maryn asked.

"I almost did. But then I thought if I did that and things continued happening, then I really wouldn't have anything to prove it's all in there. I think it's important I hang onto it. But I don't want to read it anymore."

This wasn't a lie, exactly. She did want to keep the book around, for the sake of research, for proving it existed. But there was something else, the thing she almost couldn't admit to herself. If Violet got a message from Henry, what if it could, in some way, lead her to Ben?

"Can I see it?" Maryn was looking at her intently.

"It's really nothing special, I've looked through every single page and there's nothing weird about the way it looks—"

"I'll just take a look." Maryn's voice had an edge to it that Lara didn't quite understand.

"I don't know, maybe I am making something out of nothing."

When Maryn spoke again, her voice was softer.

"I'll read it. Then we can compare what you remember from the book and what I'm reading."

"I don't know, Mar." Lara couldn't put her finger on why, but she didn't want to give the book up.

Maryn blew out a breath. "I need to use the bathroom really quickly, be right back."

Before she left the kitchen, Maryn took her phone out of her purse and carried it into the bathroom. Lara thought that was strange. Maryn wasn't the kind of person who kept her phone with her every second.

Lara absentmindedly started wiping down the kitchen counter, wondering if she'd made a mistake by telling her friend about the book.

When Maryn returned a couple minutes later, she tossed her phone back in her purse and started telling Lara a story about a guy in one of her classes who she caught watching soft porn in class the other day. Soon the two women were laughing. They didn't talk about the book again.

Maryn

When Maryn had gone to the bathroom she'd texted Clara furiously. "Shit is starting to happen to her. I think it's a book she's reading."

As she waited for Clara's response, Maryn sat on the closed toilet lid, her legs shaking up and down with unspent energy.

Clara had responded, "Can you get the book?"

"I tried. She doesn't want to give it to me and I don't want to make her suspicious. I don't like this, Clara."

"I know. What do you know about the book?"

Maryn had filled her in the best she could, but knew if she was gone any longer Lara would worry.

She'd tried to enjoy the rest of her visit, directing the conversation away from the book. But she still felt like a terrible friend and ultimately Maryn made her excuses to Lara early, claiming to not feel well. She could tell Lara wanted to know what was wrong and Maryn felt terrible putting her off and not being honest with her closest friend. Maryn felt like a liar. She almost couldn't stand to be around Lara at all and she was reaching a breaking point. Not to mention the *feeling* in her house. That energy that called to her and repelled her all at the same time.

As she drove home, she fumed. She cursed herself for ever agreeing to meet with Mrs. White all those years ago.

Once Maryn had taken a seat in Mrs. White's small office behind the circulation desk that day, the old librarian had taken a deep breath and begun speaking.

"This is always such an awkward conversation to have, no matter how many times I've had to do it."

Maryn's heart sank. Had she failed something? Had she forgotten an application or scholarship deadline?

"Maryn, have you been having a hard time sleeping? Any unexplained behaviors you can't make sense of?"

Maryn was so surprised by the question that she just looked blankly at Mrs. White's face. The librarian looked back at her patiently, waiting for her answer.

"I ... I don't know what you mean."

"It could be anything. Odd dreams, objects moving seemingly on their own, things of that nature."

Mrs. White delivered this news so matter-of-factly that Maryn was shocked into an answer.

"Yeah. I'm losing time. And I can … it's like I feel everyone else's feelings, but so strongly it's like they're my own."

Mrs. White nodded. "I thought so, dear."

"What?" She sounded snippier than she meant to, so she tried to back track. "I mean, what do you mean? How did you know?"

"There isn't an easy way to say this, Maryn, so I'm just going to say it. Pull off the band aid, so to speak." She placed her hand gently on top of Maryn's. "It would appear that you're a witch."

Maryn laughed right in her face. "What? Okay, Mrs. White. Funny. What did you really need to tell me?"

A small smile played across Mrs. White's face. "I know how it sounds, dear. But it's true. You're a witch. Your powers are starting to manifest themselves. That's why you've been losing time, spacing out, whatever you want to call it. It's also why you're feeling other people's emotions so intensely. I would guess that you're an empath, although we'll have to confirm that, of course."

Maryn's jaw was literally hanging open. She couldn't think of a single thing to say. She was wondering how she could get out of here without hurting Mrs. White's feelings. The woman obviously had a couple of screws loose. Maryn wondered how quickly she could get to the office and tell Principal Walters.

Mrs. White's voice interrupted her thoughts. "I know what you're thinking. I'm not insane, dear. Here, I'll show you." Mrs. White reached for a small potted plant, a green leafy thing, sitting on the edge of her desk.

Mrs. White cupped her hands around the base of the plant, almost but not quite touching it. She closed her eyes.

Maryn started to feel uncomfortable. *What the hell is she doing?* She reached down to grab her backpack, and stood up, intending to leave.

"Look, Mrs. White, you don't have to—"

"Shhhh. Just look."

Maryn looked down at the plant and sat back down immediately. A green stalk was growing out of the center of the plant, a small white flower blooming at its end, right before Maryn's eyes.

"Holy shit," Maryn whispered. That flower had literally come out of nowhere.

Mrs. White smiled at her, removing her hands from around the plant. "I'm an herbalist," she said simply.

"What just happened?"

"Some of my friends don't particularly like my style of breaking the news to new witches. They think showing someone magic so quickly is too much for them to take in. But I maintain that *showing* is really the only way to overcome all the doubt and denial so we can move on."

She smiled at Maryn. "Magic is real. And you're a witch, dear."

Maryn was dumbstruck, still staring at the plant.

"You'll have a million questions, but let me give you the basics. Magic is real, but not in the way picture books make us imagine. We don't ride broomsticks or conjure up talking animals or stir potions in cauldrons. It's more of a ... religion or spirituality. We believe in nature and Mother Earth and the equality of all living beings on Earth.

"Each witch has particular powers rooted in nature. I'm an herbalist. I can help plants grow and make natural medicine. I think you're probably an empath. You forge strong connections with other humans. Other witches might be able to soothe animals or are sensitive to the ebb and flow of time. Our powers are not flashy. We convene in covens to share knowledge and pay homage to Mother Nature.

"A witch's power often manifests as the witch approaches young adulthood, which is what I believe is happening to you. I suppose you're not aware of any other witch in your family?"

Maryn just shook her head.

"Hmm. Okay. It's passed down family lines, but not necessarily from our parents or even close family members. And only a very few family members actually manifest powers. It could be an aunt or a distant cousin. It doesn't really matter."

"You're serious, aren't you?"

Mrs. White laughed, a pleasant, soothing sound. "I am. I know it's unbelievable. But the good news is that it's completely your choice about what you do with this knowledge. You don't have any obligation to me or to any of us to do anything with your power. You can go on and lead a totally normal life. Or you can join us and receive training. We're here to support you, whatever you decide."

"Okayyyy." Maryn drew out the word because she had so many questions that she didn't know where to start.

"I've maybe given you a bit too much information all at once. I'm sorry. Can you stay after school today and we can chat some more?"

Maryn nodded.

"Okay, great. Why don't you come back here after last period and I'll do my best to answer all of your questions."

Maryn stood up on shaky legs. She walked out without saying anything, Mrs. White's voice floating out to her. "It's going to be okay, Maryn, I promise."

Maryn went through the rest of her day on autopilot. She avoided her friends at lunch, instead sitting on a bench outside the cafeteria, pretending to study. But really she was trying to make sense of everything Mrs. White had said and what she had seen that plant do right in front of her. She couldn't believe it was real, but she also couldn't say it wasn't. She starting making a list of questions for Mrs. White. *Just in case she's right*, Maryn thought.

She couldn't deny that she'd known something was wrong. She'd just had no idea what it could be and had certainly never expected this kind of insanity. Because it was insane, wasn't it? There was no way magic was real and she was a witch. Right?

On the other hand, she couldn't deny that she'd watched that flower grow up from nothing. Maryn's head was spinning. She decided that even if Mrs. White was full of crap, it couldn't hurt to hear her out. If it *was* all real, then Mrs. White was the only person who could help her. If it *wasn't*, then she'd listen to the woman and then finally tell her parents she needed real help.

She spent three hours with Mrs. White that day, eventually coming to believe everything she was being told. Mrs. White gave her a brief history of witchcraft and filled her in on what it looks like in the modern day. She told Maryn that there were plenty of people who counted themselves witches or Wiccans who didn't have any actual magic powers. The witches who did have powers ("We call ourselves naturalists") operated in smaller, quiet covens.

"We lead normal, quiet lives. We're not plotting to take over the world or undo our enemies with magic. We do what we can to make our communities and the world at large a better place. We provide help when it's needed. It's really quite an amazing thing to be a part of."

Maryn also learned that she wasn't under any obligation to use her powers or join a coven or acknowledge what was happening in any way. Mrs. White could help her learn to control her body and mind so she could continue on with school. Then, if she ever decided she wanted to develop her powers, Mrs. White and the witches from the local coven would help her whenever she was ready, whether it was a month or ten years from now.

Maryn left school that day feeling calmer and more focused than she had in months. Over the next few weeks, she met with Mrs. White during study hall three times a week. They told the school it was an extra credit project, an independent study. Maryn learned to quiet the power within her, essentially compartmentalizing it in her brain so she could concentrate.

By the time the end of the school year was approaching, Maryn was back to her old self, had brought her grades back up to almost all As, and had filled out numerous college applications. She'd decided she didn't see the benefit of focusing on her powers while she had so many other things going on in her life and had told Mrs. White as much when they met for their last study hall.

"I guess I really don't understand how being an empath and developing my powers more, can help me. I mean if I could make flowers grow, I could become a hell of a gardener. And I guess if I wanted to be a therapist or something my powers would help ... but I don't. I really just want to be an engineer."

Mrs. White had just smiled at her and said, "Yes. Sometimes the true purpose of our powers doesn't become clear to us until we've had a bit more time to ... experience life. You might yet change your mind. If you do, we'll be here for you."

Maryn successfully completed her senior year and went on to college, graduating and beginning her career. She met Tim, fell in love, got married. She never worked to develop her powers, although she had discovered that she was always able to read a room perfectly, which *had* helped her. She'd be able to tell who was frustrated, who needed a shot of confidence, and, most importantly, who she should stay away from.

Maryn wasn't naive enough to think she was lucky or special. She'd risen in the ranks both at school and in her career through a lot of hard work, but her ability to know who she needed to align herself with and how to be of the most use to everyone on her team didn't hurt. She knew it was her powers manifesting in small ways.

When she was honest with herself, the thought of fully developing those powers scared her. If she could do these small things that helped her in her everyday life, what would she be able to do if she really concentrated? She didn't think she wanted that kind of responsibility.

She'd kept in touch with Mrs. White, just in case she ever was in a position where she wanted or needed help. But she'd never felt like anything was missing from her life or that her magic would help her in any way.

Then Will died.

Maryn had arrived back home and was sitting in her driveway, lost in her thoughts. She felt miserable. There was no good answer to the current situation she found herself in. She had an obligation to Lara as her friend. Her first obligation had been to the coven, but how long could she let Lara go on being scared and not tell her what might be going on?

Maryn made a decision. Last week, Clara had cancelled their Tuesday coffee date, claiming that something more pressing had come up. Maryn thought it was because Clara wasn't ready to make a decision, but didn't think she'd be able to put Maryn off in person. She texted Clara. "I'm done. I'm telling her. I don't know if she's safe."

Clara had texted back "Do not tell her. We need to meet first. Please. Give me just a couple of days."

Maryn agreed, but not happily. "Fine. But we need to do something soon. In two days, if you don't have an answer for me, I'm telling her. And I won't give you a warning."

She fought back tears as she got out of the car and walked up to her front door.

CHAPTER SEVENTEEN

Lara

Lara turned on some music, set her phone on the counter, and began cleaning up the kitchen. She didn't want to think about why Maryn had left so early and had been acting so weird. Instead, she thought about her conversation with Alex. She knew she wasn't going to convince him of anything unless he saw it for himself. She couldn't blame him, really, because it *was* crazy. And she still held out some hope that it was possible it could all be explained.

In spite of the pep talk she was giving herself, Lara felt uneasy. So uneasy, in fact, that she brought Tessa into bed with her. She hated feeling uncomfortable in her own home. She thought about the book, down in the basement, and tried not to imagine what it meant that she was experiencing the same things someone had experienced in a book written in 1890.

Even after watching two episodes of *The Office* her eyes still had not grown heavy, so she got up and took a sleeping pill. Eventually she fell into a fitful sleep.

She woke early the next morning, laying still, listening for anything out of sorts. She didn't hear anything. She got carefully out of bed, not wanting to wake Tessa. She walked slowly down the hallway and entered the kitchen. Nothing was out of place.

Lara fell into a quiet depression. Maybe depression was too strong a word, but she did withdraw. She was quiet, cautious, peering into a room before she entered it, jumping at every noise. She started keeping lights on all over the house at night and leaving doors and even shower curtains open so nothing could jump out at her. She called George to her every time she had to go to the basement or in the garage and had started letting him sleep in Tessa's room.

Her behavior did not go unnoticed by Alex. "What's going on with you?" he finally asked one morning as she walked into the kitchen. He was drinking coffee before he left for work. "You left a bunch of the cabinet doors open in here last night and all the living room lights were on when I got up."

Lara's face was pale. "I didn't leave the cabinet doors open."

"Well, they were wide open and you cleaned up in here after dinner last night."

"It wasn't me, Alex." Lara didn't say anything else, hoping he would fill in the blanks. His eyebrows drew together and he looked around the kitchen.

"You must have just forgotten."

"I didn't. But whatever," she finally said, barely louder than a whisper. Alex looked away, slowly getting up and putting his cup in the sink. He took his lunchbox off the counter and leaned over and kissed her on the top of the head.

"You know, I'm really proud of you, babe."

Surprised, Lara looked up at him. "Why?"

"I know how hard therapy has been for you and how hard you have to work some days. I can't really imagine how hard it's been. And I feel like we've gotten something back here, you know?"

Lara nodded. "Yeah, I feel that way, too."

"Good. I just ... I don't want you to focus too much on ... on ... something else, to replace how much you were focusing on Ben, you know?"

Lara was confused for a moment, until she realized what he meant. He thought she was obsessing about the book, about the weird stuff happening as some kind of replacement for the grief that had taken up so much of her time and focus for so long. Lara barked a laugh and shrugged. She didn't even have the energy to argue with him about it.

"Look, I believe that you think something is going on. I understand.

But you're acting like a kid scared of the dark and I just don't know how to help you. I don't understand it."

"I get it," she said. "Have a good day."

She could feel him looking at her for a long moment before he quietly turned and walked out.

After he left, she put her head in her hands and cried.

****

"So you're noticing some similarities to what's happening in this book and what's going on in your life?" Dr. Moore asked the next day in therapy.

"No. Not noticing some similarities—" She mentally placed finger quotes around her words. "It's exactly the same. Strange things are happening in my home, either right before or right after I read about them happening to Violet. ." Lara held up her hand when she saw the look on Dr. Moore's face. "I know how it sounds! Trust me. I know. But I don't appreciate everyone suggesting I'm crazy."

It was a couple of days later and Lara had decided that if Alex and Maryn weren't going to help, she'd tell Dr. Moore. She thought now that might have been a mistake.

"No one is saying you're crazy here, Lara. It just sounds … fantastical."

"Yeah. That's one word for it."

"Well what do you think you can do about it?"

"I have no idea. Get rid of the book? Check myself into a mental hospital? Who knows!"

"Well let's talk about what you *can* control. You *could* get rid of the book. I'm assuming the mental hospital crack was a joke so we'll table that for now." Lara smiled, appreciating his attempt at humor. "Is there anything else?"

"I guess I could try to find out more about the book. I don't really want to get rid of it. As weird as it is, it's also kind of …

162

compelling, I guess? I don't know. I can only read it in short chunks because I'm too afraid of what will happen next." Lara laughed uncomfortably. "It's weird to be afraid of a book, right?"

"It's unusual."

"You don't believe me."

" It's not that I don't believe you. I think you're dealing with a lot. You're making great progress in therapy, but that can cause a lot of feelings that are usually pent-up to come to the surface and leave us feeling … a bit unstable."

Lara sighed. Clearly, she wasn't going to convince anyone this was really happening to her. She changed the subject and killed time for the rest of her session. When she got up to leave, Dr. Moore stopped her with a hand on her arm.

"I don't usually share something like this with my patients. But I think it's appropriate here. I do believe that … strange … things can happen in this world. Things we can't explain, that don't quite make sense with what we know to be true of the world. So let's not minimize what you're experiencing, okay?"

"Thanks, Dr. Moore." Lara felt relieved that even if he didn't totally believe her, he also wasn't recommending she check herself into the hospital, which, she supposed, was something to be thankful for.

Over the next couple of days, Lara decided that researching the book was one way she could do something practical and useful, rather than just sit around waiting to see what would happen next. She used every resource available online that she could think of to find out where this book had come from.

But there were a few problems. Well. More than a few. For starters, the book had no copyright page. No publisher information, no ISBN number, just the year 1890—basically nothing. An online search for the book title, *Memoriae,* brought up nothing more than the Latin translation, which was *memory.*

When she searched Violet Marsh's name the same thing happened—there were lots of Violet Marshes in the world, but none whom she could directly tie to the book. There were a couple of references on sites like Ancestry.com and Geneology.com, indicating that maybe she had actually been a real person, but she could find nothing in relationship to Grafton. She tried to locate census information about Jersey County and Grafton to see if she could verify that the Marsh family existed, but couldn't access anything without paying for a subscription to some website or another. There was nothing. Well. Almost nothing.

She took a picture of the book and performed a Google image search. Buried deep in the results, about four pages in, she saw a picture of the cover. There were the gold embossed letters, *Memoriae*. When she clicked on the link, it took her to a 2003 online event calendar for Jersey County. Specifically, for a book fair at a church. The picture of Violet's book was alongside a picture of *The Da Vinci Code*, which Lara remembered being a huge hit that year. The event page linked to a simple flyer, advertising, "There's something for everyone! We'll have everything from classics to bestsellers. All proceeds to benefit the St. James Church Mission Trip. For questions, contact Maisie Beck."

When she saw Maisie's name, she gasped. What were the odds that Lara would find her aunt's name on this flyer? Maisie was very involved in her church and helped with all of their fundraisers. Lara had found the book in Grafton, so it wasn't totally insane that she'd found this flyer. It had probably made its way from this book fair into Great Rivers Antiques and had sat forgotten ever since. Chances were slim that Maisie would know or remember anything about the book, but it was at least a place to start.

Lara picked up the phone to call her aunt, but then put it back down. What would she say? *Hey, Aunt Maisie! I have this book that I think is…* What would she say? It was haunting her? *Anyway, I'm trying to track it down and found a picture of it on a book fair flyer from 2003. Know anything about that?*

She decided she wasn't ready to bring her aunt into it. Maisie would demand an explanation and her aunt didn't abide with "ghost and goblins craziness," as she called it. Lara remembered asking Maisie once when she was a child if she believed in ghosts. Maisie had made it clear that she did not and would not talk any more about it.

Lara sighed. No, she couldn't call her aunt yet. But one thing was clear. If she was going to find any additional information about the book, she'd have to go back to the source—back to Grafton and back to the store where she'd bought it.

For the next couple of days Lara tried to ignore what was happening around her. One day, George had stood at the garage door and barked for ten minutes. Lara couldn't pull him away from the door or get him to stop barking. Not even the promise of a treat or a walk would break his concentration. She'd had to clip his leash on and pull him away.

Another time she'd heard knocking coming from the garage and hadn't even gone to investigate. She'd found her shoes and Alex's shoes and Tessa's shoes lined up neatly when before they'd been in a pile on the floor. She and Alex had heard Tessa calling out three more times, only to find her fast asleep.

It was after yet another time Lara had gone to Tessa's room while she was napping one afternoon to investigate that she finally asked Alex if he still didn't think something weird was going on.

"I admit we're hearing *something*," he said. "But maybe Tessa is just having nightmares or something and falling back asleep."

"And all of the other stuff I've been telling you about?"

Alex shrugged. "I'm sorry babe, but I think you've convinced yourself this stuff is happening so you look for it."

"I really wish you would at least entertain the thought that I'm not making this up. It's not fair to me. You should trust me."

"I do trust you. But ghosts, Lara? Come on."

"You're minimizing my feelings and I don't appreciate it."

"Lara—"

"No. I'm done. Talking in circles isn't going to help. I'm going to get some work done."

She walked out before he could respond. She sat at her desk and pulled up an internet browser window. She didn't think she could really work. It was Saturday and she didn't feel like it and Tessa would be waking up soon anyway. But she didn't want to be around Alex either. Minutes later, she heard his phone ring. He walked into her office and said, "That was work. I'm going in." She didn't say anything and he went into their room to get dressed.

Before he left, he popped his head into her office where she was pretending to edit a logo. "I'm leaving."

"Okay. Be careful." She didn't look at him.

He heard him sigh. "Lara, I don't know what you want me to say."

"Nothing. Just don't say anything. You don't believe me. I'll deal with it by myself."

"Maybe you need to try to understand what you're asking me to believe, here. A haunted book? Come on."

"Just go, Alex. I'm not going to argue about this anymore." This time, he left and she heard his truck start up and pull out of the garage. She put her head in her hands. She hated fighting with him. And he was right—she was asking him to believe something that did sound totally insane. She knew that. But she also knew she wasn't making it up.

She jumped when she heard a crash from Tessa's room and her heart started pounding. But when she heard Tessa laughing, crying out, "Mommmmmmy! I awake!" she smiled. *It's just Tessa,* she thought. *For real this time.*

KRISTINA BRUNE

Lara felt bad about sending Alex to work after an argument. She always worried that if something happened to him and the last words she'd said were in anger, she'd never be able to live with herself. After Ben died, she'd replayed their last conversation over and over. It had been normal, nothing particularly special to note or remember. But she was glad that they'd ended their conversation by saying I love you. If Alex died and she had to replay their argument in her head forever, she didn't know if she'd be able to live with that.

Alex was still at work after she put Tessa to bed later that evening, so she called him, hoping he would answer.

"Hello?" he sounded distracted and more than a little aggravated.

"Hey, babe. I know you're busy, I just wanted to say sorry. I hate fighting with you. I know how I sound. But I also know I'm not imagining things, so … I don't know. I just don't know what to do about it." She jumped when she heard a loud crash and Alex yell, "Shit!" She heard voices in the background and then someone laughing.

"Sorry," he said. "Johnny just dropped a wrench and damn near broke my foot. Hold on." She could hear the voices fading as he presumably walked away from the guys on his crew.

"Okay. I'm sorry too. It's not that I don't believe you. I believe you think this stuff is happening. It's just hard to believe. And you know how I feel about that stuff."

"I know. You think it's crap," she laughed to show him that she was making light of it.

"I do. But I'm always going to be honest with you. And I think it's stress."

"I understand and I appreciate that and I don't expect you to pretend to believe something you don't. But I guess I just need you to believe that I'm struggling with it. And I'm sure you're right. It's probably nothing."

167

She heard voices calling out to Alex.

"Hey babe, I've gotta go," he said. "We're good, okay? We're almost done with this job, but just got a call for another one, so I won't be home until morning. I'll pick up some bagels on the way home, okay?"

"Sounds good. Be careful. I love you."

"Love you, too." Alex hung up.

Lara felt a little better, but as she put the dinner leftovers away, did the dishes, and wiped down the countertops she tried not to listen to every little noise in the house. She tried not to imagine that everything she saw in her peripheral vision was somebody or something standing next to her. *Damn it, Lara*, she thought. *Stop.* Being home alone had never bothered her before and she certainly wasn't going to be one of those women who couldn't function without her husband around all the time.

She walked into the laundry room to put the dirty dish rag in the laundry basket. As she closed the laundry room door behind her and walked back into the kitchen, she screamed.

Five cabinet doors were open. Two drawers were pulled all the way out. Lara hadn't heard a thing and she had her back turned for less than thirty seconds.

"Oh my god," she moaned, her hands over her mouth. Lara ran down the hallway to Tessa's room, picked her baby up and brought her into the master bedroom, locking the door behind her. She cried silently into the top of her sleeping daughter's head. She didn't know what to do. She wanted to call Alex, but she didn't know how he'd respond. He'd probably say that she'd just forgotten to close them as she was cleaning the kitchen. She *knew* she had closed all the cabinets—she'd cleaned the entire kitchen and had left it spotless.

Lara sat down on her bed, still holding Tessa and forced herself to calm down. She decided that this might be an opportunity to give Alex some evidence. He might still try to write it off as her not remembering, but she could try. Lara set Tessa on the bed and opened her bedroom door. She stood still, listening. She didn't hear anything and began to slowly walk down the hallway.

When she entered the kitchen, she saw that the cabinets and drawers were still open. She took a picture with her phone, trying to still her shaking hand. She forced herself to check all that all the doors and windows were locked, taking George with her as she moved through the house. She tried to stay calm.

Lara went back to her room, bringing George in and locking the door. She washed her face and got ready for bed, climbing in next to Tessa.

She went back and forth between wanting to leave the house and wanting to confront whatever this was head-on. At one point she even got up and got dressed, intending to leave. That seemed like a good plan until she considered how she would explain it to Alex: "Yeah babe, while you were at work last night, I got freaked out and took the baby out of the house in the middle of the night." He wouldn't believe her. In the end, she settled on staying in her room for the night and leaving all the cabinet doors open. Alex might not believe she hadn't done it but he could at least see how it looked.

It was a long, long time before she was able to fall asleep.

Maryn

Maryn wasn't sleeping. She couldn't concentrate on school. Being around Lara—being in her house—was becoming almost unbearable. The energy, the low vibration of that *thing*. It was too much to take. And no one seemed very interested in helping her figure out a plan. Maryn hadn't felt this angry in a long time. Since after Will died.

In the weeks after his death, Maryn had spun out of control. The pain and trauma became too difficult for her to ignore and she was taking on everyone's emotions. She'd never told Tim about her magic, but she'd been forced to when she started to break down, unable to leave the house, or even her bed, for days. She'd called Mrs. White who'd graciously come to her house and spoken with Tim. It had taken him a while, but he'd eventually come to accept it.

So Mrs. White began her instruction all over, working with Maryn to practice managing her emotions in the midst of her grief. They also worked to develop her powers. Mrs. White thought it was vital that Maryn further develop her powers so she could navigate the turmoil around her. Maryn got better and better at filtering out other people's emotions and suppressing her own when they got overwhelming. After she could keep herself level, she began to discover what she could *do*.

It started out small. She discovered she could affect how the people around her were feeling. Not in a big way, at first, but small things.

She'd be in line at the grocery store, a crabby old man in front of her giving the cashier a hard time about his total. Maryn would simply … calm him. Suddenly, he'd take a deep breath, mutter, "Never mind, it's fine," to the cashier, and walk away.

One time, she was at a Starbucks, trying to study. A couple was sitting next to her and the man was quietly but forcefully telling the woman how all of their problems were her fault. Maryn tried not to listen but after twenty minutes, she couldn't take it anymore. She reached out and gave the woman a jolt of confidence. The woman said, "You know what, Chad? Not everything is my fault. I might be dramatic, but you're an asshole." And she got up and walked away.

Maryn would go to visit her parents, whose grief was so strong it threatened to overwhelm everyone in the room, not just Maryn. So Maryn would reach out and, like a soothing pat on the back of a dog's head, settle them.

She practiced in this way until she could do it with little to no effort. But she always, always felt guilty. Mrs. White assured her that she was well in control and wasn't doing anything harmful. She had to practice. But Maryn felt that it was invasive, so she never wanted to take it any further.

Until one day, shortly after the year anniversary of Will's death, she lost control for a moment. It had been a bad day. She and Tim had been fighting the night before, she had a final coming up the next day that she wasn't prepared for, and she missed Will something fierce.

She'd been waiting for the L. Standing not too far away were two black teenagers, handsome, in baggy jeans and ball caps. Just the two of them, talking and laughing, watching something on an iPhone, sharing a pair of white Apple headphones. Maryn smiled at their youth, thinking they reminded her of Will.

They were standing near the bottom of the station stairs and as Maryn watched, an older white woman stumbled on the last two stairs, quickly falling to her knees and crying out. The young men pocketed the phone in a flash and they both knelt down to help her up. One of them grabbed her phone from where it had fallen out of her hand, wiped it on his jeans, and handed it back to her. She smiled at them, thanking them profusely, clearly embarrassed.

Then the cops walked up.

Two fat, old, white guys. And they clearly had taken one look at these young black men, each holding the elbow of this white woman, and decided they knew exactly what was happening.

"What's going on?" one of the fat cops bellowed.

The young men both put their hands up immediately, one of them saying, "She just fell. We were helping her up."

"Make sure I can see your hands!" the other cop yelled, even though they both had their hands up in front of their chest. The station had fallen quiet, people watching the interaction. Maryn thought, *Not today, motherfuckers. You are not going to take down these good black boys just for being black today*, and took out her phone and began recording.

One of the cops turned to the older woman, saying, "Ma'am, are you okay? Are these boys bothering you?"

"No, absolutely not!" The woman tugged her purse onto her shoulder and stood up straighter. "I fell coming down these stairs and they helped me up."

The cops looked at the boys suspiciously. "Go ahead and put your hands against the wall."

"Can I ask why, sir?" one of them asked politely, showing more self-control and restraint than Maryn could have mustered in the same situation.

"Fucking do what I say," he responded. As he patted the boys down, the other cop looked around, noticing they were getting attention and noticing, too, that Maryn was recording the whole thing.

"Put the phone down!" he yelled at her.

Maryn ignored him, instead looking to the two boys, who could now see the writing on the wall and looked at her and her phone gratefully.

"I said put the phone down."

"I don't have to," she responded. "I saw exactly what happened and they've done nothing wrong."

"Exactly," the old woman said meekly. "They just gave me my phone back."

The other cop, done with the pat down, told the boys to put their hands behind their back.

"Sir, I don't understand why," one of them said.

"Because I fucking said so," he responded. "Are we going to have a problem?" His hand slowly, but deliberately, moved to the butt of his taser gun. His partner followed in kind, taking his eyes off of Maryn and looking at his partner.

And all of a sudden, Maryn was so angry she was literally seeing red. These boys did a good thing, right in front of everyone, and these cops and all the other assholes watching weren't going to do anything about the way they were getting treated. *Not today*, she thought again. *Not today.*

So she reached out to the cop who had done the pat down and, in a way that felt like the flicking of a switch, she forced him to drop his hand from his gun. His own hands went up by his chest and began backing slowly away. *Now apologize*, she thought.

"Look, guys, I'm sorry. Sorry. Just wanted to check in that everything was okay. I'm sorry."

His partner looked at him in confusion, his hand still on his gun, until Maryn forced him to do the same. *Hands up, back away. Apologize.*

"Uh. Yeah. Sorry guys. You all have a good day." Brows furrowed, they both turned and walked away.

Maryn let out a breath. She stopped recording and put her phone back in her purse. She walked over to the boys, who were standing there, a little dumbstruck. The old woman said, "Thank you boys for helping me," and walked away.

Maryn asked them, "Are you guys okay?" Maryn wanted to say more, to tell them it wasn't fucking fair, that she was sorry that had happened to them. But they knew the game. They weren't surprised. They were clearly just relieved. They nodded, and moved away to stand near the wall.

Maryn's whole body was shaking. She was angry —no, livid— and part of her wanted to follow those cops and see what else she could make them do. Maybe make *them* feel a little helpless. But as she calmed down, her outrage was replaced with a stunned kind of disbelief at what she'd done. She'd *made* those cops back off and apologize. She *made* them do it.

When she'd relayed this story to Mrs. White the next day, she was quiet for a long moment. "Well. Clearly your powers as an empath are a little stronger than we thought. Maryn, honey, it's going to be up to you to determine how much you want to develop this."

"I can't even imagine what this means or what I can do. I don't know if I want to know."

Just a few weeks later, she and Tim decided to move to St. Louis and her time became preoccupied with logistics. She and Mrs. White decided not to actively develop her powers any further. Maryn didn't want to manipulate people. She didn't want that kind of power. She didn't want to know what might happen if her emotions got away from her.

Mrs. White did connect her with the coven in St. Louis, so she would have a support system should she need it. Maryn contacted them about six months after they'd moved, just to meet people and have someone to talk to. There were a couple of younger ladies in the coven and Maryn slowly started to make friends. She'd grown particularly close to Clara, but now Maryn was questioning everything she thought she knew about the coven and their real intentions or, at the very least, about their commitment to helping Lara.

Chapter Eighteen

Lara

When she'd woken the next morning, the cabinet doors had all been shut. She almost laughed out loud. It felt like this thing was messing with her. When the next couple of days passed uneventfully, Lara didn't say anything else to Alex and she tried not to act out of the ordinary. She felt suspended in time, like something was going to happen, but she didn't know what or when.

About a week later, Alex called her from work.

"Did you hear about the ice storm in Mississippi and Arkansas? It's bad. Almost an inch of ice. There's a whole transmission line down and almost 500,000 people out of power. They're pulling for a crew to head down there tomorrow morning."

"Do you think it will get to you?" Lara asked. Alex's and his co-workers' overtime was tracked on a rotating list, based on how much overtime they'd worked over the last week. When overtime was available, they would ask the first person on the list, moving down the list until the spots were filled.

"Yeah, I think so. They're sending four guys and I'm fifth on the list. Johnny won't take it because the baby is due any day."

"Okay. I'll make sure your laundry is done and start putting some stuff together." She sighed, quietly enough so he couldn't hear.

On a normal day, Alex and his co-workers maintained power lines, occasionally responding to trouble. There were call-outs in the middle of the night or on weekends and if a storm blew through, taking out tree limbs and power lines, he might work extra-long hours for a few days or a week, coming home just to sleep. A storm call was different. A storm call—whether it was a hurricane, tornado, or ice storm that pulled down the power lines—meant weeks away from home, but also extra money as he put in eighteen-hour days on double time.

She could only remember a couple of times she'd actually been nervous about him heading out on a storm. Katrina in '05, when he went on the third wave of crews and there was looting and unsafe water and he was sleeping in the back of a tractor trailer, eighteen bunks deep. Then again in 2006, when he headed to work in the middle of an ice and snowstorm that, when it was over, would pull down power lines all night, snapping them like matchsticks and leaving hundreds of thousands of people out of power. But it was part of the job and the extra money was always nice.

This time she was nervous for a different reason. She didn't want to be home without him. Usually Lara loved her independence and looked forward to time alone to recharge, watch trashy TV, and drink wine in bed. But with all of this craziness happening, the thought of facing a week or more home alone every night made her nervous.

"Babe? You okay? You want me to go, right?"

"Of course! Mama wants a hot tub," she joked, trying to cover up whatever hesitation he was sensing in her voice. "I'll just miss you."

"We'll buy two hot tubs, how about that?"

She laughed.

"They're telling us to pack for two weeks. You sure you're gonna be okay for two weeks without me?"

"This isn't my first rodeo," Lara said. "I just wish things weren't so crazy around here ..." Her voice trailed off. She didn't want to get into a fight while he was at work and especially if he was leaving tomorrow. But she couldn't stop thinking about it.

"Lara," he sounded resigned.

"No, I just meant busy in general. I've got those new clients—"

"That's not what you meant, babe," his voice was kind, now, trying to be patient.

"No. I guess not."

"You know I don't think you have anything to worry about. I wouldn't leave if I did. But why don't you see if your mom wants to come stay at the house for a while? She might like the opportunity to hang out with Tessa."

"Yeah. Maybe. I don't know. It's hard to be around her sometimes … It'll be fine, I'm being stupid."

"There's nothing to worry about, babe. Will you check my work clothes and make sure I've got enough clean?"

"Yep," Lara said, forcing some false cheer into her voice. "I'll see you when you get home tonight. Let's go out to dinner."

"Sounds good. I'll see you when I get home. Love you."

"Love you, too." Lara ended the call. Behind her, in the kitchen, a cabinet door slammed. She was the only one in the house.

Lara spent the afternoon doing laundry, making sure Alex had enough clothes for the trip and making a list of what he'd need—phone charger, soap, deodorant. She did all of this on autopilot, her mind occupied elsewhere.

She was not happy about being alone in the house for who-knew-how-long. Not that Alex was any closer to believing her, but when he was there she at least knew that if something really crazy happened, he'd be there to help her. If he was gone, she worried that something bad would happen and it would just be her and Tessa with no one to help.

Lara decided she had to try to convince him one more time. She wanted him to believe her if something happened while he was gone. She needed to be able to tell him and know that he'd get someone to help her.

When Alex was packed and he'd tucked Tessa in and joined Lara in the living room, he asked, "Did you hear that?"

"Hear what?"

"I swear I heard knocking coming from our room. I thought you were in there messing with me."

"No, I've been sitting here." Lara was scared, but she thought, *Maybe if he experiences something himself, he'll believe me.*

"Huh. That's weird. I wonder if there's a tree branch knocking against the window or something."

"Is that what it sounded like?"

"Not really. But I do need to trim the tree on that side of the house."

"It could be something else."

He didn't respond right away and she stayed quiet, hoping he would catch on.

When he realized what she was suggesting, he said, "It was just something outside."

She realized he wasn't going to believe her, no matter what she said at this point, so she decided not to say anything after all.

"Yeah. Maybe."

He put his arm around her and said, "I'd admit it if something really bad had happened."

"Sure," she said.

The next day, Alex was up early and woke Lara to say good-bye. She hugged him and kissed him and told him to be careful, waving as he pulled away.

Lara called Maryn that afternoon, telling her if she had any time to hang out, she and Tessa would be available.

"Are you not looking forward to being home alone?" Maryn asked. "You don't sound happy about it."

"Not really. Things are getting really weird, Mar. And now Alex is gone …"

"What happened?"

Lara paused. Everything else—the shoes, the voices, even the dining room table—could be explained by her misremembering or some other logical explanations. But the cabinet doors had shown her that whatever this was, it was capable of making things happen right under her nose and that scared the shit out of her.

"Lara?"

"Yeah, I'm here. Sorry. Something happened the other night that I really, really can't think of an explanation for. And of course, Alex wasn't home and when I told him he still didn't believe me."

"What was it?"

"I was putting dishes away and cleaning up the kitchen the other night. Alex was at work. and I put Tessa to bed and after she was asleep, I did all the dishes, cleaned out the sink, put all the food away, everything. I was cleaning it all up and that's important. Because I *know* I was cleaning up, okay? I closed all of the cabinet doors and drawers. Every single one. I wiped down the countertop last, like I always do. I went to put the dishrag in the laundry room and when I walked back into the kitchen ..." Lara was fighting the tears threatening to fall.

"Yeah?"

"Five cabinet doors and two drawers were open. Wide open, Maryn." She heard Maryn suck in a breath and then let it out slowly.

"Lara ..."

"I know. I know what you're going to say, okay? Maybe I left them open as I was putting dishes away. But I know I didn't. I took a picture of it. They were all wide open. And the creepiest thing is that I didn't hear it! I mean, the laundry room is right there off the kitchen, I should have heard something!" Lara took a deep breath. "Alex doesn't believe me. I sent him a picture and he still doesn't believe me. I mean, does he think I'd actually stage something that elaborate?"

"Lara, are you and Tessa safe there?"

"I don't know! The rest of it seemed harmless. Like a prank. And it's not that open cabinets are threatening or something. But it just happened so fast and so ... so quietly."

"I'm only asking this because I have to. But you're sure this is somehow tied to the book?"

"Yes I'm sure!" Lara's response was snippier than she'd meant it to be.

"I had to ask."

"I know." Lara sighed. "I'm sorry. I just don't know what to think."

"What are we going to do?"

Lara felt instantly better that Maryn had said "we." If Alex didn't believe her, at least Maryn did.

"I don't know. I feel like the stupid girl in the horror movie, trying to explain it all away when it's clearly happening right under my nose. I don't know if I should leave the house or what."

"Look, Lara ..." Maryn stopped mid-sentence and didn't say anything for so long that Lara looked down at her phone to make sure the call was still connected.

"Maryn?" she asked.

"Yes. Sorry. I just ... well I guess we start with the book."

"What do you mean?"

"Well if everything that's happening is tied to the book we need to track down who wrote it, where it was published, all of that."

"Yeah. I had the same thought. I've actually started research already and I—"

Maryn cut her off. "What did you find?"

"Nothing, really. There's no evidence of the book online or that it was ever traditionally published."

"You said 'nothing, really.' Did you find anything at all?"

"No. I couldn't find anything about the book or Violet Marsh."

"Well where did you look?"

Lara was silent for a moment. Maryn had been acting so strange and Lara was starting to feel like this was an interrogation.

"I just looked online."

"What do you think you're going to do next?"

Lara was starting to feel uncomfortable. She didn't know exactly why, but she didn't want to tell Maryn any more.

"I don't know. There's not really anything to do about it, I guess."

"I'd be happy to take it for you. I don't know if it's good for you."

"I'm okay."

"I really don't know if you are."

"Look, Maryn, what's going on with you? You don't seem like yourself, I feel like you're interrogating me here. It's okay if you don't believe me—"

"I'm sorry, Lar. I'm sorry. I just … I have a lot going on right now. I do believe you. I just want you to be safe." Lara heard her sigh quietly. "I don't know if it's good for you to keep this book around, that's all."

"What's going on, Maryn? Something is."

"I'm just … I'm just not ready to talk about it yet. I'm sorry."

"Okay. That's okay. But are you alright?"

"Yeah. I'm fine."

Lara didn't know if she believed her. Maryn always seemed to be holding it together so well, when it came to losing her brother and being in school and all of it. Lara considered whether or not she should push Maryn, worried that she might be on the verge of a breakdown or something.

"You know I'm here for you, right? I mean, you can tell me anything, I understand if you're having a hard time."

"Yeah, I know. Of course. Will you keep me updated, let me know if anything changes? Anything at all. I think we need to be careful and pay attention if things get … worse, I guess."

"Okay. Yeah I will."

Lara felt uneasy when she ended the call. Something was going on with her friend, but Lara didn't know what to do about it right now.

Lara opened up the file she had on her computer with everything she'd found out about the book. The "file" consisted of a screenshot of the book fair flyer and one single-page Word document that had a list of questions and very little actual information.

What We Know

- Book published in 1890
- Marsh family did exist in Grafton, but don't know names or what happened to them
- Picture of the book was used for a book fair flyer in Grafton in 2003. Maisie knows something?
- Key parts of the book are definitely different from the first time I read it.

Questions

- What happened to Violet?
- Will the rest of the book tell me what happened?
- If I keep reading, will things get worse?
- Are there any other copies of the book?
- What does Maisie know?
- What does the store owner know?
- How did the book get into the bookstore?
- What would happen if someone else read it?

Lara sighed. She didn't know anything and she wasn't going to find any answers online. She knew now what she had to do. She needed to go to Grafton. Maybe the store owner would have some information. She could even try to track down some kind of historical association. There had to be something like that.

Now she'd just have to figure out how to tell Alex she was going and what to tell Maisie about her visit.

Maryn

Maryn hung up the phone and slipped it back into her bag. The rest of the coven looked at her expectantly as she walked back into Clara's living room. Maryn tried to keep her face neutral.

"Everything okay?" Clara asked.

"No, Clara. It's fucking not. That was Lara. She's freaked out. Her husband just left town indefinitely and something is messing with her in her own house and we aren't doing a single thing to help her. So, no, everything is not okay."

Clara sighed. "Okay. It's time to figure out what our options are. Even if this book isn't exactly what Amabel thinks it is, it's obviously something. And maybe something dangerous."

"We take it from her!" Maryn yelled. Her patience was worn thin.

"Maryn you yourself said that wouldn't work. She'd still be suspicious and it sounds like she doesn't want to let it go."

"Fine. Then we tell her everything. Now. And let her decide what to do."

"We can't tell a non-witch about this," an older, grey-haired witch said. "I'm sorry, dear. I know you're worried about your friend. But we can't just tell her, especially when we don't even know what we're dealing with."

Maryn was silent, worried about what would come out of her mouth if she spoke out of anger.

"Willa is right," Clara said. "At the very least, we need more information. I've tried to get hold of Amabel, but she won't respond to me. What do we know about her? Anything?"

Willa spoke up now. "I seem to remember Amabel mentioning she was from Oklahoma. I know she's lived in Grafton for a long while, but I believe that's where she's from. Maybe we can reach out to the coven in Oklahoma? See if they know anything about her or this object?"

Clara was nodding. "That's a good idea. I'll do that tomorrow. What else?"

"I want to keep her away from it as much as I can," Maryn said.

"I think that's a good idea, too," Clara agreed. "Will you use your powers?"

"No, Clara, I will not. I won't lie to my friend *and* manipulate her—"

"Maryn, it's not manipulation—"

"Yes, it is. No, I'll figure something out. But I'm only giving it a few more days," Maryn said, picking her purse up from the floor. "Then I'm telling her and I don't care what you all say."

She walked out of Clara's house.

Maryn drove home in silence, her knuckles gripping the wheel, her heart pounding in anger. They were manipulating her friend and now she needed help and they refused to give it to her.

Maryn thought back to when it all started, trying to figure out where it had gone wrong and what the hell she could do about it now.

There weren't that many witches around, so covens tended to convene in larger cities. Because the woman from Grafton, Amabel, was so far away she wasn't a regular at their meetings, but she'd made a special trip that October to meet with the coven, tell them what was happening, and ask for their help.

As far as Maryn could understand, a woman had found some item that might or might not be linked to some powerful, ancient magic tied to the afterlife. All Amabel would say is that there had been rumors of its existence, but no one had ever been able to confirm whether or not it was real. When Clara tried to push her for more information, Amabel was cagey. She kept saying they didn't really need to *do* anything at this point. If it was real, she didn't know what would happen. If it wasn't real, then everything would be fine. She said that until they knew more or something happened, they should just keep an eye on it. But that was the problem—they couldn't very well follow this woman around or even ask her for the book outright.

Maryn had a few problems with the story right away. First, Amabel didn't tell them how exactly she'd tracked this Lara person down. Second, she had a feeling that Amabel knew much more than she was letting on. And finally, Maryn thought that the coven was putting a little too much stock in what she was saying, with no real proof.

"Look, I don't know why we can't just tell this Lara person the truth!" a young witch in the back of the room yelled out. "We could offer to buy the thing, whatever it is, and be done with it."

"We can't do that," Amabel said. "You know we don't ever want to attract attention. What do you suggest we do, call her and say, 'Did you buy an item while you were visiting Grafton that's now acting strangely? If so, we'll buy it from you!' She obviously has no idea magic is even real so she won't believe us anyway and would likely call the cops or otherwise cause a fuss. It's not an option."

"So we're just supposed to wait and see what happens? What if it's real and she figures it out? We can't just let that out into the world," another witch said.

"We need to keep tabs on her without keeping tabs on her," Amabel responded.

"Oh that's helpful." And then they were all talking at once and no one was listening to each other. Maryn didn't really believe this was a real thing. If they couldn't even identify what it was, it was ridiculous to be causing such a fuss about it. She was getting ready to say as much when Clara finally spoke up.

"Listen! This is getting us nowhere. We really just need a way to cover our ass in the event it's real and this woman somehow manages to … to … I don't even know. What would it *do*, Amabel?"

When the older woman just shrugged, Clara sighed and briefly closed her eyes. "We don't need to interfere in her life. We just need to watch her." Clara looked down at her notebook where she'd taken some notes.

"She's in her early thirties, married, one child. She works from home as a graphic designer. Her husband is in construction or something. Her brother died about a year ago." At this last, Clara's voice faded away and she looked right at Maryn, but said nothing.

When her silence became uncomfortable, Maryn shifted in her seat and said, "What?"

"Sounds like the two of you would have a lot in common."

Maryn felt her face grow hot at Clara's words. "I doubt it."

"Do you think you could befriend her?"

"How the hell would I do that? And why? Should I make friends with her and then ask, 'Hey, so have you had any weird magical stuff happen to you lately?'"

Clara's mouth drew into a tight line at Maryn's sarcasm. "I was just thinking that if you could get to know her, you might pick up on something if she started accessing some kind of power."

"No. I'm not going to trick this woman into being my friend. It's dishonest."

A witch sitting near Maryn said, "It's not a bad plan. You would just have to spend a little time with her every once in a while. If she did break something open you'd know right away. That's it."

Maryn shook her head. "I'm not a spy."

Amabel sighed. "Maryn, I know I don't know you very well, but would making a new friend really be the worst thing in the world? And with your powers, you could keep her calm if things got out of hand, maybe even … help her give the thing up if it came to that."

Clara interrupted. "We try not to use our powers to manipulate," she said softly. Clara had always supported Maryn in her conviction to not take advantage of people and Maryn appreciated her standing up for her now.

Amabel laughed sharply. "Okay. Well I still don't see the harm in what we're asking you to do."

Maryn stood up. "I'm done. I'm not going to use the death of her brother—or mine—as some kind of cover to be her friend. That's cruel." Maryn realized that's what was really pissing her off. She started to stand up to leave.

"You didn't feel it," Amabel said quietly.

"What?" Maryn asked, turning to her.

"You didn't feel it. That night. It was so strong. I've never felt anything like it. I knew right away that something was there. I don't know how it can be nothing. Maybe it's not exactly what I fear. But it's something. And we can't pretend like it's not there. And we certainly can't do nothing."

There was something in the woman's voice that made Maryn sit back down. It wasn't until later, when she'd had time to think over the meeting and everything they'd talked about that she realized it had been fear and desperation.

In the end, Maryn had very begrudgingly agreed to intentionally cross paths with this woman. She'd told the coven that she had some conditions.

"First of all, I'm not going to force it. If we don't hit it off, I'm not going to torture this poor woman trying to become her new bestie. Second, I'm not going flat out ask her anything about it. If we really don't want to draw attention, it's going to be super weird if I start questioning her. And finally, I'm not going to lie to her about anything. If some weird shit starts going down, I'm not going to leave her in the dark."

The coven had agreed to her conditions. She got the impression that no one except Amabel thought this was a big deal and the other witches assumed all of this planning was for nothing. Maryn hoped they were right.

Of course, if only they'd known, they might have handled things differently.

Now, sitting here in her driveway, Maryn was furious with herself and with the other women. They'd been so, so stupid. And she was starting to think that Amabel hadn't told them everything.

She wasn't going to ask Clara to help anymore. She'd figure out how to be a friend to Lara on her own.

CHAPTER NINETEEN

Lara

The days passed quietly with Alex gone. Lara tried to avoid thinking about the book and didn't touch it or read it. She still occasionally walked into the kitchen to find cabinet doors open. She'd once found George shaking and whining under the kitchen table and had to coax him out with the promise of a treat. But that was it. She was busy with work and Tessa came down with a cold, so Lara kept her home from daycare for a couple of days. They cuddled on the couch and watched a mind-numbing amount of *Paw Patrol* and *Sofia the First*.

They FaceTimed with Alex every night before bed. Alex didn't ask about the book and Lara didn't bring it up. He was working sixteen-hour days and it was cold, so he was exhausted every night and she didn't want to fight or worry him.

A few days after Alex left, Maryn came over.

"So what's been going on?" she asked.

"It's actually been kind of quiet." Maryn looked visibly relieved at Lara's words. "But I've had the book hidden out in the garage. I don't know. I'm starting to think I need to go to Grafton and see what I can find out about where it came from."

"Lara, if nothing weird is happening when you just, I don't know, ignore it, I think it's clear that if you just get rid of it, all of this will stop."

"I know. But do you know what it means if this is all really happening?"

Maryn tilted her head back and forth in a maybe-maybe-not gesture.

"It means ghosts or magic or whatever the hell is real. I don't know if I can just destroy it."

"Well then let's call Ghost Hunters or something. It's just ... the more I think about it, the more nervous I get about you taking this any farther."

"I don't know." Lara squirmed in her chair. She didn't want to flat-out tell Maryn what had been churning in her mind over and over since it became clear that what was happening in the book was also happening to her. Because if the terrifying things that happened to Violet were also happening to Lara, wouldn't it follow that the *other* things that happened to Violet could also happen to her? Like getting her memories back?

Maryn smiled. "I understand why you want to figure it out. But I guess I'm worried that you're going to try to ... to ..." she seemed to be struggling with what to say.

"You think I'm going to try to do that ceremony to tap into all my Ben memories?"

"Well ... yeah."

Lara laughed. "Well it's not like there's step-by-step instructions. And also, I can believe in ghosts, but spooky ceremonies in the woods? Actual witchcraft? That I don't know about." Her protest sounded weak even to her own ears. It didn't feel logical to believe any of this could actually happen, but she felt far beyond logic at this point.

Maryn shifted in her seat and looked away. "Yeah. I guess I just don't want you to focus on this too much and get wrapped up in the idea that there's something in this book to help you."

"I think—" Lara was interrupted by a large crash from the garage. She looked at Maryn, whose eyes were wide.

"What the fuck was that?"

"I don't know," Lara said, her heart pounding. She began to move toward the door to the garage. She could feel Maryn behind her. She opened the door quickly, wanting to just get this over with.

The cabinet in which she'd put the book was open. Three cans of spray paint lay on the ground, one still slowly rolling toward the tire of Lara's car.

"Jesus," Maryn whispered.

Lara sighed and closed her eyes. The book.

Maryn didn't want to leave Lara alone in the house. Lara didn't blame her. They hadn't been talking about the book for more than fifteen minutes before it was making its presence known.

"I never doubted you, but we were sitting right in here …" Maryn's voice trailed off. She was hugging her arms to her chest and kept shaking her head back and forth. "That is some creepy shit, Lara. I don't like it. Now that I've seen it for myself, this doesn't feel like a spooky ghost story anymore. It feels—purposeful. I don't like it."

"Maryn, I'm fine. If something else happens, I'll move it or something." Lara was trying to sound confident, but she didn't feel all that confident. If she was honest with herself, she felt scared. She wanted a drink. "You want a glass of wine?"

"Absolutely." Maryn got up to get the glasses while Lara got a bottle of sauvignon blanc from the fridge. "How long are you going to let it go, Lara? What if it becomes dangerous?"

"It hasn't been dangerous yet, Mar."

"Yet. And are you willing to hinge Tessa's safety on *yet*?"

"It's never done anything to Tessa. She has not been affected by what's going on. I just need to get some answers."

"I don't want you to be the dumb woman who runs back up the stairs in the horror movie. I think we need to seriously consider that we're dealing with something we might not be able to control."

Lara shook her head. "Maybe I am being naive. It's scary, but I also think there are some answers to be found, Mar. And I'm not—" Lara held her hand up because Maryn had been about to argue— "I'm not willing to ignore what's happening. But I'm not going to be reckless."

Maryn cocked her head to the side and raised her eyebrows.

"I'm not! I just want to see what I can find out in Grafton. If I can't find anything out up there, I don't think I ever will. So if I go up there and it leads to nothing, I'll get rid of the book."

Maryn sighed, clearly not convinced. "When are you going to go?"

"I guess I'll have to see if Alex's parents can keep Tessa for a night, so whenever they're free."

"And what are you going to tell Alex?"

Lara sighed. "I could just tell him I'm going to visit Maisie. But I really don't want to lie. I don't know."

"Look. I'm leaving Friday for a two-day conference in Kansas City. Why don't you and Tessa come with me? You guys can swim in the pool and take naps and go to Legoland while I'm at the conference and when I'm done we can go to dinner or order room service and stay in our pajamas all night. You need to get out of this house."

"You don't want us tagging along. Won't you want to go out with all of your engineering people for drinks and stuff?"

"Seriously? Girl, clearly you have never seen the crowd at an engineering conference. I'll be the youngest, blackest, woman-est person there and they'll either all run away from me or try to hit on me." She shuddered. "Gross. *Please* come with me, you'll save me!"

Lara laughed. "I'll think about it." When Maryn just looked at her, Lara said, "I'll let you know tomorrow, okay?"

"I'm serious, Lara. I don't want to leave you here this weekend. You need to get out of this house for a while or get rid of the book."

Lara eventually let Maryn persuade her and she and Tessa joined her in Kansas City and they had a great time. Tessa loved sleeping in the hotel and they kept busy swimming and exploring the city.

While she was gone, Lara was able to put the book out of her mind for the most part. But on the drive home, Maryn had brought it up, speaking quietly because Tessa was sleeping in the backseat.

"So when are you leaving?"

"I think I'll leave on Tuesday. I need tomorrow to get caught up on work. I'm going to drop Tessa off with Alex's mom Tuesday morning."

"What did you tell Alex?"

Lara sighed when she recalled their conversation. She'd known it wasn't going to be pleasant. But of course, she had to tell him. He hadn't loved the idea, but eventually said, "If you think it will make you feel better, then fine. But can this be the end of it? If you don't find anything, can this just be the end of it?"

Lara had agreed, but didn't make any specific promises. She was going to see this through.

"What are you hoping to find out?" Maryn's voice broke through her thoughts.

Lara didn't answer right away. She'd been thinking about it a lot, what possible explanations there were for what was happening to her. She'd thought about what the witch had said to Violet in the book about the threads of time and memory, but she couldn't make sense of it, though she'd had a couple of fleeting theories. Maybe Henry's or Violet's spirit was tied to the book. Maybe there was some other ancient kind of spirit there. Maybe the book had a mind of its own. Maybe it really was in her head.

But in the end, the conclusion she always came back to was that she didn't know if the hows and whys really mattered all that much. If the book could really help her get her memories back, if it could provide her with any comfort at all, then she thought it was worth trying.

"I'm going to start with the guy we bought the book from. And I guess I'll have to tell Maisie why I'm there. She's not going to believe it, either."

Maryn

Lara changed the subject and Maryn was glad. Tessa had woken from her nap and demanded *Paw Patrol.* As Lara turned to help her with the iPad in the backseat, Maryn let her thoughts wander.

She felt wound tight. She didn't know what she was supposed to do. She'd checked in with Clara while they were in Kansas City. Clara had been relieved Maryn had bought them some time and gotten Lara away from the book. It had given them a chance to do a bit of digging.

The coven in Oklahoma had shed a little bit of light on Amabel's story. The witch they'd spoken to there said she had heard rumors of the magic they thought they were dealing with, but always thought it was just old stories passed down from generation to generation. She had, however, confirmed that Amabel had spent some time on a reservation there when she was younger, and thought that was probably where she'd heard about the book in the first place. She'd also told her that Amabel's childhood had been troubled, but she didn't know many details.

She said that during Amabel's time with the coven, she'd kept to herself, which they'd all thought was odd for a witch so young. She'd asked to see all their old records and had spent months poring through them. When they'd asked her what she was looking for, Amabel had been cagey and dodged their questions. When she left she made copies of a large portion of their records, specifically records of some meetings with representatives of the tribes in the area in the eighteenth century.

That was all she remembered. "I've never forgotten her, you know," the witch had told them. "She was so focused on whatever it was she was looking for. I never imagined it was related to *that*— whatever it is."

And this is where Maryn and the other witches had gotten frustrated. They still weren't sure what they were dealing with. Maryn was beginning to think that the answer lay in the book itself. If the coven would just let her tell Lara now, then they could read the book and see if it held any answers.

Lara had been hoping that Clara would have found out more. Nothing they'd discovered about Amabel really helped them and she still didn't have a way to talk Lara out of continuing to investigate. Now Lara was going to Grafton and Maryn couldn't stop her.

Maybe that's what needs to happen, Maryn thought. Maybe if Lara shakes enough shit up and starts asking questions, it will push Amabel or Clara into action. *I'll just need to keep an eye on her,* she thought. *I need to be right there.*

Lara

Lara dropped Tessa off with Alex's mom, and cheerily talked about how she was so looking forward to spending some time with her aunt. She didn't want Lynn to question what she was doing.

When she returned home, she tried to clear as many items off of her to-do list as she could so she wouldn't feel too guilty about taking a day off work.

As she finished packing, she called Alex and told him what had happened in the garage when Maryn was visiting. For the first time, he didn't immediately try to tell her she was imagining things. She supposed it was because Maryn had witnessed it.

He'd asked her what she needed him to do and she'd told him nothing, that she just wanted him to know. He wanted to know if she thought Tessa was safe and she said yes. She thought maybe he was coming around until he'd said, "Look, Lara, I think I'm going to come home."

"What? I thought you said you had at least another week's worth of work."

"We do. But I'm going to talk to my boss and see if I can leave tomorrow morning and be home by five or six."

"Why? You never come home in the middle of the storm."

"I just feel like I need to check on you guys. I'm worried, Lara. I'm sorry, but I'm worried. I don't understand what's going on."

"No, you just don't believe me."

"Of course I don't! Do you realize how this sounds? It sounds totally insane. I'm sorry, but it does. Like, committed to the psych ward kind of insane."

"I cannot believe you still don't believe me. Do you honestly think I'm just making this up? Why would I do that, Alex?"

Propping the phone between her chin and her ear, she started shoving pants and shirts and underwear into a duffle bag.

"Listen, Lara—"

"No, *you* listen! You're supposed to be the one who stands up for me! I know how this sounds. I know you don't *want* to believe it. *I* don't want to believe it, for fuck's sake! But it's happening and I have to figure it out. And I can't do that from inside a mental hospital, Alex."

She heard him inhale deeply, and let it out slowly through his nose. *Here it comes,* she thought. *The calm, cool, and collected Alex, ready to make peace, talk his wife down from the ledge, and fix the problem.*

"Lara, come on. I'm not going to put you in a mental hospital. I did call my mom. She said she could come stay with you for a while. We just want to keep you and Tessa safe. We don't see another way to do it. After everything—"

"We? WE? Who is helping you make these decisions about *my* life, Alex? Because I know damn well I wasn't consulted at all. And having your mother stay here is not the answer. It's enough that she's watching Tessa for me now."

She slung the bag over her shoulder and headed down the hallway, taking her purse and keys from the bench.

"Did you think other people weren't worried, Lara? Don't you realize I've been fielding phone calls for a year? Everyone is concerned. It's clear that you're not well and—"

"Well if things are so *clear* to you, Alex, then please, explain it to me, because that's all I want is for someone to explain this to me!"

She took a deep breath. "I won't be home if you do come back. I'm not going to let you shut me up or pretend like this isn't happening. I have to figure out what's happening to me, even though you don't seem to give a shit." She ended the call, wishing she could slam the phone down.

Shoving her phone into her purse, she walked out the back door and slammed it behind her.

When she got onto the highway, she called Maryn.

"Alex called me," Maryn said quickly. "Just before you did. He's worried, Lara."

"I know. But he doesn't believe me and I don't know what to tell him. He's not here to see it and he isn't taking me at my word."

"I get it, trust me. I wish he'd believe you. But he's been working far away from home and can't be here for you. It's hard for him, too. I think you need to call him back."

Lara sighed. "What's the point, Maryn? He thinks I'm having some kind of breakdown. There's nothing I can say over the phone that's going to change his mind."

"Just do it. Don't get defensive, tell him you understand he hasn't seen it happening with his own eyes. And just tell him what your plan is. Ask him to just trust *you* even if he doesn't believe what's happening is happening."

"I don't think it will work."

"Well, if you don't try, he's going to come home and he might try to stop you from finding out more about the book. I don't know … maybe that's not a bad thing."

Lara was torn. She wanted Alex to believe her and she knew the only way that would happen was if he saw it with his own eyes. But she also knew that he would try to deny it and come up with a logical explanation for as long as he could. She wanted some time to try to figure it out. Maybe she could stop it before he even came home and they could put all of this behind them.

"Alright. I'll call him. Thanks, Maryn."

"Love you, girl."

"Love you, too." Lara hung up, took a deep breath, and dialed Alex. He answered on the first ring.

"What the hell, Lara?"

"I'm sorry. I was pissed off. I'm going up to Grafton. I'm going to stay with Maisie and see if the guy who owned the store where I bought the book has any information about it that might help me figure out what's happening."

Alex didn't say anything. "Look, Alex, I know you're having a hard time believing what I'm telling you. And I understand. But I need you to trust *me*. I believe it's happening. Maryn believes it's happening. She's seen it. So I have to figure it out. I just have to. There's no harm in me just trying to find out more information."

"I don't even know what to say, Lara."

Lara struggled to keep her voice calm. She was pissed off he still wouldn't just trust her, but she knew that anger would only further convince him he was right. "You don't need to come home. I promise I'm fine. I'm going to go to Grafton and hopefully get some answers. I want to put this behind me."

"Okay. Okay. I give up. If it makes you feel better, fine. But when I get home, I think we need to call Dr. Moore, okay?" He sounded resigned and a little pissed off.

"Fine. Whatever. He doesn't believe me either, so I'm sure you two will have a lot to talk about."

He sighed. "I love you."

Lara closed her eyes for the briefest of moments. She wanted to cry. She wanted to end the call, but she also wanted to tell him to come home and help her. But she was on her own.

"I love you, too."

CHAPTER TWENTY

Lara

Lara parked the car and saw the front door swing open as Maisie came out to greet her.

"Hi, Lolly." Maisie was moving slowly and stopped at the bottom of her porch stairs. "I can't wait to hear what this mystery visit is about."

Lara hadn't told Maisie why she wanted to come stay, just that she needed to spend the night and she'd explain more when she got there. She didn't know how Maisie would react.

Lara wanted to visit Great River Antiques first. She wanted to talk to the store owner and see what he could tell her that she could then share with Maisie. Maisie dealt in facts and Lara needed to be armed with all the information she could get her hands on, lest Maisie treat her the way Alex had been.

"Thanks, Aunt Maisie. You're the best," she said, kissing her aunt on her soft cheek. "I have to run out really quickly, but I wanted to drop my bags off and see what you'd like for dinner. When I'm done I'll get some food and a bottle of your favorite wine from Aeries."

Maisie looked at her, clearly trying to decide if she was going to let Lara off the hook. Before she could demand answers, Lara said, "I promise I'll tell you everything tonight. And don't worry, I'm fine, Tessa's fine, Alex is fine. I just need to run out really quickly then we'll get drunk and I'll tell you everything."

Maisie relented. "Okay."

Lara took her bags up to the guest room, kissed Maisie on the cheek again, and headed back to her car.

She parked in front of Great River Antiques and got out. The sign on the door read Open and the bell tinkled as she pushed it.

The man was sitting exactly where he had been last time, maybe even wearing the same clothes. He looked up as she walked in, and she couldn't make sense of the look on his face. Was he angry? Annoyed? Scared? Lara took a deep breath.

"Hi. I don't know if you remember me or not, my husband and I were here a while ago. I'm Maisie's niece—"

"I know who you are."

"Okay. Well, Mr —."

"My name is John."

"Okay, well, um, I'm here because I bought a book back in October, when I was here with my husband."

Lara reached into her bag and pulled out a picture she'd snapped of the book and printed on her computer at home. She hadn't wanted to bring the book with her. As soon as she set it on the counter, John jumped back away from it, nearly falling off the stool he was sitting on.

"Where the hell did you get that?" he demanded.

"H-here," Lara stammered, surprised by his reaction. "I found it on the floor, behind that shelf over there." She pointed vaguely to the bookshelf.

"There's no way you found that in my store. I haven't seen that—no, you did not find that here. I would remember selling that to you."

"I did. But I had tucked it into a case and just told you it was in there. I never showed it to you."

He was shaking his head as if he didn't believe her.

She pressed on. "I was hoping you could tell me where you got it from. I can't find any information about it online or anything. It doesn't have a publisher or any additional information. I was hoping to find out something about the author."

"I can't help you. I don't know how it ended up here. It

shouldn't have been here at all."

Lara was getting annoyed. Clearly he knew something about it.

"Look, any information you can give me would be great. I just need to know—"

"No, I can't," he said loudly. Then shook his head and must have felt bad for how short he was being with her, because he lowered his voice and said, "I really don't know anything that could help you. Sorry. I'll give you your money back."

Frustrated, Lara said, "I don't want my money back. I don't understand why you won't tell me whatever it is has made you so upset."

"I can't," he said simply.

Lara picked the photo up and said, "Fine. Thanks for your time." She turned to go.

"Ask Maisie."

Lara's heart jumped at his words and she turned to look at him. "Maisie?"

He nodded.

"Okay. Thanks." The bell tinkled again as she left the store.

Lara got into her car but didn't start it. She gripped the steering wheel, looking out the windshield, but not really seeing anything in front of her. What the hell had John meant and why wouldn't talk to her? What did Maisie have to do with any of this? Now she clearly had no choice but to tell Maisie everything and ask her what she knew.

Lara got their food and a bottle of wine and headed back to her aunt's. As she parked the car, she felt nervous. Maybe Maisie wouldn't believe her. Or maybe she was more afraid that Maisie would tell her some awful, evil story that would make her more scared than she already was.

She smiled at Maisie as she walked in the door, but Maisie wasn't stupid and she knew Lara better than anyone. Her aunt could tell right away that something was wrong. She didn't ask questions as

Lara set out the food, making small talk, purposefully avoiding what she really needed to say.

When they'd finished eating and cleared away the dishes, Lara excused herself to use the bathroom and change. She washed her face and put on her pajamas. After that, she realized she couldn't stall anymore and went out to the living room. Maisie was sitting in her favorite chair, wrapped in her favorite old sweater and holding a glass of wine.

As Lara sat down on the couch and pulled a blanket over her legs, Maisie said, "Okay. Now tell me what's going on."

"I don't know where to start. I guess it really began with a fight between Alex and me last fall. It was really bad. I was not doing well. I don't think I was even honest with you about how hard things were for me at one point. I was barely leaving the house. I wasn't cooking or cleaning or even working all that much. I wasn't even able to *read* and you know how much I usually read."

Lara reached behind her and pulled her hair into a sloppy bun on top of her head. "Looking back, I was obviously depressed and needed help processing what had happened to Ben. Anyway, that night I ended up locked in my bathroom, counting all the pills we had left in the medicine cabinet." She heard Maisie's sharp intake of breath but couldn't look at her. Lara pulled her hair out of the bun.

"I was thinking about killing myself. I don't know if I would have ever really gone through with it. I was just tired. So, so tired. I didn't want to die, but I did think it would be easier for everyone if I just wasn't around anymore. I didn't want to keep hurting so much. I realized as I sat there, counting those pills, that things were bad and I needed help. The next day I made an appointment with Dr. Moore and things have slowly gotten better. I've been working hard at it ever since."

She looked up at Maisie, who looked near tears. She nodded.

"One of the things I was trying to focus on was spending time with Alex. That's why we came up here in October. I didn't really want to come, but I forced myself to. And we had a great time. That Friday, Alex and I went to Great Rivers Antiques just to look around. And you know Alex, we walked out of there with a bunch of crap we didn't need."

Maisie laughed.

"I found this old book, on the floor, shoved behind a shelf. I don't know what made me pick it up, but I did. It was really old, published in 1890 or something. Or printed in 1890 I guess I should say, there isn't really a publisher's page. Anyway. I picked it up and opened to the first page and the first lines were about how difficult it was when the narrator's brother died."

Maisie was sitting very still and not saying anything. Lara continued. "I thought it was a sign or something stupid like that. So I bought it and I started reading it that night. And it felt so good, to finally be reading again. I read a lot of it that weekend and finished it a few days later. It was really comforting. It was all about this woman, Violet—" At the name, Maisie made a noise and Lara looked up at her. Maisie just shook her head and gestured for her to continue.

"... this woman, Violet, and her attempt to find meaning in her life after her brother died. She eventually gets help from an old witch in town. What I thought was really cool is that it must have been written by a local writer because the whole thing is set in Grafton." Lara stopped then, looking at Maisie and waiting for her to say something.

"What did it look like?" Maisie asked.

"The book?"

Maisie nodded. Lara thought it was a weird question.

"Um. It's green, leather-bound. With a gold leaf and tree design on the cover." Lara couldn't read the emotions on Maisie's face. "Maisie?"

"What happened next?"

"Well, I read it that week and then put it away for a while." Lara paused. "A few months. The counseling was definitely helping and I was in a much better place than I had been before. I still have really hard days—sometimes I have hard weeks. I was having one of those days, a couple of weeks ago. And I remembered that the book made me feel so much better, so I thought I'd read it again."

Lara took a deep breath. "But this time when I read it, it was … different. I read the first couple of chapters and remember thinking that it was weird because I didn't remember much of the story. The major plot points were the same, but there were a lot of scenes that were completely unfamiliar to me. Then, as I got farther into it, it started to become creepy and made me feel unsettled. That definitely didn't happen the first time."

"So you just didn't remember it."

Lara was surprised at Maisie's tone. It was accusatory and almost angry.

"Obviously that's the first thing I thought. But I really don't think so. When I read it the first time it made me feel better. The second time, I did not feel good. But that's not even the weirdest part. And look, I know how you feel about supernatural, paranormal stuff—" Maisie interrupted her with a snort, making her feelings clear. Lara ignored it. "So I don't expect you to believe me right away. But I'm not lying and I'm not making it up." She took a drink of her wine.

"The creepy things that were happening in the book—that definitely weren't in there the first time—started happening to me. In my house."

Maisie just looked at her. So Lara told her everything. The shoes, the diary, the dining room table, the cabinets. The knocking. She didn't hold back and she didn't try to apologize. When she was done, she pulled a blanket tight around her shoulders and decided she was going to wait for Maisie to respond.

After a few moments, Maisie turned, set her wine glass down on the end table, and folded her hands in her lap. "So, what do you think is happening, Lara? This book is haunting you? Are you sure you haven't imagined these things? What does Alex say?"

This response was very unlike Maisie. Maisie always said that people had a right to feel the way they feel, whether you agree or believe it or not. She always said that as humans, it was our job to at least try to understand how someone else was feeling and not discount their experiences. So her taking this sarcastic, disbelieving tone shocked Lara.

"I don't know what I think," Lara tried and failed to keep any defensiveness out of her tone. "Alex doesn't believe me and he's explained everything away. And now he's been gone for over a week and hasn't seen all of this firsthand. But I guess no one believes me. Whatever. I know it *sounds* crazy, but I'm not a liar."

"Honey, I'm sorry you're having a difficult time. But it's just not possible."

"Damn it. This is why I came up here today. When this started happening and started to feel dangerous, I decided I needed to look into it and track this book down. Well, it's not in print anywhere. There's no record of it online and I can't find anything out about the author or figure out if any of the people in the book were real or if the whole thing is made up. The only thing I could find was an old flyer for a book fair in 2003. Here in Grafton. And your name was on the flyer."

Maisie looked surprised. "What?"

Lara showed her a screenshot of the flyer on her phone. Maisie's hand was shaking when she handed the phone back to her, but she didn't say anything, so Lara kept talking.

"So I decided to come up here and do some research. I went back to Great Rivers Antiques this afternoon. I talked with John.

There's no better way to say it other than he freaked out when I showed him the picture of the book. Told me I shouldn't have it. *Then* he said something that makes me think your act right now—like you don't believe me—is total crap."

The color had drained from Maisie's face. She turned her head, looking out the window. Neither woman said anything for almost a full minute. Maisie finally said, "What did John tell you?"

"Not much. He just said, 'Ask Maisie.' So what do you know, Maisie? And why are you acting like I'm the crazy one when clearly there's way more to this whole thing than you're letting on?"

"Lara, I don't want to do this."

"Bullshit!" Lara hadn't meant to raise her voice but she couldn't help it. She was so tired of everyone acting like she was making all of this up.

"I swore I would never talk about it. You have to understand that, Lara. It's not going to do any good to bring this all up again. Let's just get rid of the book."

"No. Do you know what this means, Maisie? It means that ghosts are real. Or something. And what if it means something more. Something about Ben? I can't just ignore that! Why did John tell me to ask you?"

"I don't know, Lara. He's always speaking out of turn and feeding the gossip mill. Don't put too much stock in what he said." Maisie clapped her hands together lightly and stood up. "I think you need to get rid of the book and let this all go. Ghosts aren't real." Maisie began moving toward the kitchen.

"Maisie. Wait. Are you serious?" Lara had never been angry with her aunt before and she felt guilty about it now. But there was something Maisie wasn't telling her and she needed to know about it. "I think you do know something and I don't know why you won't tell me."

"Lara, I told you. I don't know anything. And you know how I feel about ghosts. Now, I'm tired and I'm going to bed. I love you. Good night." Maisie made her way slowly down the hallway. Lara didn't call after her.

Lara couldn't believe that Maisie was willing to just flat out lie to her. Was she going to hit a dead end every time she tried to find out more?

John

John's hands were shaking. How in the hell the book ended up in the store? Did Maisie know Lara had it?

"Dear god," he whispered, putting his head in his hands. He was too old to deal with this shit again. After Lara left, John had closed up the shop and gone upstairs to the small apartment where he'd lived since Virginia died and he sold their house to his son. He fixed a TV dinner, but only took a couple of bites before throwing it in the trash. He felt sick to his stomach.

Seeing the picture of that book, Lara holding it so casually—well, it had been shocking to say the least. He'd barely held it together and he could see that Lara wasn't convinced by his insistence that he didn't know anything about it. John turned on the television, stopping on *Casablanca* on TCM. He watched it distractedly, not really paying attention. As he thought through what it meant that the book had resurfaced, he realized he was going to have to talk to Maisie.

After she'd broken his heart all those years ago, they'd kept their distance from each other. At least as much as they'd been able to in a town as small as Grafton. He'd realized, eventually, what had actually happened between her and CiCi. He and Maisie had spoken about it once, when they'd both been more than a little tipsy at a church picnic. She'd told him that she'd realized much sooner than CiCi that she was gay and that was why her and CiCi's friendship had suffered during high school. She told him that CiCi felt the same, but was too scared to admit it. Which was why she'd married William and tried too hard to deny her true feelings.

It wasn't until William left for the war and they'd started spending time together again that she'd admitted how she felt about Maisie. They'd found a way to cobble together a life as much as they could in a small, conservative town. John had told her he was happy for her, although that was still kind of hard to admit.

Now, just as Humphrey Bogart said, "Louis, I think this is the beginning of a beautiful friendship," John heard a knock on his door.

John walked slowly through the kitchen to the back door of his apartment. His shop was downstairs and there was an interior staircase, but there was also a set of stairs on the outside of the building.

John pushed aside the curtain and was shocked to see Maisie standing there. He was so surprised, in fact, that he just simply stood there, looking at her.

"Well, are you going to let me in or are you just going to look at me?"

John unlocked the door and opened it for Maisie, who walked in, took off her coat, and set it on the back of a kitchen chair. "I'm sorry to bother you so late, John. But I'm assuming you know why I'm here."

"Yeah. Your niece gave me the shock of my life tonight, just talking about that book like it was nothing at all."

"How did it end up in your store, John?"

John was silent. He didn't know what to say. He pulled out a chair and sat across from Maisie. "I'm sorry, Maisie."

"Why are you sorry? How did the book end up here, John?"

"I went back and took it."

"You did what?"

"I went back there. To the cave. I found the book, still wrapped up in the sack and I took it." John rubbed his hands over his face.

"Why?"

"I never stopped thinking about it. I never stopped wondering if there was something more to it, if there was a way to … to use the magic in there. And after Virginia died, I was so lonely—"

"Wait. After Virginia died? *That's* when you went back to get it?"

"Yeah. I was too old at that point to trek up to that cave, but I did. And there it was. All of the other stuff—the blankets and pillows were still there, too. It was eerie." John shuddered. "Anyway, I took it. I read it over and over but nothing ever happened and eventually I gave up and tucked it away in a box."

"When did Virginia pass?"

"2005."

"But that's impossible …" Maisie whispered to herself.

"What?"

"Nothing." Maisie shook her head. "So did you put it down in the shop on purpose? Why would you do that, John?"

"I never meant for it to end up there. It was in a closet, along with some other old books I wanted to save. My son was here a couple of months ago helping me clean up and organize and he must have found that box and assumed it was meant to go in the store. I didn't know what happened until Lara came in here and showed me."

"She asked me about it tonight. She told me that ever since she bought it, things have been happening to her, John." Maisie told John some of what Lara had told her.

When she'd finished, John was silent for a long moment. "I'm so sorry, Maisie." He shook his head. "I thought we'd never have to think about all of this again," he said so quietly that Maisie barely heard him. "But she says it's about a woman whose brother died? What the hell? That book was about a dad who died in the war."

"Yeah. I know. John, when you read the book was it scary?"

"Not really. A little creepy, maybe. But not scary."

Maisie nodded.

"She needs to get rid of the damn thing! You need to tell her to get rid of it. Burn it and dump the ashes in the river."

"I don't know if she's going to listen to me."

"You have to make her."

"If only I could."

Lara

The next morning, Lara woke early when she heard Maisie in the kitchen. She put on a robe, used the bathroom, brushed her teeth, and headed to the kitchen. Maisie was standing at the stove, making scrambled eggs. Lara picked up the fresh pot of coffee and poured a cup. "Morning, Maisie." Lara added creamer to her coffee.

"Good morning, Lolly." Maisie sounded exhausted.

"Are you okay?"

"I didn't sleep well, love." Maisie scooped some scrambled eggs onto two plates, adding some toast and bacon.

"You didn't need to go through all this trouble for me," Lara said.

"You know I love to take care of you." Maisie sighed. "That's why I need to talk to you this morning, dear."

Lara looked up from her plate.

"I wasn't honest with you last night. There is something … I do know something about that book."

"No kidding."

Maisie laughed off her sarcasm. "Clearly I'm not a great actress. I just didn't know how to explain this. I was hoping I'd never have to tell anyone this story. I'm sorry I didn't do more to protect you."

"Protect me? What do you mean?"

"I've read the book. When I was thirteen. My friends—CiCi and John—and I found it in a cave up on Sutter's Acres."

"Wait," Lara interrupted her. "John? As in John who runs Great River Antiques?"

"Yes."

"Then he lied to me, too! I knew it!"

"I know. We just—"

"Maisie, what the hell is going on? I tell you I think I'm losing my mind because all of this weird stuff is happening to me and you tell me you have no idea? And this John person is in on it, too? What—"

"Lara!" Maisie had raised her voice and Lara was so surprised she stopped talking immediately. "I'm *sorry*, honey. But you have to understand. What we went through back then … We were just kids. I've spent many, many years convincing myself that we imagined it and that it never happened. CiCi and I hardly ever talked about it, in all those years. So when you started telling me about it, I panicked. I didn't want to think about it and I certainly didn't want to be reminded that it was all real."

"What happened to you?"

Maisie sighed. "We're going to need more coffee," she said, taking the pot and topping off their cups.

Then she told Lara exactly what happened back in 1946.

CHAPTER TWENTY-ONE

Maisie

They'd found the book in their secret spot. Maisie's family home sat on two acres of land that butted right up against Sutter's Acres, high on a bluff overlooking Grafton. At the very back edge of the property, there was a small cave, carved into the bedrock of the bluff.

Maisie, John, and CiCi had spent hours exploring that land, discovering streams and giant boulders to climb and had built countless forts and hideouts. They'd stumbled upon the cave years ago and had explored it a bit but had been scared to venture too far in. Now they were thirteen and thought they were much, much braver. And they desperately wanted somewhere that was all their own. Maisie's father was on the rampage every other day. John's mother was struggling to take care of her family. And CiCi was just trying to be there for her friends.

One cloudy fall day, John had suggested it was time to go back to the cave and explore it properly. It was the perfect place for a secret hideout. To their knowledge, no one else knew it was there and no one would ever bother them. Maisie's father wouldn't be able to find her and John could get away from the pressure he felt to help his mother and his sisters.

Two days later, they met after church. It was still warm, but the air had that crispness to it that spoke of the coming winter chill. They'd packed snacks and flashlights and even brought some blankets and a few old pillows to sit on. Maisie and CiCi had grand plans to decorate. John was hoping to find long-forgotten treasure. Maybe something to help his mom catch up on the bills.

As they trekked through the woods, they talked about what they might find in the cave.

"Maybe we'll find some old Indian drawings on the wall," said John. "I'd love to find a real arrowhead, too."

"Maybe we'll find the Piasa bird," said Maisie. The Piasa bird was an old Native American legend in the area, a huge dragon-like bird that devoured men.

"I hope not," said CiCi, who was the least adventurous of the three by far and scared easily.

"It's not real," said Maisie.

"But if it is, at least we'll die together!" said John, throwing his arm around CiCi's shoulders.

"Not funny, John!" she said, pushing him away.

After a fifteen-minute hike through the woods, they arrived at the mouth of the cave.

"It's pretty dark in there." CiCi wrapped her arms around her waist and peered nervously into the mouth of the cave.

"Time to see what's back there. I'll go first." John walked confidently into the cave, shining the light ahead of him. It was just tall enough for them to walk without stooping—an adult probably would have had to bend over. The cave was quiet, the sounds of their footsteps muffled but bouncing off the walls. There was a nearly imperceptible sound of dripping or running water. The cave smelled of earth and leaves and the temperature became noticeably cooler the farther they went in.

Maisie was shining her light up and around her, looking at the cave walls.

"It's so quiet," whispered CiCi, turning around to look back at the opening, trying to reassure herself there was still a way out.

"I don't think it goes back much farther," said John. "I think I can see the end right up ahead."

John was right and they reached the end just a minute later. The cave was just about eighty yards long in total, ending in a small, circular room. They could touch the top if they reached up on tiptoe. It was surprisingly cool and totally silent.

"Wow," said Maisie.

"This is so cool," John said.

"I feel like nothing can find us in here," said CiCi, laughing a little.

They got to work setting up the items they'd brought. They tucked blankets and pillows against the rock. John put an extra flashlight and some matches in a steel box and placed it on the ground. They also gathered some sticks and larger pieces of wood to stack against the mouth of the cave in case they wanted to have a fire.

When they were done, Maisie began shining her flashlight around the walls of the little room. She spotted something tucked behind a large rock on the floor of the cave. "What's that?" she asked, kneeling down and picking the object up. It was a burlap sack, the kind rice or flour might come in. It was folded around something.

"Don't open it!" cried CiCi, just as John said, "What's inside? Open it!"

Smiling at her friends, Maisie unfolded and opened the sack. She poked around inside before drawing out a small green book. She carefully set it on the floor of the cave.

"Well, it's not buried treasure. But this looks super old." John opened the book to the first page. "*Memoriae,*" he said, reading the title. "Written by Violet Marsh, 1890." He turned it over in his hands. "There's no book description. Wonder what it's about."

"Why would someone put a book in a bag and hide it all the way out here?" CiCi asked.

"It's weird," said Maisie.

CiCi, who had taken the book from John and was now thumbing through it, said, "Guys. Listen to this—'The day my father died was the day I felt like I lost my grip on the real world.'"

"Whoa," said John.

"So weird," agreed Maisie. "I'm totally taking it with me. I need to read it."

John smiled, but CiCi looked nervous. "I don't know …" CiCi trailed off. She had a weird feeling.

"CiCi, don't spoil my fun! It's a book, what could possibly happen? I want to know why the book was tucked away up here and back so far. Clearly it wasn't meant to be found."

"Yeah, CiCi! What if this is, like, a super great find?"

"Fine," she said reluctantly.

John started exploring the rest of the cave and Maisie paged through the book, thinking maybe one of the owners of one of the antique shops in town could tell them more about it.

The trio didn't find anything else exciting in the cave, save for a few scribbles on the walls that didn't really look like anything and very easily could have been dirt drawn down the side of the cave by drips of water.

"Well, I guess I'm not going to find any arrowheads today," said John.

"Alright, let's head back," said CiCi, who was more than ready to get out of there.

As they walked back they discussed why someone might hide a book up there. They were excited to have a bit of a mystery to solve and talked about how they might find out more about the book. Even CiCi started to join in the discussion.

"For starters, I need to read the book," said Maisie. "Then we'll see what it's all about and what we can find out."

Two days later, Maisie had finished. She told John and Maisie at school that she was done and they should meet up so she could tell them about it. They agreed to hike back to the cave, not only so they would have a private place to talk, but also so they could drop off some more stuff to really outfit their new place.

They trekked up to the cave. They lit lanterns, got comfortable against the blankets and pillows, and settled in.

"So?" asked CiCi. "What's it all about?"

"Well," Maisie began. "it's a diary by this girl named Violet Marsh. She lives in Grafton, so it's someone who might still have family in the area. She's seventeen and her dad ..." CiCi looked at each of her friends then looked down at her hands.

"Well, her dad came home at the end of the Civil War and I guess he ... wasn't well. He married her mom when he got home and she and her twin brother, Henry, were born about seven years after the war was over. She and her dad were very, very close. He couldn't work, because of his ... issues. Her mother's family had money and that's what supported them. Violet and her father spent a lot of time together. The diary starts in 1889, two months after her father died. She doesn't say how he died."

The three kids were silent for a long moment. They'd lived through the war and they were all still dealing with the aftermath, as were so many people all around the globe. CiCi's father had not gone overseas. He was a police officer and so was exempt from the draft, as he was deemed necessary to the community.

But John's father had died in Okinawa. Maisie's father had come home, but he was sick. He could be violent and drank too much. Her mother told her that he was struggling to deal with the memories of what he'd seen during the war and that he just needed more time. But it was difficult and Maisie mostly just tried to steer clear of him, which made her sad because before the war, they'd been close.

"So what does she write about?" asked CiCi finally.

"Mostly about how much she misses her dad and that she doesn't know how to get on without him. It doesn't seem like she's very close to her mom and she and Henry are just sad all the time. Then one day she's walking along the river and meets this witch, who tells her that she can help her talk with people who are dead."

"Whoa," said CiCi, wrapping her arms around her stomach.

"That's creepy."

"Yeah, a little bit," said Maisie. "But it wasn't really. She and Henry go with this witch who helps them remember a bunch of stuff about their dad and it makes them feel better. They share all their memories with their mom, who is sad, but in the end they write this book about their life with their dad and how great he was." She looked down at her hands. "There are lots of parts that really made sense to me. I even underlined a few and wrote some notes for you, John."

"Well that's kind of cool," said CiCi.

"I guess," said John, who was looking toward the mouth of the cave, his lips pressed tightly together. He got up and walked toward the mouth of the cave. "I thought I heard something out here."

Maisie and CiCi looked at each other and Maisie put the book back in her bag. "Maybe I shouldn't have said anything. I didn't think about it upsetting him. I'm a dope."

CiCi patted her hand. "It's okay, Maisie. He'll be okay."

A few minutes later John joined them and asked to see the book. "Does the book tell you how to get the memories back?"

"Not really," said Maisie. "They talk about some weird ceremony in the woods, but not how to do it."

"I want to find out more," said John.

"Okay," Maisie said, although she wasn't sure it was a good idea.

Over the next couple of weeks, Maisie, John, and CiCi tried to find out more about the book and the Marsh family, but didn't come up with much. They went to the library and found some records of a Marsh family that used to live in Grafton, but there wasn't any record of Violet. They also checked the library at school but couldn't find any other copies of the book.

They looked through the antique shops in town, trying to find another copy, but they couldn't find one anywhere. John talked about it constantly. By then he'd read the book more than once and he started researching witchcraft and the history of witches. But nothing led them to any more information.

Things were getting worse at home for Maisie and John. Maisie's father was now starting to leave the house and not return for days. Her mother, a nurse, was doing her best to keep the house together and care for Maisie and her sister Ruth, but it was getting harder and harder. Maisie suspected that her mom had had to bail her dad out of jail more than once and she'd heard them arguing about money. Her dad was a mechanic at his brother's shop in Alton, so he would never be without work. But if he wasn't there, he also wasn't getting paid. These days, it seemed like he was at home or at the bar far more than he was at work.

John's mother was working seven days a week at three different jobs. John had started doing odd jobs around town for a dime here and there, just to help out. He'd said the owner of the house they were renting had been by more than once in the past two weeks to ask about rent. Focusing on the book was the one thing they could feel in control of and take their minds off their worries.

Eventually, Maisie began to read the book again, hoping to find some clues she'd missed the first time. That was when the story began to make her feel uncomfortable. Violet and Henry's story had been a sad story, but one that ultimately ended well as they found a way to connect to their father through their shared memories of him and memorializing him in their journal.

But it seemed like Maisie had misremembered the story. After Violet and Henry's run-in with the witch, they'd grown depressed and withdrawn, spending time only with each other.

Eventually, Maisie couldn't believe what she was reading. The beginning of the book was the same. But when Violet met the witch the book started to feel different. Maisie remembered the witch wanting to help Violet. This time, she still wanted to help, but Violet and Henry got scared during the ceremony in the woods and were chased out by a cold, screaming wind. They ran back home without finishing the ceremony. In the days that followed, odd things began happening to Henry and Violet at home. It started when Henry and Violet heard someone talking in the living room, but there was no one there.

When she read about a mysterious knocking Violet and Henry heard coming from the back door in the kitchen, the pantry door, and the ceiling, Maisie closed the book and threw it to the foot of her bed. Her heart was pounding and she felt goosebumps on her arms. *None of this happened the first time I read it!* Her blood went cold and her stomach clenched in fear. She felt a tingling in her fingers. She couldn't figure out why she was having such an intense reaction to this book. All she knew was that she did not remember any of this. Maisie began taking notes in the book, circling the things she didn't remember and making notes about what she thought had happened the first time.

When strange things started happening to Maisie, she didn't tell anyone about it. Her mother had too much to worry about and Ruth was too little. She knew John would want to know, but CiCi would just be scared. For a while she convinced herself she was just imagining it. It started with small things, anyway. She'd found a pair of shoes set side by side in the middle of the floor that she was sure hadn't been there before. Once she found a dining room chair stacked on top of another when she thought for sure she'd been the only one home. These things were easily explained and Maisie didn't want anyone to think she was crazy. She also suspected that re-reading the book was just putting creepy ideas into her head and she didn't want to admit to anyone that she was scared.

She wasn't surprised when, one chapter later, Violet and Henry found a dining room chair stacked atop another. But she could not, no matter how hard she tried, remember either reading this part the first time or stacking her dining room chairs atop one another. Still.

There was no other explanation. She had to be doing it herself or it was someone else in the house.

It wasn't until she felt something in her house with her that she started to admit it wasn't in her head. She'd been reading in her room. For once, her dad was home and relatively sober. He'd fallen asleep on the couch with the paper laying across his chest. Her mother was reading a book and Ruth was in bed. Her bedroom door was partially open, light from the hallway spilling into her room.

Maisie heard two soft knocks on her door. Thinking it was her mom, but hoping it was her dad. He used to come into her room a lot before she went to bed, chatting about their days or reading together. He hadn't come in for one of their late-night talks in months. She said, "Come in." No one came in and no one responded.

"Hello?" she called. Maisie set her book down and went to the door. When she opened it fully, no one was there. She looked down the hallway toward Ruth's room and back toward the living room. There was no one there. Thinking she surely must have imagined it, she went back inside her room and returned to her book.

Just a few minutes later, she heard two soft knocks. On her window. Jumping up this time, she stood next to her bed staring at her curtained window. Too afraid to pull the curtain back, she stood frozen, waiting to see if she would hear the knocks again. Sure enough, moments later, she heard the same two soft knocks on the ceiling, then again on the wall next to her bed. Her eyes moved wildly back and forth, chasing the knocks with her eyes. Next she heard multiple loud raps, much harder this time, on her closet door. This knocking seemed to go on forever, loud and violent, shaking the door. Finally, she was able to move and ran out of her room.

As she dashed into the living room, her mom looked up from her book and quickly put a finger to her lips, gesturing to Maisie's dad, clearly not wanting Maisie to wake him.

"Mom!" Maisie whispered urgently. "Something is in my room! I keep hearing knocks on the door and the window and the walls!"

"What? What are you talking about?" Her mom put her book down.

"I'm hearing knocking everywhere in my room! I'm serious. Will you please come check it out?"

Her mom got up slowly. "I'm sure you're imagining it, honey. Or it's just the pipes or the house settling. But we'll take a look."

They went into Maisie's room and stood still, looking around and listening. Nothing happened. Her mom pulled back the curtain and peered out—nothing was there. She opened the closet door—nothing was there, either.

"See? Everything is okay. You've been reading too many spooky stories," her mom said, kissing her on the top of the head. "Why don't you get ready for bed, it's getting late."

Maisie did as her mom asked, but it was a long time before she fell asleep that night.

The next day was Friday and Maisie debated whether or not she should tell John and CiCi what had happened. She decided she had to tell someone, so asked them to meet her at the cave the next morning. They agreed.

On Saturday, Maisie packed the canvas satchel she used for school with snacks and water, preparing for their day in the cave. At the last minute, she put the book in her backpack. *Just in case*, she thought. *Maybe I'll leave it up there in the cave.*

When the trio had congregated at the cave, Maisie filled John and CiCi in on everything that had been happening.

"I knew that book was bad news!" declared CiCi.

John was laughing. "No way, Maisie. None of that happened in the book when I read it."

"I'm not imagining it. The stuff happening at my house was real and I only read the book for the first time a few weeks ago—I couldn't have forgotten it all so quickly! And like I told you guys, the first time I read it, it was nice and had a happy ending."

"Maybe we should tell our parents," said CiCi.

"CiCi, your mom and dad are probably the only ones who aren't too busy to listen to us. And even then, there's no way they'd believe us. I guess I should just get rid of it …" Maisie's voice trailed off.

"No," John said, his voice raised and eyebrows furrowed.

"Why?" asked CiCi.

"I don't know. For some reason, I don't feel like we should. What if we can—" John seemed to stop himself from saying anything further.

"That doesn't make any sense! There's no reason to keep it," CiCi said.

Maisie shook her head. "I think I'll just leave it here in the cave and see what happens. Maybe once I quit carrying the book around with me all the time, everything will stop. And anyway, I'm too nervous to keep reading it, I don't want to know—"

Just then, they heard the loud ringing of a bell. CiCi screamed, a short, high yelp and she clamped her hands around her mouth. The bell began to clang violently, a high, echoing sound that made John cover his ears.

"What is that?" Maisie yelled.

"I brought up an old bell I found in the barn," John said over the din of the bell. "It's hanging up in the front of the cave!"

Then, under the sound of the clanging bell, they could hear what sounded like feet running and stomping on the dirt-packed floor of the cave. CiCi screamed again and grabbed onto Maisie's arm. Maisie stifled her own scream as she peered toward the mouth of the cave. The cave curved slightly, so she could only see a small portion of the entrance and didn't see anyone standing there.

"CiCi, stop screaming," Maisie whispered into her ear. She clutched John's arm. "John, turn out the light. If something is here, we don't want it to be able to see us." John flipped off his light and Maisie did the same. Plunged into darkness, they could only listen to the deafening sound of the bell and the footsteps that still hadn't stopped.

"What are we going to do?" John whispered into her ear. "We'd have to run right toward it to get out of the cave!"

"If someone was really running that fast, they would have made it down here by now," Maisie whispered. "Whatever it is, I think it's just trying to scare us."

The three of them sat frozen, hearts pounding, waiting for another sign of an intruder.

"I think we need to get out of here," CiCi was whimpering. Maisie put her arm around her and said, "I know, I know."

Abruptly the bell and the pounding footsteps stopped. The sudden silence was jarring and CiCi cried out. They sat there for a few more minutes, clinging to each other and listening for any noise that would tell them they weren't alone in the cave. Maisie thought she heard something else beneath the sound of their rapid breathing. Something that sounded like moaning. Or a deep, guttural keening that seemed to be building into a scream. But John and CiCi didn't say anything, so she didn't ask if they heard it, too.

Eventually, John said, "I'm going to go check it out."

"Not alone you're not," said Maisie. She took CiCi's hand and they stood up. "We'll go together. Don't turn on your lights."

Picking up their bags and linking arms, the three walked slowly toward the mouth of the cave. They were able to see just enough in the fading afternoon light to make their way.

When they reached the mouth of the cave, they stopped suddenly. It looked as though a huge animal had dragged its claws down the outside of the cave entrance. Three huge gashes were gouged deep into the rock on either side of the entrance. The cowbell lay in two pieces on the floor of the cave and leaves and branches had blown in, carpeting the cave floor.

The cave was silent, as were the woods around them. Maisie's heart was pounding; her flesh stood up in goosebumps. A chill fall breeze blew toward them. They stood quietly observing the damage. Maisie's body felt taut, pulled tight. She was ready to run. "I think—"

A scream coming from the back of the cave cut short her thought. It was loud and piercing and sounded only partially human. Maisie thought it was traveling closer and closer to them.

"Run!" she screamed. They ran into the woods, not slowing until they were nearly a hundred yards away and standing behind a huge oak tree.

"What just happened?" CiCi cried.

"I don't know!" John and Maisie said at the same time. They were silent as they tried to catch their breath. CiCi wiped tears from her cheeks. "M-maybe it was just wind?" she asked.

"That was *not* wind!" yelled John. "That bell was bouncing back and forth like crazy!"

"Oh no," said Maisie, touching the bag slung around her hip.

"What?"

"The book is in my bag. I wanted to leave it in the cave."

"I'm not going back in there," said John.

"Neither am I," Maisie said. "I'll leave it somewhere else. But that bell started ringing as soon as I said I was going to leave the book in the cave."

"I don't want it anywhere near me," said CiCi.

They made their way quickly back into town. When they reached Grafton's main street and stood at the corner, John asked, "Where are you going to leave it?"

Maisie looked around. "I'm not sure. There's that old falling-down shed behind the church that no one ever goes in. It might be good to keep it by a church, I guess."

"I really think you should burn it or something," said CiCi. She was near tears.

Just then, CiCi's mother spotted them from across the street and called out to them. "Why don't you three come by for some cookies? I just made a fresh batch of oatmeal, CiCi's favorite." The three kids looked at each other nervously.

"What's wrong? You never hesitate when it comes to cookies," CiCi's mom was looking at them suspiciously.

"Sure, mom, cookies sound great." They crossed the street to join her and began walking toward the small house tucked back from the street. When she stopped to talk with a friend, John, Maisie, and CiCi huddled together.

"Are we really just going to hide that thing and hope nothing else happens to us?" CiCi asked. Her voice was shaky and she'd wrapped her arms around her stomach again.

John looked nervously up the street at CiCi's mother. "I don't know what happened. Did you guys hear that—"

"Stop," said Maisie. John and CiCi looked at her curiously. "Let's just not talk about it right now. If anyone is ever going to believe us, we have to be sure they can't accuse us of making up a story. Let's wait until we get to CiCi's house and we'll each write down what we heard and what we saw. Then we can compare and see if we all saw the same thing."

"I don't want to think about it anymore!" cried CiCi. "Ever again."

"Just this one thing, CiCi. Then we don't have to talk about it anymore, I promise." Maisie squeezed her arm. CiCi, resigned, just nodded.

CiCi's mom let them into the house and served them milk and cookies. None of them wanted to eat, but they forced down some cookies.

"You guys are awfully quiet. What's going on?" None of them answered and just before the silence got really awkward, CiCi said,

"Just tired, I guess. We were in the woods exploring for a while." The phone rang then, and her mother went to answer it, saving her from saying any more. Just a minute later, they headed to CiCi's room.

John passed out three pieces of notebook paper and three pencils. Without saying a word, they started writing. When they'd all finished, they compared notes and found they'd all seen and heard the same thing. They'd heard the bell ringing, then pounding footsteps. Once the noise had stopped, they'd also heard a moaning sound, coming from all around the cave. Finally, they'd all seen the broken bell, the gashes in the stone around the entrance, and the mess of sticks and leaves. And they knew they'd all heard that scream.

"Okay then," said Maisie, taking a deep breath. "That settles it. We all experienced the same thing. I don't understand it."

"I don't think we should try to figure it out. You need to get rid of the book. I'm done talking about it." CiCi stood up. "I'm going to do my chores now."

"CiCi, wait."

"No, Maisie. I'm done. I don't know how I'll ever sleep again, but I definitely don't want to talk about it anymore." She walked out of the room.

John looked at Maisie. "What are you going to do?"

"I don't know."

Two days later, CiCi met Maisie and John at the school steps. "Did you get rid of it?" she asked Maisie.

"Not yet. I haven't had a chance to get away. Yesterday was a bad day with my dad."

"I've been thinking about it. And as much as I hate the idea of thinking about it anymore, I think we need to finish reading the book," said CiCi.

"What?" John yelled so loud that a couple of kids standing

nearby stopped talking and looked at them. "Sorry. But what? You said you never wanted to see it again!"

"I know. But if the book really is … predicting what's going to happen or what's already happened to Maisie, shouldn't we know about it? Isn't it better to know?"

"I don't know," said Maisie. "That makes me really nervous."

"We'll read it together," said CiCi. "Then at least we'll know. Let's meet at my house after school."

CHAPTER TWENTY-TWO

Lara

"Okay? Then what happened?" Lara asked. Lara felt like she'd been holding her breath throughout Maisie's whole story.

"I don't think I can finish right now, Lara. I need to lie down."

Lara bit back what probably would have been a not-so-patient reply, realizing that Maisie looked exhausted. She had a hundred questions, but decided to let it go for now.

"Okay, I understand. I'm going to go out today and see if I can find anything out.'

"What are you looking for, Lolly? What do you want to find?"

There was so much she could say to her aunt. She could say that she wasn't sure what she wanted to find. If Violet was real and it was possible that all of these things had really happened to her, then Lara couldn't ignore the fact that the *magic* was real. But was it good? Evil? If it was real, she was in over her head. But if Violet wasn't real and this all really was just a story, then what did it mean for Lara and the things that had been happening to her? Was she really losing her mind? So, no. She really couldn't define what she wanted to find.

"I don't really know." She stood up and kissed Maisie's cheek. "Is it okay with you if I stay another night? I have a feeling I'm going to need more time than I think for research."

"Of course, dear."

Lara went up to Maisie's guest room and got dressed and ready to go out. She thought she should probably finish reading the book, if only to know what was in store for her, because by now she had no doubt that the rest of the book would be totally different from what she'd read the first time. And judging from all she'd learned from Maisie, it was only going to get worse.

But there would be time for reading when she returned home. She needed to take advantage of the time she had left in Grafton. She decided to start at the Jerseyville Public Library. She needed to track down the Marsh family, if they'd existed, and try to verify whether or not Violet had been a real person.

After she was done putting on makeup and wrangling her hair into a bun, Lara called her mother-in-law and asked if Tessa could stay with them one more night.

"Hi, Lynn."

"Hi, honey. How are you?" Lara unexpectedly felt her throat tighten up at the sound of Lynn's soft voice.

"How's Tessa?"

Lynn gave her the full rundown of everything they'd done, everything Tessa had eaten, and when she'd slept.

When she was done, she said, "How are *you*, Lara?"

"I'm okay." *Might as well address the elephant in the room.* "I'm ... Look, I know Alex told you what's been going on. I'm not crazy, Lynn."

"Honey, no one is saying you are. It's just ..."

Lara didn't want to hear any more about how concerned they all were about her, so she cut her off. "I know. I know how it all sounds. But I'm okay. Even if it turns out to be total bullshit." Lara laughed. "At least I tried, right? At least I did *something.*"

"I understand that." Lynn paused. "Did I ever tell you that after my mama died, I dreamed about her every single Thursday night?"

"No, I don't think you ever told me that."

"She died when Alex was just a baby and I was in the thick of raising all those kids and it was so hard. I relied on my mama to tell me what to do when one of them was teething or wouldn't sleep or James and I were fighting. So when she died, it felt like my whole world was going to fall right apart." She was quiet for a moment.

"It was always the same dream. We'd be sitting on the porch

swing of the house I grew up in. We never said anything at all, we just sat there, swinging. It was the most wonderful gift, just having her there with me. I don't know why it was every Thursday and I don't know whether or not it was just my subconscious trying to make me feel better, but it went on for years, until all of my babies were grown.

The last time I dreamed of her, she spoke to me. She said, 'Lynn, honey, you did a great job and I love you. You're gonna go on and have a bunch of grandbabies now. I'm proud of you.' Then she hugged me and I smelled her perfume and I woke up. The next day Alex's brother called to tell me he and his wife were expecting a baby. My first grandbaby."

"Wow."

"Yes. I know strange things happen and sometimes it's just what we need. I also know my son and I know he's not going to accept any of this easily. But I also know he loves you. He's just worried."

"I know. I'm being careful."

"Okay. And Lara, honey?"

"Yeah?"

"I'm not going to pressure you into telling me about everything that's happening to you, but we know how difficult the past year has been for you and we wish there was more we could do. If there's anything you need, all you have to do is ask. We love you, you know that, right?"

Lara felt tears welling up in her eyes at the kindness in her voice. "Thanks, Lynn. I love you guys, too."

Lara hung up, stunned at the unexpected turn that conversation had taken. She wiped tears off her cheeks, threw her phone in her purse, and headed downstairs.

Lara hugged Maisie as she walked toward the front door.

"I really wish you'd just let it go."

"I know you do. But I'm sorry, I can't."

"You don't have to be sorry. I just can't bear the thought of anything happening to you." Maisie looked down at her hands. "I miss Ben, too, you know."

"I know that. I'm sorry I've put you in a position where you have to relive all of this."

"I should have taken care of it long ago."

"Will you ever tell me what happened in the end? Maybe if it's scary enough you'll talk me into destroying the book." Lara smiled at her.

Maisie looked at her for a long moment. It seemed she was about to start talking. But she just shook her head, one small, quick shake. "Maybe," she said eventually. "But I don't think you'd change your mind even if I did. And I'd rather not relive it if I don't have to."

"My god. That bad, huh?" As the words came out of her mouth, Lara realized that perhaps she should take her aunt's warning more seriously. But just as soon as the thought appeared, it was gone. Lara had a singular focus now and it was figuring out what this book was. And how it might lead her to Ben.

Lara drove to the library in Jerseyville, hoping she wouldn't run into anyone she knew. She approached the library's front desk. A young man was standing behind the desk, probably college-aged, handsome, with a shaved head and short beard. He wore stylish black-framed glasses and was wearing a well-ironed plaid button-down shirt that was open in the front, showcasing a gray T-shirt that read: "Don't let the muggles get you down." Lara smiled, appreciating the Harry Potter reference.

"Hi. I was wondering if you could tell me where to look if I wanted to find out about the families that lived in Grafton in the nineteenth century."

"Sure! You'll want to start in our genealogy room. It can be a bit overwhelming, so go ahead and take a look and come back out to get me if you need help." He looked around conspiratorially and, not seeing anyone, stage-whispered, "I'm not supposed to spend too much time back there, I'm supposed to help man the front desk, but between you and me, I am bored. To. Death. Today. So *please* come and get me. My name is David."

Lara laughed and assured him she had no idea what she was doing so she'd most definitely need him. She followed his directions back to the far wall, walking through the door marked, Genealogy Room. A small hand-written sign taped beneath it read: "PLEASE no food or drink."

Lara spent a couple of minutes walking around the room, inspecting the shelves that lined the walls. She spied old landowner records, census records, tax ledgers, blueprints, and books that were yellowed and looked like they'd been printed a million years ago. She quickly realized that David needn't have worried. She really did not have any idea where to start.

She walked back out to the main room. David saw her coming and turned to the older woman next to him, and said, "Alice, I have to go help in the genealogy room. I'll be back."

As it turned out, David was an historical linguist, working on his PhD in history from University of Missouri St. Louis. He was back in town for the semester to work on his thesis, about how family names change over time. She couldn't have asked for anyone better to help her.

He clearly knew the genealogy room well. Lara told him that she wanted to find out whether or not Violet was a real person and, if so, what happened to her. She told him about the Marsh family, including Henry's death, their ship building business, and that they'd lived in a house in Grafton. Once she explained what she needed to find, he moved expertly between stacks, pulling down books and binders and ledgers one after another.

He paged through them, seeming to know exactly what he was looking for. Lara felt a little helpless so she began paging through random binders, scanning names and birth and death dates. One thing that stuck out immediately was how young everyone died back then. They were lucky if they got thirty-five years.

It was only a matter of minutes before David exclaimed, "Jackpot!" and pushed a photocopied page toward Lara.

It was a census record for Violet's family. There was her father, Walter, and her mother, Louise, along with Violet and Henry.

As she stared at the page, Lara couldn't decide whether she was terrified or relieved to discover that Violet Marsh had been a real person. Violet had existed. Lara's stomach tightened. If there had been no record of her, Lara wouldn't have had anywhere to go from there. She would have been able to stop. The decision would have been made for her. Now, she had to consider what she already knew in the back of her mind. This was all real. Everything that had happened to Violet and everything that had happened to her.

Lara sat back in her seat and felt her stomach clench. She felt like she might be sick. What did this mean? *Well at least I know it's not in my head,* she thought. Followed very closely by, *Am I getting closer to Ben?* As her thoughts churned, she realized David was talking.

"You're lucky," David was saying. Lara shook her head slightly to clear the roaring in her ears and focused on him.

"Sorry, what?"

"I said, you're lucky. The first census in the U.S. was taken in 1880, so this is the first census record ever taken and your girl is here."

Lara nodded. "Yeah. Lucky."

"Are you okay?"

"Sorry. Yes, thank you so much for finding this, it helps a lot."

David looked at his watch and poked his head out the door briefly. "There's still no one out there. Alice is fine. Let's see what else we can find."

David pulled some books about the history of Grafton and the surrounding areas. He told Lara chances were slim they'd find anything in these, but if the Marsh family business was as big as she said, there might be something. He instructed her to search the indexes for Violet's name.

"While you do that, I'm going to search for death records. Well not actual death records. Unfortunately those weren't widely kept until early in the twentieth century, but you can almost always rely on newspaper announcements. I'll be over here on the microfiche machine."

Lara nodded and kept paging through the books. They passed about ten minutes in companionable silence and Lara let her mind focus on the task at hand so she wouldn't start freaking out.

In the end, they got lucky again.

David found death announcements for Violet's whole family; Henry in 1887, her mother *and* father in 1889. But nothing of Violet. *Her whole family was torn apart in just three years,* Lara thought. *Whatever happened to Violet, clearly her parents didn't survive it.*

Lara thought it was odd that Violet's parents seem to have died so closely following the events in the book, but she hadn't mentioned it in her book.

In one book, published in 1950 about the history of Grafton and its early settlers, Lara found a letter from Violet Marsh to a friend who had moved to New York. It was dated a little more than a year after Henry's death. Most of the letter was mundane and talked about Violet's day-to-day life and gave no indication of whether or not she was being haunted by a damn book. But she did mention a new project she was undertaking.

I've found something to occupy a bit of my time. I've been doing some writing and, you might think me crazy as a loon, but I've been delving into the history of this place. Did you know that witches claim to have lived here for a whole century before Grafton was settled? Imagine the magic they could weave!

Violet's letter then quickly changed subjects and that was the only time she referenced anything unusual going on in her life.

After more than an hour, Lara stretched and told David she didn't want to take up any more of his time and thanked and profusely for his help.

"Please, this is the most actual work I've had to do in weeks. Nothing ever happens here. It was fun!"

They walked back toward the front desk. Lara asked him what had brought him to Jerseyville.

"I grew up in Alton," he said. "I got my undergrad at U of I and moved to St. Louis to get my PhD. I moved back home for a semester so I could work here and finish research for my thesis. Being closer makes the research easier, but I am ready to move back to St. Louis. My boyfriend is there and let's just say the night life in Jerseyville is less than exciting."

Lara laughed. "I know, I grew up here. The only thing we had to do back then was steal a six-pack from our parents and drive around on the back roads." She shuddered. "I really hope kids aren't still doing that. So stupid."

"I wouldn't know, I spend most of my time here and usually go back to St. Louis on the weekends. But now I know I should stay off the back roads." He paused. "Do you mind me asking why you're interested in the Marsh family?"

Lara hesitated. She didn't know what to say. She definitely didn't want David to think she was insane, but she had a sneaking suspicion that he'd probably believe her. She decided to give him just a piece of her story.

"I found this old book in a store in Grafton, apparently written by Violet. It's really interesting and has … had an impact on me. But I haven't been able to find any other copies of the book or any evidence of who published it. I just wanted to find out more about who she was."

"Hmm. That's interesting," he said. "Well, now I'm intrigued. I'll keep digging when it gets slow here and I'll try to find out more about what happened to her and her family."

"Oh, you're so busy, please don't take a lot of time out to do this for me. I know it's a lot of work."

"Please. Look around. There isn't exactly a line of people waiting for my help." He smiled at her.

"I'd love to pay you for your time."

"No, no. I'm actually interested in learning more about the Marsh family anyway. I'm kind of surprised I haven't heard about them before. Trust me, it will give me an excuse to look like I'm working really hard. Why don't you give me your number and I'll let you know what I find out?"

"Well I definitely appreciate it," Lara said, taking a stubby library pencil and piece of scrap paper from a container on the counter. She wrote down her number.

Thanking David again, Lara left the library, squinting in the sunlight. She ate a quick lunch and headed back to Grafton.

As she'd left the library David had suggested she visit Mystic Rivers, a shop in downtown Grafton.

"It's advertised as a 'spiritual and metaphysical' gift store. She sells crystals, tarot cards, candles, incense, all of that stuff. You know, for wannabe witches."

He said the store owner, Amabel, knew as much as anyone about the history of Grafton. Lara knew vaguely of Amabel and her shop, but she was a bit of an enigma in town. She kept herself to herself, as Maisie liked to say, and no one was really sure how she spent her time when she wasn't in her shop. Even Maisie, who was friends with everyone, had very little to say about the woman and had once even told Lara, "That woman and her store don't belong here."

Lara didn't love the idea of talking to this Amabel woman before she told Maisie everything, but she was determined to track down any lead that came her way, so she wasn't going to wait now.

Lara again drove down the main street of Grafton and quickly found a parking spot. She walked up to Amabel's store. Most of the stores in Grafton were old houses and the owners didn't seem to do much to commercialize them. Mystic Rivers was a small, one-story building that had clearly once been a small house. Narrow but long, it was painted yellow with white shutters and had a porch that wrapped from the front of the house around the side.

Lara pushed through a small gate that ran the length of the front yard and over the sidewalk and climbed two steps to the porch. The porch was covered in hand-carved wooden totems, dream catchers made out of bent twigs and branches, dried branches, and more detritus whose purpose wasn't clear to Lara. A wind chime tinkled when she opened the door.

The store was narrow but ran almost the full length of the house. It smelled strongly of incense and the shelves that lined the walls and tables in the middle of the room were piled high with a mishmash of items. Lara saw books, candles, arrowheads, precious stones, small Indian totems, jars of incense, all manner of silver, turquoise, and beaded jewelry, tarot cards, dream catchers, artwork, scarves, candles, and more.

A woman stood behind the counter. She was the kind of woman who was obviously no longer young, but you couldn't be sure just how old she was, either. Her gray hair was pulled into a loose bun at the nape of her neck. She wore a long, flowing black dress, with a colorful scarf wrapped around her neck. Rings adorned almost every finger and the bracelets on her wrist clinked together every time she moved. Large, beautiful turquoise earrings hung from her ears. The woman smiled warmly at Lara as she walked toward her.

"Hello, dear. How can I help you?" Her voice was raspy and soft.

"Amabel?" When the woman nodded, Lara went on. "David from the library in Jerseyville said you might be able to help me. I don't …" but that was as far as she got. She didn't quite know what to say. How could she explain all of this? If Amabel had no idea what she was talking about she would think Lara was out of her mind.

"I'd be happy to offer whatever assistance I can. Just ask," she said softly. Her quiet voice belied her intense gaze. She was looking at Lara, eyes wide, her body stiff.

Lara reached into her bag and pulled out the picture of the book. Amabel's eyes widened as she looked at the picture.

"I have this book. And I think it might be tied to something … well, I don't really know. But some odd things have started happening to me—"

"What do you mean?" Amabel cut her off.

"Well, in the book, this woman—"

Amabel cut her off again. "What do you mean things have been happening to you?"

"I'm not sure how to explain it. It's just been …" Lara struggled for the right word. She didn't want to give away too much to this woman. "Unsettling."

"How did you get it?" the woman demanded.

"Do you know something about it?"

The woman looked toward the door. A family of four had walked in, mom, dad, and two teenage kids who looked less than ecstatic about being dragged around antique shops.

Glancing once more at the picture in Lara's hand, Amabel seemed to struggle to tear her eyes away from it. Eventually, she smiled thinly at the family. "Can I help you find anything?"

The dad said they were just looking, but the mom said she'd always been curious about how tarot cards worked. Lara saw one of the kids, a girl wearing Ugg boots and a puffy vest, iPhone clutched in her hand, roll her eyes at her younger brother.

Amabel stood up and began heading around the desk. She briefly turned her attention back to Lara. "I will be back in a moment. Please wait here."

She walked over to where the mother was holding a pack of tarot cards and began explaining their history and how they'd been used since the eighteenth century for divination. In spite of themselves, the teens began listening and Lara smiled when she saw them inch closer to Amabel. Her soft voice was melodic and she was a great storyteller.

"Everyone around here knows the history of the Illini tribe of Native Americans. But one thing a lot of people don't know about this area is that witches lived here alongside the Native Americans before the settlers came."

Amabel picked up an arrowhead and told them a story about the arrowheads, how the natives used them for hunting, fishing, and fighting. She told a wild tale about them fighting the settlers and how during one particular battle, a coven of witches helped entrance the white men, commanding them all to walk into the river. The family was hanging on her every word. By the end of her tale, their hands were full of items. She sold them a pack of tarot cards, three arrowheads, and a dreamcatcher.

As Amabel rang up their purchases, Lara roamed around the store, touching objects, admiring the art and jewelry. When the family finally left, Lara returned to the desk where Amabel had perched on a stool and was clearing away some paperwork so the countertop was clear. "Please tell me how you came upon this book," she said.

Lara told her the story, about Ben and finding the book in John's shop and how she'd loved it the first time she read it. Then she told her what had happened when she began reading it the second time and how it had been different. She almost told her Maisie's story, but for some reason held back. She was laying everything else out to this woman she didn't know, but she knew how difficult it had been for Maisie to tell her what happened all those years ago. She didn't want to break her trust. Not to this woman whom she suspected Maisie didn't care for.

Lara also stopped short of telling Amabel that she didn't want to get rid of the book. She hoped she wouldn't ask why she hadn't done so yet.

Amabel was silent for a moment after Lara had finished talking. When she spoke, she placed her hand lightly on the picture. She looked into Lara's eyes. "We aren't meant to engage the dead."

"Well, I don't—I mean, that's not really—" Lara stuttered, not sure what to say. She agreed, in theory. But when it came to her own brother, well …

"I said we aren't *meant* to do so. That doesn't mean we don't *want* to. Losing a loved one can make us desperate, make us obsessed with what happens after we die. It's a question that all peoples, in all lands, have grappled with since the beginning of time. Right along with, 'Why are we here?'" She sighed, taking her hand off the picture and absentmindedly wiping it on her scarf as though it were dirty.

"How do you know about this book? It's been lost for years, as far as I know."

"I don't know much. I've heard rumors. There were stories about Native Americans and witches, who, centuries ago had attempted to … to … connect with the dead. However, no one thought it was real. Over time, the stories died into just whispers. But …" Her voice trailed off, but her eyes were back on the picture. *She looks … hungry*, Lara thought.

"So what should I do? Should I—should I destroy it?" Suddenly, Lara was glad she hadn't brought the book with her on this trip. *She'd take it from me*. Lara wasn't sure where that thought had come from but it felt true.

"I'm not sure if I can help. You heard the story I told that family, yes?"

Lara nodded.

"I embellished, of course," Amabel smiled. "I do love a good story. But, as with all stories, there was some truth within it. There was a small group of witches"—Amabel didn't even stumble on the word—"that did move to this area in the early eighteenth century, not long after the witch trials in the east. For a hundred years they did live here peacefully, alongside the Native Americans who lived here. There were some instances in which they did intermarry and share their ancient knowledge. But when it came to our magic, each had their own knowledge and rituals and did not want to get involved with the witches, so it wasn't common."

Lara shuddered as she listened, both amazed and frightened by how similar Amabel's story sounded to what the witch told Violet in the book.

"When the area was settled in the early nineteenth century, the Native Americans were, unfairly, of course, moved off the land. A handful of the witches moved along with them, and some simply faded into the community here, remaining silent about their power. My family was one of those that moved. My ancestors settled in a town near a reservation in Oklahoma, which is where I was born."

Amabel was staring over Lara's shoulder, her mind clearly looking back into the past. Lara remained quiet, wanting her to continue.

"One of my cousins, who had lived in this area his whole life came to visit many years ago and I became interested in our family's history. So I returned here as a young woman. I didn't intend to stay, but I met my husband and, as they say, the rest is history." She shrugged, but still didn't meet Lara's eye.

"Much of my family's history has been lost as we've scattered all over the country. But I have some old letters and documents that have been passed down by the women in my family. I haven't looked at them in years. I can't recall if there is any information that might be helpful to you, but I will find them. Perhaps they will help."

"Can I leave you my contact information? Would you be willing to keep me updated with what you find out?" Lara asked.

"You don't have the book here." It was a statement, not a question.

"No." Lara again suspected that there was something—perhaps many somethings—that Amabel wasn't telling her.

"Yes. Well. Can you come back tomorrow?" Lara agreed to come back before she left town in the morning.

Amabel nodded. "My people—witches—were good and peaceful people," she said. "But there is also dark magic in our history. If the rumors about that book are true, I must caution you again against keeping it." She held up her hand when Lara started to interrupt. "I can see my words fall on deaf ears. So allow me to suggest one thing. Do not keep it on your person. Not in a purse or a pocket. Keep it away from your family. Lock it away. Okay?"

Lara felt chilled by her words. "Okay," she said quietly.

Lara left the store then, her mind reeling with everything she'd learned. Violet was a real person. The things that had been happening to her, Lara—and the things that had happened to Maisie and John and CiCi—were real. This was all real. She wanted to know what it all meant. She wanted to know what it could do. She wouldn't stop until she had answers. But she had a sinking suspicion that she was in over her head. Way over her head.

Amabel

"Those bitches," Amabel muttered.

When Lara walked out of the store, Amabel sat heavily on the stool behind the front desk. Her hands were shaking and her heart was pounding. She took deep breaths. Amabel didn't know where to start. Her thoughts were a jumble and she couldn't sort them.

That was the same woman she'd seen on the street that morning all those months ago when she'd been woken by the strange energy. It was the same woman the coven in St. Louis was supposed to have been keeping tabs on. She'd just walked into her store and asked about the book. Why hadn't the other witches warned her? Had they stopped following her? Did they know she'd come here?

Amabel hadn't heard from the coven witches so she'd assumed nothing had ever come from it. But now she knew they had either not been keeping good tabs on Lara or they were keeping information from Amabel.

The woman had the book and it was real and it was clearly powerful if it was manifesting things in her life. It was real. She'd been right. All of the speculation, all of the research, all of the time. It was real. She still didn't understand it and she didn't know how the book itself was responsible, but it was real.

Amabel moved to the front of the store, flipping the sign to Closed. She had a lot to do.

CHAPTER TWENTY-THREE

Lara

When Lara returned to Maisie's, she smelled spaghetti sauce as soon as she opened the door. It was Lara's favorite meal and one that Maisie always made when Lara was having a difficult time.

"Maisie? Is that your spaghetti I smell?"

"Yes, dear." Lara heard Maisie call from the kitchen.

Lara set down her bag and took off her coat, draping it over a living room chair. She glanced at her phone, seeing a couple of missed calls and texts from Maryn, but ignoring them. She had to talk to Maisie.

Lara walked into the kitchen where Maisie was standing over the stove, stirring her famous sauce. Lara helped Maisie finish dinner and they ate together in amicable silence, Maisie's big band music playing softly in the background. When they'd cleared the table, Lara poured them each a cup of coffee and they sat at the table together.

"Maisie. Listen. I did some research today and I think I have an idea of where the book came from. I think it's all true, everything that happened to Violet. I think it originated with some kind of magic."

Maisie didn't answer for a long moment. "Over the years I was able to convince myself it wasn't as bad as we'd thought at the time," she said. "We were kids. Time heals a lot and memories fade. Most of the time, I was even able to believe that I didn't believe in ghosts or spirits or whatever. Nothing strange ever happened to me again, so it was easy enough."

Maisie was squeezing her coffee mug, staring into it intently. "I need to tell you the rest of what happened to us back then. I never wanted to think about it again, but I think you need to know." She took a deep breath.

****

Maisie, John, and CiCi sat together on CiCi's bed and opened the book between them. Maisie opened to the last page she'd read, where the knocking seemed to be chasing Violet through the house. Maisie took a deep breath and began to read aloud.

They only made it about halfway through what was left in the book, taking turns reading aloud. Maisie kept pausing to point out the discrepancies in this version to John and CiCi. John, who'd read the book, agreed it was different.

After they'd been reading for more than an hour, CiCi, trembling and scared, closed the book and threw it to the end of the bed.

"I can't read anymore," she said. "I don't want to know what happens. You need to get rid of that thing, Maisie!"

"They talked about the ceremony in the woods," said John quietly.

"What?" asked Maisie.

"You read a part about the ceremony. They said they had to take three of their father's things and put them in a circle. That must be how they got their father's memories back."

"Yeah. The first time. Not this time. This time they just got scared to death!" retorted CiCi.

John didn't respond.

"We're getting rid of it," CiCi said firmly.

"But don't we want to know what's going to happen?" Maisie asked.

"I thought we did. But now I'm not so sure. What if by reading it we're giving it … I don't know … permission or something? To continue?"

"Are we really saying we think a book is haunting me? How is that even possible? I don't even believe in ghosts, let alone haunted books!"

"How else do you explain it?" Cici challenged her.

Maisie didn't have an answer.

"The logical solution is to get rid of it."

"And if the weird stuff doesn't stop?" Maisie retorted.

"Then, well … we'll have to figure something else out."

"Okay. But where do we take it?"

This time, CiCi didn't have a good response.

"I think it needs to go back to the cave," said Maisie.

"No. You're insane if you think I'm going back there."

"Whatever was there sure did seem to want it back. Or something."

"Or something! It wanted to kill us!"

John had remained silent throughout their exchange, looking down at the book and turning it over in his hands.

The more Maisie thought about it, the more sure she was that the book needed to be returned to where they'd found it. "I'm taking it back. I understand if you don't want to go with me. That's okay."

Without saying a word, CiCi got up and stormed out of her room. Assuming CiCi was angry with her, Maisie began gathering her things to leave. To her surprise, CiCi walked back in a few moments later, carrying her bag. "Of course I'm not going to let you go by yourself. But I'm not happy about it. John, are you okay with this?"

"Yeah, John, let's go. Safety in numbers, right?" Maisie gave a weak laugh. "Even though it didn't seem to help last time."

John said, "Let's go." He looked pale and unsure.

"We're going to run in, leave it, and run out, okay?" Maisie tried to reassure him.

"Okay."

They went to John's and waited while he packed his bag, this time grabbing his BB gun and some BBs. When Maisie looked at the gun skeptically, John muttered, "Just makes me feel better, okay?"

They made their way through the woods and to the edge of Sutter's Acres. All of them moved slowly, as if by unspoken agreement they would try to put off the inevitable for as long as they could. But eventually they reached the cave and stood outside of the opening, huddled together. They peered in as far as the light reached and listened intently.

"Well. No screaming. No footsteps. I guess that's a good sign," said John.

"Look, guys. I'll take it in there by myself. I got us into this mess," said Maisie, taking a deep breath and standing up tall.

Shocking all of them, it was CiCi who said no. "We all found it. Safety in numbers, right?"

Holding their flashlights in front of them, arms linked, they stepped into the cave.

They were halfway in when all of their lights died. They had just turned the bend, so light from the cave's opening was dim at best. They froze on the spot and didn't make any noise. They couldn't hear anything.

"What should we do?" Maisie breathed in barely a whisper. "Are the lights totally out?"

John flicked the on/off button on his light several times but had no success. "Mine's out." CiCi and Maisie tested theirs with no better results.

Maisie heard CiCi rustling around in her pack. "I grabbed this just in case," CiCi said. Maisie heard the flick of a match and a candle flared into life. CiCi cupped her hand around it and whispered, "Let's move fast. I don't know how long this will last. It's just one of my mother's table candles."

The trio began moving again, taking less care about where they stepped, focusing more on moving forward. Maisie let John's arm go, intending to get the book out of her bag so she could drop it and go. She moved items aside, her fingers closing on the book. She tucked it under her arm as she closed her bag and put it back on her shoulder. It was then she realized she could no longer hear the sound of John and CiCi's footsteps.

"Guys?" she whispered. They didn't respond. "Where did you go?" Nothing.

Heart pounding, Maisie turned around in a circle but couldn't see the light of the candle or the light to the entrance of the cave. Where had they gone? They had just been right beside her. She didn't know what to do. She wasn't even sure which way was forward.

Suddenly, from far ahead, what must have been nearly to the end of the cave, she heard CiCi scream. "Maisie! Maisie!"

"CiCi!" Maisie was frozen to the spot. There was literally nothing for her to do because she couldn't see. She moved tentatively in the direction of CiCi's scream, but her foot immediately ran into something solid. She threw her hands in front of her and felt the stone wall of the cave. She turned slightly to her right, reaching out again and feeling solid wall. She turned slowly in a circle, hands outstretched, reaching out again and again but feeling nothing but wall all around her. She was enclosed in a space just big enough for her body. But there was no room like this in the cave, they'd explored all of it. Where the hell was she? She was spinning in circles, beginning to panic.

John and CiCi, their arms still linked, had continued to move down the cave.

"Maisie?" John whispered.

"What?" said CiCi.

"Maisie let go of my arm. Where is she? Maisie?"

John and CiCi called her name, but they didn't hear her respond. CiCi spun around, holding the candle above her head, but they didn't see her, and couldn't see anything beyond the candle's weak flame.

"John, where did she go?" CiCi was holding back a sob.

"I don't know. I don't know." John was paralyzed with fear. How does someone just disappear in the middle of a cave?

Maisie felt her bag ripped off her shoulder. She dropped the book and it landed by her feet. Then she heard it being thrown, over and over, against the wall of rock right by her head. Maisie put her hands over her ears and began to cry. She wasn't touching the book but it was flying around the small space. The book slammed into her back, then her leg. When it slammed into her stomach, she grabbed it quickly and, with a scream, threw it as hard as she could, hoping that it wouldn't bounce off the wall and back into her face.

She heard it land somewhere in the depths of the cave. Air whooshed around her as whatever walls had been closing in on her disappeared. She spun around behind her but didn't see anything.

John and CiCi's arms were wrenched apart as something flew between them. It was a cold, not-quite-solid mass of energy. And suddenly, the cave erupted in noise. They could hear Maisie screaming their names and they yelled back. A wild wind was rushing through the cave, howling and echoing of the walls.

Maisie saw a small light coming toward her and began to make out the outline of her friends. She ran toward them.

"What the hell, Maisie?" John yelled. "Why did you run away from us?"

"I didn't run away!" Maisie said, crying. "All of a sudden you guys were just gone. I was stuck in this super small space, there was stone all around me. I—I ..." She was crying too hard to continue.

"Where's the book?" said CiCi. She looked terrified, trembling in the light of her candle.

"It's gone. Something ripped my backpack off. I think it wanted the book, so I threw it. I don't know where it is."

John took the candle from CiCi, shining it around on the floor of the cave. He spotted Maisie's bag and picked it up by the strap. It was torn, shreds hanging off it. He shone the flashlight on the ground and then rummaged around in the bag, finally declaring, "It's not here."

"Let's get out of here," Maisie said.

"But the book—"

Maisie cut John off. "It's here somewhere and this is where it can stay. We're leaving and we're not coming back."

They left the cave quickly and ran through the woods. They agreed to never talk about it again and never told anyone.

When Maisie finished her story, she looked over Lara's shoulder, looking for all the world like she was there, back in the past.

"We were afraid for our lives. You need to get rid of the damn book, Lara. Burn it. Throw it in the river. Something."

"But aren't you at all curious about what it *is* and what it all means? What if—"

"No, Lara! We can't. Don't you understand what that *thing*—" she spat the word—" is capable of? You need to destroy it like I should have done seventy years ago. If I were younger, I'd demand that you give me the book—hell, I'd fight you for it—but I won't pretend I could win that battle now. You just need to believe me that you *have* to get rid of it."

"Then why didn't you destroy it? If it's so bad, why didn't you go back and find it and make sure it was destroyed?"

Maisie suddenly looked every bit of her eighty-three years— exhausted and beat down and overwhelmed. "I don't have a good answer for you. I was really struggling with what was happening to my father. I was terrified and fascinated all at the same time. But then after what happened in the cave … I thought if the scary stuff stopped after we left it there, then there was no harm in just leaving it there. And it did stop! Nothing like that ever happened to me again." She shook her head. "I was *thirteen!* John and CiCi and I didn't know what to do." She sighed a deep, heavy sigh. "I don't have a good explanation. But I wish more than anything we had destroyed it."

Lara didn't know what to think. There were so many questions swirling around in her head that she couldn't pluck one out to ask.

She wanted all of this craziness to stop. She didn't want to be scared anymore, she didn't want Alex to think he was losing her. She thought she probably should destroy it. But she couldn't stop thinking *what if*. What if she had one more chance to remember her life with Ben? What if what happened to Violet in the book was meant to scare her away from the real power it held?

"Hiding it away didn't work for you. What makes you think it will work now?"

"It *did* work for me," Maisie said insistently. "Nothing ever happened to me again after we left it there in the cave. But because we didn't actually destroy it, it's back."

"What if it's not all bad?"

"Lara, please. Nothing good can come from this."

"Here's what I understand. All of this scary shit feels like it's more about getting our attention and not actually about hurting anyone."

"It felt harmful when I was locked in some stone room that never existed!"

"Maybe. But it didn't hurt you. You flung the book away and it went away. It wants the book. Or the problem *is* the book. I don't know."

"You're being naïve, Lara. Maybe it stopped, but it had the power to *not* stop. Do you understand me? I don't know why it did, but it had the power to hurt me. And if what you think happened to Violet's family is true, then you need to be far more careful than you're being. It keeps coming back. Thinking you can stop it or control it is wishful thinking. It doesn't make sense, Lara."

"I know. Which is why I want to figure it out." Lara bit her lip, not wanting to say this next thing, but knowing she needed to. "Violet got all of her memories of Henry back, Maisie," she said quietly. "I can't forget that."

"What?" Maisie nearly yelled this question, startling Lara.

"The book. Or at least the first time I read it. She gets all of her memories of Henry back. She remembered everything."

"What do you mean? That's ridiculous. This whole thing is ridiculous!" Maisie stood up and began putting away the remains of their dinner, slamming cabinets and throwing dishes into the sink.

Lara began speaking quietly, telling Maisie about the end of *Memoriae*. Well. The first ending.

"Oh, Lara. Listen to yourself. This all sounds impossible. And anyway, how do we know any of this actually happened to Violet?" Maisie looked distraught and overwhelmed.

"It sure feels real when I'm at my house and terrifying stuff starts happening. It sure felt real to you when you were stuck in that cave, you said so yourself. If we acknowledge that this is happening to us, then there's no reason to think it didn't happen to Violet just the way she wrote it. If it's possible for me to get my memories of Ben back, I can't let it go. I can't let that go."

"What do you mean get them back?"

Lara put her head in her hands, upset she had let that slip. She told Maisie how she'd lost her memories of Ben and how it had been eating away at her.

"Oh, Lolly. Honey, they're still there. You don't need to go through all of this!"

"There's something here, Maisie. I'm sorry you don't like it, but there's something going on and it's real. Violet Marsh was a real person. I think everything actually happened to her."

Lara told her what she and David had discovered at the library.

When she was done, she said, "Then David suggested I try to talk to Amabel at that store in town, so I—"

"You talked to her?" Maisie interrupted sharply.

"Yeah … she told me witches are real and that this might be tied back to some ancient—"

Maisie interrupted her yet again. "Listen to yourself, Lara! Damn it!" Maisie stood up quickly, clutching the back of the chair to steady herself. "This is ridiculous," she mumbled, more quietly.

Lara didn't understand Maisie's anger. "I know how it sounds. I can't even imagine what I'm going to tell Alex. But I think there's something here to be discovered. Something that might help us … end whatever this is. I don't know what it is yet. But there's something."

"No. I'm done listening to this, Lara. I've told you I don't want you to keep pursuing this. I don't like it and I think you should stop. It's ridiculous, Lara."

"If it's ridiculous, Maisie, then you're saying none of that stuff that happened to you was real. And I don't think you believe that."

Maisie sat back down in her chair and closed her eyes, rubbing her fingers across her forehead. Eventually, she said, "I love you, but I don't want to have any part of this."

"I understand," Lara said, though she didn't. She was angry. "I'll figure it out. I'll go back and talk to Amabel. Then I'll find out what happened to Violet and prove to you and everyone else that I'm right."

CHAPTER TWENTY-FOUR

Amabel

Amabel only slept for two hours that night. She couldn't stop her thoughts from spinning out of control. She wanted to know where the book was and how Lara was making things happen to her. She wanted to know how much Lara really knew about the book and whether or not she'd figured out a way to use it. She wanted, most of all, to get her hands on it.

When she thought about what she should do next, she couldn't see a clear path. She thought, of course, about using magic to force Lara to tell her where it was. The problem with that plan was that Amabel didn't know how involved, if at all, Maryn and the rest of the coven witches still were. She didn't want to try to stand up to all of them.

In the end, she thought her best bet would be to try to get Lara to trust her, make her think they were in this together. In order to do that, she'd have to give Lara some information, make her think she was going to help.

So Amabel had found the letters and chosen a couple to show Lara. She'd tell her just enough to make Lara think she could be trusted. It was a risk, for sure. Especially considering what the letters contained. But it was clear to Amabel that Lara wanted to keep the book. She didn't want to give it up, likely for the same reasons Amabel wanted to get her hands on it.

Lara

The next morning, Lara packed up her car and told Maisie goodbye. She could tell her aunt was scared. Maisie hugged Lara, clinging to her for a long moment.

"Please, *please* be careful, Lolly. I don't know how to tell you how dangerous I think this is."

"I know." Lara squeezed her tighter, feeling guilty for worrying her aunt so much. "I'm sorry I've brought this all back up for you. But I can't just let it go. I'm sorry."

After leaving Maisie's, Lara headed back to Amabel's store. It was still early, so the store wasn't open yet, but Amabel opened the front door as Lara walked up the porch steps.

"Good morning," Amabel said with a tight smile.

"Morning." Lara wasn't sure how to read Amabel's expression. She looked … angry. But Lara didn't understand why she'd be angry. She found herself thinking she didn't trust this woman, though she couldn't put her finger on why.

The women walked to the front counter and Amabel took her place behind the counter.

"I found the letters. I honestly didn't expect to find anything of importance, but I think you'll be happy to learn that there is a record of sorts of your book."

Lara felt her heart leap at Amabel's words. "Really?"

"Yes." Amabel placed her hand on some papers and looked at Lara. "But I have a confession. I wasn't totally honest with you yesterday. I've argued with myself all night. My original plan was to tell you that I couldn't find the letters when you arrived this morning."

Lara had known Amabel knew more than she'd let on. She stayed quiet, letting Amabel take her time.

"As you know, the world has moved on. Technology has replaced religion and we only believe what we can see, what we can understand, what we can put our hands on. Our ancestors may not have had electricity or understood how diseases are transmitted or even known that the earth is round, but they did know how to strike a balance between the physical world we live in and that of the world we can't see. So those of us who still believe hesitate to share that information."

Amabel made sure Lara was looking her in the eye. "It is real, Lara. All of it. What happened to Violet and what's happening to you."

Lara's heart started hammering in her chest and goosebumps raised along her arms. Wanting Amabel to continue talking, Lara said nothing.

"I know what you must be thinking. Witches aren't real, magic doesn't exist. As humans have moved on and science explains and understands more and more about the world, no one has ever been able to explain or understand witchcraft or the afterlife or any of that so they've decided it simply doesn't exist. But it does.

"We're not talking about Harry Potter. But it does exist. Our power, such as it is, has become … watered down over the years, I suppose you could say. We're not flying on broomsticks or putting curses on our enemies. Modern witchcraft is spiritual, like a religion. For the most part."

Lara had no idea what to say. Did she really think this was possible? Three months ago, she would have said absolutely not. But was it really that crazy? Like she'd told Maisie, if she denied that it existed, she'd be as good as admitting nothing weird had happened to her.

"What do you mean, *for the most part*," Lara asked.

"What?"

"You said modern witchcraft was spiritual 'for the most part.'"

For the first time, Amabel's cool exterior seemed to falter a bit. Her eyes went wide and then she looked away. She picked and pulled at the end of her scarf. She was quiet for a long moment before she spoke again.

"There are rules among my people about the types of information we can share with outsiders. Modern witchcraft *is* a religion. We strive to connect with Mother Nature. We are feminists. We practice self-love and visualization and use the power of herbs and crystals to better our lives and the lives of others. All of those things sound normal to you, I'm sure."

"Normal enough."

"Right. So that's what we tell people we're all about. And we do practice all of those things. But there is ancient magic also. That I cannot tell you about. Suffice it to say that we don't practice the type of witchcraft Hollywood likes to portray, but we're not altogether powerless, either."

Lara nodded. "So … the book? I imagine that falls into the category of what you can't tell me about?"

Amabel tilted her head back and forth in a maybe/maybe not gesture. Then she looked away, seeming to battle with herself, eventually coming to a conclusion.

"There's always been rumor and speculation about that book. I've never known exactly what it contained or what it looked like. But it was assumed it was an embellished story. The magic it would take to achieve that kind of communication, well …" Amabel's voice trailed off.

"Well, what do you think it is? Is it a spellbook? What are those called? Isn't there a word for it?"

"Yes, I suppose it could be something like that. Without looking at it more closely and bringing it to my sisters, I can't really say for sure."

Lara considered, for a moment, what it would mean to hand the book over. It would mean giving up any chance, small though it might be, of talking to Ben again. Of getting her memories back. She had a suspicion that if she did hand it over, she wouldn't get it back.

Amabel, sensing her hesitation said, "I can tell you don't want to give it up. But I'm not sure how much more I can help without looking at it myself. I did make copies of those letters that contained information I can share with you. There were only a couple."

She slid the papers across the counter and Lara picked them up. They were printer copies of what Lara could tell were very old letters.

"Like I said, my ancestors were among those who moved out of the area, so much of our history was lost during that journey. I did find these letters from an old witch who lived in this area for the entirety of her life. She gave them to me before she died, but she didn't give me any additional information."

Lara began to read the first one.

Dear T,

I'm afraid this letter has been long delayed, as I was unsure what to say or how to explain. Your assumptions and fears were correct. It does exist.

I had long suspected it was possible. And when I met her, there was something ... I cannot explain it. I knew you and the others would never agree so I made a decision. One I may regret for the remainder of my days. That is the extent of the explanation I feel comfortable giving via post, without the benefit of speaking with you in person. Please tell me when we can meet.

With my sincerest apologies,

A

"There's no date on it and we can't be sure they're talking about your book, but I thought it was interesting." Amabel handed Lara another piece of paper. "There's one more that you should see."

Vee –

It's more powerful than we thought. We must rid ourselves of it. I cannot help you as I am under strict orders to bring it directly to my superiors. I think we both know I cannot do that. You know what to do.

A

Lara read the sentences again and looked at Amabel. "So if they're talking about the book, there is a way to destroy it." Lara didn't know if she was relieved or disappointed.

"It seems so."

"Do you know what it is? You said these were the only letters you could share with me."

"These are the only ones I can share."

"Okay. But do the other ones have the answer?" Lara was grateful for Amabel's help and didn't feel comfortable pushing her, but she also wanted the answers and knew, somehow, that Amabel knew much more than what she was sharing.

"I'm honestly not sure. The other documents do contain references to magic, but it's unclear exactly what it is for or whether or not it's the solution you're looking for." Amabel looked at her closely. "Do you really *want* to destroy it?"

"I don't know. Whatever is happening is obviously escalating. I don't want to put myself or my family in danger by keeping it. On the other hand, it's difficult to think about destroying that ... that kind of power."

"Yes, I understand. My people are taught from an early age how to strike that balance between what we want and what is safe. And to determine when it's best to put safety ahead of power."

Lara understood the slight reprimand. Amabel was saying Lara was in over her head. "Can I ask why you can't tell me what's in the other letters?"

Amabel sighed. "Lara, it's 2016. We're centuries out from the witch trials. Even so, it is ingrained in us, either from birth or from the first days our powers manifest themselves, to not speak about our beliefs. Now, that is slowly changing. More and more witches are speaking out about what they're calling 'modern witchcraft,' but they're speaking about it in a way that the rest of the world can accept. Modern witches are feminists, naturalists, spiritualists, yogis."

Amabel laughed quietly. "And most of us *are* all of those things. Those things are safe. It's how little shops like mine can exist without making anyone uncomfortable. But the real stuff? The actual magic? We don't talk about that with anyone who isn't a direct descendant of a known and trusted witch. It's simply the way it is." She looked at Lara and her gaze felt cold. "You wouldn't understand it anyway."

Lara nodded, resigned to the fact that Amabel had given her as much information as she was willing to. "What should I do?"

"If you really won't let me handle it, I really don't know."

Lara sighed. "You've already told me more than I ever could have hoped for. Thank you." Lara wanted to leave. The way Amabel wouldn't take her eyes off her was making her uncomfortable. All the same, Amabel was the only person who'd given her any valuable information at all. She picked up her purse. "Can I, I …" Lara stumbled over her words a bit. "Can I come back if I need to?"

"Of course. Please do," Amabel said, unsmiling. She took a business card from the stack on the desk. "Call me if you change your mind and want me to take a look. And you should give me your number, too. Just in case I come across anything else that might be helpful."

Lara scribbled her number down and left the store.

Lara drove to her in-laws' house from Grafton in complete silence. She never even turned any music on, she was so preoccupied by thoughts of what she was going to do next.

She wasn't sure what her next step was, if there was any step at all. How was she supposed to figure out what to do with the book if none of the people with the information she needed could—or would—help her? And she was sure she couldn't just Google "How to use a spellbook" and find an answer. Not to mention, she was going to have to explain all of this to Alex and he was not going to believe any of it.

And then there was the book itself. Lara felt such contradictory feelings about whether or not she should keep it that she didn't know what to do. On one hand, it felt dangerous. On the other hand, she couldn't possibly destroy it or give it away. Not when she thought there was even the most remote possibility it could lead her to Ben. She'd sacrifice a lot for that. Not Tessa's safety. But she had to admit that she would flirt with her own safety.

She visited with Lynn and James for a while and let Tessa show her the cows and the pigs. As she buckled Tessa into her car seat and turned to tell Lynn thank you, Lynn surprised her by wrapping her in a big hug.

"Are you okay? You know both of you can stay here until Alex gets back."

Lara smiled. "Thank you, but we're okay. I've just got a lot on my mind."

Lynn looked back at her, then down at Tessa. She clearly wanted to ask more but she wouldn't. "We'll take her any time, you know? You too, honey."

"I know. And I love you for it."

On her way home, Lara called Maryn.

"I need to fill you in on what I found out in Grafton. Are you home?"

Maryn told her to come straight to her house.

"What are you going to do?" Maryn asked when Lara finished telling her everything that had happened. She'd stared at Lara intently as she'd told the story, asking almost no questions, just listening.

Lara laughed without smiling. "I have no idea. I don't know where to start."

"Well you've gotta figure out what happens next in the book, right? That has to be the next step."

"Yeah, I guess so. I don't really know if I want to know," Lara admitted. "I'm scared about how bad it's going to be. You should have seen Maisie talking about what happened all of those years ago, Mar. She was still scared, even though she was trying to play it off as no big deal."

"You could give it to Amabel and be done with it."

"Yeah. I could."

"But you won't."

"No. Not until I finish it. I have to know if I can … if it's possible …" She didn't know why she found it so hard to admit that she just wanted to know if she could talk to Ben again. In spite of everything, it still sounded impossible.

"I get it. Okay …" Maryn's voice trailed off. "Lara, I—" She stopped.

"Yeah?"

"Nothing. Never mind. So you need to finish reading the book. Then we need to figure out what we do next."

"Yeah. And I have to figure out what the hell to tell my husband."

"I don't envy you that job," Maryn said with a small smile.

When Lara got home, she and Tessa ate a quick dinner and then went to the park. Lara found herself wanting to keep Tessa out of the house as much as she could. As long as that book was there, she didn't feel entirely safe.

Then why the fuck aren't you getting rid of it?

Lara had been having the same argument with herself since she'd left Grafton. She couldn't deny something beyond what she thought of as the real world was happening here. There was no ignoring it. But she still couldn't totally believe it. So, did she believe or didn't she? And if she believed, why would she put her family in danger? *Because Ben.*

It always came back to Ben and the big what if.

When Alex called them that night, he talked to Tessa for a minute before she ran off to play. When Lara picked up the phone and looked at his face, she nearly started crying. She so badly wanted his advice, but she didn't know how he'd react to everything she'd found out in Grafton. She didn't bring it up and was hoping he wouldn't ask, because she didn't yet know what to say. But of course, he eventually asked her how her visit had gone.

"It was fine. Interesting. It turns out that Maisie actually found this book a long time ago, way back in 1946."

"Wait. Seriously?"

"Yeah. Kind of crazy, huh? Some pretty scary things happened to her, too."

Alex was silent for a long moment before he said, "Maisie doesn't believe in that shit."

"I know. That's what I thought, too. She didn't want to tell me at first, but she finally admitted that she found the book when she was thirteen." Lara told him an abbreviated version of Maisie's story. She left out Amabel and everything she'd told her. Witchcraft might push him over the edge.

"This is …," is all he said when she'd finished. "I don't even know what to say, Lara."

"Just don't say anything. I don't have it in me to fight about it."

"What are you going to do?"

"I'm not sure." Did he believe her now? Lara held her breath, wondering what he'd say next. She looked at his face in her phone screen, the face she loved so much, and she felt desperate to hear him say, *I believe you.*

"I want you to get rid of it. Right now. I think it's just a book, but clearly you've created this story around it and for whatever reason, Maisie has decided that after eighty-three years she suddenly believes in ghosts or something. I don't know what's going on, but I think if it's gone we can just get past this."

Lara closed her eyes and felt the fight drain out of her. She didn't even want to argue. "Maybe you're right. I don't know."

"I think you'll feel better if you just get rid of it."

"I'll think about it." She changed the subject quickly, asking him how work was going. She forced herself to be cheerful and normal. She didn't want to talk about it with him anymore. Alex said he'd be gone a while longer, maybe four more days.

Before they got off the phone, she told him she loved him and she couldn't wait to see him. She did miss him. But she was glad she had another few days to try to get some answers.

Maryn

Maryn had felt like a caged animal while Lara was in Grafton. Lara hadn't called her, hadn't texted. She'd wanted Lara to go, to try to figure things out. But what if Amabel did something terrible to her? What if she convinced her to hand the book over?

Maryn's thoughts swirled. *Damn it, I should have gone with her! I should have told Clara! I should never have gotten involved in any of this!*

She was near tears. She didn't know what to do. Then the phone rang and Lara showed up at her house, and told her what had happened. When Lara and Tessa left she was *enraged.*

To keep her hands busy, Maryn picked up the snack Tessa had eaten. If she didn't keep herself moving she was afraid her rage would boil over and she'd do something she'd regret.

Amabel had armed Lara with enough information that she was going to inch closer to the truth and *still* Maryn wasn't supposed to tell her. She found herself wishing her power was time travel so she could go back and change her mind.

She picked up her phone and texted Clara. "Meet me at my house in 20 minutes or I'm telling Lara everything. She went to Grafton. She talked to Amabel."

Maryn watched the three little dots blink on her screen until Clara's reply came through. "Give me 30."

As Maryn waited for Clara, she tried to gather her thoughts so she wouldn't just speak out of anger. She wanted Clara to hear her, not put her off like she'd been doing.

The doorbell rang and Maryn opened the door. Clara at least had the grace to look ashamed and nervous.

"How are you, Maryn?"

"Not great, Clara."

Clara sighed. "I'm sorry. I know this has been difficult."

"No, I really don't think you know *how* difficult it's been. Lara has become one of my closest friends and you're asking me to keep lying to her. Which is so stupid."

Clara nodded. "I know. Can I come in?"

Maryn stepped back and they walked back to the kitchen.

"Do you want some coffee?" Maryn asked.

Clara said yes and sat at the small table in Maryn's breakfast nook.

Maryn poured two cups of coffee and joined her.

"Lara knows something is going on. And if it's what you all think it is, she has a right to know about it so we can help her."

Clara was nodding. "I really do understand. It's just that we're still not sure what the book is and until we know we don't know how to proceed. Believe me, we don't want anything terrible to happen to Lara either."

"Amabel told her all about witches! She's got enough information to start to figure shit out, Clara!"

"She what?" Clara's hands stilled with her coffee cup halfway to her mouth.

"Yeah. She told her *all* about witches and showed her some letters." Maryn told Clara everything Lara had told her. She felt like she was betraying her friend's trust—again—but didn't see an alternative. As pissed as she was at Clara, she still trusted her and it had gotten to the point now that Maryn didn't think she had a choice. If she was going to help Lara, she had to have Clara's help.

"Damn it," Clara muttered quietly when Maryn was done.

"Yeah. So now I'm supposed to act surprised by all of this magic shit, like I don't know anything about it? I just keep lying to her, Clara, and I'm done. I. Am. Done."

Clara was looking out the window and didn't say anything.

"Lara is going to read the rest of the book, Clara. I told her to. We need to know what happens. But then what? What if it gets really dangerous? What do we do then?"

Clara's lips drew together in a tight line. "You're right, Maryn. It's time to step in. I can't figure out why Amabel would tell her some of it and not just tell her everything. I don't understand the game she's playing."

"So what do we do?"

"I'm not sure yet. I meant what I said earlier. We don't know enough about this thing to make an informed decision. But Maryn, there is one thing that I think we've all overlooked."

"What's that?"

"Lara has to be a witch."

Maryn sat back in her chair, shocked by Clara's words. "What?"

"Think about it. If the book is what we think it is—"

"Which you still haven't really explained that to me," Maryn cut in.

Clara ignored her question. "Then it's powerful magic that wouldn't just work for everyone. And the book didn't—misbehave—for anyone but Lara and Lara's aunt. John had the book both as a teenager and an adult and nothing ever happened to him. The logical conclusion is that only a witch can manipulate it."

"Then Maisie is a witch, too."

"Perhaps. I mean, I suppose it's possible it would work for anyone, but I doubt it. Not this kind of magic."

Maryn sat quietly for a moment, thinking about the implications. "If Maisie is a witch, she either doesn't know or purposely didn't tell Lara."

Clara nodded.

"Okay," said Maryn. "What do I do?"

"Will Lara give you the book?"

"No. I really don't think she will. I think she wants to know what's happening, but I also think a small part of her doesn't want to get rid of it and miss the chance to communicate with Ben again."

"I know the answer, but I'm going to ask anyway. Can you take it from her?"

"I *could*. It's *possible*. But I won't." Maryn looked down at her coffee. "In the months after Lara and I met, I was able to forget that our whole relationship started out as a lie, because it didn't really matter. Nothing out of the ordinary was happening. I was just her friend. Not a spy. But now ... now I've been flat out lying and keeping things from her for months. I won't steal the book, too."

"I understand. Just know that the longer she has it, the more likely she is to get more deeply involved, to find out more about the book and about us. And we're going to have to come clean."

At her words, the anger flared up in Maryn's chest again. "Oh, believe me, Clara, I know I'm going to have to come clean. We should have done it weeks ago. I'm ready."

"I really am sorry you've been put in this position. I know you didn't want to do this in the first place. But you have to see that it was the right thing. What if all this was happening to Lara and we had no idea? Or had to find a way to get to know her *now*? Now, we know what's going on and we can help her."

Maryn nodded grudgingly. Clara had a point.

"We can't ask Lara to stop and we can't take the book. You're right—she's going to keep investigating, she's probably going to keep reading, so it might get worse before we can step in. Here's what I think we should do. You need to help her, be there for her however she needs you right now.

"I just need a few more days. I need to talk to Amabel and make her tell me what she knows. There's some ulterior motive here. Something she's not telling us. I'm starting to think Lara might discover some information for us and I want her to tell you all about it. In a few days, we'll tell her everything. Together."

Maryn considered her words, trying to decide whether or not Clara was just putting her off again. But she believed her.

"Okay. But Clara, please tell me what you think this thing is."

"I think it's a portal into the other side."

Amabel

Letting Lara walk out that door without demanding access to the book was the single hardest thing Amabel had ever done. Now that she knew she was so close to everything she'd ever wanted, she could practically taste it. But this was a marathon, not a sprint. If she came on too strong, Lara would never trust her and would never let her get close enough to the book.

In a day, maybe two, Amabel would call Lara, claiming she'd stumbled upon something … some source of magic that was somehow tied to the book, blah, blah, blah. She'd make something up that Lara would believe. She'd convince her to bring the book to her and then she'd do what she had to.

Chapter Twenty-Five

Lara

Lara put Tessa to bed and took a shower. She got the book from the garage where she'd been hiding it from herself and climbed into bed. On her drive home today, she'd thought long and hard about everything Amabel had told her. Before Ben died, she would never have considered taking any of this seriously. She would never have believed. But Ben's death had broken something open in her.

Before, she would never have believed that a healthy thirty-four-year-old man could drop dead on his kitchen floor after going for a run. But it had happened. She would never have believed that she could survive it. But she had. She realized now that there was plenty in this world that she *thought* she understood, but the reality was that she understood nothing. So why couldn't witches and magic be real?

It was true, what she'd said to Maryn about being scared to find out what else happened in the book. But now, she at least knew that there was information out there. Lara couldn't see the entire path to figuring out what was happening, but she could, at the very least, see that a path existed. Whatever the rest of the book contained, she wouldn't get any answers until she read it.

Lara knew that this was going to come down to her. Everyone else—Alex, Maisie, Amabel, even Maryn—they would all prefer that she just get rid of the book and be done with it. But she was an adult. What was happening now was impossible, yes, but that didn't mean there was something wrong with her. She didn't need to doubt herself. She had survived the past two years with help from other people, but ultimately because she did the work. She'd pulled herself back from whatever brink she'd been on. She was beginning to understand that she'd survived some of the worst life could offer.

She could handle anything and didn't need to justify her choices to anyone.

The only thing left to do now was read the rest of the book. She was scared, and after Amabel's warning to keep the book far from her family, she felt guilty reading it here in the house. But not guilty enough to stop.

Memoriae

Two weeks later, I woke one morning to a silent house. That in itself was not all that unusual. It was, after all, only the three of us. However, the silence had a heaviness, a complete and total stillness that left me feeling short of breath.

I got out of bed, pulled on my dressing gown, and walked into the hallway. "Mother? Father?" But there was no response.

I made my way slowly to their room. The door was cracked partially open. When I pushed it the rest of the way, my eyes took in the scene all at once and I started screaming.

Mother and Father lay on their backs, side by side. Their hands were folded identically across their chests. They were very clearly dead. Faces blue, eyes open—and mouths wide in screams of terror. Above the bed, written in blood were the words, *Don't. You can't. Don't.*

I do not remember how the next two weeks transpired. Helen, along with Reverend Miller, handled everything for me, asking only my opinion about these flowers or those, this dress or that. My entire family was gone and *alone* was not quite accurate enough to describe my place in the world now. The constable questioned me about the message on the wall, but I had no answers. He eventually assumed that either my mother or father, consumed by grief over the loss of Henry, had taken some kind of poison, writing the message as warning.

I didn't care. My life was over. Whatever evil had been unleashed in this house was out now. I had no doubt that I would be next. But I wasn't going to go down easily.

I needed to find that witch.

She'd said that I would not see her again. I did not know if that meant she would disappear or simply that she would not seek me out. I couldn't ask around town, so I was going to have to try to find her. And she *would* give me answers.

I finally summoned up my courage and headed toward the river one bright morning. I began walking along the bank, heading toward the spot where I had first laid eyes on the witch. As I approached the rock I had first seen her sitting on all of those weeks ago, I could see immediately that she was not there. I headed farther along the river, looking for the copse of trees in which her house had sat.

When I could see the trees up ahead, I slowed and began looking around me. I did not want to be caught unaware. I could see nothing, but every sound made me jump. I heard a twig crack and the wind blowing through the trees sounded like the rustling of clothes. Taking a deep breath, I walked into the woods. I saw the witch's shack there, right where it had been before.

Everything was as it had been before, although it all looked just a little shabbier. The wood pile had tumbled to the ground and the dreamcatcher had fallen onto the porch. No smoke rose from the chimney. I stood still for a moment, looking at the house and wondering if I really wanted to knock on the door. Before I could decide, it slowly swung open.

I could see Amelia's face in the doorway.

"Who's there?" she called.

"I-I …" I was suddenly frightened but let my anger fuel me. I cleared my throat. "It's Violet Marsh."

The woman came out of the house and walked toward me, faster than I thought she would have been able to. She was soon standing right in front of me.

"What are you doing here? I told you I'd given you everything you needed."

"I know what you said, witch. I know what you said, but something is happening. Something went wrong. There is something in my house, it is following me and my parents are *dead.* Do you hear me? They are dead and you will tell me—"

"Did you follow my instructions?"

"Yes, exactly. Except, nothing really happened. There was a terrifying wind and I felt—something. But then nothing happened. Until I came home and—"

She interrupted me again. "Let me see the book."

I shoved it at her. She flipped through the pages, running her fingers over my lines of writing.

"You wrote in it!" She sounded furious.

"Well, I—yes. You told me to write down my memories."

"And only your memories! You've written pages!" She slammed the book shut and held it out to me. I did not take it. I did not want it.

"Take it back. Destroy it. It has already ruined my life. But it definitely did not *work.*"

"Oh, it worked, girl. It most certainly worked." She shoved the book in my hands and I had no choice but to take it. "I told you exactly what to do. You chose to do the one thing I instructed you *not* to do. Now you have to deal with it."

She started to turn away, mumbling, "I knew we should have destroyed it. I knew it was a mistake to hand it down to such an inexperienced—" I couldn't hear her last words as she made her way back toward her house.

"Wait! Do not walk away from me! You have destroyed everything!" I screamed, louder and more forcefully than I've ever screamed in my life.

"It was not me, I can tell you that. Follow me, girl. There is not much I can do to help you, but I can tell you what I should have told you weeks ago."

We entered her home and everything was much the same as it had been before. She sat in the same chair and I sat across from her.

"Do you remember everything I told you, about my people and you being the last in line?"

I nodded, clenching my hands in my lap until my knuckles were white. The rage, as she sat there so calmly, threatened to overwhelm me.

"You being the last in line does not mean that you are the last witch. There are small groups of us here and there. We are working toward a common goal of getting organized and coming together. We feel like it is safe to do so. Quietly, of course. We have created a governing body of sorts." She shook her head.

"I discovered an artifact, long ago. It was a spell, essentially, written ... no, embedded, into a piece of cloth. It was the magic I told you about, the magic born of the partnership long ago of my people—*our* people," she said pointedly. "The magic that opens a door to the dead. To *all* the dead. Good *and* evil."

She said this as though I should understand what she was saying. When I looked blankly at her, she blew out a frustrated breath and muttered, "You really know nothing. It was magic that could open doors to angels, demons, ghosts, anything you can imagine. And it was an *open* door. We could get in, but oh, they could also get out. Oh, don't look at me like that. You don't want to believe in angels and demons, in spite of what you've been through? Do not be dense."

"It was decided that this particular piece of magic, when I discovered it, should be—handled. It could not fall into the hands of just anyone. I wanted to destroy it, but I was forbidden from doing so. They did not want to destroy something so powerful, however, we knew we couldn't let it be widely known that it existed. It had to be hidden."

She shook her head. "The council, in their infinite wisdom, decided to pass it along to someone who would not ask too many questions. Who had no experience. Who could not possibly discover its power. Well, you were all of those things, but clearly the plan didn't work as they intended."

"This is insane. Why did they not just hide it somewhere? Why didn't *you* get rid of it the moment you realized what it was? What were you possibly thinking, giving it to me?" The questions were pouring out of me. I was so, so angry and I wanted to know why I had been dragged into this mess.

"I discovered it not far from here, in a cave up in the bluffs."

"I have never seen you in town before. Why did you come here?"

With that question, she became clearly uncomfortable and clenched her hands together in her lap. She didn't answer me for a long moment.

"Back in Oklahoma, one of my closest friends was from the local tribe there. She had heard rumors of a powerful, dangerous magic that was created a century ago, by a small group of witches. No one really believed it existed, but her grandmother, who had only recently passed away, had been delirious in her last days and spoke over and over again of a piece of muslin cloth and a cave and paint and blood. Cloth, cave, paint, blood. She repeated those words over and over. My friend had heard enough about how they had conjured the magic to know that that was likely what her grandmother was talking about.

Her grandmother was from this area."

She looked at me, then. "My sister died in childbirth when we were still young. All these years later and it feels as fresh as though it just happened." She sighed. "I'm old. I'm sick and I'm scared. I decided I had nothing to lose and I wanted the comfort of my sister …" She looked away again.

"So I traveled here. It was a difficult journey. I asked some young witches from the local coven to assist me in finding the cave. Once we found it, I pretended it was not the right one, even though I knew it was. I sent the young witches away and went back the next day. I found a large piece of muslin cloth wrapped in elk skin, sitting in a small niche in the back of the cave. A stone had been rolled in front of it. The stone had writing and symbols on it. The cloth itself was stiff and saturated in what I can only assume was dried blood."

I shivered at that.

"There was script written carefully on the back of the elk skin. Much of it was faded and ruined, but I was able to decipher some of the writing. Enough to know what I had to do, so that I could ... how can I describe it? So I could open a pinhole in the door. Right to my sister. See her again. Speak with her." She shook her head back and forth.

"The temptation was too great. As I am sure you understand. So I did it, the same ceremony you performed in the woods, and it was—magical." She was smiling now. "Memories of my sister flooded back to me, the way she looked, her laugh, the way her hand felt in mine as we walked to school ... It was like no time had passed at all. It was almost as wonderful as having her back."

She shook her head a tiny bit, breaking the spell of her memories. "It was a bright, sunny day, the day I completed the ceremony. As my memories came back to me, I was prepared to tell everyone what I had found. I could not wait to share it. I thought I had discovered the solution to grief. If we couldn't forget those we lost, if we were able to conjure up their memory anytime we wanted, and feel as if they were *right there with us*... well. That would make it all bearable, do you not agree?"

I nodded, though I wasn't sure I did actually agree.

"I did what I thought was right and I took it with me. I immediately wrote to some of our leaders, who made plans to come here and see it. While I waited, I tried to figure out how to transport it, how to keep it safe, how we could use it more broadly. The day I actually manipulated the cloth—refolding it, attempting to find a way to transport it and conceal it, it became immediately clear that whatever dark magic was contained within was working against me."

"What happened?"

"Much the same events that happened to you, I would imagine. By the time my superiors arrived, it was clear that the boundary between life and whatever lies on the other side had been broken open and the magic was not quite as innocent as I had first believed. After we examined the cloth, we realized that the magic it contained could, in fact, help you find the thread that connects to a lost loved one. At the end of which seems to be a well of every memory you have, which is the best alternative to actually communing with the dead. But like I said, it also works both ways. And if we are not careful something could get out that is far more dangerous than my sister or your brother's memory. That's why you write down three memories—just enough to open that link. We came up with a plan to manipulate the cloth into the cover of that notebook—"

"I have been carrying that ... that ... *thing* around with me all this time?"

"Yes," she said, not meeting my eyes. "Some of my superiors further studied the text and we realized that if it was manipulated in any way other than three simple memories, it seemed to weave a different sort of thread. A bigger one, one of pain and anger and grief. I suppose it's because the threads are so close and the magic so volatile that it doesn't take much. It invites something else in."

"How do you know?"

Amelia shook her head. "One of my sisters got carried away. She performed the ceremony five times. Something got out. Something that attached itself to her. She killed herself, or so they said. But her injuries—well—I never believed it."

"But why me? I still do not understand."

"They wanted to hide it in plain sight, in a sense. Any witch who was aware of what it was would have been too tempted to examine it, to use it. But they also believed that it had to be in the hands of a descendent. Just in case. In case of what I do not really know—magic in the hands of an untrained witch is worse than a normal human. They also felt that if we gave it to you then we would, technically, not have any knowledge of where it ended up and could claim innocence if it was ever discovered."

Heat rose to my face at those words. These women had used me, had put me in danger and exploited my grief. "Why would you tell me to use it? Why would you give me those instructions, knowing what it was, and then just send me away unprepared?"

Amelia looked into my eyes and I saw that they were no longer filmy and white as they'd been weeks ago. They were clear. And bright blue. "I could feel your pain. I understood that pain and I was so sad for you. I wanted to help. I thought if it worked, that would be wonderful for you. If it did not, I assumed you'd never tell anyone, because it would, I am sorry to say, make you sound a bit mad." Amelia sighed. "I should not have done that. Or at the very least I should have told you about your heritage—"

"What does that *mean*? Are you saying that I'm a witch?"

"You're descended from a witch. I knew your great-aunt, on your mother's side, long ago. It was another reason I made the journey here. I knew there would be witches in the area."

"My great-aunt? I never even knew her."

Amelia shrugged. "She once mentioned a niece in this area. I wrote to the local coven and they confirmed you were still here. And grieving, which of course worked in our favor."

"Well I am so glad my brother's death was so convenient for you. But your plan did not work. I didn't even get any of my memories of Henry back. All I seemed to do was invite something evil into my life and now my parents are dead! None of this makes any sense. I do not even understand what I did!"

"Of course you don't! We put powerful, dark magic into the hands of someone who has no idea what it is or how it works." She sighed. "Did you start writing in it before you did the ceremony?"

I nodded. "I couldn't decide if I should actually attempt it. So I started writing about Henry and my life and meeting you. It was … healing, I suppose."

She shook her head. "It was a mistake. I should have fought my superiors more aggressively. I shouldn't have told you anything. You wrote down the story of your anger and grief, and it was too much. It wove the threads of pain."

"This is too much!" I yelled and stood up quickly. "This is ridiculous. I don't want any part of it any longer. I am leaving and best of luck to you." I turned toward the door, intending to leave.

"Sit down." The force in her voice surprised me so much that I did stop and looked right at her.

"You have to be the one to bind it. It is bound to you. If you are not the one to contain it, it will not leave you alone."

I stared at her for a long moment. "This is ridiculous!" I said again. "How dare you put me in this position and then expect me to fix your mistake!"

"It is my mistake." She finally had the decency to look ashamed. "I am sorry, Violet. I should never have agreed to their plan." She took a deep breath. "It is bound to you, however, so we have to manage it together. I will not involve the coven this time. We just need to neutralize it. I am forbidden from destroying it, but we can hide it …"

Her voice had trailed off and she was no longer looking toward me. She was deep in thought and I did not say anything. She kept saying "we." How I could help her I had no idea. I wanted to run away. I had so many questions. I was so angry. But I wanted this thing gone and if what she said was true and I had to be the one to bind it, I couldn't do that without her. Thus conflicted, I simply stayed frozen.

"I have an idea," she said. "We just need to take it one step further than I did. Have you ever wanted to write a book?"

And so we created a plan. We wove the threads of this story and the threads of the magic into this book.

If you are reading this, I hope you see mine as the cautionary tale it is. When we lose a loved one, it is a horrific and crippling loss. One I know well. But it cannot be changed. There is no magic that will make it better. There is no God who will comfort. Only time can heal—or, at the very least, dull the pain enough so you can move on and create some semblance of a life. But we will never be whole again. The best advice I can give is to find a way to accept that and create a life anyway.

Chapter Twenty-Six

Lara

Lara set the book down on the nightstand, tears pricking at her eyes. *This* is how the book ends? This hopelessness? No indication of what Violet and Amelia's plan was? Violet's whole family destroyed, and she got no answers at all?

Lara felt angry and sad and hopeless herself. Mostly because it gave her no comfort and also because she felt like this was the end of the road. Lara couldn't see that there was an answer for her. She thought for sure Violet's story would, at the very least give her some sort of path to follow. But this was it: *And we created a plan.* What did that even mean?

And above all, now she was scared. Violet seemed to think something from the book killed her parents. *I've got to get Tessa out of here.*

Lara looked at the clock. It was one in the morning and she wasn't tired at all. She wouldn't be getting to sleep any time soon. Lara took the book with her into the living room. She began to flip through the pages towards the beginning, re-reading certain passages and looking for what, she wasn't sure. Did she really think the book would change before her eyes? Could it be different *again*?

Lara's eyes landed on a page detailing Violet's conversation with Helen, the maid.

Helen's hands stilled for a moment, then resumed their work. "Not recently, miss, no. I will admit that in the weeks after he passed, I did spend some small amount of time there, just dusting and, well, it was … nice."

I looked over at her, but she wouldn't meet my eyes. Helen

had been with our family for almost twenty years. Of course she was missing Henry as much as the rest of us. I patted her shoulder and said, "I understand."

"But one day, oh, I suppose it was about six months ago, I did decide to do a bit of dusting. And I heard … I heard." Helen shook her head. "Never mind, miss. It was surely my imagination. I'm an old woman, you know."

"What was it, Helen?" I had to know what she had heard. I had to know if I was the only one experiencing these strange things.

Helen must have heard desperation in my voice, or at least a willingness to believe her. "I thought I heard a voice saying, Don't. Don't. Don't. Over and over, miss. It was soft, almost as if it was in my ear …" Her voice trailed off. "But surely it was my imagination getting the best of me. I did leave quickly, though. And I haven't been in his room since then."

Lara shook her head. She'd read this same passage not two weeks ago and this wasn't in there. The book was changing more and more rapidly, adding pieces of a story. But why? Were any of these changed excerpts leading to an answer? If she read the book *again*, would there be even more changes? Would there be an answer? If only she could go back and compare every single scene that was different from the original, maybe it would tell her something. But she didn't know if that would even help at this point, because she had no idea how much the book was changing each time she opened it. How long would she go on reading it, the book changing more and more and things getting scarier and scarier for her?

With a frustrated groan, Lara threw the book on the coffee table and sat back on the couch, closing her eyes. A moment later, she heard the rustling of pages and her eyes flew open. The book was lying open on the table, the pages turning rapidly as though there was a strong breeze. Lara sat up straight, and just watched, helpless and terrified. Her stomach clenched and she felt frozen. She didn't want to touch it. When the pages stopped suddenly, Lara looked down at the book, slowly leaning over. It was open to the page where Violet goes into Henry's room.

Light held before me, I made my way to Henry's room. I slowly pushed open the door and peered inside. At first, I noticed nothing out of place. His bed was made and an overcoat was hanging on a hook on the back of his door. His wardrobe was closed and his Sunday shoes placed neatly on the floor under the window. On his nightstand sat a pitcher for water, a book, and an open notebook. It wasn't until I looked more closely at the notebook on the nightstand that I realized something wasn't quite right. It was open to the middle of the book and dark, black words were scrawled across both pages, reading, You can't. Don't. Don't.

I stepped back quickly. It was Henry's handwriting, of that I was sure, but it was messy and I could tell it had been written in a hurry. What I couldn't accept was that it was there at all. I suppose it could have been there all along, but I had spent a lot of time simply sitting in this room, surrounded by his things, but not touching anything. I hadn't been able to do so much as pick up the things on his nightstand, but I was sure that this notebook had not been there before. Who had put it there? And why had Henry ever written those words?

The passage was the same as the first time Lara had read it, of that she was sure.

But now, there were dark words scrawled in black across the page. *"You can't. Don't. You can't. Don't. You can't. Don't."*

It was Ben's handwriting. It was *Ben's* handwriting. Lara felt two things all at once: absolute, abject terror. And elation. The latter feeling won out. It was Ben. It was Ben. Tears began streaming down her face. She picked the book up and clutched it to her chest. Was he warning her? And what was he warning her about? What shouldn't she do?

"What should I do?" she whispered. "What should I do?"

Lara woke up some time later, on the couch. The book had fallen to the floor. She squinted at the clock on the mantel, seeing it was almost four in the morning. She quickly picked up the book, turning rapidly through the pages, looking for the writing, wanting it to be there and also not wanting it to be there. There it was. Ben's writing. She ran her fingers over the words. Ben was here. She'd been right. This had something to do with Ben.

She was excited and scared and confused. She set the book on the table. She was tired and not thinking clearly. Tomorrow—well, later today—she'd figure something out. But for now, Ben was here.

She collapsed on her bed and fell into a fitful sleep.

****

Later that morning, Lara awoke to her alarm, feeling groggy and sluggish. Now that she was awake, the light of day streaming through her windows, she tried to think clearly about what had happened last night. Some of the elation had faded, fear quickly taking its place. It was Ben—she was sure about that. But it had happened *right in front of her*, which left her feeling uneasy and nervous in the house. She wanted to get Tessa to daycare as soon as she could.

After dropping her off, Lara tried to work, but it was useless. She couldn't concentrate on anything. She looked through her to-do list for the rest of the week and decided it could all wait. She didn't have any pressing deadlines. Lara fired off a couple of emails to her clients, telling them she was taking some personal time and would be in touch early next week. Then she closed her email, saved and closed her work documents, and opened an internet browser. She was just desperate enough that the time had come to search "grimoire" on the internet.

An hour later, Lara had gone down some dark internet holes and learned more about modern witchcraft and its more fantastical history than she even knew was available, but she found nothing to help. She was frustrated and mad and she didn't know what else to do.

Lara opened the Word document with her list of questions. She wanted to add what she'd learned and add all the new questions she had.

What We Know

- Book published/written in 1890??
- Marsh family did exist in Grafton, but don't know what happened to Violet
- Picture of the book was used for a book fair flyer in Grafton in 2003.
- Maisie found the book in 1946.
- Scary stuff happened to Maisie, CiCi, and John
- They left the book in the cave.
- There were witches in Grafton in 1889.
- There were rumors of something that contained powerful magic to do with communicating with the dead.
- There is a way to destroy it.

Questions

- What happened to Violet?
- How does the book change?

- Why was the story I read different from what Maisie read?
- Will the rest of the book tell me what happened? NO.
- If I keep reading, will things get worse?
- Are there any other copies of the book?
- What does Maisie know?
- What does the store owner know?
- What does Amabel have to do with witches? What is Amabel not telling me?
- V. and Amelia had a plan, clearly something to do w/ V. writing the book. What was the plan and how did it solve their problem?

Lara let out a frustrated groan. She still didn't really know anything. Or maybe it was right in front of her and she just couldn't see it.

As Lara saved and closed the document on her computer, her cell phone rang. She looked at the caller ID and saw that it was David, from the library.

"Hello?"

"Lara? Hi, it's David. From the library."

"Hi, how are you?"

"I'm good, listen, I think I found something you need to know."

Lara's heart began to beat just a bit faster.

"Great! I haven't been able to find out much of anything."

"Well, it's kind of weird. Um. How much do you know about your family tree? Like, ancestors going way back?"

Lara laughed. "Next to nothing. I spoke to my grandparents a few times about their lives during the war for school projects, but that's about it."

"Okay. Well, I found a record of Violet Marsh. And I think you're related to her."

Lara's mouth dropped open. "What?"

"Yeah. Let's see …" Lara heard the rustling of paper. "Okay. I actually had to start with Violet's mother, since there was no record of Violet after 1890. She had a sister named Rose. Who had a baby named Cynthia. Who had a baby named Ruby. Who had a baby named Iris. Ringing any bells yet?"

"Who had babies named Maisie and Josephine," Lara said, almost in a whisper. "Josephine was my grandmother."

"Bingo," David said quietly. "Isn't this kind of an odd coincidence?"

Lara couldn't believe it. She was related to Violet Marsh. Distantly. But still. "Yeah. It is."

"Well, that's not all I found out. I tracked down the Marsh family's business. It was sold to a company in New Orleans, so that part is all correct. They kept pretty good records and have some correspondence from when Violet's father died. I guess he stayed on as a consultant right up until he died. This letter I found was addressed to Violet, but at an address in Oklahoma. Now, I searched Oklahoma death records, but struck out. There is nothing about Violet Marsh after 1890."

Lara felt a sinking weight drag her down. She'd been hopeful that the first version of the book was the reality—that Violet had gone on to get married and have kids and lead a happy life.

"David, I don't know how to thank you enough. This is so much more than I hoped for."

"I'll email you all the documents I found. Did you talk to Amabel last week?"

"Yes, and she was very helpful, thank you for recommending that."

"Sure." David paused, seeming to want to ask her more. "Lara, look, I know we don't know each other very well, but I'm so curious about all of this."

Lara sighed. "If I told you, you'd think I was nuts. Trust me."

"Honey, I'm a gay man from southern Illinois and both of my parents still talk to me. Crazier things have happened than whatever is going on with you and Violet Marsh." David laughed. "You can't tease a history doctoral candidate like this, it just makes us more curious."

Lara laughed, too. "You've helped me more than I ever expected. As payment, I'll tell you everything when this is all over. I promise. You probably won't believe me, but you have my word."

"I'll hold you to it!"

They hung up and Lara opened her Word document back up, adding: Violet Marsh is my great-aunt, four times removed?

Lara stared at the screen, trying to figure out what this might mean, but it was too overwhelming. She needed to tell Maryn.

Lara picked up her phone and opened the messaging app.

"Finished reading the book and I'm still alive."

"What happened to Violet?"

"I don't know. It wasn't helpful. I also found out something … want to tell you in person. Coffee tomorrow?"

"Let's just meet now. I really want to know what's going on."

Lara didn't respond right away. She was trying to wrap her head around everything that had happened. What did it mean that Ben had tried to send her a message that was clearly a warning? He wanted her to stop, that much was clear, and it was safe to assume he meant stop messing with this, whatever *this* was. But how could she stop? How could she pretend like all of this wasn't happening when it was *Ben*. It was Ben! Just like she'd hoped. Lara put her phone down on her desk and looked out the window into the backyard.

What did it mean that she was related to Violet Marsh? Did it mean anything? Is that why the book changed for her? She had too many questions and she felt like her brain was on overdrive. She couldn't make sense of anything right now. Lara put her head in her hands and wondered if she should just get the book and burn it in the firepit in the backyard, then call Alex and tell him everything was over.

Glancing at the clock, she realized Alex was probably at lunch right now. She opened the FaceTime app on her Mac and called him. When she saw his face smiling from beneath his yellow hardhat, she wanted to cry. She missed him.

"Hey, babe," he said, the camera shaking as he walked.

"Hi. Can you talk? I just wanted to say hi."

"Yeah, hold on," Lara saw a glimpse of his bucket truck as he opened the door and climbed in.

"Okay," he said, taking his hardhat off and running his hands through his hair. "You look sexy. I miss you."

Looking at her image on the computer screen—hair in a messy bun, no makeup, wearing Alex's old sweatshirt—she laughed. "Yeah right. I'm a mess."

"You're my mess. How's everything going?"

"It's okay. Fine." She forced a smile. "We miss you."

"I miss you guys, too. This storm is brutal. It seems like all the major damage has been fixed, but now we're moving onto all the backyard poles that take forever to get done. It's muddy and cold and some of these customers have been out of power for a week and a half now, so we're getting stopped and yelled at a lot." He sighed. "I understand why they're frustrated, but we're doing our best."

"That sucks. For everyone. How much longer do you think you'll be there?" From somewhere in the house, Lara heard a scraping noise and she stiffened.

"I'm not sure—what's wrong?"

"Nothing, sorry, I just heard something. Probably just George. Anyway. What were you going to say?"

"I'm not sure how much longer. At least another three days. I'm ready to come home, though. What was that?"

A loud thump had come from somewhere in the house. Lara felt like a deer in the headlights. She'd hoped Alex hadn't heard it. She didn't want to argue about it.

"Um, I don't know …"

"Babe, what's going on?"

She shook her head. "I don't know. Just weird stuff." She looked toward the door of her office.

"Did you get rid of that book?"

"No."

"Why not?"

"I don't know, to be honest. I finished reading it. The ending was entirely different. The whole thing was."

He didn't say anything for a minute. "You're sure, aren't you?"

"Yes." She looked into his eyes, hoping he would see that she was clear-headed. Hoping he would believe her.

"Shit. So what—I mean. I don't know …" He was struggling with what to say.

"Someone who helped me do some research when I was in Grafton the other day called me this afternoon. He tracked down Violet Marsh. She's—Alex, she's my great-aunt, four times removed or however the fuck you say that. I'm related to her." Lara hadn't intended to tell Alex all of this, but she found the words pouring out of her mouth.

"Are you serious?"

"Yes. On my mother's side. It's crazy, right?"

"Holy shit. So what—"

Behind Lara, the door to her office slammed shut. She whirled around in her chair, breathing hard. Alex, who could see the door behind her, yelled. She turned back to the computer, eyes wide. The house was silent now.

"What the fuck was that?" Alex said. He was leaning into the camera.

"I don't know," Lara said miserably, shaking her head.

"Oh my god," Alex said. "I don't know what the hell is happening, but get out of there, Lara. Or go get rid of that fucking thing." He looked scared. "I'm serious, get rid of it. I don't know what the fuck is going on, but get rid of it."

"It's not hurting me."

"Lara, don't be stupid. Jesus, I can't believe I'm having this conversation. What's the point of hanging onto it?"

Lara was so tired, all of her defenses were down, and it all came out of her. About Violet and how she got her memories back. How she wanted to keep it just in case there was something there and that she couldn't stand the thought of destroying something that could help her.

When she finally finished, Alex looked shell-shocked. "I don't know what to say."

"Do you believe me?"

Alex laughed humorlessly. "I think maybe I'm starting to. I don't know. Jesus. Who cares if it does have magic or some shit? It's fucking with you. And I don't want Tessa around it. I can't believe I'm saying this."

"But Ben. What if—what if it has something to do with Ben?"

Alex's face softened and he took a deep breath. "I understand. But how long do you let this go on?"

"I don't know." Lara heard a knocking coming from the phone and Alex said, "Hold on babe." He rolled the window down in his truck and leaned his head out, talking to someone. His voice was muffled as he said, "Yeah, we can eat. Where? ... Okay. Give me five minutes."

His face came back into the frame and Lara smiled, needing to convince him that she had this under control. Because as she'd talked it out with him, an idea had started forming in her mind. She couldn't grasp all the details yet, but she thought she knew what to do next.

"I'm okay, babe. I'm meeting with Maryn in just a bit and we're going to come up with a plan. I'm going to figure something out. If anything else happens today, Tessa and I will go to Maryn's. Okay?"

Alex didn't look convinced, but he nodded. "Promise me if it starts to feel dangerous, you'll leave." He shook his head. "I cannot believe I'm having this conversation. I feel helpless here."

"I'm sorry. I love you."

"I love you too. Call me tonight, okay?" She agreed and they hung up.

Lara called Maryn.

She picked up right away. "Hey, do you want me to come over?" Maryn asked.

Lara looked toward the door. "No. Not here."

"Okay. Where?"

They agreed to meet at Starbucks in twenty minutes. Lara hung up, let George out, then gathered her purse, computer, and notebook. She looked into the living room as she walked by, where she'd left the book laying on the coffee table last night. It wasn't there.

She rushed toward the table, heart hammering. She looked on the floor, the couch, it was nowhere.

Heart hammering, she began to search frantically all around the house, terrified. Tessa hadn't touched it, she'd been in Lara's sight all morning. Lara certainly hadn't moved it. Where the hell had it gone?

Finally, she opened the door to Tessa's room and scanned the area. When her eyes landed on Tessa's little white bed, she froze. The book lay there on Tessa's white and pink polka dotted pillowcase. It was closed and placed neatly in the center of the pillow, looking out of place among her stuffed animals and the copies of *Goodnight Moon* and *The Very Hungry Caterpillar* Tessa insisted on sleeping with.

Immediately, the fear faded and Lara got *pissed*. This felt like a message. Or a threat. And whatever was going on, it was not going to mess with her baby.

Lara stalked over to the bed, picked up the book and walked out to the backyard, putting it in the small storage shed they had out back.

Today, she'd plan. Tomorrow she'd get that thing out of her house and she'd get some answers.

CHAPTER TWENTY-SEVEN

Lara

Lara sat at a table in the corner of Starbucks. Maryn joined her shortly after and sat down. After they'd ordered, Maryn asked, "Okay, what's going on, Lar? You're kind of freaking me out."

Lara told Maryn what David had found out.

"You're fucking *related* to Violet Marsh?" Maryn was sitting back in her chair, looking at Lara with wide, shifting eyes. She couldn't stop moving. She picked up her cup and put it down. Grabbed her phone, flipped it over, then over again. She crossed and uncrossed her arms. Lara was unnerved by her behavior.

"I know. It's unbelievable."

"Uh, *yeah it is.*" Maryn was shaking her head back and forth. "That's ... that's unbelievable. What do you think this means?"

"I don't really know. But it definitely means there's more to all of this than just coincidence."

"Yeah, I guess so."

"So," said Maryn. "What happened at the end of the book?"

Lara sighed. "Not much, really. Nothing that helps me." She told her about the disappointing ending and Maryn agreed that it didn't seem to have any answers.

"What are you going to do?"

"I don't know."

"Let's lay out everything we know. I think we need to have a plan before I—"

"Before you what?" Lara asked when Maryn didn't finish her sentence.

"Um. Before I can try to help."

"Maryn, what—"

293

Maryn cut her off. "We know the witches in the coven did something to Violet's notebook, somehow wove the cloth into the cover, right?"

"Yeah, that's right," Lara said.

"Okay. But we don't know if the book you have is actually the same book as Violet's notebook."

"Right."

"And we don't know what Amelia and Violet did to make everything stop."

"We also still don't know what happened to Violet."

"And how did the book end up in the cave for Maisie and John to find?" asked Maryn.

"I guess that's where Amelia and Violet ended up leaving it, after they did whatever it was they did." Lara let out a frustrated groan. "There are still so many questions and I still don't know what to do." She began tearing her napkin into little pieces and making a pile.

"You know, one thing we haven't really considered is *why* all of this is happening to you, Lara," said Maryn.

"What do you mean?"

"Like, why is the book making things happen to you? It seems— angry. But why? What does it want? Why you?"

"I don't know. Because I read it? Because I reread it? Because I'm related to Violet?" A thought occurred to Lara. "What if Violet was a witch, too, and she just didn't know it? Amelia kind of said as much, right? Something about descendants?"

A small smile played on Maryn's lips. "Yeah …"

"Okay. Well, what if whatever solution she and Amelia came up with had something to do with that? Like Amelia taught her some kind of magic?"

"That would make sense, I guess."

"I need to know more about this coven. I need to talk to Amabel again," Lara said.

"Didn't she say that she'd told you everything she could?"

"Yeah. But I don't believe her and that was before I knew I was related to Violet. Maybe that makes a difference?" This was the thing that had been niggling in the back of her brain earlier. Maybe being related to Violet was what made her susceptible to it.

"What do you mean?"

"Well, I mean, if she could be responsible for it, maybe I am, too? Because we're related?"

Maryn was staring at her. "Are you saying you think you're a witch?"

"God. No!" Lara laughed. "I think I'd know that by now. I just mean, maybe if it's related to our family in some way, that means I could—I don't know—fix it?"

Maryn sighed and Lara couldn't read her expression.

"I need to go back up there. Want to go with me this time?"

"I don't know if that's the best idea. I think … Lara, maybe it's time to get rid of it."

"What?" Lara couldn't believe what Maryn was suggesting after they'd spent the past twenty minutes talking about doing the exact opposite.

Maryn wouldn't meet her eye. "This is all getting weird. Maybe it's time to just let it go."

"Well, I don't think so."

Lara looked at her friend for a long moment. She'd been acting so strangely. She'd been helpful through all of this, but also distant at times, and Lara was sure she was keeping something from her.

"Maryn, are you okay? We've been talking about what's going on with me constantly. I don't think I've been a great friend. But to be honest, you've been acting really weird."

Maryn laughed. "Thanks."

"Sorry, but you have. What's going on?"

Maryn looked miserable. She opened her mouth like she was

going to say something, but closed it again.

"What?" Lara asked.

Maryn shook her head. "Nothing." She looked like she was going to cry.

"Maryn, Jesus, what is wrong with you? You can tell me. What is it?"

"I have to go," Maryn said. "I'm sorry. Sorry." And she got up and left without another word.

Lara felt like she might cry herself. She picked up her cup and threw away her trash. *Guess I'm on my own,* she thought. But the thought didn't upset her as much as it might once have. As much as she hated feeling like they were in a fight, she couldn't force Maryn to tell her anything and Lara had bigger problems.

Lara called Alex's mom. Lynn agreed to keep Tessa for as long as Lara needed her to, but Lara could sense the hesitation in her voice.

"Honey, are you okay?"

"Yes. I think so. I don't really know. Something weird is definitely happening, Lynn. I can't explain it. I think …" She took a deep breath. "I think this trip will be it. I'll figure it out and this will all be over."

"What's happening, Lara?"

"If I told you, you'd think I'm crazy. Maybe one day I'll tell you the whole thing."

"Okay." Her mother-in-law still sounded hesitant.

"Can I bring Tessa up tomorrow?"

"Of course. Bring George, too, I don't want you to have to worry about anything."

"Thanks, Lynn. I promise I'll tell you everything one day. I think out of anyone, you *might* believe me," Lara said with a laugh.

She ended the call and immediately called Alex. He picked up on the first ring.

"What's up?"

"Hey, babe. I just wanted to let you know that I'm going back to Grafton tomorrow. Your mom is going to keep Tess. I'm going to get some answers and this will all be over."

"Are you sure you're okay for tonight?"

"Yeah, I think so." She purposely didn't tell him about finding the book in Tessa's room. "If anything happens, we'll go to Maryn's. Well. Maybe. Or maybe we'll just head to your mom's."

"Huh?"

"Maryn's been acting really weird, Alex. Not like herself at all."

"How so?"

"I don't know how to describe it, really. She's been super tired and looks like hell. I've been telling her everything that's going on with this book and it's always like she's holding something back, but then leaves or ends the conversation. I don't know."

"What do you think's going on?"

"I don't know. I just want this to be over. It'll be over soon." She said this mostly to convince herself.

"Okay. I guess. Lara, I ..." He didn't seem to know what to say. "I'm sorry I didn't believe you. I keep thinking about that door just ... just slamming closed."

"It's okay, babe. I really don't blame you. None of this makes sense." She felt relieved to finally have him on her side.

"Just be careful, okay?"

"I will."

She ended the call and took a deep breath. Time to make one last call, the one she'd been dreading. She had to tell Maisie she was coming back before she just showed up tomorrow. Lara called her. When Maisie answered, she sounded tired.

"Hey, Maisie. It's me."

"Lara. Are you okay?"

"Yes, I'm fine. I'm okay. Listen, Maisie, I've found out some more stuff and I need to come back to Grafton. Can I come up tomorrow and stay for a couple of days?"

"You're always welcome here, Lolly, but why? Can't you just be done with this?"

"Amabel didn't tell me everything and things have gotten— worse. I need some answers and I think she has them."

"What do you mean things have gotten worse? What did you find out?"

"I'd rather explain it all in person."

"Okay," her aunt sighed. "I wish this had never happened. I should have burned the damn thing." Maisie sounded miserable, and suddenly Lara was sure she'd been beating herself up ever since Lara had left her house.

"Maisie. None of this is your fault. It's going to be okay."

"It is my fault. If I'd gotten rid of it, none of this would be happening."

"Stop, Maisie. Everything is okay. I'm fine."

"I just don't have a good feeling."

"I'll see you tomorrow, okay?"

Lara ended the call.

She and Tessa spent a quiet night at home, got into their pajamas early, played, and watched movies. Nothing happened. No noises and nothing moved around when she wasn't looking. As she lay in bed that night, sleep feeling very far away, she thought maybe she should just forget the whole thing.

But the what ifs played on an endless loop. What if she could get her memories back? What if magic was fucking real? What if? What if? What if?

The next morning Lara texted Maryn.

"What happened yesterday? Are you okay?"

Lara waited for a reply while she got Tessa ready to go to her in-laws. She waited while she drove. She waited while she visited with

Lynn and got Tessa settled.

After she kissed Tessa goodbye and got back into her car, she texted Maryn again. "Heading to Grafton now. I'll keep you updated. If you want."

It was a little bitchy, but Lara was starting to get a little pissed. She was mostly worried about her friend, but also couldn't shake the feeling that Maryn needed—wanted—to tell her something, but wouldn't. And if she somehow knew something about all of this, Lara wanted to know.

****

Lara parked the car in front of Mystic Rivers. As she walked up the steps, she felt nervous, but also excited. Ready.

As she approached the door, Lara saw the *Closed* sign.

"Shit!" She couldn't believe she hadn't thought of this. Everything in Grafton is closed on Mondays. "Shit!" Lara said again.

She decided to try knocking, just in case. Tentatively at first, but then harder. At first, she didn't hear anything but after a few long moments, she heard footsteps from inside.

"Sorry, we're closed," Amabel started to say as she pulled the door open. She stopped speaking when she saw Lara standing in the doorway.

"Lara. Hello."

"Hi, Amabel."

"What can I do for you? Is everything okay?" Amabel had opened the door, but was standing in the doorway, not inviting her in.

"I need to talk to you."

"Well, I was just finishing up my inventory—"

"Amabel, please. I think there's something you need to know. I need answers and I think you can help me." Lara looked at her, not breaking eye contact.

Amabel put her hand on the door and for a second, Lara thought she was going to close it in her face. But she swung it open, saying, "Come in."

Lara walked through the door and expected Amabel to follow her, but the woman was looking out toward the street, right at Lara's car. Her body was rigid. *She looks like a dog on a scent*, Lara thought.

"Amabel?" The woman didn't answer and didn't move. "Amabel!" she said, more loudly this time.

After what felt like a long moment, the woman turned around and shook her head. She closed the door and pushed past Lara, taking care not to brush up against her.

Amabel led her to a small room in the back of the shop. It was clearly used for extra storage. Boxes lined the floors along the perimeter of the room, stacked two and three high. A row of shelves along the back wall held extra inventory and office supplies. There was also a small table in the center of the room, four old office chairs gathered around it. A ledger, catalogs, and a notebook sat on the table.

Before Amabel was able to gather the items and stack them on the shelves, Lara saw photocopies of letters, pages covered in writing she couldn't read and symbols she'd never seen before.

"Please sit down," Amabel said.

When they had settled, Amabel spoke. "I have to admit, I'm feeling a little ambushed here." She smiled, but it didn't quite reach her eyes.

"Sorry to barge in like this. After I left Grafton last week, things didn't get better. I finished reading the book and there weren't any answers there. Then I found out some information that made me think there's a lot more to this."

Amabel looked at her expectantly. Lara picked up her bag from the floor and pulled out some documents.

"Someone at the library tracked down Violet Marsh and her family for me. There isn't a whole lot of information about her, but

I was able to track her family. And I'm, well—I'm related to Violet Marsh."

Lara wasn't sure how she'd expected Amabel to react to this news, but she certainly wasn't expecting her to look calmly back, completely unsurprised. "You knew that already." It wasn't a question.

"I didn't know it. But I suspected you had to be related to all of this somehow."

"Then why didn't you tell me that? Didn't you think it was kind of important?"

"Perhaps. I wasn't sure. I was hoping you would give me the book, to be honest. When you refused, I suppose I hoped you would let it go eventually. I assumed that if you didn't, and things got worse, you would come back."

Lara let out a short bark of a laugh. "So you just let me go, without all of the information. Do you know what I've been going through?"

Amabel sighed. "I'm sorry, Lara. There's no protocol for handling something like this, and then I just did what I thought was best."

Amabel's words were calm, her voice quiet. But Lara saw that her fists were clenched so tightly her nails had to be digging into her palm.

"What is it, Amabel? What do you know about this?"

"There's so much you don't know," Amabel said, ignoring her question. "It's just so much to tell."

"Try me," Lara said, crossing her arms. A thought occurred to her. "You know, I had a feeling you knew more than you were telling me. You told me quite a bit that last day I was here. Why didn't you just tell me you knew nothing about the book; send me on my way? You told me you couldn't tell anyone anything, unless they were a direct descendant of a witch. If you weren't going to tell me everything, why did you tell me anything at all?"

"Like I said, I suspected, but I didn't know anything for sure. I knew that if the book was manifesting things in your life, it was likely that you had some kind of connection to us."

"Oh my god," Lara said. "Maisie."

Amabel's eyes snapped up to hers as she said, "Maisie?"

"Maisie. My aunt. That's why she experienced everything she did. She's related to Violet Marsh, too." It was so obvious and Lara was pissed at herself for not thinking of it right away.

Amabel was leaning over the table now. "Maisie is your aunt? How much does your aunt know about what's been happening to you? I know she had her own experiences with the book, but what does she know about what's happening to you?"

"I've told her everything. Why?"

"Just curious," Amabel leaned away from her, which seemed to take some effort. She took a deep breath, but didn't say anything.

"Wait, how did you know Maisie had the book?"

As Amabel started to reply, they heard a knock at the front door. No, not a knock. A pounding.

"What now," mumbled Amabel, getting up from her chair. But before she even made it out of the back room, they heard the front door slam and footsteps stalk through the store. Amabel went out to meet whoever this person was in the small hallway.

"Is she here?" a voice asked.

Lara heard Amabel respond quietly, but couldn't hear exactly what she said. But Lara recognized that voice.

"Maryn?" she called out. In the next moment, Maryn appeared in the doorway.

"Maryn?" Lara repeated dumbly. "What are you doing here? I thought—"

"We need to talk," Maryn said.

"Maryn, are you really going to do this now?" Amabel asked.

"Wait," Lara said, holding up her hand. "You know each other?"

"Yes, Amabel, I'm fucking doing this now. It's gone on too long. I'm done."

"What the hell?" Lara said.

Amabel crossed her arms and said, "It might make *you* feel better, but is she ready to hear it?"

"I really don't care what you think, Amabel. You drag us into this, tell us *nothing*, when clearly you know what's going on, then you stop communicating with us at all. But I'm done. I don't care what you or Clara or anyone says—"

"STOP!" Lara yelled. "Stop talking about me like I'm not here, and tell me what the hell is going on."

"I'm sorry, Lara. I'm so sorry." Maryn sat down next to Lara. She started to reach for her hand, but seemed to stop herself. She shook her head sadly. "I'm so sorry."

"What? Why are you sorry?"

Maryn took a deep breath. "I'm a witch. Or part of this coven, or whatever," she said, gesturing toward Amabel.

"What?"

"When you found the book, Amabel knew it right away. She came to us and told us it could potentially be something powerful. But none of us knew what it was exactly. We also didn't know who you were. All we knew was that you had something they needed to keep tabs on. They needed someone to keep an eye on you."

Maryn paused here and looked at Lara.

"I don't understand. Someone's been watching me?"

Maryn looked away again, toward the wall, and Lara watched as tears formed in her eyes. "It was me. They sent me." And Maryn told her everything. How Amabel, armed with information about Lara, had come to St. Louis and it had been decided Maryn would befriend her. How Maryn had been fighting to just come clean about everything and how the coven had managed to convince her to wait just a little longer.

With each revelation, her words felt like a punch to Lara's gut. Her friend, her rock through everything that had happened over the past months, had been lying to her the whole time.

"So … you … you were spying on me? Reporting back on everything I was doing?" Lara's voice was cold and hard. Tears appeared in the corners of Maryn's eyes, threatening to spill over. Lara looked away from her, not wanting to feel sympathy. Lara's heart was pounding and heat was rising in her face as she realized that the most important friendship in her life had been fake.

"No. Lara, no. All I was supposed to do was report back to them if you started struggling with anything. If odd things started happening. That's it. I didn't tell them anything else about your life."

"I trusted you."

"I know." Tears were streaming down Maryn's face now. "I know, and I'm so sorry. But you have to believe me when I say that I might have come into your life because of all of this bullshit, but our friendship is real. After the first day I met you, it stopped being about all this other shit and became about you."

At this, Lara looked at Maryn and said, "Did you even have a brother?"

Maryn recoiled as if she'd been slapped, sitting back hard in her chair. "Yes. Jesus, Lara. I wouldn't lie about that. I never lied to you about—"

"Never lied to me? How the hell did you all even know who I was, where to find me? How did you know I'd be at that support group?"

Amabel stepped in then. "I was able to convince someone at the Ruebel to give me your name. We found you in St. Louis and, honestly, social media and the internet did the rest of the leg work for us. We found out about Ben and we, well, we used our resources to find out about the support group."

Maryn broke in. "That was all. We didn't dig into your past or personal records. We didn't even know you were Maisie's niece."

"Oh, that's all? Well, I guess I should count myself lucky that you didn't run my credit or call my employer." Lara began gathering up her things to leave. She couldn't stay in this room with these people who had so callously betrayed her trust. She didn't care anymore if they could help her figure out what was going on with the book. She was done.

"We wanted to keep you safe," Maryn said quietly.

"Right. Safe from something that you couldn't even identify? Safe from something you didn't even know was real or not? It sounds to me like someone knew exactly what I had and just wanted to make sure no one else got their hands on it."

Maryn looked at Amabel then, eyebrows furrowed in confusion. Amabel looked back at her calmly, not saying anything.

"Amabel?" Maryn asked. "Did you know how dangerous it was?"

The older witch didn't look away. "I had my suspicions."

Maryn shook her head, disgusted. "I'm so fucking stupid. You lied to me. To all of us."

"I didn't lie."

"Okay, well you didn't give us all the information."

Amabel shrugged.

"Why? So she wouldn't go running to the cops about witches and magic being real? So we wouldn't draw attention to ourselves? Great. Fine. But what about *her*?" Maryn said, gesturing to Lara.

"She's fine, isn't she?"

"Oh, come on, Amabel! Yeah she's *fine*, but she's been terrified by what's going on. If you had given me all the information, I could have actually helped rather than just sitting on my ass, wringing my hands and worrying."

"I didn't need you to intervene. I wanted that book."

"Look," Lara cut in. "I'm done. This is fucking ridiculous. I don't understand anything you're talking about."

Lara turned to go.

"Where is it?" Amabel said sharply.

"What?" Lara asked.

"Where is it? Where's the book?"

"Not here." Lara wasn't going to help this woman.

"You need to just give it to me."

"I don't need to do anything for you. I'm done."

"Give it to me, Lara or it's not going to end well for you."

Lara looked at Amabel for a second, startled by the intensity of her tone. Then she walked out of the room.

Maryn

Maryn turned to Amabel. "What is wrong with you, Amabel? Why did you threaten her? Clara's going to be pissed about this."

Amabel rolled her eyes. "Do whatever you have to do, Maryn."

Maryn walked out of the room, but turned back. "I'm going to tell Lara everything I know, what little there is. You have two options, and you need to decide what side of this you want to fall on. You can tell us everything you know and try to convince her you can help so we can get rid of the thing. Or you can keep playing these fucking games and we'll figure it out ourselves without you. And we'll destroy it."

"You have no idea what you're dealing with."

"Maybe not. But you have a decision to make." Maryn walked out, following Lara.

As she left, she heard Amabel slap her hand on the table and yell, "Shit!"

CHAPTER TWENTY-EIGHT

Lara

"Lara, wait! Please!" Maryn ran down the front stairs of Amabel's store. Lara was opening her car door and getting ready to step inside. She didn't say anything.

"Can we talk?" Maryn asked.

"I don't know." Lara was trying not to cry. She was overwhelmed. Maryn was probably the one person she *wanted* to hash all of this out with. She could have the answers. But getting past the confusion and betrayal? Lara wasn't sure she was ready for that yet.

"I'm so, so sorry, Lar. You have no idea. There's so much I want to tell you. Can we please talk?"

Lara wasn't sure what she wanted, what was the right thing to do. But when it came down to it, this was Maryn, someone she'd trusted all these months, someone who had been a good friend, whatever the reasons she'd come into her life. Plus, she clearly had information Lara needed. It couldn't hurt to hear her out.

"Okay."

"Okay. Thank you," Maryn said. "Where should we go?"

"There's a bar down the street."

"Okay."

They each ordered a beer and Maryn started talking as soon as they sat down. "In the beginning, I thought I was doing the right thing. I thought that if you did have something that you wouldn't understand or be able to deal with, it would be better to have someone to keep an eye out for you. Then we became friends and I was so thankful for you. And nothing weird was going on, so I thought I could just put that part of it behind me."

"Would you have ever told me about the coven and ... and all of that?"

"Would you have believed me?" Maryn asked with a smile.

"Probably not."

Lara shrugged. "I don't know where to start. So ... what does it mean to be a witch?"

Maryn told her everything, how it had started in high school and how she'd worked on developing her powers, all the way up to what had happened recently.

"I resisted getting involved in a coven for so long. I didn't want any obligation to use my powers. I don't like to. I don't ever want to manipulate people."

"Have you ever used it on me?"

"No." The force of Maryn's voice told Lara that she was at least being honest about that. Lara didn't respond and Maryn spoke again. "Lara, I haven't. Not on you or even in your presence. And look, I'm going to be honest. I could do it right now—I could make you forgive me, make you hug me and act like everything is normal. But I'm not going to now or ever. I would never do that."

Lara was quiet, thinking about what Maryn had just said. It wasn't a threat. She believed her and Maryn was one of the best people she'd ever known. Lara realized the world was lucky that this particular power had fallen into the hands of someone like Maryn. She just wasn't sure she could forgive her for coming into her life under false pretenses and waiting so long to tell her. They'd shared so much over the past months and Maryn had been such a large part of her healing. Lara couldn't stand the thought that it was all based on lies.

"I don't know what to say, Maryn. I feel betrayed."

"I know. Ever since you first told me about the book and the things that started happening, I've been fighting them, trying to convince them to let me tell you."

"Why didn't you just tell me, in spite of what they said?"

"I should have. I know that now. Hell, I knew that then. I just let them convince me that it was better to keep you in the dark a little longer. Lara, you don't realize what that book is, what it can do. I'm starting to think I don't even understand."

"Well, no I don't, because no one explained it to me." Lara couldn't keep the bite of sarcasm out of her voice.

"You're right," Maryn said. "You're right." She shook her head. "They told me we needed more information. They didn't want to tell you too soon because we didn't know what the tipping point would be for you … what would make you believe. They thought it would be easier to convince you to give the book up if you knew something was really wrong and you needed help. They figured you'd either get rid of it on your own or start seeking answers and we'd intervene."

"If it's so terrible, why didn't you just take it? You had plenty of opportunities to do it."

"That's not what we're about, Lara. I know it doesn't feel like it, but we're not out to manipulate you. I mean, don't get me wrong. It was suggested that I could just take it. We felt like we were stuck between a rock and a hard place. Witchcraft is, for the most part, about community and women helping women. Above all, we wanted to keep you safe. It really wasn't about tricking you or using you. The book was in your possession. And for a long time, we weren't even sure what it was." Maryn shrugged. "We just wanted to make sure it didn't get out of control, didn't hurt you. That's why I was there."

Lara took this new information in. If all of this were true, then she could maybe understand. She sighed. "I believe you, Maryn. But I'm still upset and confused."

"I understand. And you have every right to be." She sighed. "Can I tell you everything I know about the book and the magic and we'll go from there?"

Lara nodded. Maryn told her about the coven's suspicions that it was just as Amelia and Amabel had said—ancient witches had somehow created hundreds of years ago. She explained that their biggest fear was that the magic could actually allow someone to communicate with the dead. To open doors that should remain firmly shut.

Lara asked what the big deal would be. Selfishly, she couldn't think of anything she'd like more. But Maryn explained that they simply didn't understand enough about how it worked. It could open doors to spirits intent on destroying the living, and there was just no way to know.

"Clara, the leader of our coven, believes that if the information we have about the book is accurate, it's dangerous because the good magic is too closely intertwined with the bad."

"What do you mean?" Lara asked.

"It's like the witch said in the book. There are threads of magic that link us to the past, the living to the dead. But they're threads, like a rope. Intertwined and crisscrossing each other. So let's say you tried to use it to communicate with Ben. You might find the thread that leads you to him, but there's no telling what you'd unravel along the way."

Lara nodded, not sure what to say.

"This kind of powerful magic isn't used anymore, at least to my knowledge and what I understand from Clara. It's actually kind of frowned upon. Most of us believe in the power of supporting each other and doing good in the world. Not using magic to get what we want."

"Most of you?"

"There are outliers, of course. There are those witches who definitely want to get their hands on the most powerful magic out there. But magic is a responsibility. It's not a right, and it's not a means to an end."

"So do you think there's someone who might want this magic to actually use it?"

"To be honest, I never really considered it until a couple of days ago. I trust Clara and the other coven leaders. They're good people, Lara. They support each other; they support good causes; they use their power for good. When Amabel first came to us with this information, we all agreed we wanted to just make sure you were safe and wouldn't force the issue unless we thought it became dangerous.

"At first, Amabel went along with it. She agreed to not do anything and seemed okay with me keeping an eye out. But when things just kept getting worse for you, I was done. I was ready to tell you no matter what they said. But Clara called Amabel and she was adamant. She wanted me to take the book from you, to use my powers to get you to hand it over.

"I refused and Clara supported me. At this point, we had all deferred to Amabel a bit, because she knew the most about the book. She was the one who had felt it first. I had, of course, picked up on the book's energy each time we spent time together, and I reported back that it was getting stronger. I convinced Clara and everyone else to just tell you in the hopes we could convince you to give it up. But Amabel refused. She didn't want you to know."

Maryn furrowed her brow. "Now that I say that, it's odd, isn't it? Amabel has been so insistent that we need to get the book back, then all of a sudden, she didn't want us to tell you. She said it was because she thought if we told you now, you'd get upset and destroy it."

"I wonder why she changed her mind?"

"I don't know ..." Maryn's voice trailed off.

The women were quiet for a moment and Lara thought back to what she and Amabel had been talking about before Maryn arrived.

"I need to go back to Maisie's. Amabel said something odd before you got to the store. I need to talk to Maisie."

"Okay."

Lara stood, but paused as she turned to go. She wasn't sure how she felt about everything she'd learned today. She was still upset that Maryn hadn't been honest, but she believed Maryn cared about her and that she could trust her. She knew their friendship was real, no matter how it had started. Lara took a deep breath and said, "Do you want to go with me?"

Maryn smiled in relief. "Yes. Please." She grabbed Lara in a hug. "I really am so sorry, Lara. It's been eating me up."

Lara pulled away and nodded. "Just, be honest from now on, okay?"

"Absolutely."

Amabel

Amabel was frantic. Maisie was Lara's aunt. How had she not seen this before? This might be the answer to everything.

When Maryn and Lara ran out of the store, Amabel considered going after them, and even followed them into the main part of the store, but stopped when she got to the door. They wouldn't listen to her, anyway. Not right now. She needed time to prepare.

She needed that book. She'd spent so long looking for it, devoting years to research and tracking it down, and now it was so close. It had been right in front of her, here in Grafton in a musty closet all along, and she'd only sensed it that one time. She still didn't know what that meant, but it was here now, and she wanted it. She *needed* it, but no one could know why.

She couldn't do as Maryn said and come clean because then she'd have to tell the rest of the coven exactly how much she knew. And maybe even *why* she wanted it so badly.

Amabel had been so stupid. How had she not seen it? How had she not even thought to keep a better eye on Maisie, to learn everything about her? It was clear now that the book must somehow be related to the women's bloodline.

Now everyone was pissed off and wouldn't be likely to help her.

Amabel was probably going to need their cooperation, whether they chose to or not.

She returned to the back room and opened a small, hidden safe on the far wall and pulled out a book of her very own.

Lara

When Lara and Maryn arrived at Maisie's house, Lara made introductions and the women sat down at Maisie's kitchen table.

"Maryn, it's so good to meet you. I've heard a lot about you. I'm glad Lara has such a good friend."

Maryn smiled. "Well. I've maybe not been the best friend. But I'm here for her now."

Maisie looked a question at Lara, who took a deep breath.

"I've got a lot to tell you, Maisie. You're not going to like it."

Maisie just nodded and Lara started talking. She told her everything that had been happening at home, what she'd found out about witches and the book. Maryn told Maisie her own story, looking down at the table when she came clean about how she'd come into Lara's life.

Maisie was silent for a long moment and then put her hand on Maryn's. "You're not the only one who's held back trying to protect her, dear."

Maisie turned to Lara. "I just wanted this to stop, Lara. I didn't want to revisit any of this; I told you that."

"I know." Lara wasn't sure where Maisie was going with this, and she was more stunned that Maisie hadn't had anything to say about Maryn admitting she was a witch.

"I've known it was all real from the beginning, honey. I wanted so desperately for you to not be involved."

"What are you talking about?"

"I knew that Amabel was a witch." Maisie sighed.

"Are you serious, Maisie?" Lara was working to keep her voice under control.

"Yes. I'm sorry, dear. I should have just told you everything. But I just wanted to convince you the book was bad news. I was just hoping you'd realize how dangerous it was on your own."

Lara shook her head. "I don't know what to say." Lara couldn't work out her feelings. It was another betrayal. On the surface, she could understand why both Maisie and Maryn had done what they'd done, but it didn't make it any easier to accept.

Maisie clutched her hand. "I haven't lied to you, Lara." Lara let out a sharp breath, skeptical.

"I know how that sounds. But everything I've told you is true. I just left this one thing out."

"Kind of a big thing."

"I know." Maisie took a deep breath.

"We went back to the cave once, to look for it. I was going to burn it."

"Who did?"

"Me and CiCi. We'd never talked about it again after that last day. And we weren't close with John anymore, after everything that happened between the three of us.

One night, probably almost twenty years after everything happened in the cave, it must have been about 1975 or so, CiCi and I got drunk—even then we were too old to just be getting drunk on a Friday night, but this was back when we had nothing but time ..." Maisie smiled, the look in her eyes far away. She shook her head and continued.

"For the first time we talked about everything that had happened back then. We'd both always privately thought that we had exaggerated how scary it had been—a product of our very active thirteen-year-old imaginations. So we decided to be brave and go back up to the cave." She shook her head and smiled.

"Oh, we were funny. Stumbling up the hill, laughing. We

thought we'd find the book, tossed on the floor of the cave. We thought maybe we'd even find John's old broken cowbell." Maisie laughed again.

"The cave was untouched. It was exactly the same as we'd left it." Her voice fell to a whisper. "We didn't find the cowbell, but the marks at the mouth of the cave ..."

Maisie took a deep breath.

"We'd forgotten to bring a flashlight, of course, but CiCi had a cigarette lighter. We used its tiny bit of light and walked into the cave. It seemed so much smaller than we'd remembered. Of course as adults we took up more space. All of our things were still there. The pillows and blankets we'd used. The steel box, the flashlight. It was all still there. I couldn't believe none of it had been touched in all those years. But the book was gone."

Lara felt the hair on the back of her neck rise, and goosebumps broke out on her arms.

"The book was gone," Maisie repeated. "When we realized it wasn't there, we got scared and left quickly. We never found it. Never saw it again. I always wondered if John took it. I asked him once, the one time we talked after everything that had happened. We got drunk at a church picnic. Hmm—it seems like a lot of my stories start off with, 'We got drunk,'" Maisie laughed again, and for a moment Lara could see what she must have been like as a young woman—brash and bold, not afraid to laugh, not afraid to do exactly what she wanted, everyone else's opinion be damned.

"Anyway, John and I talked for a long time that night. I told him everything then, about CiCi and I going back up to the cave. I asked him if he'd gone back and taken the book. He was shocked. He said he'd forgotten all about it. He'd said he thought it was destroyed. CiCi and I had told him we'd burned it, so he'd had no reason to look for it. And surely it couldn't have really been as dramatic as we remembered. I agreed with him and believed him at the time. But when you told me you'd found it in his store, I thought for sure he'd lied back then, that he had gotten it from the cave and kept it all these years."

"And? Did he?"

"He lied. He had gone back for it." Maisie told Lara how the book had ended up back in John's shop.

"Okay, so he got the book out before you went back to look for it and held onto it all these years."

"No. John didn't go back until 2005. *After* CiCi and I had tried to find it."

"That doesn't make any sense."

"I know. I was sure the book wasn't there." Maisie's voice trailed off. "At least, I was at the time. But we were pretty drunk. I suppose we could have missed it." She looked into space, thinking. "I think we must have missed it. Especially because of what happened shortly after CiCi and went up there."

"What?"

"This is the part I didn't tell you, Lolly."

Chapter Twenty-Nine

Maisie

A couple of days after CiCi and Maisie went back to the cave, Amabel approached Maisie on the street. She was new to town. No one really knew her and no one knew quite what to think of her. She was young and beautiful, in her early twenties, but she dressed funny—long skirts, flowers in her hair and feathered earrings. Woodstock had been six years earlier, but she would have fit right in there. Instead, in Grafton, she stood out.

She also didn't go to church. Either one of those things in a town like Grafton was enough to cast suspicion on anyone. Maisie had only spoken to her once before and thought she'd seemed nice enough, even if it seemed like she was taking the hippie thing a little too far, even for the seventies.

Amabel had already rented the place for her store and came running out when Maisie walked by. She took Maisie's arm and said, "Sister, have you found something?"

"What?" Maisie pulled her arm out of Amabel's grasp. She had no idea what the woman was talking about.

"You didn't feel it?"

Maisie looked at the woman, who was clearly excited. She was smiling expectantly, as if she was waiting for Maisie to confirm something for her.

"No. I'm sorry; what are you talking about?"

Amabel's smile faltered a bit. "The other day, I felt—when I saw you and that other woman walking—"

"What?"

"I felt it, I felt ..." Amabel looked confused, now. "Can you just tell me what it was?"

"I have no idea what you're talking about."

"No, no, that's not right. I felt it. You have to know something. You can tell me. It's okay. I know." Amabel smiled what she clearly meant to be a reassuring smile, but it gave Maisie an odd feeling.

"I'm sorry, but I don't have any idea what you're talking about." Maisie started to walk away, wanting to get away from this woman as fast as she could.

"I'm one of you!" Amabel called after her.

Maisie spun around. *What does she mean she's one of us?* Her first thought was that she meant she was gay. Is that what she was referring to, that she saw Maisie and CiCi together? But how would she *know*? They were so careful when they were in public.

Maisie started walking back toward her. "You're one of us?"

"Yes," Amabel said with relief, smiling again. "I'm so glad to find others here. I wasn't sure I would find anyone in a town this small. The others in St. Louis weren't sure, you all hadn't registered yet, so ..."

"The others?" Maisie was so confused. She and CiCi had some friends in St. Louis who were gay, but what was this woman talking about registering?

Amabel hadn't stopped talking. "If you all didn't feel it, I'm not sure what that means. I *thought* I knew what it was I was feeling, but maybe I was wrong. I was just so sure. Do you want to come inside?" She paused her speech to look up at the darkening sky. "Hmm ... it's almost a full moon, but not quite. Damn. It would be better if it were totally full, but we can still try a ceremony—"

At that, Maisie finally stopped the woman. "Amabel! I have no idea what you're talking about. I'm going to go now." Maisie had never wanted to escape from talking with someone so much.

"Maisie, it's okay. I know we're typically more discreet, but come on, we both know, so it's okay!"

"I don't know how many other ways to say this, but I have no idea what you're talking about. I know we don't know each other very well, but quite frankly you don't sound well."

At this, Amabel's smile faded and she seemed to understand Maisie was serious.

"You don't know what I'm talking about?"

"No. I don't. Sorry. Have a good night."

This time Amabel let her walk away.

Maisie wasn't sure what had just happened, but the woman was definitely off her rocker. And how had she known Maisie and CiCi had been in the woods? When she returned home and told CiCi about the strange encounter, they decided to just avoid Amabel.

That worked for two days.

It was Sunday and Maisie was sitting on her porch, enjoying the first cool evening in a long time. Summer was on its last legs and she was relieved for the break in the heat and humidity that had seemed a long time coming.

When she saw Amabel walking up her street, she almost ran inside, but the woman had seen her sitting there and picked up her pace. "Damn it," Maisie mumbled under her breath.

Amabel walked up to Maisie's porch steps, stopping just short of coming onto the porch.

"Maisie, I'm sorry to bother you." The woman looked tired. Her hair was disheveled and there were bags under her eyes.

"What do you need, Amabel?" Maisie tried to keep the annoyance out of her voice, but she did not want to talk to this woman.

Amabel took a deep breath and said, "You really don't know what I was talking about the other day?"

"No, Amabel, I don't."

The woman closed her eyes and shook her head. "Then I must have sounded crazy."

"A little bit."

Amabel sighed and sat down on the top step of the porch. "I'm sorry. There's not really an explanation I can give you that would make sense to you. Have you ever had to keep a secret, even though you didn't think you should have to?"

Maisie let out a startled laugh. "Yes. Yes, I have." She thought about CiCi, how painful it was some days to not be able to just live her life the way she wanted, to love who she wanted out loud and in the open like everyone else.

"So is the woman I saw you with the other day your sister? Your friend?"

"She's my closest friend. We've been friends since we were kids. Made it through two wars together. Now we're both nurses. Her name is CiCi."

Amabel nodded. The women were quiet for a minute. From Maisie's house at the top of the steep hill, you could see the river, wide and swift, the sun dipping lower and reflecting off its churning surface.

"Can you just tell me what you and CiCi were doing in the woods?"

Just when I was warming up to her, Maisie thought. "Look, Amabel, I don't know how you know we went into the woods, and I don't mind telling you it's a little odd. We weren't doing anything."

"I can't explain how, but I know something happened there, Maisie. I need to know."

"I don't know what you're talking about," Maisie said again. The conversation was starting to make Maisie uncomfortable. She'd never tell this woman anything about the book, but she was starting to wonder if Amabel had information about it. She wasn't sure what it all meant. All she knew was that, for reasons she couldn't quite articulate, Maisie did not want to tell this woman anything about the book or the cave.

"You don't have to acknowledge or agree with what I'm about

to tell you. I don't expect you to. Clearly you're not going to tell me anything. But you know something, Maisie." Amabel looked at Maisie, making sure the woman could see her face. "I'm a witch. You were doing something with powerful magic up there, so I know you're lying when you say you don't know what I'm talking about. I don't know—"

Maisie interrupted her with a loud laugh. "You're a witch? Do you hear yourself, Amabel? Come on. I don't know what you're implying, but I don't believe in that nonsense. And *I* am definitely not a witch."

A small smile played around Amabel's lips. "Laugh if you want. Like I said, I didn't expect you to admit anything. But I know what I know. I don't care what you think about it."

Amabel stood up. "I need to know. And I'll find out, Maisie. If it happens again, I'll know and you'll have to tell me."

Maisie didn't respond, but her heart was pounding. "I don't much like what you're implying."

"Not implying anything. Just being honest." Amabel walked down the stairs, but turned around when she reached the last step. "Be careful, Maisie. Whatever it is that you're not telling me, it's probably not something you fully understand. So be careful."

Maisie didn't reply as she watched Amabel walk down the hill toward town.

Lara

"She and I avoided each other after that," Maisie told Lara and Maryn. "We never exchanged more than polite hellos in town. But whenever I saw her, I could feel her watching me and CiCi. She always seemed like she was *waiting* for us to do something. Now I guess it makes sense."

"What do you mean it makes sense?" Maryn, who had hardly said anything the whole time, asked.

"Well she thought we were witches and were doing something—who knows what—in the woods."

Maryn nodded. "She sensed the book and suspected what it was."

Maisie shook her head slowly. "I never wanted to believe any of this was real. I made myself forget what she'd said about being a witch. I convinced myself we'd blown it all out of proportion. Lara, when you came to me and told me what was going on with the book, I really didn't connect it to Amabel."

Lara sighed. "To be honest, I don't know that it would have made a difference if you had. Other than I maybe wouldn't have gone and told her everything, because now I have a feeling she's going to do whatever it takes to get it from me." Lara rubbed her hands up and down her face. She felt exhausted.

"There's still so much I don't understand. And none of this really gets me closer to figuring out what the book even is or why it's happening to me."

"I've been thinking about something," Maryn said. "We—well, I for sure—don't know much about what the book actually is. You've heard Amabel's theory and that's what she told us when she originally came to the coven asking for help. But Clara has done some independent research. Amabel gave us a weird vibe so Clara wanted to try and confirm what she told us. Amabel is desperate and no good magic ever came out of desperation."

Maryn leaned down and took something out of her bag. "Lara, like you already know, covens are organized by location. And one member is responsible for keeping track of our historical documents. There's not much left, so it's not as big of a job as it sounds. The letters Amabel showed you should be a part of our records. I don't know how she got her hands on them. But we have two that seem to be part of the same set of correspondence. It's not much, but it did give me an idea."

Maryn slid two pieces of paper across the table. They were both photocopies of letters. The first was just two lines.

A –

I am available next Thursday for tea. I will meet you at the hotel.

Bring the book.

T

"That seems like a response to one of the letters Amabel showed me. Whoever T is asked to meet A in person."

Maryn nodded. "The next one tells us a little more."

A –

We have reached a unanimous decision and you aren't to return. What you have done, how you have betrayed the coven, it simply cannot be forgotten. We cannot force you or her to do our will. That is not what we are about. I can only hope that you will soon come to your senses and force her to do the right and responsible thing.

You seem to be taking some comfort in the fact that only she can really "use" it, so to speak, but I don't understand why. She is untrained, untested, and unstable. So while you believe you've contained it, you've really just made it a tool. I cannot see how that is any safer.

I do not want you to become involved in something you cannot handle. Or that is dangerous, for you or for the world as a whole. Please see sense. I'll be prepared to help you when you do.

T

Lara read the letter twice then handed it to Maisie. While her aunt read the letter, Lara thought about what it might mean. It didn't seem to shed any light on anything.

When Maisie was done reading, she looked at Maryn and said, "Okay. It's interesting, but how does it help?"

"I guess Amelia is A? In the book, Amelia helped Violet. But who is T?" Lara interjected.

"Amelia seems to make sense. I don't know who T is," Maryn responded. "Clara can look back at our records."

"Do these letters help us at all?" Lara asked.

"Well, something that's been bothering me is how John could have it in his house all those years and never experience anything odd. Nothing. He forgot about it. And then why was it in your house for so long, Lara, without anything happening? So I've been trying to figure out what changed or what circumstances cause it to start making trouble."

Lara nodded. "Yeah that makes sense. I don't know."

"In the letter, T says, 'only she can really use it.' That leads me to believe that the magic is tied only to one person. Who has to be Violet, right?"

"That might make sense," Lara said. "But what did I do that made all of this start?"

"That I don't know," Maryn said. "Can you think of anything you started doing differently the second time you read it?"

"No, not really." Lara was silent for a long moment, trying to think of anything at all. "I don't know. I wasn't doing so great the first time I read it. I was depressed and emotional. The second time I was feeling better. I was more clear headed. I did start taking notes, kind of journaling as I read the book, figuring out some of my own feelings and nailing down some of my memories of Ben."

"You were keeping a journal?"

"No. There are a ton of blank pages in the back of the book.

Like, almost a whole notebook's worth. I just started writing there."

"Lara, that's it!" Maryn said. "That has to be it. You started manipulating the book itself. That must have activated the magic. Woken it up. Whatever you want to say. That's common in some grimoires and spell books. A witch can change or tweak the spells best by writing directly in them. That has to be it."

"Wait, I thought you said that you all weren't the fairytale kind of witches. That sounds a lot like fairytale magic."

Maryn smiled at her. "It does. It's not common. We don't have libraries full of spell books. In fact, I've only ever seen one. And they're not full of love potions or spells that can help you get revenge on your enemies. They're usually for getting plants to grow or helping with fertility. Natural herbs and stuff. No rat's ears or dragon tears."

The women laughed, and Lara thought again how utterly unbelievable and strange this all was.

"I need to call Clara," Maryn said. "This is far beyond my knowledge. She might know what to do. But it's important she knows this."

Maryn took her phone out of her purse and walked into the living room.

"I'm so sorry," Maisie said, taking Lara's hand.

"It's okay. I know that everyone has been trying to help me, protect me. Of course I wish everyone could have just been honest from the start, but I do understand."

"I can't believe any of this, if I'm being honest. Witches … Lara, I feel like I've been living in the dark this whole time, my head in the sand. And in spite of everything, I still don't know if I actually believe it."

Lara laughed. "Yeah I get it." The two women sat in silence for a couple of minutes, lost in their own thoughts. Lara thought about Maryn's theory, that she had altered the book in some way by writing in it. What would it mean if Maryn was right? She knew literally nothing about magic and she'd managed to, what—wake the dead? Give life to some evil magic? She shuddered involuntarily.

Suddenly, she was scared and felt very helpless. She realized she was at everyone's mercy here; Maryn, Clara, even Amabel. They all knew more than she did, they were all much more capable and skilled than she could ever be. It made her uncomfortable. They could tell her anything—ask her to do anything—and she wouldn't know whether or not it was the right thing. She wasn't sure she trusted any of them enough to have that much blind faith.

She thought about the book, sitting in the trunk of her car. What would happen if she turned it over to them? She'd *maybe* miss out on a chance to talk to Ben? She still didn't even know if that was even possible, so was it worth keeping the book around? Maybe she should just turn it over to the witches, let them deal with it. On the other hand, it felt like abandonment. Here was this amazing, terrifying, unbelievable thing that had come into her life, that had changed her. And of course, there was still the *what if.*

Lara put her head in her hands and groaned. "Maisie, I don't know what to do," she mumbled quietly. She felt her aunt take her hands and pull them gently away from her face.

"I know you don't. You know how I feel about it, but I do understand why you're hesitant to give it up." Maisie looked toward the living room, where they could hear Maryn speaking quietly. "You can trust her, though. She cares about you and won't put you in danger. Maryn strikes me as the kind of person who's not going to take any bullshit, especially when it comes to the people she loves."

The relief Lara felt at her words made her realize she'd been looking for this assurance. It had been hard to trust her own feelings, but hearing that Maisie trusted Maryn eased some of Lara's concerns.

"I do not trust Amabel, though," Maisie continued. "There's a reason she wants to get her hands on that book so badly, and I think she'll do, well, whatever it takes to get it. It's just a feeling. All those years she spent watching me and CiCi—she's been waiting for this for a long time." Lara nodded in agreement.

Just then, Maryn came back into the room. "Okay," she said. "Clara is going to come up here. There's a lot to figure out and she's concerned about Amabel. She thinks that I'm probably right, that you writing in the book woke it up, for lack of a better word ..." Maryn's voice trailed off, and she twisted her phone around in her hand, unlocking the home screen and closing it again. She looked around the room, clearly needing to say something but not sure how.

"Maryn? What is it?"

"Well, Clara thinks ... Maisie, did you write in the book when you were reading it?"

Startled by her question, Maisie looked thoughtful. "Yes. I highlighted a couple of lines, mostly the parts about what Violet did in the woods. We were trying to figure out how it worked, you know."

Maryn nodded. "Okay. Well, have you—either of you—ever noticed anything odd happening around you?"

Lara laughed. "You mean aside from the creepy haunted book I've been living with for months?"

Maryn smiled. "Yeah, aside from that. Like, before all this started."

"Like what kind of things?"

"I don't know." Maryn looked uncomfortable. "It could be odd feelings you get, a foggy head, objects moving ..." At this last, Maisie and Lara looked at each other, both shaking their heads.

"No. Nothing like that," Lara said.

Maisie agreed. "Nothing at all. I've never believed that any of this was real."

"Okay. Well, Clara thinks, maybe, because you are both related to Violet ..." She turned away from them again, still playing with her phone.

"Maryn, what?"

"Clara thinks maybe you're both witches."

"What?" Lara nearly yelled at the same time Maisie burst out laughing.

Maryn smiled weakly at them. "I know how it sounds. But hear me out." Lara and Maisie were both shaking their heads, but they remained silent as they waited for Maryn to continue.

"Clara thinks that the reason the book could stay in John's house for so long and in yours, Lara, without anything happening, is because it doesn't work for everyone, and it doesn't work until something happens to wake it up. The magic is probably tied to witches and maybe even only those descended from Violet herself. Like, Clara's not even sure she or I could use the magic in the book."

Lara let that sink in. "Wait, so you think *I'm* the only one who can use it?"

"Well, you and Maisie. But we don't know for sure. Clara wants to examine it, get a feeling for it. But she suspects maybe that was the safety Amelia and Violet put into place. So they didn't have to destroy it, but they could ensure not just anyone who got their hands on it could use it."

Lara didn't know what to say. Clearly, neither did Maisie, who was staring openly at Maryn, her mouth even hanging open a little.

"So, she's going to come here tomorrow. She'd like to meet both of you, if that's okay. She doesn't want anything bad to happen to either of you and wants to make sure we can protect you until you decide what to do."

"Until *I* decide what to do?" Lara asked.

"Yes. We're not going to force you to do anything, Lara. I told you, that's not what we're about. Which leads me to the other thing. Clara is concerned that Amabel has been as forceful with you as she has. She's … not happy about that. She suggested we keep the book with us at all times."

Lara's stomach tightened. "Okay. That makes me a little nervous." Lara looked at her aunt. "I don't know if you want it in the house, Maisie."

Maisie smiled at her. "I can handle it, dear. As long as you both plan to stay here with me, I think we'll be okay."

"Of course we will," Maryn said. "When Clara gets here tomorrow, hopefully we can get some answers and get this all figured out once and for all."

CHAPTER THIRTY

Lara

Lara got the book out of her car. When she touched it, she could feel a thrumming, something she hadn't noticed before. It wasn't quite a vibration, but that was the closest sensation she could liken it to. It gave her chills. She didn't like it.

Lara dropped the book on the table and they all stared at it for a long moment. Maryn's face was very pale and she was rubbing her hands together as though they were cold. Lara noticed Maisie's hands shaking a bit and she again questioned whether or not it was fair for her to be putting her aunt through this.

"Maisie, are you sure you're okay with it being here tonight? We can go stay at the Ruebel instead."

"I'm fine, dear," she said. But she gathered her arms around her middle, rubbing them.

Lara and Maryn put the book in Maisie's basement, shoved onto a shelf in the back of the musty room.

"I don't like having it here," Lara said. "Damn it. I feel so guilty."

Maryn patted her back. "You didn't know, Lara. There was no way for you to know."

The women got ready for bed, Maryn and Lara each taking one of the guest rooms. Lara had an overwhelming desire to ask Maryn to stay with her, but she didn't. She got into bed and tried to distract herself with Netflix streaming on her phone, but the service was so bad the video kept buffering. She tried to read, but that felt a little too on the nose. Eventually she gave up and just stared at the ceiling until she started to get drowsy, eventually falling into a fitful sleep.

She awoke suddenly, some time later, but wasn't sure why. She felt as though a sound had woken her, but she didn't hear anything now. Her heart was pounding, but there wasn't anything wrong that she could tell. *Must have been a dream.*

She lay back, but she had to go to the bathroom and she wouldn't get back to sleep until she did. She swung her legs over the bed, cursing her tiny bladder. She shuffled down the hallway, navigating mostly by memory in the dark. She flipped on the light and one of the two bulbs in the fixture popped and burnt out.

"Damn," she muttered, making a groggy mental note to change it for Maisie in the morning.

Lara used the bathroom and made her way to the sink to wash her hands. She looked down, rinsing off the soap. As she shut off the water, she looked up and into the mirror, taking in her tousled hair and puffy, sleepy eyes for a split second before she noticed the shadow standing behind her.

With a gasp that caught in her throat before it became a full-fledged scream, she spun around on instinct. But there was nothing there. Just the shower curtain. Heart pounding, she looked back in the mirror. Nothing.

Lara closed her eyes and leaned on the counter for a moment, convincing herself it must have been her sleepy mind playing tricks on her. All the same, she didn't look back in the mirror as she stepped to the bathroom door and turned off the light.

She made her way back down the hallway. Still unsettled, she sank gratefully onto the bed, hoping she'd be able to fall back asleep.

As she lay her head down on the pillow and closed her eyes, the mattress next to her sank. As though someone had gotten in next to her and sank their own head down. Lara's blood ran cold and she began to shake, too afraid to look over at the other side of the bed and too afraid to get up.

She tried to speak, to scream, but nothing came out. Nothing beside her moved, until the bed squeaked and she felt the unmistakable pressure of someone rolling towards her on the bed.

That was enough for her to finally move.

As she sprang out of bed, she heard a piercing, terrified scream come from outside the door to the room. Lara yelled, "Maisie? Maryn?"

Just as she opened her door, Maryn opened hers. "Was that you?" And seeing her friend's face, she said, "Lara, what happened? What's wrong?"

"Something in my room. In my bed. I don't know. I didn't yell though. What was that? Where's Maisie?" Lara stammered, running toward her aunt's room. "Maisie?" Just as she reached the door, it swung open and Maisie, bleary-eyed, looked back at her.

"Lara? What was that? Are you okay?"

"You didn't scream?"

"No. Is that what woke me?"

Lara looked back at Maryn.

The scream sounded again, this time from the main level of the house.

"Jesus!" Maryn yelled. "What the hell is that?"

"I don't know. It has to be the book. Son of a bitch, I knew I shouldn't have kept it here. Maisie, I want you to go back to your room," Lara said. "Lock the door."

"Lara, don't treat me like a child. *You* stay here." Maisie walked back into her room and moments later returned, carrying a small, silver pistol.

"Maisie!"

"I'm an old woman who lives alone, Lara. Don't look so surprised. I've never had to shoot the thing, but I've got it and maybe it'll come in handy tonight."

Lara knew there was no use arguing once Maisie had made up her mind. The three women crept down the hall toward the stairs. The house was silent, but Lara sensed something waiting. She didn't know how she knew, but she did.

"Maryn?" she whispered. "Do you feel that?"

"Yes. There's something here."

As they made their way down the hall, they began to hear a quiet hum of noise. It was almost like when you leave the television on and fall asleep—background noise that doesn't really register. A mix of voices and music, collating together.

"What is that?" Maisie whispered.

"I don't know."

They crept down the stairs, through the living room, and into the kitchen. As they stood in Maisie's bright kitchen, the heart of her home, the basement door swung open violently on its hinges and the low hum of noise became clear. It was voices. Hundreds, maybe thousands, of voices. All screaming, yelling, crying, calling out.

"Oh my god," Lara said quietly.

It got louder and louder. Lara could feel it in her bones, hear it inside of her head. On and on it went. The women stood in the kitchen, waiting for it to end, unsure what to do. Lara felt like the sound was going to rip her apart. The terror, the screaming, it was the manifestation of every desperate and terrible thought and feeling she'd ever had. She felt herself start to give in, open up to the darkness. If she could just let it in, the sound would stop. She was sure. The noise faded, bit by bit. Her eyes drifted closed—just let it out of the book and into her—

She felt Maryn squeeze her arm and lean in close to her. "Lara, we have to go get the book. You know that's what it is." Lara jumped, eyes opening. (*When had she closed her eyes?*) She shook her head. The sound rushed back, making her clamp her hands over her ears. What had just happened to her?

Maryn was in her face, looking like she was waiting for an answer. What had she said?

"Lara? We need to go get the book and get it out of here." Lara could hear banging now, coming from the basement. She shook her head. *Get it together,* she thought. She nodded at Maryn and looked at Maisie, who was standing wide-eyed, looking at the basement door.

Lara grabbed her hand and yelled in her ear, "We're going to go get the book. Stay. Here." She expected Maisie to argue with her, but her aunt just nodded. "Keep that"—she gestured toward the gun still clutched in Maisie's hand— "thing's safety on unless I yell otherwise." The last thing she needed was her aunt freaking out and shooting wildly around the room. Maisie nodded.

Lara headed toward the basement stairs. She could feel Maryn close behind her. When her foot hit the first step, the sound came to an abrupt stop, the sudden silence more terrifying than the noise. Lara heard Maryn breathe, "Jesus Christ." Lara couldn't tell if it was a prayer or not, but she thought it wouldn't be a bad idea.

As they crept down the stairs, a knocking came from the basement. *Step. Knock. Step. Knock. Step. Knock.* Lara didn't want to keep going, but she had to. They couldn't leave it down there all night. She didn't know what would happen if they didn't get it out of the house.

When they reached the bottom step, they stood together, side by side, looking toward the shelf where the book was sitting. The knocking continued, picking up speed. What was making that noise? It sounded like something hard hitting something soft. A pillow on wood? A fist on flesh? No. A book on an old wooden shelf.

Knock. Knock. Knock knock knock knock knock KNOCK KNOCK *KNOCK KNOCKKNOCKKNOCKKNOCKKNOCK.*

Lara was frozen. She stood there, stock-still, her shoulder touching Maryn's, and listened to the knocking. She listened. *KNOCK KNOCK KNOCK.* She heard Maryn's voice, calling her name, but it sounded like it was coming from far away. She couldn't move her legs or her arms. She closed her eyes. *KNOCK KNOCK KNOCK*

Lara's eyes flew open when Maryn suddenly rushed forward,

pushing Lara behind her. "Go back upstairs!" she yelled. "You can't touch it!"

Lara watched as Maryn walked toward the shelf where the book still lay. *What the hell had she been doing, standing there like that?* Lara thought she should try to help but just as she went to move forward, Maryn yelled, "Lara, I said stay there!" The knocking was, impossibly, getting louder and Lara fought a desire to put her hands over her ears.

Then, Maryn had the book in her hands. "Where should I put it?" she yelled.

"I don't know!" Lara fought the fog in her brain as she tried to think of a solution. Why the hell hadn't they talked about this before rushing down here?

She heard Maisie's voice floating down from the kitchen. "Lara! Tell her to take it out back and put it in the Millers' old house!"

Lara nodded and told Maryn, "Come on, follow me."

The women made their way up the stairs, past Maisie, who handed Lara a key and a flashlight, and went out the back door, the knocking following them all the way. Maryn's face was contorted like she was in pain, but she kept the book held tight to her chest and shook her head when Lara offered to carry it. As soon as they were outside, the knocking stopped.

Lara led Maryn through Maisie's backyard, explaining as they walked around Maisie's garden and toward the back of her property.

"There's an abandoned house back here, no one's lived in it for five years. The people left Maisie with a set of keys when they moved and for some reason have never sold it. We'll put the book in there and lock it." Maryn just nodded.

"Are you okay?"

She just nodded again, but still didn't say anything.

When they reached the porch, skirting the holes in the rotted wood, Lara tried to insert the key into the lock, but her hands were shaking so badly that it wasn't until her third attempt, after she heard Maryn suck in a breath and stifle a moan, that she managed to steady her hand and open the door.

Maryn threw the book on the floor of the foyer, where she could just glimpse a dark hallway and set of stairs, before Lara closed the door again and locked it. Maryn leaned over, breathing heavily, her hands on her knees.

"Maryn? Are you okay? What's wrong?"

Maryn took a shaky breath. "It's hard to have that much physical contact with something that powerful. That's all."

"Oh." Lara thought for a moment. "Why isn't it hard for me to touch it?"

"I have no idea. I honestly have no idea what the fuck just happened, to be honest," Maryn replied. The women made their way off the porch and headed back toward Maisie's house.

"Hold on," Lara said, grabbing Maryn's arm. "Do you hear that?" Lara could hear something coming from the direction of the old Miller house. It sounded like voices again.

"Yeah, I hear it," Maryn said. "Let's go."

Amabel

It was late. Amabel was rifling through her notebook, going through boxes, bottles, jars, when she felt a jolt of that same energy, stronger than she'd felt before, so strong she dropped the papers she'd been holding and they scattered all over the floor.

"My god," she breathed quietly. She closed her eyes, taking in the feeling and trying to gather any information she could. It was unlike anything she'd felt before. It was good and bad and it felt barely contained, like the river threatening to spill over its banks during a flood—a force of power and energy that couldn't be held back.

After a minute or two it receded again, and Amabel sat heavily in a chair in the storage room of her shop.

"This is it," she said aloud to the empty room. It wasn't until she said the words did she realize that there had still been a small seed of doubt there. Having not seen the book, she still wasn't entirely sure it was what she thought it was. But now there could be no mistake. And now she knew she had to do whatever it would take to get her hands on it.

She'd spent the night planning, trying to figure out how she could outsmart—or simply overpower—Lara and those other witches. She realized overpowering them wasn't likely. She was outnumbered, for one, and they were much younger than she was. She'd have to use her brains and her knowledge of magic—magic she knew they didn't have.

Her main concern was that they'd call in reinforcements. If it was just Clara, Amabel had no doubt she could overpower that uppity witch. After all, she was willing to … compromise … and use magic that holier-than-thou Clara would frown upon. But if they called in the rest of the coven, it might become a problem.

She'd discovered a powerful summoning spell years ago, that could make objects appear whenever and wherever she wanted them, so long as the object was a reasonable distance away. She thought this might be her best bet. If she could just get close enough to the book, she would use the spell, and once she had the book in her hands, she'd simply run.

Clara was the type of witch who would call the spell "Hollywood magic," something flashy and unnecessary in normal circumstances. But witches like Clara didn't understand the power that lay literally at her fingertips. She'd never want to draw attention to their power, never want to use it for anything but good, and always advocate for only using magic when it was absolutely necessary.

Amabel had gone along for years, mostly not to rock the boat and stay on the good side of the coven in case she needed them. She'd lived her life quietly, running her store, living in this small sleepy town that, to her surprise, she'd come to love. She would miss it. But behind her quiet life, she'd been gathering information like squirrels gather nuts before winter. She had an arsenal of spells and everything she needed to execute those spells stored in a large trunk in the back room of her store. There was untold power contained in that trunk and she was ready to put it to good use. She'd been waiting her whole life.

Amabel felt she deserved this power. Her life had been one misery after another, after all, and if magic could finally help her leave some of that pain behind, she was willing to do whatever it took. She wished the lie she'd told Lara about a cousin and a husband and ties to Grafton were true.

As she inventoried the contents of her trunk for what was probably the fourth or fifth time that long, long, night, Amabel spoke to her sister, as she often did when she was trying to think through a problem.

"It's time, Eloise. I think I've got everything I need packed here. I just have to figure out where they are. It shouldn't be too hard, there's only so many places they can go. I'll wait until morning, then scope out Maisie's house. Wasn't there a tracking spell we saw not too long ago ..."

As Amabel flipped through her spell book, her mind wandered again. She and Eloise had been eleven and nine when their parents were killed in a car accident near their hometown in Oklahoma. Until then, life had been good. They'd not been fancy or rich but they got by and their parents, who were both teachers, had loved them.

After the accident, the girls had no close family to speak of so they'd been shuttled off to an orphanage where they were too old and no longer cute enough to be seriously considered for adoption, so they sat there, enduring harsh treatment from the nuns. They would be placed in the occasional foster home where each of the girls experienced untold horrors. By some miracle they were always placed together, which was rare in the system, but they were still too young to protect themselves or each other from the adults around them.

When they'd been in the system for four years, they began plotting how they would run away. As the big sister, Amabel felt responsible for finding a way out, but she didn't know how. She was still too young to get a job that would support them and they had no resources at all. She thought their best bet would be to run away to a bigger city, maybe Tulsa or Oklahoma City and find something there.

Then they'd been placed in the final foster home either of them would ever see. They'd been there less than two weeks when, one night, she awoke to a scuffle in the room the girls shared. She looked to Eloise's bed where she saw a man, their foster "father," looming over her sister's bed. A pillow was over her sister's face and he was trying to do something to her that Amabel didn't want to register at the time.

That's when it happened for the first time. Amabel was overcome with anger—no, rage—and she cried out, screaming at him to get off her sister. She picked up a lamp and, feeling a powerful energy surge out of her body as she reared her arm up, the lamp flew out of her hand and hit him square on the side of the head. He collapsed instantly.

Amabel pushed him off the bed, his body crumpling to the floor. She barely noticed how the side of his head now didn't look quite right.

She yanked the pillow off of Eloise, but she could see right away she'd been too late. Her sister's face was blue. She wasn't breathing. Amabel screamed, gathering her sister in her arms, not even aware that her foster mother and the four other kids in their care were all trying to enter the room, all of them screaming. She focused her energy on them, pushing them all away from her and her sister, and they stumbled, terrified now, and running out of the small space.

Amabel slammed the door shut, and took another minute with her sister's body, tears pouring down her face, before she realized that she had to leave and she had to leave now. They'd try to pin all of this on her.

Amabel kissed her sister's face, told her she was sorry, so sorry, and climbed out the window.

She'd started running, not caring or knowing where she was going. Eventually, she'd come to a small dirt road that, as it turned out, led to a Native American reservation. Just as the sun was peeking over the plain, a dusty pickup truck that looked like it had maybe once been red, stopped. An older Native American man was driving and as he rolled the window down, his dark brown eyes looked kindly at her.

"Are you okay?"

Amabel was too exhausted to come up with a story or consider what she was doing. "No. I'm not," she answered honestly, before the tears started up again. The man got out of the truck and helped her into the passenger seat.

He'd taken her to his home, where he and his wife listened to her story. They were a childless couple who lived quietly on the reservation and they were the first people to show Amabel kindness in years. They took her in, concocting a story that she was a friend's child who'd been orphaned.

There had been a halfhearted search for her after Eloise and her foster father died, but from what little information she and her caretakers could glean from town, the cops seemed to believe she'd killed that man in defense of her sister. But she didn't want to risk having to answer questions or get placed back into the system.

While she was on the reservation, she kept to herself. She made no friends and participated in few activities. Her heart and her mind felt broken, like she'd never be whole again. The only thing she had was the powers she'd discovered on that most terrible of nights.

Amabel didn't understand what was happening to her. All she knew was that she could move objects without ever touching them. She'd go out into the prairie and practice, throwing around various objects and honing her power so that it was eventually easy to control. She could move one blade of grass apart from the rest, roll one small rock in whatever pattern she chose. Her power had limits, however, and she couldn't move large objects. But it was something to hold onto. She never told anyone what was happening to her.

Amabel stayed on the reservation until she was eighteen and decided to leave when she heard about the book.

The old woman would tell her stories of her ancestors, who had been forced to scatter all over the country. Amabel's heart ached for what the Native Americans had been put through, these amazing people who had shown her such kindness, and she listened intently to the tales, thinking that if just one part of their story lived on in her, then that was a kind of a testament.

One day, the old woman told her a story—a rumor, really— about some magic that could let you speak with the dead.

"It's thought to be a book—a book that contains magic old and new, good and evil."

"How do you know about it? Where did you hear about this?" Amabel tried to keep the excitement out of her voice, but the way the old woman's eyes peered into hers told her that she hadn't been successful.

"A tribe member from Illinois told me of it. That from where she is from, there were witches, long ago, whose magic was melded somehow with that tribe's connection to the spirit world." The woman's face was cold, her mouth a grim line. "I know what you've been doing, girl."

Amabel was startled by the abrupt change in subject. "What?"

"Moving things around, without ever placing your hands on them. It's not natural. It's evil. You're a witch."

Amabel was struck speechless for a moment. The thought had never really occurred to her before, but it opened up a whole new world of possibilities.

The woman began talking again. "We've taken you in, provided for you. We care for you. But we don't approve of *that.*"

Amabel could only nod. A plan was already forming in her mind. "Where is this book?"

The woman didn't respond right away. "I don't know. I don't even know if it is real."

"Can you tell me anything else about it?" Amabel pressed.

"All I know is that it's thought to originate in Illinois, at the place where two great rivers meet. That's all I know."

It wasn't long after that conversation that Amabel set out. They'd agreed to let her have their old truck and she had squirreled away enough money to last her at least a few months, if she was very, very careful. She'd loved her time with the old man and woman and told them so, and hugged them goodbye, knowing she could never repay them, and also knowing that she'd never come back here.

As Amabel had turned to go, the woman had grabbed her hand and said, "I think it was a mistake to tell you about that book. Don't go finding trouble in something you don't understand." Amabel had just nodded, gotten into the truck, and headed east.

Thoughts of finding the book had consumed her in all the years since. She'd headed to St. Louis from Oklahoma, gotten a job in a hotel, and spent her free time researching where she might find the place where two great rivers meet. It didn't take long to realize that Grafton fit the bill. It was close enough that she could visit often, waiting for—something, anything, to indicate the book was real or that it was somewhere nearby. She researched the Native Americans in the area and got to know their beliefs and customs. She also found the coven.

Amabel got a crash course in witchcraft from an old coven

member in her first months in St. Louis. The power was intoxicating. Amabel wanted to develop her powers as much as she could, learn as much about witchcraft as possible, and she wanted to use it. She couldn't understand why the witches insisted on living so quietly, when they could do so much more—they could change the world. They could have whatever they wanted. But she was met with resistance every time she suggested they use their power on a broader scale.

Amabel realized quickly that she'd be on her own if she ever wanted to really use her powers to their full potential. So she never told anyone about the book. She knew they wouldn't approve and when she was being totally honest with herself, she didn't want to share it when she found it. She had plans. First, she'd talk to her sister and her parents. Then, she'd get rich and get everything she'd ever wanted and never had.

She moved to Grafton three years after she'd arrived in St. Louis, recognizing an opportunity to open the store. It would be a perfect front for her research. The years since then had been frustrating and she'd grown bitter. It hadn't been long after her arrival in town when she realized Maisie knew something about the book, she just knew it, she could feel it. But the bitch wouldn't tell her anything and Amabel's hatred for Maisie had become a thing that lived inside her.

The first thing she'd do when she got her hands on the book was unleash something to make Maisie pay.

Now, standing in the back of her shop, Amabel shook her head clear of the memories. All of that was done.

She'd gone along with the coven leaders these past months. But she was done complying. It was time to do what they'd been made to do and Amabel knew there were witches all over the country who were ready to break out and join her. She just had to get her hands on the book and she could go.

The years of research and waiting and frustration were finally going to pay off. Today.

CHAPTER THIRTY-ONE

Lara

When the three women woke the next morning, they were bleary-eyed and slow moving. Sleep had felt impossible after what had happened and all of them tossed and turned.

Lara woke and considered what you should wear for a day you planned to confront an evil, haunted book. She laughed to herself at the thought, wondering again if she was actually losing her mind. She took an old T-shirt of Ben's from her suitcase. One that was worn soft and smooth, and as she pulled it on, she instantly felt better.

Maisie was in the kitchen making coffee when first Maryn, then Lara stumbled in.

They were meeting Clara at 9:00. Lara and Maryn waited until 8:50 before they reluctantly retrieved the book from the abandoned house. They'd stood at the porch steps, staring at the door, mostly listening for any indication the book was there, causing trouble.

"Why is it quiet sometimes and terrifying the next?" Lara asked quietly.

"I have no idea."

They wrapped it in an old dishcloth and dropped it in a backpack. Neither of them wanted to touch it if they didn't have to.

Maisie had insisted on going with them to meet Clara. After what had happened last night, Lara just wanted to get the book away from her and let her rest. She'd never forgive herself if something happened to her aunt because she'd brought this book back into her life. But Maisie felt an obligation to help end what she should have ended all those years ago, and couldn't be talked out of it.

"We'll be in good hands with Clara," Maryn had reassured Lara. "She's much, much more powerful than me or even Amabel. It'll be okay."

Eventually Lara had given in, but she wasn't happy about it. Lara drove to the Ruebel, none of them saying a word during the short drive.

Clara was waiting for them outside of the hotel. Maryn made introductions and Lara was instantly grateful for Clara's calming presence. She'd hugged each of them warmly and said, "I'm sorry to meet under these most extraordinary of circumstances. But I'm glad I could be here to help. We'll get this figured out."

The town was quiet, still. Very few places were open this early on a weekday, but they could get coffee and scones at a small shop down the street from the Ruebel. There were only a couple of other patrons, but still the women took one of the small wrought-iron tables on the empty back patio, where they could see the river, but, more importantly, where they could be alone.

Once they'd placed their orders, Clara said, "Okay. Maryn filled me in over the phone last night. I have a lot of questions, but one thing I can tell you right now is that there is absolutely something here. Something I have never felt before." She looked at Lara and Maisie. "I know this is all new to you so I'll try to explain as best I can." Looking thoughtful for a moment, she said, "Do you know the feeling in the air, right before a thunderstorm?" The women nodded.

"It's a hard feeling to explain, but it's a current in the air. Electric, waiting. That's the closest thing I can liken this feeling to. When there is powerful magic nearby, we feel it as a current in the air. Those of us who are more experienced can follow that current and find out where it's coming from. Right now, it's very clearly right here at this table. Do you all feel it?"

At her words, Maryn nodded and rubbed the goosebumps that had quickly spread along her arms. Maisie was shaking her head, but Lara paused. "I felt something when I touched it last night. I hadn't felt anything before that, but last night—I guess that's what you're describing."

Clara nodded and turned to Maryn. "It's so strong. How have you been able to stand it?"

Maryn smiled weakly. "It's not been easy. And we need to tell you about last night."

Together, they told Clara what had happened in Maisie's house. She listened intently, asking a few pointed questions.

When they were done, Clara said, "We need to address this today. As quickly as we can. It's escalating and I can guarantee that Amabel felt it. She knows something is happening and I don't trust her. She wants to get her hands on that book, badly. We can't let that happen."

Clara reached into her purse and pulled out a book. *Now that is definitely the stuff of fairytale magic,* Lara thought. The cover was made of old, cracked leather. The edges were worn and the spine looked as though it might crack at any moment. It looked stitched together, somehow, as though there was more than one notebook, more than one spine woven together. Symbols were etched into the leather, some of which Lara couldn't make out, but the ones she could see clearly, she didn't understand. She couldn't take her eyes off of it. She had the same feeling she'd had when she picked up her book last night.

Clara could tell she was staring and smiled. "Lara, dear, I know this is all a lot for you to take in, but I can tell by your reaction that you know this is something special. And it is. This is our coven's ..." She seemed to be struggling for the right word. "Record-keeper, I suppose. We track our members, their families, any incidents of particularly important or concerning magic. We keep notes about any effects witches have had on world events or predictions about future events. It's all here."

For some reason, Lara wanted to touch it. Something in her was calling to something in it. Maryn lightly touched her hand and said, "I felt the same thing the first time I saw it, Lara. I think Clara's hunch was right. I think you're probably a witch."

Lara was shaking her head. "I don't think so. I mean, wouldn't I have known by now?"

"Not necessarily," said Clara. "Sometimes we just don't notice our power manifesting, especially if we don't have someone nearby to help us develop it. Sometimes, a witch might not have anything odd happen at all and lives her whole life never knowing."

Maisie interrupted. "Well, I don't feel a thing. I think it's safe to say I am not a witch." They laughed and it was a nice break in the heaviness of the conversation. Their waitress came out then with their breakfasts, and they waited until she'd left to resume the conversation.

"Maisie, our powers are on a spectrum. Some of us are more naturally powerful than others. You could just be … slightly less powerful. The fact that you had such an intense experience with the book when you were a child tells me there's something there, slight though it may be. And Lara, whatever the reason for your powers just now coming to light, dear, we can help you figure it all out. But not today. Today we have to deal with Amabel."

Clara took a sip of coffee and continued. "I first want to give you a little more background information. It's important you know everything before we move forward. I know Maryn has told you about her powers of empathy. I am a clairvoyant, for lack of a better word. I can't predict the future or speak with ghosts, but my powers are rooted in knowledge. I tend to just—know the things I need to know when I need them. Not every time, but often enough. I first realized I was different when I was sixteen and got a flat tire on my dad's old Ford pickup truck and just changed it on the side of the road." She laughed. "No one had ever taught me. I just knew."

"Well that's a pretty helpful power to have," Maisie commented, her eyes wide.

Clara smiled. "It is. Over the years I've gotten better at homing in on what I need to know in any given situation. It helped me get through college with a perfect GPA, but it's far from a perfect science, and it doesn't *always* come to me."

Maryn cut in. "She's being modest. It's an amazing power to have. She always seems to know the right thing to do and never steers us wrong."

"Then I'm glad you're here," Lara said gratefully.

Clara squeezed her hand. "I also want to tell you about Amabel. I was suspicious of her when she first got in touch with us, but I didn't listen to my gut like I should have. I try not to rely on my powers when it comes to people. People are unpredictable and sometimes I've trusted my gut and people surprise me. Our behavior is very rarely rooted in any kind of logic or sense." The women all laughed at that truth.

"So I try to give people a chance to show me their true selves before I rely on my own impressions. But Amabel rubbed me the wrong way from day one. I could tell she wasn't telling me something."

Lara shuddered. She was suddenly very glad that she'd never let Amabel touch the book.

"I found out a bit about Amabel's history," Clara went on. "She had a very difficult childhood. Her parents and only sister died when she was young. I'm not sure where she spent her teenage years. When she landed here in Grafton, Maisie, she was probably very lonely. If she already had a sense of what this book might be able to do, I'm wondering if she wants to use it to speak with her family."

Lara felt sympathy for Amabel. She certainly understood.

"My suspicion is that Amabel found those letters first. She touched them and got a sense of what it might all mean and has been on a quest to track it down ever since."

The women sat in silence for a few moments, finishing the last of their meals and thinking about what Clara had told them. When they had finished and cleared the table, Clara opened the book and turned it to a page somewhere near the middle. "I believe our sisters have known about this magic since its inception. As Amabel said, there have been rumors of a magic like this for years. Very little is known about it, and it sounds like Amabel told you almost everything."

"Almost?" Maryn asked. "Did you find something new?"

"I think so. Amelia, who, by the way, I was able to locate in our records here, said in the book that it was magic borne out of Native Americans and witches coming together, and the witches went rogue. When I first heard that I thought it was ridiculous. That's not really how things work. At least not to my knowledge. But after I talked to Maryn last night, and she told me how Amabel acted yesterday and how she's treated Maisie all these years, it became clear to me as it did all of you, that Amabel knows more than what she's letting on.

"I'm far from being the most experienced or educated witch, but I do know a lot about our history and this kind of magic had only ever been a rumor. The kind of thing passed down from generation to generation, mostly by women brand new to witchcraft. But Amabel's behavior made me think she'd found something somewhere along the way that made her think it really is real. So last night, after I got off the phone with Maryn, I went back through our book here and came across a letter. Just one page, no more than a few lines. And I think, based on the letters she showed you, Lara, it's part of that correspondence. It doesn't tell us much, but now I think I know why Amabel wants to get her hands on it so badly."

Clara opened the book and turned it so Lara could read. It looked like the same handwriting as the letters Amabel had shown her.

Dearest Vee,

I hope this letter finds you in good spirits. I received your last note and was happy to hear that you're seeking—and finding—comfort in those pages. I am here for any further questions you might seek the answers to.

I know I shared similar sentiments the last time we met, but I must caution you. We created a solution. But it is a dangerous and powerful one. It would be a simple task to become overwhelmed by and lost within that power. I am sure I do not have to state explicitly what could happen if it was placed in the wrong hands. You must use the utmost caution and care, not only for your own safety, but also to keep the book within your singular possession at all times. As you know, the power exists now and cannot be destroyed by any means other than that which we discussed. Please bear that in mind.

I wish you all the best and look forward to our continued friendship.

With love,

A

Lara read the letter again and looked at Clara. "This seems like the missing letter Amabel didn't have. Well. I guess it's the one she didn't show me." She looked down at the letter again. "So there is a way to destroy it. Something specific."

"Yes," Clara said. "But what I'm still unsure about is what that is. And what exactly Amabel knows." Clara paused. "There's one more thing in here that I think sheds a bit of light on what, exactly, the thing is capable of."

Clara flipped to another page. This was another handwritten document, but it wasn't a letter. It looked like a transcription of some sort.

"These are meeting minutes," Clara explained. "Occasionally someone will get in the habit of keeping minutes from coven meetings, though it tends to go in waves. If no one volunteers, it just kind of stops. We have full transcriptions of some meetings, going back a long time. It's only a very small record of all the meetings we've ever had, but I happened to find this small paragraph."

> Regarding the matter of sister Amelia, she claims to have found magic long since believed to be only speculation. We have asked for, but not yet received, proof of this object. She refused to bring it to us. If it is what she claims, we are in agreement that it must be contained and possibly destroyed. If a power such as this exists, it not only mustn't fall into the wrong hands but also mustn't be used by anyone, ourselves included. We have agreed to —

And there the paragraph abruptly ended. The next paragraph was asking for volunteers to help a new member who needed some additional support in developing her powers.

"It's like someone changed their mind about documenting their plan," Lara said.

"Yes, I thought the same thing." Clara sighed. "So that's all I found. I wish there were more. I wish we knew exactly what to do with it."

"What do you think will happen if I just destroy it? Burn it, maybe?" Lara asked.

"I really don't know. I don't know if whatever failsafe Violet and Amelia used prevents it from being destroyed or if they simply found a way to keep the magic from being used. It's not clear."

"Lara, maybe it's time to just try to stop it," Maisie said quietly.

Lara looked at Clara, who was clearly conflicted. "Lara, the decision is yours. It's your ancestry, your possession. You can decide what to do with it. But I will be honest with you. Selfishly, I don't want to destroy it until I've had a chance to examine it. If it can do what we think it can—well. That's more powerful than anything I've ever known. But I will honor your wishes."

Lara looked at Maryn. "What do you think?"

Maryn looked at Clara then at Lara. "I think if you don't at least try to understand it, you're probably going to wonder about it and regret it for the rest of your life. Because I know what you've been thinking this whole time, because I've been thinking it, too."

What if, Lara thought. What if she could talk to Ben, even just one more time? She nodded and turned to Maisie. "I'm sorry. I just want more answers. I need to know."

"I understand, Lara. I do. I just don't have a good feeling."

Lara took her hand. "I know. I just have to know."

Against Lara's protests, the women headed back to Maisie's. Lara wanted her aunt out of this mess completely. But not only did Maisie refuse to let them handle it alone, she insisted they not go somewhere else to do it. And Clara thought it was possible that having Maisie involved might help them in the end, since she also had ties to the book.

When they got back to the house, Maisie began making tea and the women settled around her kitchen table. Lara said, "I'm going to go get it. I left it in the car."

"Lara, do you want me to?" Maryn asked. Lara knew she was thinking about what happened last night and she loved her friend for wanting to protect her.

Lara smiled and said, "Thanks, Mar. But I need to do it."

Lara walked outside to her car, approaching it slowly, listening for any sounds. She didn't hear anything. She stopped a few yards away and clicked the button on her key fob that opened her trunk and watched as it rose slowly. When nothing jumped out, she slowly stepped closer. She felt ridiculous.

With each step that nothing happened, she began to breathe a little easier. But when she took the bag from the trunk a feeling of dread and foreboding overcame her and she had to resist the urge to throw it down. She forced herself to walk back to the house.

When Lara walked back into the kitchen, Maisie and Maryn were looking at Clara, whose face was pale, her hands shaking.

"Is she okay?" Lara asked, rushing to the table.

"I'm fine. I'm okay," Clara said quietly. "It's just—very powerful and not at all what I expected. It's dark. I've never quite felt anything like it." She looked at Maryn. "How did you do it? How did you spend so much time …"

"I know. I just never really touched it," Maryn explained. "The few times I was physically close to it, it was hard, but Lara kept it hidden away much of the time."

Clara nodded. "Lara, can you set it on the table?"

Lara gladly set the book down, then backed away a bit. Maisie did the same.

Clara took a deep breath and placed one hand tentatively on the book. She jumped a little, but then pressed her hand more firmly into place. She closed her eyes and was silent for almost a full minute. When she opened her eyes and removed her hand from the book, she rubbed her hand on her pants, like there was something on it.

"Well. I'm not quite sure what to say. It's absolutely some powerful magic. There is dark and light, all wrapped up here. And there's something close to the surface. It's dangerous." Clara's brows furrowed in confusion. "It's odd. I felt so much clarity when I touched it, along with a sure sense that everything we thought about the book is true. It's been a long, long time since I felt something so clearly. I felt magic that was most definitely ours, but also something else … our suspicions seem to be right. There's definitely a power here that is connected to the past and to the dead."

Clara looked at Lara, Maryn, and Maisie in turn. "We can't let Amabel get her hands on this. If I can get all this information out of it, I don't know what she'd be able to do."

The women all nodded and Lara felt her stomach turn. "So what do we do?"

Clara sighed. "I'm not sure. Any ideas?"

"I was hoping that's what you're here for," Lara deadpanned. No one laughed.

The room was silent, until Maisie said quietly, "Why don't we ask it?"

No one said anything for a moment, until Clara said, "What do you mean?"

"Well, it's clear to me that whatever this thing is, it has been trying to send a message—communicate—from the beginning. It tried to get Violet's attention, my attention, Lara's attention. Now, I have no idea *why*, but it's trying to say something."

Maryn was nodding. "That makes sense, I guess. But how?"

"And how do we do that safely?" Clara asked.

Lara took a deep breath, unsure if what she was about to say was insane. "If it's Ben, it'll be okay." All this time, she'd been acting as if it was a *what if*. But as soon as she said the words she knew them to be true.

"It was Ben's handwriting in the book. It's him. He's there. I can ask him."

"I don't know," Clara and Maryn said at the same time. Lara expected them to be skeptical. "Look, I think at this point it's safe to say that we can't just hide it away or destroy it. We'll never be sure we really got rid of it. It's clear there's a lot more to what's going on, right?" She looked at the women for confirmation. They both nodded.

"So we need to figure something out and I think Maisie's right. I think we go right to the source. Save ourselves trying to speculate and figure it out. The longer we sit with it, the more chance that Amabel will get her hands on it." Lara reached out for the book tentatively, touching it lightly and sliding it across the table to her seat.

"Clara, is there a way to do this? I mean, I know you don't know a lot about it, but anything you think I should know?"

"I don't really know. I do wish we had a bit more information about your powers. Heading into this not knowing makes me a little nervous. It makes everything a bit unpredictable."

"How so?" asked Maisie.

"If there's something here—" Clara gestured toward the book— "that somehow enhances her power, she's untested, unpracticed. I don't want it to totally get away from her." Clara looked back to Lara. "Can you tell me if *anything* odd has happened in your life, anything that you couldn't explain. It could be physical, mental, anything."

Lara was quiet for a long moment as she thought. She couldn't think of anything more than a couple of times when she'd thought about a specific song on the radio and it had come on. She shook her head. "Nothing. I'm sorry."

"Lara, wait," Maryn said. Lara looked at her, head cocked to the side.

"Do you remember when you told me that you used to feel Ben by you? Over your shoulder?"

"Oh. Well, yeah. But that's just in my head. It's not like I see dead people."

Clara leaned forward. "No. Wait. Let's not discount anything. Tell me about this feeling, Lara."

"I don't know." Lara shifted uncomfortably in her seat. "It's just a feeling. Like I just know he's there. I don't hear or see anything."

"Do you meditate?" Clara asked.

The question confused Lara. She wasn't sure what that had to do with anything. "I've tried it. But every time I do, I just start daydreaming and my thoughts seem to get more intense rather than calming. So I always quit."

"Do you have intense dreams?" Clara wanted to know.

"Yes she does," Maisie interjected. "She always has. She used to tell me the craziest stories when she was little."

"Ohhh …" Maryn breathed quietly.

"What?" Lara asked.

Clara looked at Maryn and the women nodded at each other. "You might be a hedge witch," Clara said.

"What the hell is that?"

Clara sighed. "Don't freak out."

"Oh, fantastic," Lara said, rolling her eyes.

"Hedge witches can cross the divide. Jump the hedge. Reach into worlds beyond this one. Some of them can speak with the dead, specifically their ancestors. Some of them who have really honed their powers can astral project. Hedge witches draw their power from the power of connection to this world and the next."

Lara was shaking her head. "No. Nope."

"And memories, Lara. Hedge witches are tied very closely to their memories."

Lara blinked. "But my memories …"

Maryn nodded. "I know." She turned to Clara. "Lara has lost her memories of her brother. She can't recall anything unless someone tells her about it."

"Oh my," Clara said. "I'm so sorry. That must be terrible. I wonder if when Ben died, your powers, I don't know, shut down. To protect you. It would be too painful. I don't know. Unfortunately, we don't always have a great understanding of how our powers truly work."

Lara didn't know what to say. This was all too much to take in. She was a witch? And *that's* why she couldn't remember?

Clara smiled kindly. "Don't worry. You don't have to worry about any of this. It does not have to change your life at all. We don't really have time to find out if my hunch is right today anyway. But it's good to at least have a theory to work with."

Clara looked back at Maryn. "If she is a hedge witch, she's going to be very susceptible. It's going to open very easily for her. I think it's important that Lara is alone while she tries this, but we'll need to be close by. Very close."

Clara focused on Lara again. "Lara, when a witch uses a grimoire or casts a spell, it's important she has complete concentration. One wrong word or move can have a profound effect on how it turns out. Grimoires are known to—reshape themselves. I think that's what's happened here, why the story changed for you, Maisie. It gives the reader what they need." She fell silent for a moment.

"When we attempt this, we have to be aware of that. You're not exactly casting a spell and we don't have any kind of protocol to follow, but I still think it's most important that you concentrate on your brother and his spirit."

Lara nodded dumbly, unsure if she was even fully understanding what Clara was telling her.

Clara looked worried. "I'm really not sure about this. I'm wondering if we should wait, calling some of our other sisters ..." Her voice trailed off.

Lara was not reassured by her hesitation. Luckily, Clara seemed to gather herself.

"Maisie, is there somewhere we can go? I would rather not do this in your house. Whatever we're about to open up here, I think you'd rather not have it in your home."

Before Maisie could answer, Lara jumped in. "I know where to go. The cave. It's tied to that location already and it's private." Maisie's face paled even as Maryn and Clara nodded.

"Lara—" Maisie began.

"I'll be okay, Maisie. Trust me. I have a feeling it's going to be okay."

"Well," her aunt said, "I do not."

The women gathered supplies; flashlights, a lantern, an extra notebook and pens. Maisie wanted to show them where the cave was, convinced that they wouldn't find it otherwise, but Lara was adamant that Maisie not be involved.

"It will be too much for you and you have nothing to gain from this. This is my bad decision. Not yours."

Maisie had finally relented, secretly glad because she wasn't sure her old bones could make it all the way to the cave and back. She gave them detailed directions and watched from the front porch as they took off toward the woods.

The trio found their way to the cave with ease. Lara was surprised that the woods seemed to have changed so little since Maisie's last visit—Maisie's directions were spot on and they found the cave with no trouble. The women explored the outside, noting the marks around the cave's dark entrance, just like Maisie had described. The mouth yawned open, pitch black.

Lara stood staring at it, flanked by Maryn and Clara. The backpack thrummed, gently vibrating her hand. The book wasn't going to let her forget it was there. If she didn't do it now, she might never do it. She took a deep breath.

"Okay," Lara said. "I'm going in."

"Stay out here," Clara said instantly. She'd been quiet since they'd arrived at the cave and her face looked drawn and pale.

"Clara, are you okay?" Maryn asked.

"Yes. It just doesn't feel like a good place. I don't like it. I don't want to go in."

"I think I need to go in," Lara said. "Didn't you say I should be by myself?"

Clara nodded. "I did say that. But I was wrong. There's too much bad tied too closely to the good. If you're alone when it opens, I don't know what will happen. I have to be able to control it." Clara's face became even more tightly drawn, her eyes wide with fear. "I think we should wait. I think we need to call more women in from the coven."

Lara was unsettled by Clara's fear. It was almost enough to make her consider going back. But all the same, Lara felt like this needed to happen today. They didn't know what Amabel was doing or what her plan was. They needed to deal with it *now*.

"Look, I've come this far. I'm not going to stop now." Lara smiled, even though it felt fake. "You'll be right here. If it will make you feel better, maybe you could just stay at the mouth of the cave? Not go too far in, but close enough to me to help?" Lara mentally crossed her fingers, hoping Clara would agree so she wouldn't really be in the cave alone."

Maryn squeezed her hand. "I think she's right, Clara. We don't know where Amabel is. If we can deal with this now, we should."

Clara nodded and took a deep breath. "Maryn, we need to sit together, and concentrate on a binding spell. Whatever—comes out of that thing—we'll need to be prepared to contain it."

Maryn nodded and Lara watched as the women sat down on the ground just outside the cave, and began pulling items out from their bag. Herbs and candles and a pentagram made out of sticks. She shuddered, unsure if she was terrified or fascinated.

When they were set up, Maryn nodded at Lara. "Okay. I think we're ready."

Lara took a flashlight out of her bag. Taking a deep breath, she walked toward the mouth of the cave.

Amabel

Amabel finished packing the trunk and put the few items she needed into an old backpack. She'd put on dark jeans, a black jacket, and boots.

She intended to start at Maisie's house. As she headed in that direction, she reviewed her plan. She'd try to reason with them first. Tell them that if they'd just give her the book she'd leave, go somewhere far away and they wouldn't have to think about it again.

WEIGHT of MEMORY

She didn't expect that to work, of course. They'd be high and mighty, say that this kind of power needed to be contained, that it was too dangerous.

Next, she'd try just a little persuasion spell, see if she could force them to hand it over. If *that* didn't work, she had a containment spell ready and waiting. She'd subdue them by force, take the book, and go.

It sounded simple enough. Of course, there were about a million things that could go wrong and for the first time in all these years, she wished she had someone to help her, someone who recognized that what she was doing was important and was going to change the world.

Stop worrying about things you can't change now, she thought. *Time to focus on getting this done.*

She approached Maisie's house cautiously, stopping a few houses down the street to listen and see if she could feel anything. Nothing yet. She watched the house for a few minutes. Nothing happened. It appeared to be quiet. She considered her next step.

In the end, she decided to just walk up and ring the bell. After all, if she was going to try to handle this with reason first, sneaking and skulking around wouldn't help.

Amabel walked up the steps and stood in front of the door, listening again. Still nothing. She raised her hand and knocked.

CHAPTER THIRTY-TWO

Maisie

Maisie was sitting at the table, gripping a now-cold cup of coffee, staring into space. She was wondering if she should call Alex or even the police. All this talk, all this madness about witches and magic and a haunted book had her questioning everything she'd ever believed about the world. And she'd never forgive herself something happened to Lara and she could have done something to stop it.

When she heard the light rap at the door, she jumped up, heart pounding. *They're back!* Was her thought as she moved toward the front door. But as she reached out her hand to turn the knob, she stopped and looked at her watch. They'd only been gone about forty-five minutes. It was hardly enough time to get up to the cave, let alone carry out their plans and get back. *And Lara would never knock.*

Maisie stood frozen. Whoever it was knocked again.

"Who's there?" she called out, thankful that Lara had insisted she lock all the doors after they'd left.

"It's Amabel, Maisie. We need to talk."

"I don't think so. I don't have anything to say to you."

"I know you all have it. I know they're there with you."

"No one's here, Amabel. Just leave."

"Look, Maisie, I'm not going to go away and I'm going to get in there, whether you want me to or not. Let's just be adults about this."

Maisie didn't say anything. As she stood there, frozen in uncertainty, she heard the click of metal against metal and realized it was the tumbling of the front door lock.

"Shit," she whispered. She looked around, wondering if she had time to get her gun from where she'd stowed it in a kitchen drawer, but before she could move, the doorknob was turning and the door swung open.

Amabel stood there, a small smile on her face. "That wasn't so hard, was it?"

"Amabel, what do you think I can do for you?" Maisie was more calm than she would have thought possible given the situation. She supposed that everything she'd learned and experienced had finally convinced some part of her brain that a woman opening a door without touching it really wasn't all that odd.

Amabel looked around the living room and walked toward the kitchen. "Where's your niece?"

Maisie didn't answer.

"Look, just tell me where it is and I'll go. That's all I want. I'll take it and I'll leave and none of you will hear from me ever again."

"Well, as lovely as that last part sounds, I can't help you. The book's not mine and it's not here anyway."

"Okay. Then tell me where Lara took it and I'll go."

"You think I'm going to send you after her? After all the years you watched me and CiCi? And now, after you threatened my niece, you think I'm just going to tell you?"

"I don't *want* to make you, Maisie, but I will."

Maisie laughed. "Get out, Amabel."

But Amabel didn't. Instead, she looked into Maisie's face, her lips just barely moving. Just as Maisie was about to turn away, to lock herself in her room or finally call the cops, she found her lips moving instead.

"They took the book to the cave. Up by Sutter's Acres." And just like that, she gave Amabel the same instructions she'd given Lara and the other witches. She was horrified at herself, but couldn't stop the words from coming. They poured out of her, even better directions than she'd given Lara.

Amabel smiled at her. "Thanks." And just like that, she turned and walked out of Maisie's house.

Lara

Lara walked slowly into the dark cave, a flashlight held out in front of her, the beam shaking as her hand trembled. She listened hard for any noise, any rushing, screaming wind, but there was nothing. It felt like an interminably long walk, but she reached the end of the cave quickly.

She shone her light around the walls and floor. She saw old pillows. A blanket. She smiled. Maisie, CiCi, and John's stuff really was still here. When she was sure she was alone for the moment, she opened her bag with one hand and took out an old battery-powered lantern Maisie had had in her garage. They'd put fresh batteries in, but suddenly Lara was sure that it wouldn't turn on. She clicked the power button and was relieved when a weak yellow glow lit up a small circle around her.

She sat down, her back to the wall of the cave, and set the lantern down on ground. Next, she took the book and pen out of her bag, setting them on her lap. She opened to the page with Ben's writing and traced his words with her fingers. "You can't. Don't. You can't. Don't. You can't. Don't."

I'm sorry, Ben, she thought.

Lara gripped the pen and at the top of one of the blank pages in the back of the book wrote, "Ben?"

Her heart started pounding. Her body felt cold. She was terrified. She didn't know what she was waiting for. Would the words just appear? Would she see a disembodied hand reach out, Bic grasped tightly in its fingers? The thought caused a hysterical giggle to escape, and she immediately clamped a hand over her mouth. She sat still and silent, her eyes moving from the book to the space around her, listening, watching, waiting.

Nothing was happening. *Maybe I need to put the book down.* She set it down on the dirt floor in front of her, staring at it intently. She remembered what Clara had said about concentrating on nothing but

Ben, so she closed her eyes and brought his face to her mind, smiling, handsome. The feeling of safety she always felt when he was around.

Then, just like that, the pages began flipping, over and over, from the front of the book to the back, eventually stopping on the same page she'd started. Lara's heart was racing and her breath was coming fast and shallow. Tears sprang instantly to her eyes when she saw that there were new words on the page.

"Lolly. Love you."

She wrote, "Ben is it really you? I love you so much. I miss you so much." This time, she set the book down immediately and watched the pages turn, faster this time.

"It's me. Suck it up, buttercup. I'm okay."

She smiled. It was him. It was Ben. And just like that, Lara wasn't afraid anymore. It was Ben. Tears poured out of her eyes, as the wish she'd had for so long, the wish that had seemed harder than impossible, was coming true.

"Ben. I miss you so much. It has been so hard without you. Are you okay?"

None of that was helpful. None of that would get her any answers about what was happening, but she had to tell him. She had to talk to him, tell him everything that had been building up in her since the day he died.

When the pages settled this time, it said, "I'm okay, but this is hard. Need to stop, Lolly. Ur not safe."

"No, please talk to me. Please. Don't go."

"Not going yet, but can't do this for long. Hard to do this. Can't. Holding it back is hard."

"Holding what back? What is it? How do I stop it?"

"I'm not the one scaring you. You opened a thread to me, but it's not just me. It's the weight of all the good memories of the world. But it's also the weight of the bad memories, it's the weight of evil. It wants out, too. Have to stop."

Then, on the next line, "You can't keep this open. Don't. Let me go." The last *o* was sloppy, not quite coming together in a full circle, the ink trailing off into a squiggly line, as though something had stopped him mid-letter.

Tears were streaming down Lara's face. This was what she'd wanted. She was talking to Ben and now he was telling her to stop.

"Please don't go. I need you back. I can't remember you Ben I need you back. Please." Her words were sloppy. She couldn't see the page through her tears.

"I'm always in your memory, whenever you need me. It's enough, Lolly. I promise. But you have to stop. You have to—" The words stopped there.

"What Ben? What do I do?"

The pages flipped for a long time this time. So long that Lara was terrified that it would never stop and Ben was gone. When they quieted, the words were on a different page, a page that had Violet's story on them. Ben had underlined two lines, that read: "into this book."

Then, in the margin, he'd sloppily written, "Unweave the threads."

"I don't understand," Lara wrote.

"Unweave them. Have go. Love you much, Lolly."

Lara sensed it was coming to an end and sobs shook her body as she wrote.

"Please don't go. You were the best brother. I love you, Ben."

"Love you, Lolly. Love so muc—"

As Lara read his final words to her, the pages started turning and didn't stop, moving so quickly it was blur. Lara stood up and moved away from the book, unsure what she should do. She was sobbing. She wanted to write more to Ben, but she was afraid to touch it and she sensed he was gone. It began to lift off the dirt. She knocked it out of the air and it fell to the floor. The pages stopped turning.

She sank to her knees, sobbing. It had been *him*. After all this time, she'd been talking to him and now that he was gone it felt like she'd lost him all over again. She cried for what felt like a long time. Eventually, she was able to take a couple of deep breaths and leaned down to pick the book up. As she did, she heard a scream coming from inside her head and from the book, all at the same time.

Her heart skipped a beat then began pounding wildly in her chest. Terror coursed through her. She wanted to run, but she was frozen. This was not Ben. *What do I do? What do I do?* She heard stomping and wind was rushing through the cave.

She listened hard and as the wind quieted a bit, she heard Maryn's voice floating down from the mouth of the cave. "Lara? Are you okay?"

"Stay out there!" Lara yelled. She didn't want Maryn or Clara walking through the cave, only to meet whatever this was head-on.

"Lara?"

"Just stay out there, I'm fine!" Lara grabbed the lantern and spun in a circle, looking around the alcove at the back of the cave and spinning back toward the mouth. The book lay innocently on the floor. She did not want to pick it up, but she couldn't leave it. She was positive now that it mustn't fall into Amabel's or anyone else's hands.

When Lara bent down to pick it up, she felt a push from behind and she stumbled forward, tripping on a rock. She just managed to steady herself a bit on the cave wall, breaking her fall but banging her knee.

"Shit!" she yelled. She had to get out of the cave. Now. She gripped the book tightly and began running down the cave, stumbling and running her hands along the wall. She'd dropped the flashlight somewhere. As she drew closer to the mouth, she saw a shadow blocking the light. She couldn't make out Maryn and Clara's forms on the other side.

Lara screamed and came to a stop and stood still, her back against the wall of the cave. She could hear footsteps behind her and, impossibly, in front of her. "Fuck, fuck, fuck," she whispered. She was too scared to move forward. The shadow had no recognizable form, but it was tall and wide. And she felt that it was advancing toward her.

"Clara?" she yelled.

"Lara, are you okay?" Clara's voice sounded muffled, like it was coming from farther away from than it really was.

"I don't know. Something's in here, I don't know what to do. I don't want to walk by it. What should I do?"

"Hold on, Lara! When I say go, run toward us, okay?"

"Okay!" Her chest heaved. She hadn't realized tears were still streaming down her face. She didn't want to take her eyes off the thing at the mouth of the cave, but when she looked at it for longer than a second or two, the terror overtook her and she had to look away.

When Lara heard the murmur of Maryn and Clara's voices start to get louder, she pushed off cave wall and stood clutching the book to her chest, preparing to run when Clara said go.

"Okay, Lara, run!"

At Clara's words, Lara took off down the cave, her eyes on her feet so that she didn't trip and so that she didn't have to see what exactly she was running toward. In a matter of seconds, she was back in the sunshine. She dropped the book and fell to her knees, breathing hard, heart pounding. She felt like she might never stop crying.

She felt Maryn's hand on her back, heard her say, "Lara, it's okay; you're okay; you're okay."

Then, speaking to Clara, Maryn asked, "Should I help her?"

"I think maybe a little bit," Clara responded quietly.

A moment later, Lara felt a bit more calm. Her heart rate slowed and the overwhelming sense of panic eased a bit.

"Take a deep breath," Maryn said quietly. Lara did as she was told, shakily drawing in air and letting it out slowly. She stopped crying and wiped her eyes.

"Did you just magic me?" she asked Maryn, trying to smile.

"I did a little bit. Sorry, I could tell you were panicking, I didn't want you to have a full-blown panic attack. I won't do it again."

"No, it's okay. I don't know how I would have calmed down on my own." Lara stood up, brushing off her pants.

"What happened, Lara?" Clara asked. Clara's face was pale and she was sitting with her back against a nearby tree. She looked exhausted.

Lara told them what she'd experienced in the cave, reluctantly picking up the book and showing the pages where she'd communicated with Ben.

"Oh my god," Maryn said quietly, reaching out a hand and not quite touching Ben's words. "It was really him?"

"Yes, I know it was. It was him, Maryn." Her voice broke and tears began quietly rolling down her face. She looked at her friend and she recognized the longing in her eyes. She wanted to know if she could talk to Will. She wanted to grab a pen right that second and tell her brother that she loved him, one more time, that she missed him, and that nothing would ever be the same without him.

Lara put her hand on Maryn's arm and said, "I know what you're thinking Mar. I know. But we can't do it. We can't. There is something really terrible here, right alongside whatever good there is. I'm so sorry. But we can't."

Lara turned to Clara. "We need to figure out what we can do to get rid of it. Now. If Amabel gets her hands on it, she's going to unleash whatever that thing was in the cave and we can't let that happen. We can't. We need to figure out what Ben meant by 'unweave the threads' and we need to do it."

Clara nodded. "Okay." Clara stood and Lara saw that she was unsteady on her feet. She looked more closely at Maryn, and saw she was swaying slightly, and looked—drained.

"Are you two okay?"

The two women looked at each other. "We had to use a lot of our strength to push back whatever that was, is all," Clara explained.

"How did you do it?"

"I pushed out every ounce of happiness and good feeling I could muster," Maryn said. "Clara performed a powerful containment spell. It should stay—well, we don't really know if we contained it back in the cave or back in the book, if that's where it came from. But it went away. For now. We're fine, just tired." Maryn's eyes went back to the book again. "I'm so sorry I let you have that thing in your house for so long, with your baby. I should have known. I can't believe I didn't know."

Lara saw her own feelings mirrored in Maryn's face—fear, confusion, regret, and longing.

"I know we need to destroy it," Maryn said. "But it's not going to be easy, is it?"

"No, it's not," Lara agreed. "But we have to."

"Let's figure out what we know," Clara said. "We know enough to know that there's good and evil here. We know there's ancient magic here, that it's contained in the book somehow. We know it wants out. We know it can allow you to talk to the dead. I think the answer lies in what Ben told you. 'Unweave the threads.'"

"Unweave the threads," Maryn repeated thoughtfully.

Unweave them, Lara thought. She looked at the words Ben had underlined. *Into this book. Into this book.*

"That's it," Lara said with a sigh.

"What?" Clara asked.

Lara began laughing quietly. "It's right here. It's been right in front of us. Ben said we have to unweave the threads. And Amelia and Violet wove the threads of the magic *into* the book. Right into it."

"Oh my god," Maryn said.

"Into the book," Clara repeated.

Lara nodded. "Whatever original object contained the magic, I think it's here in the book. But I'm not sure how. Is it like a … transfiguration spell?" Lara asked.

Maryn laughed. "Harry Potter. *Again.*"

"We need to deconstruct the book," Clara said. "Whatever it is, it's in here."

"What's going to happen if we do that?" Lara asked. "I don't know if it's safe. Won't it—come out?"

"I think it can only be activated when you're intentionally calling the *magic*. When you wrote to Ben today, when you wrote down your memories, when Maisie took notes in the book, when Violet wrote in it." Clara paused for a moment, thinking. "That's what awakens the magic. I think we can deconstruct it as long as we don't call on the magic. It must be part of the spell."

"Do you really think that will work?"

"I think so. We need to take it apart."

"Okay." Lara said. "I'm going to do it. We'll need a knife I guess?"

"Yeah, I think—"

Just then, they heard stomping in the woods. Someone was coming and they weren't coming quietly.

CHAPTER THIRTY-THREE

Lara

All three women turned to look at the figure emerging from the trees. It was Amabel, of course.

Clara stood, stronger on her feet. "Amabel, you need to leave."

Amabel smiled. "Not a chance in hell, Clara. Just give it to me. You all don't care as much as I do. Let me have it and I'll leave you all alone."

"We can't let you have it and you know it. Just go."

The smile was gone from Amabel's face. "I need it. You don't."

"Why do you need it, Amabel?" Lara asked, stepping around Clara.

Amabel's eyes flickered to Lara. "My parents are dead. My sister ... My sister is dead. I need it. I deserve it. I looked for it for years, it should be mine."

Maryn looked at her in sympathy. "I understand, Amabel, but can't you feel it? Can't you tell it's not so simple? That it's dangerous?"

Amabel looked away, not meeting their eyes. "It's fine. I don't care. Just give it to me."

It was then Lara felt a tug on the book that was in her hands. It was pulling away from her, toward Amabel.

"Amabel, stop." Clara spoke forcefully, her eyes locked onto Amabel's face.

"You bitch," Amabel muttered. She closed her eyes, her lips moving silently, and Lara felt the tug on the book grow stronger. She also felt her grip weaken, almost like she meant to ...

"Maryn, help," Clara shouted. Maryn focused her attention on Amabel, whose face was strained, her mouth a tight line, her brows furrowed in concentration.

As the women battled, Lara wanted to help but she didn't know how. She began to back away, toward the cave, thinking she could throw the book in there and trap Amabel if she went after it. It was the best she could think of.

Suddenly, both Clara and Maryn cried out and clutched their heads with their hands. "Shit!" Maryn yelled.

A small smile spread across Amabel's face. "I thought that one might neutralize the two of you," she said before spotting Lara by the cave.

"Come on, Lara," she said. "Let it go. These two aren't going to be able to help."

Looking into her eyes, Lara knew she couldn't let the book fall into Amabel's hands. Even if she did only want it for her own selfish purposes, the woman was unhinged. She glanced at Clara and Maryn, who were shaking their heads and trying, unsuccessfully, to get to their feet. She was on her own.

Lara looked back to Amabel, who was advancing slowly toward her. Lara gripped the book, and stuck her right pointer finger in between the pages, opening it just slightly, hopefully slowly enough that Amabel wouldn't notice. She thought, *Ben, if you're there. I need help. She can't get her hands on the book. I know what to do. I just need a little help.*

As soon as she'd finished her thought, she heard it. The wind, kicking up from the back of the cave. A quiet noise that sounded like a moan, building to a scream. The book began shaking and it fell out of Lara's grasp.

Just then, three things happened at once.

First, Maisie stepped out of the woods. Her face was pale, and she was breathing heavily, leaning on a tree. "Lara!" she cried out.

At the same time, Clara and Maryn finally got shakily to their feet. They grasped hands and turned to Amabel.

Finally, Amabel rushed forward, picking the book up from where it had fallen. Lara reached out to try to stop her but she missed.

"Lara, move!" Maryn shouted.

Lara jumped out of the way, just as the scream rose up from the cave. Amabel, still clutching the book, flew backwards into the cave, landing with a sickening thud against one of the side walls. She slid to the cave floor, the book falling open by her feet.

The pages began moving, faster than Lara had ever seen, and Amabel's head jerked back against the rock. The pages fell still, the screaming stopped abruptly, and Lara sank to her knees.

Clara rushed over to Amabel, kicking the book out of the way, and felt for a pulse in the woman's neck. She took a deep breath and nodded, looking at Lara. "She's just unconscious."

Lara felt relief and then remembered Maisie. She stood and spun around, where her aunt was standing open-mouthed. "Maisie, are you okay?" Her aunt nodded and Lara looked at Maryn, who smiled at her and said, "I'm okay."

"Maisie, why did you come all the way up here?" Lara asked. Her aunt looked exhausted and Lara couldn't think what had made her come all the way to the cave.

"Amabel came to my house first and she … she opened the lock on the front door, I don't know how. Then she forced me to tell her where you all were." Maisie closed her eyes for a moment and swallowed hard. "I came here to make sure you were all okay. I'm so sorry. I didn't want to tell her."

"She did what?" Maryn asked, at the same moment Clara said, "What do you mean she *forced* you?"

"The door was locked and she just—opened it. Then, she kept trying to get me to tell her where you all had taken the book. I knew I couldn't and I wasn't going to. But then the words were just coming out of me and she left. I'm so sorry."

"God damn it," Maryn muttered.

Clara didn't say anything, just looked at Amabel lying there.

"What the hell happened?" Lara asked Clara.

Clara had picked up the book and was holding it cautiously out in front of her.

"I'm not entirely sure. Amabel was using some powerful magic, both on Maisie and up here. I can't believe she's developed those spells..." Her voice trailed off for a moment before she shook her head and said, "Maryn and I couldn't stop her. She started to overpower us, then she used something that stunned us."

"The pain in my head was unbelievable," Maryn said quietly.

"I guess that's when I summoned Ben," Lara said sheepishly.

"You did what?" asked Clara.

"I could tell you two needed help but I didn't know what to do. So I opened the book and asked Ben for help. I think that's how Amabel was thrown back into the cave. I know it was dangerous, but—"

"I think you did the right thing," Clara said. "But that wasn't all." She turned to face Maisie. "When you got here, all of a sudden, I felt more powerful. I was stronger, I, I ..."

Maryn cut in. "I felt it, too. It was like my powers on my best day, times ten."

"You're an amplifier, Maisie," Clara said.

"I don't know what that means and I honestly don't care," Maisie said.

"Fair enough," Clara responded. "But the combination of Maryn and I trying to force Amabel away from Lara into the cave and whatever came out of that book to help you, Lara, that really overtook her and her black magic."

Lara shuddered. "Is she going to be okay? I really didn't want to hurt her."

"I think so. But we need to take her away from here. And we

need to keep her and that book as far away from each other as possible."

Just then, they heard a moan from Amabel.

Lara nodded. "When she wakes up, you three take her back to town."

"I'm not leaving you here alone," Maryn said.

"No, you have to. I'm fine here. You two will need to subdue her and just in case she's still got some trick up her sleeve, you'll want to have Maisie if she really does amplify your power."

"She's right. I don't know what options we have," Clara said, looking in Amabel's direction. "I don't want to get into a position where she overtakes us and comes back up here. I think the two of us, with Maisie's help—"

"I honestly have no idea how to help. I didn't *do* anything," Maisie insisted.

"It's okay, Maisie, you don't have to do anything," Clara said. "You just need to be with us. And I promise this will all be over soon."

Maisie just nodded. The fight seemed to have gone out of her.

Clara didn't look happy about it, but she eventually agreed to leave Lara at the cave. But not before giving her some very specific instructions.

"When I get back, we'll take it apart. I think we need to do it here. The magic is obviously amplified or something here, and if we have to bind it, I want to be close enough to bind it here. It was harmless here for four decades so it seems like a good plan B."

Lara agreed. They waited for Amabel to wake enough to stand up. Oddly, she didn't say anything. She looked off into the distance, seeming not to see anything. She didn't protest when they led her out of the cave or when they took the bag from her shoulder. She said nothing as they walked toward the trees or when Clara asked her if she was going to give them any trouble. She seemed dazed, catatonic. Hopefully she'd stay that way.

The women set off through the woods. Lara was alone.

She took a deep breath and opened the book to one of the last remaining blank pages. She was going to do what Clara said. She would wait to pull this book apart, piece by piece. But for now, she'd try to do the one other thing the book promised her. Get her memories back. It might be reckless. Her friends might return to find her unconscious or injured or worse. But she had to try.

She wrote down her three favorite memories of Ben.

When he held Tessa for the first time, like she was a tiny football made of the thinnest, breakable glass. The moment he kissed her sweet, smooth forehead.

When their parents had been in the middle of the darkest days of their divorce and Lara would want to cry herself to sleep. Instead, she would crawl into Ben's bed every night and they'd listen to music quietly. Nirvana. Soundgarden. Sublime. Reel Big Fish. Anything and everything that would drown out their parents' angry voices.

His laugh and his smile, both of which were always easy to come and could brighten even her darkest mood.

She didn't have three items of his, but she had her locket, she had his T-shirt on underneath her jacket, and she had herself. That was enough.

She sat down on the grass, leaving the book open in front of her. She closed her eyes, put her hands on either side of the book, in the dirt, and she waited for the words to come.

And come they did. She began speaking, not knowing what she was saying or where the words came from. They poured from her.

And then it happened. She felt it—a niggling in the back of her brain, a trace of a memory. Just a sound, really, Ben's laughter echoing off the inside of an old plastic slide.

Then, her memories came flooding back to her in a wave of emotion so great, she felt like her heart would stop beating. She felt the joy and pain, the comfort and the despair. She remembered Ben holding her hand to cross the parking lot at McDonald's when she was five. She remembered a game of I Spy in the back of their family's car on a trip to Florida. Ben teaching her to drive, Ben teasing her about her first boyfriend, a fight they'd had over who got to watch TV in the basement with friends. Ben at her wedding, whispering how proud he was of her. Ben playing with Tessa. Ben. Just Ben.

Lara was crying and laughing, felt joy and pain together in a way she never had before. The weight of all Ben had done in her life, the weight of all of her memories of him, settled into her bones like a warm blanket on a cold night. He was hers, again.

She was still sitting there, eyes closed, tears streaming down her face, when Maryn appeared in the clearing.

"Lara?"

Lara opened her eyes and smiled at her friend.

"Are you okay?"

"Yeah. I had to try it, Mar."

"Try it?" Maryn looked confused. "Try what? Lara—"

"It's fine Maryn. I'm fine." Lara started to explain what she'd done, but she couldn't explain it to Maryn, how her brother was back in her soul, and not give her friend the same thing. She'd already had a chance to talk to her brother and recalling the pain and longing on her friend's face then … well, she couldn't do it again. She'd have to show her.

"Come here," Lara said.

Maryn sat down next to her, hesitant. Lara handed her a pen and opened to the last blank page of the book. "Write down your three favorite memories of Will."

"Lara, I don't think—"

"Just trust me. Please."

Maryn wrote slowly, occasionally looking at Lara, looking into the cave, looking around. Lara smiled at her encouragingly. When she was done, Lara put the book flat on the ground and said, "Do you have anything of Will's with you right now?"

Maryn touched the necklace she always wore around her neck, one that looked a lot like Lara's. "This. This has some of his ashes in it. My mom got it for us …"

"That's good. That's fine."

Lara sensed she could help the rest of the way. She walked Maryn through the steps, encouraging her, helping when she needed to. As the soft wind whipped up, Lara scooted back, away from Maryn. This needed to be hers and hers alone.

Lara watched her friend's face as the wonder and pain settled in. Then the tears. Then the peace.

****

Maryn and Lara sat together, their backs to the walls of the cave. Maryn told her that they'd managed to get Amabel back to town. She hadn't said a word. And she hadn't protested as they'd brought her to her house and cast a sleeping spell that would keep her comatose for hours.

"Clara didn't like using that kind of magic on her, but we need to deal with that—" she pointed to the book "—and she wanted to call in council leaders to figure out what to do about Amabel as a permanent solution."

"Council leaders?"

"They're like a governing body over the covens. They don't have much of a function until a witch goes rogue. But we're in a tough position. If they find out about the book there could be consequences. They might want to examine it, decide what to do with it. Clara just wants to destroy it so no one else is tempted. So she's calling everyone in. They won't be here until this evening. I told her I wanted to come back up here with you while she made phone calls. She should be back soon."

"Is Maisie okay?" Lara asked.

"I think so. I took her home. She poured herself a glass of whiskey and sat down in her chair."

Lara laughed quietly. "She's fine then."

"So, Lara ... what just happened? I don't know what just happened."

Lara smiled at her friend. "We got our memories back. It gave us everything back."

"It's amazing."

"Yeah. Getting rid of it ... I feel ..." Lara shook her head, not sure how to articulate what she was feeling.

"Guilty as hell?"

"Exactly. I know we have to. But it feels selfish."

"It's the right thing," Maryn said. But she didn't sound sure.

A few moments later they heard Clara walking through the woods.

By unspoken agreement Maryn and Lara didn't tell Clara what they'd done. They knew she wouldn't approve.

They discussed how best to disassemble the book. They'd need to cut the cover off, take the pages apart, and see what was inside it.

"Maryn and I will cast containment spells while you're doing it, just in case. We need to be inside the cave so we can keep it there."

Maryn handed Lara an Exacto knife she'd brought back from Maisie's. Lara took a deep breath before she began carefully cutting off the cover at the seams. As she did, the book thrummed, vibrating underneath her fingers. A wind whipped up and Clara and Maryn looked around nervously.

"You need to move faster," Clara said quietly. "Don't think, don't in any way say or do anything to make it think you need it. But move quickly."

Eventually, Lara carefully peeled back the cover and all three of them gasped as they saw what lay between the green leather and the cardboard of the book.

It was a piece of cloth, thin as the oldest, worn handkerchief. It was covered in symbols and writing Lara couldn't make sense of. Clara reached a tentative finger out and touched it, closing her eyes.

She gasped and fell back. "It's just like we thought. It's so much good and so much evil. It's ancient. It's like nothing I've ever felt before. My god."

"It's weakening," Maryn said. "I can feel it."

Clara nodded. "It is, but I don't want to take any chances. Let's take the cloth apart."

Lara hesitated. "Are we sure? It's so beautiful. So powerful."

The three women looked at it, considering, memorizing it. Maryn snapped a picture of the cloth laid out on the ground. Clara was, of course, the one to break the spell.

"We have to. I know it feels like giving up something that could change your life. But we have to."

Lara felt around the corners of the cloth, examining the ends, looking for a frayed thread to start with. When she'd located one, she tugged on it gently with her fingernails, prying and wiggling until it came free. She repeated the step, over and over.

As Lara disassembled the cloth, pulling it apart, string by string, fiber by fiber, she felt a clearing of the air. She sat in the cool cave, light from a battery-powered lantern casting a soft glow along the walls and a lightness settled into the cave as the bonds of powerful, dangerous magic were released. She felt a calm breeze, a soft sigh, a presence right there over her right shoulder. A thought occurred to her—that maybe, now, this magic could be used for good.

When she was done, she had a small pile of thousands of tiny, silvery threads.

"What do we do with them?" she asked Clara.

"I'm not sure." She looked at Maryn. "It feels like the power is gone, doesn't it?"

"It does."

"We should burn it. Just to be safe," Clara said, ever cautious and careful.

Maryn nodded.

"Can I do that alone?" Lara asked.

When Clara didn't answer right away, Lara said, "I need to do it. It helped me, Clara. I know it's bad, but there's enough good in there too. I want to do it."

Clara looked at Maryn, who shrugged.

Clara sighed. "Okay. But if you're not back ten minutes after us, we're coming back up here."

Lara agreed and she was alone yet again. She did what she needed to do and left the cave for the last time.

****

After everything she'd been through, the conclusion to the whole crazy business was anticlimactic. Lara returned to Maisie's that afternoon and sat with her aunt for a long time, talking about Ben, talking about what Lara intended to do now that she knew she was a witch. Lara still wasn't sure.

Maryn and Clara had set off to check on Amabel and wait for the other coven members to arrive. From what Maryn told her later, the council hadn't been happy Clara had destroyed the book, but there was nothing to do about it now. They'd taken Amabel away. The woman still hadn't said a word or given any indication she cared at all what happened to her now. When Lara asked if they thought it was permanent damage, Maryn didn't have an answer.

"We don't know. Time will tell."

"What happens to her now?"

Maryn sighed. "We really don't get a lot of witches misbehaving. There are places—safe houses, kind of—where they can send her.

She'll be tightly bound. She won't cause any more trouble. But really, with the book gone, she doesn't have anything to fight for." Lara felt sad for her.

Lara had stayed the night at Maisie's, wanting to make sure her aunt was okay. The next morning Maisie had looked more tired than ever and Lara had a serious talk with her about moving to St. Louis. Maybe even moving in with them. For the first time ever, her aunt hadn't automatically put up a fight.

When Lara left Grafton, she went straight to pick up Tessa, grabbing her girl in a tight hug. Tessa seemed to know Lara needed it—or maybe she'd just missed her—because she let Lara hold her, breathing her in, for much longer than she usually did.

Lara told Lynn that everything was okay now and promised to one day tell her the whole story.

"I think you'll believe me," Lara told her with a smile.

Walking into her house for the first time, without the book, and without the pallor of terror hanging over her, Lara felt like a new person. Her house seemed brighter and she was more comfortable in it. She cleaned and cooked dinner and played with Tessa. She went to bed and slept soundly for ten hours. She felt better than she had since before Ben died.

Alex arrived home the next day. He could immediately tell that things were different. He stared at her for a long moment when he walked through the door, taking in her bright smile. Then he kissed her for a long time, until Tessa ran in screaming "Daddy, Daddy!" and tugging on his pants, demanding some attention.

That night they put Tessa to bed early and sat on the porch, each with a glass of wine and Lara told him everything. She left nothing out. Alex asked few questions. When she was done, she said, "I know how it sounds. But you can ask Maryn or Maisie."

"I believe you," he said simply.

"You do?" she said, shocked.

Alex sighed. "A few days before I left, I picked that book up. I just wanted to get a feel for it, see what the big deal was. I still didn't believe you." He looked down at his hands, ashamed. "I should have. The passage I read was a memory Violet had of Henry, when they were playing by the river, balancing on a large tree trunk, running up and down, up and down the trunk. They ran faster and faster until Henry fell off. When he did, he landed just the wrong way on his ankle, breaking it, and getting a bad cut on his right elbow. Violet said the cut was shaped like a moon."

Lara shook her head. "It's amazing. That scene was not in that book either of the times I read it," Lara told him.

Alex nodded. "The day before yesterday, we were on a job site in a subdivision. A family walked up to thank us, a mom, dad, and little twins, a boy and a girl. A large tree had fallen down in the storm and the kids started running up and down the trunk. Over and over."

"Oh my god."

"Yeah. I didn't think anything of it at first, until they started running really fast. And they couldn't have been more than six or seven, so eventually the mom got nervous and told them to slow down. Right after she said that, the little boy fell off. He broke his ankle. Got a gnarly cut on his right elbow."

"Shaped like a moon."

"Shaped like a moon."

Lara got chills all over. "Why didn't you tell me?"

"I didn't want to make it worse for you. But I knew then that I'd been a complete ass and I should have believed you from the beginning. I'm sorry. Can you forgive me?"

"Of course. I don't know that anyone would have just believed me anyway. It worked out in the end," Lara said, taking his hand and stroking her thumb over his palm.

"I feel bad for her."

"For who?" Lara asked. There were a lot of "hers" in this story to feel sorry for.

"Violet. It couldn't have ended well for her, don't you think? She just disappeared. After everything she went through."

"Yeah. I guess we'll never know."

"What are you going to do?"

Lara knew he was asking about her powers. "Can you live with a witch?" she teased.

"Well, I have been for years now," he teased back, smiling at her.

She slapped him playfully on the leg and said, "I'm not going to do anything. If I am a hedge witch, I don't see how that could be of any use in my regular life. I think it would only invite more craziness in. Maryn and Clara think that's why everything got as out of control as it did. My power made the book's magic more powerful because it's so closely tied to the afterlife. I don't want to do anything that invites that back into our lives."

Alex nodded. "I'm glad. Even though I'd support you no matter what. But I'm glad."

Lara squeezed his leg.

"Lara?"

"Yeah?"

"Can you tell me a story about Ben? Do you remember that day at the lake—"

Lara laughed before he could finish. "The jet skis?"

Alex nodded, laughing already.

"We had so much fun," she said with a smile. And then she told him everything about that day—what they'd been wearing, what they ate for lunch at that marina cafe, and the colorful cuss words Ben had used when he was thrown from the jet ski and lost his pants.

She and Alex sat on their deck, in the midst of the all-consuming pain that came with remembering what they'd lost, and laughed until they cried.

EPILOGUE

Lara

Lara took a deep breath and looked around the small meeting room in the Oak Bend branch of the St. Louis Public Library one more time. She'd purposely asked for a room in the basement, where it would be quiet and she could dim the light.

The metal chairs were arranged in a neat circle, a pen and a small, bound notebook sitting on each chair. The colorful notebooks dotted the chairs like a rainbow: green and purple and blue and orange.

Pulling her phone out of her pocket to check the time—fifteen minutes until it was scheduled to start—Lara wondered, yet again, if anyone would show up. She'd advertised A New Way Sibling Support group as "Not your regular support group." The literature she designed read:

> Most support groups focus on healing, moving on, finding peace. Those things are important and have a place in the healing process, but some of us might not be ready for that. Some of us live a long time in the hardest parts of grief— the anger and the pain—and it can feel impossible to contemplate living the next hour without your sibling, let alone finding peace far down this long road. You might not be ready to imagine a world where you can move on. And that's okay.

> With a focus on strengthening your memories of your loved one, we will help you figure out what you need right now, in this moment, just to get through the next day, hour, or even the next minute.

A New Way will not force you to heal before you're ready. Grief is hard. It can be debilitating. We're going to talk about those hard things and bring them out into the open. We're going to help you find ways to honor your brother or sister while also taking care of yourself right now. We're real. We're honest. We're not your regular support group.

Lara worried it sounded a bit woo-woo. But was it really any worse than the groups that promised to help you "move on?" If Lara had learned anything, it was that there was no moving on after a tragic loss. There's moving through, and changing your path, but no moving on.

Lara rearranged a chair and a notebook, thinking, for what felt like the millionth time, that this was an insane plan.

When Clara and Maryn left her alone that last day at the cave, she'd intended to light it on fire and be done with it once and for all. She'd gathered sticks and dry brush and constructed a small pyramid. Using matches from John's old tin box, which had shockingly still worked, she held the flame to the wood and watched it catch.

She gathered a small amount of thread from the bag and moved her hand toward the flames. As she did, she heard a breeze kick up from the back of the cave and her hand stopped, hovering in midair. Was she doing the right thing? She honestly didn't know. It was too dangerous to keep. She had no obligation to anyone to keep it intact and in truth, she'd already destroyed it by tearing it apart.

Still she hesitated and the *what if* came back again. *What if* it could be used for good? *What if* other people could heal the way she had? A thought hit her, then. *What if* she could help?

Before she could think too much about it, she'd returned the threads to the bag and snuffed out the flames. The breeze from the back of the cave stopped.

When she'd returned home from Grafton and things started settling down, she'd decided to test her theory. She took one small piece of one of the strings and placed it in the binding of a notebook. When she'd first had the idea, she'd been unsure what it would mean to put this out into the world—to use the power of everything she'd learned from Violet Marsh and Amabel and about herself. She still wasn't sure now. But she'd begun writing, her favorite memories about her own life, all the things she wanted to remember and tell Tessa. And it was like a flood. It just kept coming, in great detail, in clear and brilliant color. And she was so thankful. It worked.

She didn't tell Maryn until a couple of weeks later. And they'd come up with their own plan.

Now, they were here and Lara still had no idea if she was doing the right thing. She looked at her phone again. Ten minutes.

"Stop checking your phone. People are going to start walking in any minute."

Lara looked at Maryn, who was setting out some cookies and making sure there was coffee in the pot.

"I don't know."

"Lara, it's going to be fine. People are going to love this. It's worked for me and you, right?"

"Yeah. I guess. I just don't know—"

"Girl. Stop."

As Maryn said the words, a young black woman with black wire-frame glasses and a trendy jean jacket stepped tentatively into the doorway. Her eyes were red and swollen and she was holding tightly to her purse.

"Hi," she said quietly. "Is this the support group?"

Lara felt a smile spread across her face and walked toward the woman, holding out her hand. "It is. Hi, I'm Lara, and this Maryn. We're really glad you're here."

The woman smiled and said, "I'm Kay. I-I've never been to something like this before, but it's just been … It's been …" She shook her head back and forth and shrugged.

"I know. I get it," Lara said, gently squeezing Kay's arm.

Maryn was looking over Lara's shoulder toward the doorway smiling. "Hi, please come in."

Lara turned around and saw two more people standing in the doorway, a middle-aged woman holding a Starbucks cup and an older man who took his hat off his head as he reached out to shake Maryn's hand. After that, more people started streaming in, filling the chairs. They even had to get some extra chairs and widen the circle. Twenty people in all showed up, sitting and looking expectantly at Lara and Maryn, who were standing by their own chairs at the head of the room.

Maryn and Lara sat down and Maryn squeezed Lara's hand. Lara took a deep breath and said, "Wow. I am so, so glad you are all here. This is our first group and I wasn't sure if anyone would show up to something I called, 'Not your regular support group.'" There was some laughter from the circle.

"My name is Lara and this is Maryn. We met in a grief support group over a year ago. My brother Ben died from a heart attack when he was thirty-four."

"My brother Will was killed by a drunk driver," Maryn added.

"It was your average support group—lots of talk about healing and God and finding peace," Lara went on. "It was—nice. But Maryn and I weren't feeling so nice at that point."

"We were actually just really, really pissed off," said Mary, and the group laughed in surprise. The older woman nodded her head vigorously and Kay muttered, "Amen."

"It felt like no one wanted to hear about how pissed off we were. So we never went back to that group, but Maryn and I have spent a lot of time over the past year helping and supporting each other. Eventually, the idea came to us that we would have loved a support group that didn't make us feel like we were somehow failing or falling behind because we weren't ready to 'move on' yet."

"So here we are," said Maryn with a smile. "Like we said, this isn't your regular support group. We're going to tell you about the days we ended up crying on the floor of our closet and the time I tore my brother's apartment apart because I went just a little bit crazy looking for a 'sign'"—Maryn made finger quotes in the air—"from him." More laughter. Lara thought that was a good sign and she felt some of her nervousness fade.

"We're not professionals," Maryn continued. "I'm a freaking engineer and she's a graphic designer." Maryn hooked her thumb in Lara's direction. "But we learned grief the hard way and we found something that has helped us. We're doing okay now. We just want to help other people be okay, too." Maryn and Lara looked at each other and smiled.

"So. Now that you know how we all got here, I want to explain a bit more what we're about," Lara said.

"My brother Ben was my best friend. When he died, the moment I heard the words, I was no longer the person I had been. I didn't realize it at the time, of course, but I was fundamentally changed. Everything I tried to do to heal didn't work because I was trying to heal the person I had been. I was trying to get back to my old self, but that was impossible. So I was angry and, quite frankly, a hot mess for a really long time." Heads were nodding all around the circle.

"I didn't want to move on because moving on feels like forgetting. When we move on from a divorce or a bad job, we learn the lessons we need to learn, maybe we change our behavior to avoid going through something like that again. But we move on and we leave it behind, right? And often, that kind of change opens doors to something better.

But as we all know, the thought of moving on and leaving someone we loved so much behind is unbearable. We get stuck. Eventually, we feel the pressure to be okay, to get better, to move on. So we do, even though most of the time it's an act.

We move on and we push that person to the back of our minds so the pain doesn't hurt so much and we can get on with our lives. Sometimes, it works. We go on and love again, and smile again, and even feel moments of joy again. But we are still, whether we realize it or not, mourning not just our loss, but something new—the loss *and* the shoving aside of the memories of the person we loved so much, who lived and who mattered to us and to the world." Lara felt herself getting choked up and took a deep breath.

"Not to mention, there's the unique part of being a grieving sibling that no one ever talks about. We're supposed to take care of everyone else, right? Take care of our parents, of our sibling's kids or their spouses. We're left making decisions and feeling responsible for holding everything together. It's lonely." Lara looked around and saw more shaking heads and lots of tears falling down sad faces. "Well, you're not alone. We see you and we see your pain and here, in this room, your needs come first."

Maryn took over. "As I'm sure you all know, one of the hardest parts of this really shitty thing we're all going through is facing the thought that we might forget what they look like or what their laugh sounded like. We might forget a bunch of our memories and that sucks because we don't get to make any new ones."

"But a lot of people will tell you that you can't obsess about that. That it's going to happen with the passage of time and we just have to deal with it," Lara added. "Well, I didn't want to deal with it. I didn't want to forget Ben or anything that had ever happened while he was alive. Of course I wanted to be happy again, because I owed that to him and to my husband and daughter, and part of that meant finding a way to move on. I knew I couldn't dwell on or obsess over my memories of Ben. But I didn't think that meant I had to push Ben out of my life, either."

"So we want to help you use your memories as a way to heal," said Maryn. "We've come up with some ways to draw your memories out and use them, when you need them. We want the power of the love you have for whoever you've lost to be the thing that helps you heal."

"Does that sound weird?" Lara asked with a laugh. There were smiles and shaking heads all around the circle. "Like Maryn said, we're not professionals. But we've learned the hard way, and we think we can learn from all of you, too."

Lara and Maryn asked everyone to introduce themselves and talk about their brothers and sisters. They asked them not to share how they died, but share the thing they loved most about that person. Around the circle it went, the same loop of grief and pain that made Lara's heart hurt, but this time, it also made her smile.

Kay told them that her brother, Devion, had practiced basketball in their driveway for one hour every night, because he was convinced he would make it to the NBA.

"He wasn't going to be in the NBA," Kay said with a laugh. "He was 5'8" and only made two out of every five free throws. But he was determined and dedicated and I love him so very much." She was crying, but she was also smiling.

One man told them that his sister, Betty, loved Hershey's kisses so much that his parents, two years after her death, were still finding wrappers in the couch cushions and under the car seats. "She always smelled like chocolate and nothing made her happier than buying a fresh bag and putting it in her fancy candy dish."

Rose told them about her sister, who'd been so passionate about Cardinals baseball that every year from the time she was ten, all she'd ever wanted for Christmas was season tickets. "None of the rest of us loved baseball as much as she did. But she was so adamant that my parents usually got her a partial package and we would all go to the games together. We'd end up watching her as much as we watched the game, because she knew all the players' stats, and yelled at the umps, and cheered louder than anyone."

When they had all finished, there were lots of tears but there were also many, many smiles. "Thank you all for sharing," said Maryn. "The reason we asked you to start with that is because we want that memory you just shared with us to be your anchor memory. That's going to be the memory you come back to when you're feeling most sad."

"A big turning point for me was when my therapist told me that my brother's memory didn't have to be all about the fact that he was dead," Lara added. "I hadn't realized it, but every time I thought about him or talked about him, I always started with the fact that he was dead. But he is about so much more than his death and he deserves to be remembered better than that. So that's what these specific memories are for."

Maryn and Lara asked them all to take their notebooks and write these memories down. Lara watched their faces, as they scribbled in the notebooks, small smiles on their faces. She thought, *Holy shit, this might actually work. I might actually help people the way no one could help me.*

Lara looked around the room at the rainbow notebooks and thought back to the day she'd told Maryn about her idea for this support group and how she thought they could help. Maryn hadn't hesitated.

"Absolutely. We know what it did for us. We can help. It's perfect."

And so, they'd purchased fifty notebooks to start, in all different colors: green and purple and blue and orange. Sitting on the floor of Lara's living room, they'd carefully used an Exacto knife to cut a small slit into the binding of each notebook, peeling back the cover, revealing the binding. Then they'd woven a tiny piece of a single thread into the binding of each notebook.

With it, weaving a tiny bit of the magic into the book. She hoped it would help the owners of these notebooks get back just a little bit of the memories they might otherwise forget. And they never had to know.

Lara wrote a letter she included in each notebook, where she'd gathered her thoughts about her experience and what she'd learned. She felt a little silly. After all, she wasn't a therapist. All she knew was what she'd learned by losing it all and then getting (almost) all of it back.

What do I know about grief?

What makes grief so painful is the one-two punch of longing and the unknown. We long for the ones we've lost with a depth of pain that is overwhelming and, at times, unbearable. We want them back—we want to hear their voice, feel their arms around us, just be in their presence. And we can't have it.

Then there is the unknown—so many unknowns. Why did our loved one have to die? Where did they go? Did they know how much we loved them? Could I have done anything different to protect them, to change the course of events? Will we ever see them again? Are they watching over me?

We feel powerless to change our circumstances, so we cling to anything that makes sense. Maybe that's throwing ourselves into finding out more about how our loved one died. Maybe we start raising money in their name. Maybe we binge-watch television or lose hours on the internet. Maybe we simply fall away from the world, drowning in pills or alcohol or the confines of our bed.

The one thing we have—the thing we have that is known and is true and that can't be taken from us—is our memories of the ones we lost. It's a small comfort. It's not enough.

Cruelly, memories fade over time. We forget the tenor of their laugh, the way their eyes crinkled at the corners when they smiled, how they tilted their head when they were in a deep discussion. We try to cling to them, but they slip away and it's yet another loss in a long string of things that have been ripped away from us.

It is cruel, but it is also simply the way things are. What I've come to realize is that my brother doesn't live in the specifics of my memories. When I laugh with my husband or cuddle with my daughter I am feeling the weight of them, smelling their skin, and taking in the lines and curves of their faces that I love so deeply. These are the things we think we need to cling to. But what I'm really taking in is the power of our connection—the love that ties us together and the weight of our shared experiences.

The weight of our memory, rather than crushing us, cocoons us like a blanket and will see us through.

My hope is that the work you will do in this notebook will help you remember the best things, but also learn to find comfort in the spirit of the person you've lost. And I hope it will help you find peace. Finally, peace.

ACKNOWLEDGEMENTS

I never thought I'd have a chance to actually write the acknowledgments for my very own book, even though I've written and rewritten it in my head hundreds of times. There are so many people to thank, who helped me bring this book to life, who encouraged me, and most of all, who believed in me.

First, to the baristas at the Edwardsville Starbucks. You kept me fueled, almost every single day, for years. You asked me about my progress, were excited for me, and were just lovely every single early morning and late night I was there at that little table writing. You just might singlehandedly be the reason anyone is holding this book in their hands right now.

A huge thank you to the team at Sands Press for believing in this story and being excited about it. Laurie Carter, you were a dream editor and every single one of your kind and encouraging emails made me cry.

The internet is a crazy thing. There are a few people I have to thank who started out as voices inside my computer. Suzanne DeRoulet, you've been a champion of this story from day one. Thank you for your invaluable advice and encouragement. You are one of the most talented writers I know and I cannot wait to hold your book in my hands. Peyton, Juliette, Ellie, and Dani, I'm so glad we "met" and created our kinda-about-writing-but-not-really writers group and that you tolerated grandma. I cannot wait to see your stories come to life.

To everyone who supported me on this journey—the countless family and friends who tolerated my posts on Facebook, pre-ordered books, asked me how it was going, told their friends, and were excited for me—thank you will never be enough.

Natalie and Cory McCunney, you are some of my biggest cheerleaders and I'll be forever grateful hockey brought us together. Now, since I've acknowledged you here in my very first book, will you please move home?

Derrick Shy, you were one of the first people I told about this book and instead of laughing, you told me it sounded like a great idea and talked through plot points with me. I don't think you know how important that was to me as I was just getting started. I know you're not totally happy with the small-ish role the character modeled after you ended up getting here, but hopefully this entire paragraph dedicated to you in my acknowledgements makes up for it.

My dad always had a book in hand and encouraged such a deep love of reading in me. It has been one of the most important parts of my life. My mom supports me always and without question and showed me the passion and dedication it takes to write a book. You both encouraged me to follow my dreams and I am forever grateful.

Kyle, I felt like I had to put you in here because if I didn't, people would think it was weird. Thanks for being my brother, I guess. (But seriously thank you for always listening to me and being a constant support in my life and keeping me laughing with the best, most accurate *Schitt's Creek* gifs.) (Ew, that was gross.)

To my wonderful, smart, and kind children, Caleb and Leah. There aren't words to express how proud I am of you and how much joy you have given me. Thank you for being excited about mom writing a book, for dealing with the late nights and early mornings I was away writing, and for just being the amazing kids that you are. You make me laugh, make me think, and have made me a better person. Being your mom is the greatest gift of my life.

Chip, you encouraged me to try in the first place, without question and with one hundred percent confidence in me. You sacrificed, you pushed me, held me accountable, and cheered me on like I could have never imagined. I am so thankful to you and lucky to have you. After everything, we're still here and I love you more than ever. Thank you.

To all the people who've mourned the loss of a sibling. You are not forgotten. It is the worst, most unexplainable pain. It's unfair. You are not alone.

And finally, to Nathan. I miss you every single minute of every single day. I can't believe I've lived so many years without you. You were the best person I've ever known and twenty years was not enough. I am a better person for having you in my life and I'm so unbelievably lucky that you're my brother. And oh, Nater. You should see Tyler. You would be so proud of your son. We love you so very, very much.